*T*he new Prince of Wales took the frail girl's hand in his. "Come sit with me and I will tell you why I have come." His manner was light. "My father, King Henry, has given his consent to our match, and I come here to give you this good news."

"Our . . . match!" The girl gasped.

"Isabella, my beautiful little Isabella, I love you. I want you to be my wife . . . my Queen one day. My father . . ."

She had sprung to her feet; her hands were clenched at her sides, her eyes stony.

"You . . . the son of my husband's murderer . . . you dare to come here and say this to me!" Her voice became shrill. "Your father is a murderer. You have killed my husband. You make your crime worse by suggesting that I marry you! I hate you, Harry of Monmouth. I hate you. I hate you."

"Well," said Harry with a grin, "that need not prevent your marrying me."

THE
STAR OF
LANCASTER

Jean Plaidy

FAWCETT CREST • NEW YORK

A Fawcett Crest Book

Published by Ballantine Books

Copyright © 1982 by Jean Plaidy

All rights reserved under International and Pan-American Copyright
Conventions. This book, or parts thereof, must not be reproduced in any
form without permission. Published in the United States by Ballantine
Books, a division of Random House, Inc., New York.

Library of Congress Catalog Card Number: 82-7705

ISBN 0-449-20416-2

This edition published by arrangement with G. P. Putnam's Sons

Manufactured in the United States of America

First Ballantine Books Edition: June 1985

CONTENTS

Encounter in the Forest 1

The Child Wife 30

The Lord Harry 53

The Last Farewell 84

The Forget-Me-Not 109

The Prince and the Virgin Widow 151

Hotspur 174

Isabella at the Court of France 198

Prince Hal 216

Oldcastle 249

Agincourt 268

Death At Lollards' Gallows 281

A Charge of Witchcraft 295

Katherine de Valois 303

Death of the Conqueror 316

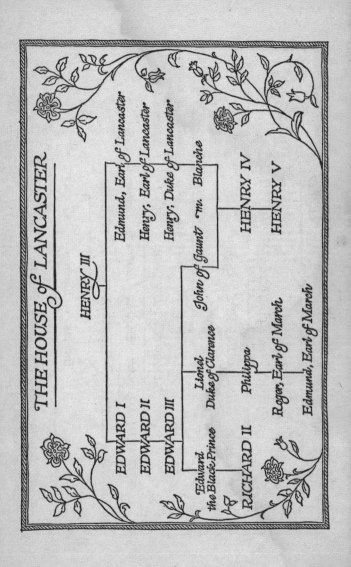

THE HOUSE of LANCASTER

HENRY III

- EDWARD I
- EDWARD II
- EDWARD III
  - Edward the Black Prince
    - RICHARD II
  - Lionel Duke of Clarence
    - Philippa
      - Roger, Earl of March
        - Edmund, Earl of March
  - John of Gaunt *m.* Blanche
    - HENRY IV
    - HENRY V
  - Edmund, Earl of Lancaster
  - Henry, Earl of Lancaster
  - Henry, Duke of Lancaster
    - Blanche

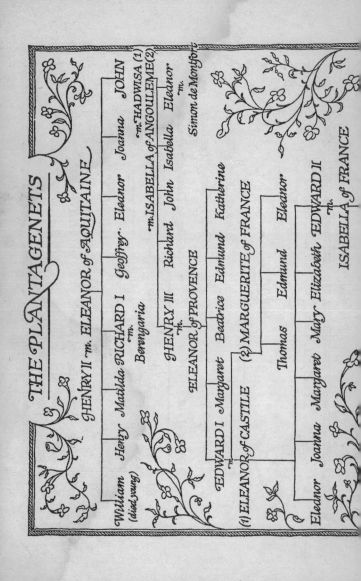

THE PLANTAGENETS

HENRY II m. ELEANOR of AQUITAINE

William (died young) Henry Matilda RICHARD I Geoffrey Eleanor Joanna JOHN
m. Berengaria
m. ¹HADWISA (1)
m. ISABELLA of ANGOULEME (2)

HENRY III Richard John Isabella Eleanor
m. ELEANOR of PROVENCE
m. Simon de Montfort

EDWARD I Margaret Beatrice Edmund Katherine
(1) ELEANOR of CASTILE   (2) MARGUERITE of FRANCE

Eleanor Joanna Margaret Mary Elizabeth EDWARD II
m. ISABELLA of FRANCE
Thomas Edmund Eleanor

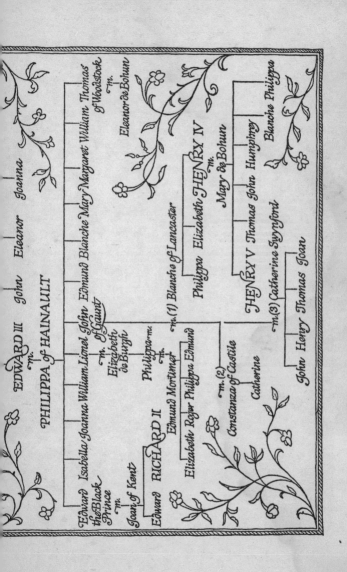

EDWARD III m. PHILIPPA of HAINAULT

Edward the Black Prince m. Joan of Kent · Isabella · Joanna · William · Lionel m. Elizabeth de Burgh · John of Gaunt · Edmund · Blanche · Mary · Margaret · William · Thomas of Woodstock m. Eleanor de Bohun

RICHARD II

Philippa m. Edmund Mortimer

Elizabeth · Roger · Philippa · Edmund

m.(1) Blanche of Lancaster

Philippa · Elizabeth · HENRY IV m. Mary de Bohun

HENRY V · Thomas · John · Humphrey · Blanche · Philippa

m.(2) Constanza of Castile

Catherine

m.(3) Catherine Swynford

John · Henry · Thomas · Joan

ENCOUNTER IN THE FOREST

The walls of the convent rose serene and beautiful among the green meadows. Close by were the grey walls of Pleshy Castle, the home of the little girl who was seated at the table, her lesson book spread out before her. How quiet it was in the convent! she was thinking. There was a peacefulness here which she found very comforting, the more so because she had become aware of a certain turmoil in the castle.

Mary had always been a little in awe of Eleanor, her elder sister, and perhaps more so of Thomas, Eleanor's husband. He was a very important man, of course; and Eleanor was proud to be his wife. She was constantly reminding her little sister that *her* children would be royal because Thomas was the King's son.

It was true. Thomas of Woodstock, as people called him because of the place where he was born, was in fact the Earl of Buckingham and the youngest son of King Edward the Third and Queen Philippa. Mary could remember when he and Eleanor were married. Her father had been alive then and there had been great rejoicing at the castle, for it was a brilliant match for the de Bohuns, even though Humphrey de Bohun was a very rich man owning as well as Pleshy Castle those of Monmouth and

Leicester and a mansion in the City of London; and, although it was because of his immense wealth that the marriage had been approved by the royal family, the de Bohuns had been well aware of the honour done to them.

Then everything had changed because her father—Humphrey de Bohun to give him his full title—had died and his vast fortune was to be divided between his two daughters for there was no male heir. Thus Eleanor, wife of royal Thomas, and ten-year-old Mary became the richest heiresses in England.

Eleanor was delighted about that; so was Thomas; Mary was amazed at their excitement. What difference did it make to them? she wondered. They had been very rich before. What more could they want?

When she asked this, she was sharply told by Eleanor not to be foolish and she was subdued for she had always been very conscious of Eleanor's seniority. Eleanor had always made her aware of it, even before their father's death. She was *much* older, Eleanor had pointed out, and Mary was only a child. She must do as she was told by those of superior knowledge and that naturally meant an elder sister.

Brooding now over those days as she sat within the peaceful walls of the convent, her books lying neglected before her, she was thinking of all that had happened since her father's death and the attitude of Eleanor and her husband towards her. It was almost as though they were planning something.

The thought made her feel slightly uneasy and she was more than ever aware how pleasant it was to be in the convent among the gentle nuns. Presently one of them would come and look at her work. If it was good, little would be said, for it was implied that they expected it to be good; if it was carelessly done or betrayed an ignorance of the subjects set there would be a gentle reproof which strangely enough hurt her more than anger and contempt would have done.

Mary liked the nuns; she liked the convent; the atmosphere fascinated her. The Abbess had told her that the Poor Clares lived only to serve. They moved about the convent like grey silent ghosts for if they wished to speak to each other they must first receive permission to do so from the Abbess. They slept on hard boards; they fasted; they followed strict laws of poverty; and it was their duty to forget their own needs and devote their time to the care of the sick and the poor.

Often she compared their lives with those who lived in her castle home. Eleanor liked luxury and so indeed did Thomas. He had been accustomed to it all his life, for his father had kept an extravagant court and King Richard's it was said was even more luxurious. Yet here within the convent walls, the Poor Clares slept on their hard boards, denied themselves food, taking only that which was necessary to sustain them that they might continue with their work, and Mary often thought how strange it was that there could be such differences in people's lives.

Eleanor loved rich clothes and her seamstresses were working constantly on new garments for her. She would spend hours discussing which two colours harmonized— for all her gowns were two-coloured now in accordance with the fashion—and fine silks would be placed to-gether and matched. Her cote hardies were very splen-did indeed and often decorated with gems. Her hanging sleeves grew longer with every fresh gown and she was happy to hide her hair—which was straight and not very abundant—under a very elaborate head-dress.

Mary often thought what the nuns could have done with the money which her sister spent so freely on adorning herself. She often compared her with the nuns in their grey gowns, shapeless and loose, held in at the waist with their linen cords which were tied with four knots to represent, and to remind them of, their four vows. She compared the serenity of the nuns with the restless activity of her sister and it seemed clear to her which of them found life more satisfactory.

It was not one of the nuns who came to her but the Abbess herself. Mary was overcome with awe and she felt that such a visitation must be of some portent.

The Abbess said: 'Well, my child, you have done your lessons for the day.' She took the books and glanced at them; then her piercing eyes were on the girl.

A beautiful child, she thought. She had inherited more than her share of the family's good looks. The de Bohuns had been benefactors of the convent for years and it was natural that this little girl should have been given over to them that they might educate her. It happened to many children of high birth and they must welcome it. Noble families were their life blood. They needed the patronage of those who in so many cases thought to expiate their sins by endowing a convent and by supporting it throughout their lives. It was ironical that such holy places were so largely dependent on sinners and doubly so that the greater the sins committed the more munificent were the gifts likely to be.

Now she was responsible for the education of this young girl; but she knew that ambitious Thomas of Woodstock and his equally ambitious wife had sent her here for a purpose.

It would be good for the convent if that purpose was successful; but the Abbess did not wish it to be so unless it was the best thing for the girl. With her dark hair and her gentle rather doe-like eyes, her heart-shaped face and her delicate features she showed signs of real beauty. Her nature was gentle but alert; she would be steadfast but the fact was that the Abbess was unsure.

As yet, she thought, she is too young to decide.

'It is a fine day,' she said briskly. 'Let us walk awhile in the gardens.'

This was strange. The Abbess had never walked in the gardens with her before, but one thing Mary had learned in the convent was not to ask questions so she shut her books immediately and rose.

She followed the Abbess through the stone corridors. They passed silent-footed nuns, who, preserving their silence, did not speak. In the gardens, where vegetables and herbs were grown, three nuns were working: they did not look up. In the bakery it would be the same, as in the wash-house and the ale house. They were all working steadily away and in silence as they would be in the still rooms where the herbs were being made into medicines for the use of the poor.

'You see, my child,' said the Abbess, 'that here we are working for others. It is our mission in life to serve God through His unfortunate children.'

'Yes, my lady Abbess, I have long been aware of that.'

'And you think it a worthy vocation?'

'Oh yes, my lady. I do.'

'There are some who take their vows perhaps too early and later regret that they have done so. The world is an alluring place my child.'

'It is full of wickedness, my lady.'

'And what do you know of that wickedness? Tell me that.'

Mary was silent and the Abbess smiled.

'You know nothing of the world save that which you have heard. But you have seen something of what a nun's life is like. And you think it a good life?'

'Oh I do, my lady.'

They walked in silence for some moments; then the Abbess said, 'How old are you?'

'I am ten years old.'

'It is too young to make decisions which would affect the whole of your life.'

'What decisions, my lady?'

'My lord the Earl has said that if you should wish to join us here he would not stand in your way.'

'To . . . join you here.'

'To become one of us. What do you think, Mary?'

The girl was silent. To live the life of a nun! To work for the poor! To speak only when given permission to do so! She did not know what to say. When she entered the calm of the convent she had felt a happiness envelop her. That was because Eleanor had said something that she had felt to be unkind; and she was aware of the friction at Pleshy. Her brother-in-law was often angry about something. He and her sister were constantly discussing some grievance and assuring themselves that the day would come when they would be avenged. It made her uneasy; and for that reason she liked to get away. But to live here always . . . never to know what was really happening in the world . . .

The Abbess said: 'My dear child, do not look alarmed. It would be years before anything was done. The Duke of Lancaster is your guardian and he would have to give his consent of course. His plans might differ from those of your brother-in-law and sister. But a great deal depends on your own wishes for we would not want you to be here against your will. The decision is yours, remember that, but there is talk of its being a suitable life for you and I thought I would tell you this that you can be more watchful of us and our ways. I think it is never too soon to think of these matters.'

'Thank you, my lady. I will think of them.'

'That is well. I believe your groom is waiting at the stables to take you to Pleshy.'

The Abbess went into the convent and Mary made her way to the stables where her horse was ready for her.

In the solarium at Pleshy, Mary was embroidering an altar cloth for the chapel when her sister joined her. Eleanor was pregnant; she was hoping for a son; she already had one little girl about a year old and she thought herself rather ill used by life because her first-born had not been a son.

She sat beside Mary and said: 'You look so happy. But you always do when you return from the convent. I believe you love that place.'

'I do. It is very pleasant there and the nuns are so gentle. They are very good, you know, Eleanor.'

'I do know it. There are no more worthy people in the world. Some of us have duties in other directions.' She sighed as though she deplored having to be a great lady, go to Court, wear magnificent clothes, and would have counted it a great privilege if she had been allowed to put on the grey robe of the Poor Clares and devote herself to the needy.

Now that was too much for Mary to accept. Eleanor thoroughly enjoyed her worldly life, but she had been planning something for some time and Mary was beginning to understand what it was. Eleanor wanted her to go into a convent; in fact she was trying to persuade her to. Her next words confirmed this.

'Oh Mary, I am beginning to think you are more fortunate than I. I do believe God is giving you a chance to lead a very worthy life.'

'You mean go into a convent? Become a nun?'

'I see you are full of joy at the thought.'

'No, Eleanor. That is not entirely true. I do think the nuns are good and I should like to be as they are . . .'

'Well then, sister, is that not what I said?'

'But there are other joys in the world. When I play with little Anne I think how fortunate *you* are to have her and then there is the new one who is coming. I do love the peace of the convent but I should love to be a mother too . . . to have babies like Anne.'

'What nonsense!' said Eleanor sharply. 'Having a baby is by no means pleasant I can assure you.'

'I know it is an ordeal but the reward is great. Sometimes I think the most wonderful thing in the world must be to have a child.'

'You are speaking of matters of which you know nothing,' said Eleanor sharply. 'I think you should begin to consider going into the convent. I could speak to the Abbess.'

'Eleanor, have you already spoken to the Abbess?'

'We have talked of your future, of course.'

'And our mother?'

'She has not given an opinion but I am sure that she would be happy for you to take up the holy life.'

'I think she would respect my wishes in that,' said Mary with spirit.

Eleanor opened her eyes very wide. 'But is that not what we all wish to do?' she demanded.

'If that is so,' replied Mary gravely, 'it is for me to decide and I have some time yet to think about my future.'

'Of a certainty you have,' retorted Eleanor. 'But I think you would be very happy to feel you had settled it.'

Mary was silent. Eleanor would be very happy, she was sure, if it was settled that her young sister should become a nun.

Thomas Woodstock, Earl of Buckingham, rode out to Pleshy to say good-bye to his wife before he left for France. He was not displeased to be going for he was of an adventurous nature and had the Plantagenet desire to do battle. He was fresh from the triumph he had enjoyed when just before Christmas he had captured eight Spanish ships off Brest. Egotistical, impulsive, inclined to recklessness, Thomas yearned to be in the centre of events.

Eleanor understood well. She shared his ambitions. She greeted him warmly and immediately commanded that the finest dinner should be served and the minstrels give of their best. She had always insisted that they should have the newest songs from Court and as they were not far from London and Westminster she usually succeeded in her endeavours.

Eleanor had married into royalty and she could not forget it nor allow anyone else to.

It was a good marriage from the point of view of both husband and wife. Thomas enjoyed her ambition and approval in all his endeavours and it gratified him that she should be so conscious of the royalty he had bestowed on her.

In their apartments he told her of his successes at sea—avoiding that part in which the squadron of which he had been in charge had been scattered by a storm.

'I am going out to aid the Duke of Brittany,' he explained. 'He is handing over the Castle of Brest to us for as long as the war shall last. But the French will take it unless I get there in time to hold it.'

'You will do that,' she said. 'I trust Richard is grateful for all you do for him.'

'Grateful! He takes everything as his right and knows little of affairs. He's nothing but a boy. A boy King of England!'

'There should have been a Regency,' said Eleanor.

'Ah my dear, you speak truth there.'

'Though Lancaster would have been in command you may be sure.'

'He would have tried to be. I should have stopped that.'

Eleanor nodded sagely. There was little love between the two brothers. John of Gaunt, Duke of Lancaster was as ambitious as his brother. Both bitterly resented the fact that they had not been the eldest of Edward's sons. It would have been different if the Black Prince had lived. He would have stepped naturally onto the throne and there would have been no question of his right to be there. But his son, this young boy—delicate and effeminate—was quite unsuited to the destiny thrust upon him; and it was particularly galling that it should be so when Edward the Third had had other sons than the Black Prince. John of Gaunt and Thomas of Woodstock believed that they were more suited to take the crown. As for the third brother, Edmund of Langley, he was not ambitious, preferring to live quietly in the country. But

John and Thomas were constantly jostling for power and it was galling to both of them to have to accept their puny nephew as their King.

Thomas was a man who brooded on his wrongs; he could never forget nor forgive a slight; and when John of Gaunt had put forward his own son Henry of Bolingbroke for the Order of the Garter and their late father Edward the Third had bestowed it on him, Thomas had been consumed by hatred of his brother—for there had been two candidates for the Order, Thomas himself and Henry of Bolingbroke, and to get it for his son, John of Gaunt had had to push aside his brother.

No, that was something which would never be forgiven.

'Well, my dear,' he said, 'my stay here is a brief one. By the time I return our little one will be born.'

'You shall have news as soon as the child arrives,' Eleanor promised. 'How I hope that this time it will be a boy!'

'If not, there is plenty of time for us. Take care of yourself, my dear. And Mary . . . has she given any indication yet?'

'I am hopeful that she will soon do so. She is happy in the convent. But the Abbess thinks she should wait awhile and not make a hasty decision.'

'The Abbess should be about her own business.'

'It may be that she would consider Mary's taking her vows as her business.'

'Once she has taken them, yes. The girl must be persuaded.'

'I am doing my best. She is young yet, and if we can only persuade her before . . .'

Eleanor frowned and Thomas said: 'You are thinking of fortune hunters. My dear wife, none could marry her without consulting us.'

'You have forgotten your brother. He is her guardian.'

'He is occupied with other matters. He spends a great deal of time with his mistress. I wonder what it is this Catherine Swynford has to cast such a spell on him. There is no doubt that he is bewitched by the woman.'

'You think she is a witch . . .'

Thomas shrugged his shoulders. 'If she had been she would have made him marry her doubtless. He knew her when Blanche died. But he married Constanza, did he not?'

'Because he hoped for the crown of Castile.'

'Yes, John has matters to occupy him. I doubt he gives much thought to little Mary de Bohun.'

'Then it is really just a matter of persuading Mary.'

'The day will come,' prophesied Thomas, 'when she enters her convent and then everything will be ours, my dear.'

His eyes glistened at the thought. So did Eleanor's.

She would persuade Mary in time. She had always persuaded Mary.

Thomas left for France. Mary returned to her lessons at the convent. She had become very much aware of everything around her, and she was beginning to believe that the peace of the convent would be very desirable.

John of Gaunt had come to Arundel Castle where he was being entertained by his good friends, the Earl and Countess.

John had recently returned from Scotland where he had negotiated peace with the Scots and he had taken with him his eldest son Henry of Bolingbroke. Henry was some fourteen years of age, a good-looking sturdy boy, and his father was proud of him.

Soon, he had thought, I must find a suitable bride for him. It would be someone who could bring him wealth. That was necessary. The richer a man was the more power he had. His brother Thomas had done very well for himself with the Bohun heiress. Those Bohun girls would be two of the richest in the kingdom. It was small wonder that Thomas had become very smug since his marriage.

John was very well aware of the extent of the Bohun fortune, the younger girl being his ward. The King had bestowed this gift on him—for gift it was, as the wardship carried with it a grant of five thousand marks and Richard had given it to him as compensation for some payments which were due to him. Thomas had been displeased about that. John smiled grimly at the memory of Thomas's disquiet. No doubt he did not want his brother to know too much about the de Bohun inheritance. Moreover it gave John a command over Mary's future.

As he rode up the high circular knoll on which the castle stood, his thoughts were on his brother and he wondered what mischief he was concocting now. Across the drawbridge under the portcullis into the castle he went where the Earl was waiting to greet him. John of Gaunt was the most powerful man in the land—under the King; and Richard as yet was but a boy.

It was the Countess who had brought up the subject of the de Bohun girls. She was their aunt and she was very interested in their future because she had heard a rumour that the younger was thinking of going into a convent.

They had eaten dinner and the minstrels were playing in the gallery; much good wine had been drunk and the conversation was of a desultory nature.

'You are my niece's guardian, my lord Lancaster,' said the Countess. 'I doubt not you would have been informed if Mary had made her decision to take the veil.'

'I have heard nothing of it,' replied John. 'And I think the girl is too young to make such a decision.'

'I doubt not,' put in the Earl, 'that she is being gently persuaded that the convent life is for her.'

'Persuaded!' cried the Countess.

'Well,' said the Earl, 'look what Buckingham would gain by such a measure. Not a half of the de Bohun estates but the whole would fall to Eleanor. She is a lady with her wits about her, so I have heard. And Thomas has a nose for money. But, my lord Lancaster, she would need your consent.'

'I should not give it unless it was the girl's own wish,' John replied.

'I am glad to hear you say that,' said the Countess. 'She is ten years old. Girls of that age can be filled with ideals. They can make a decision before they understand what it is all about, particularly if they are discreetly jostled into it.'

'I shall go and visit her,' said John. 'I shall see for myself what it is all about.'

'I believe Eleanor is a very forceful young woman,' explained the Countess. 'When she sets her mind to something she works hard to get it. Mary is gentle—the beauty of the family. Such a pretty little thing. I confess

I should hate to see her shut away with the Poor Clares. And think of all that money!'

'I am thinking of it,' said John. 'That is why I shall go to see her.'

'It would be easier if it were not known that you were sounding her,' said the Countess. 'I have an idea. Would you like to hear it?'

'We are all ears,' said the Earl. 'Is that not so, my lord Lancaster?'

John nodded, smiling.

'Why should I not ask Mary to Arundel? That will arouse little comment. I shall tell her we all want to see our nieces. There is no reason why I should not bring her to see her Uncle Richard. I will ride to Pleshy and bring her back with me. We shall have some merriment here in Arundel and we shall see whether Mary really wishes to give up the world for the veil. What think you of this plan?'

'It seems to me fair enough,' said her husband. 'What think you, my lord?'

John was thoughtful. An idea had come to him. He did not speak for a moment, and the Countess prompted: 'Well, my lord Lancaster?'

'I like this plan,' he said. 'It would be a weight off my mind to know that she was not being forced into the life. I wish to see the girl . . . away from her sister and the influence of Thomas. I want to judge for myself what is best for her.'

'Then I will go to Pleshy and when Mary is here, my lord, I will send you word.'

John was smiling. He liked the idea. He liked it very much.

Eleanor received her aunt with a certain gracious dignity.

She gives herself airs since she married into royalty, thought the Countess, smiling inwardly. She did not like Eleanor. The girl was too proud, too ambitious. Mary was quite different, charming and pretty. The Countess was glad young Mary had managed to acquire all the good looks.

'My dear Eleanor,' she cried, 'it is long since I saw you. Marriage suits you, my dear. One baby in the nursery and another on the way. I'll vow Thomas wants a boy this time.'

'We are hoping for a boy,' replied Eleanor.

'Is there news of Thomas?'

'None. You know how difficult it is to get news from France.'

'Doubtless the child will be born by the time he returns. A reward for his services to the King.'

'He is not likely to get any other.'

'Oh come, Richard is grateful to his uncles.'

'Not to Thomas.'

The Countess laughed lightly. 'It is a pleasure to see you so contented with your marriage. And Mary, how is she?'

'She is devoted to the nuns. It was so fortunate that the convent is so close to the castle. It means that we have her with us and she can at the same time indulge in her pleasure to be within the convent.'

'It was most convenient that you chose to come to Pleshy,' commented the Countess. 'It might have been one of your castles or that draughty house that was your father's in the Dowgate Ward of London.'

'You mean Cole Harbour. Yes, Pleshy is just the right place for Mary, and I am ready to stay here for that reason. I like to see my little sister contented.'

'As she is, I believe.'

'Oh very. People are fortunate when they are almost born with the knowledge of what they want in life.'

'You mean the convent for Mary. I agree with you. It is very fortunate. I look forward to seeing Mary while I am here.'

'Of a certainty you will.'

I am determined on it, thought the Countess, for it is the object of my visit.

Later that day she did see Mary.

She thought: The child is truly a beauty. It would be a pity if she were shut away in a convent just because her greedy sister and her avaricious brother-in-law want her share of the de Bohun fortune.

She was very cautious, being eager to give no sign to Eleanor that she was in the slightest degree averse to Mary's future in the convent.

She mentioned more than once the great admiration

she had for the Poor Clares and the wonderful work they were doing.

Mary spoke glowingly of them and Eleanor purred like a contented cat.

The Countess said: 'Your uncle Richard was saying that he should so like to see you. I told him that I would persuade you to come back to Arundel with me for a short visit. He said: I so long to see my dear nieces.'

'I am scarcely in a condition to travel,' Eleanor pointed out.

'Alas, that is so,' agreed the Countess. 'Mary could come though.'

Mary cried: 'I should so much like that.'

Eleanor looked a little taken aback but before she could speak the Countess said firmly: 'Then so it shall be. We will set out tomorrow.'

Eleanor said: 'Mary, you will not wish to leave your studies.'

'But, Eleanor, it will only be for a short visit. I long to go.'

'Then you shall, dear niece,' said the Countess quickly. 'Later on, when you have the baby, Eleanor, you will come to see your uncle I know.'

'Cannot he come here, my lady?'

'He will, of a certainty he will. But he has asked me so particularly to take you both back with me. He did not think that you would be unfit to travel. Men do not understand these things. I must take *one* of you back. Mary, we must leave early. It is a long journey and I wish for an early start.'

Mary was clearly excited at the prospect of the visit and Eleanor could only shrug her shoulders.

It would be but for a few days and their aunt was clearly in favour of Mary's taking the veil. Perhaps she would help to persuade her.

There was no need to worry.

It was exciting riding to Arundel with her aunt. Mary had forgotten how beautiful the Sussex countryside was. She could smell the sea and she remembered that the castle was only a short distance from the coast. The Countess had been talking about the pleasures of Arundel and the new dances and songs of which Mary had some knowledge because none could enjoy social life more than Eleanor and Thomas. There were often visitors at Arundel, explained her aunt. It was a great pleasure when they came with news of what was happening in Court. Not that she was ignorant of that, she was quick to add. Your uncle is in constant attendance on the King.

Mary did notice that, although while they were at Pleshy her aunt had talked a great deal about the Convent of the Poor Clares, stressing the good life led by the nuns, during the journey her conversation had changed considerably; and she seemed to be extolling the pleasures of life outside convent walls.

As the drawbridge was lowered and they rode under the portcullis and into the courtyard, the Countess said: 'What joy there is in coming home. I always wonder when I return what will have been happening to the place while I have been away, what visitors we have had or who will be awaiting us. One of the best things in life is coming home.'

She looked sideways at Mary, on whose face was an expression of understanding and shared excitement.

It will not be the convent life for her! thought the Countess. Lancaster will see to that.

Into the castle went Mary, to the chamber which had been made ready, there to wash off the stains of the journey and to prepare herself to go down to the great hall where the appetizing smells which pervaded the castle proclaimed that food would soon be served.

One of the women of the household arrived to say that on the instructions of my lady she had come to help her dress. My lady had set out a gown for her as her own would not yet be unpacked.

Mary was astonished at the splendour of the garment. The surcoat was of fine blue silk and delicately embroidered with birds and flowers. Under the surcoat was a less loosely fitting gown in a delicate shade of green; the sleeves of the garment made it in the height of fashion for from the elbow they hung almost to her knees.

Mary was not used to wearing such fine clothes although she had seen Eleanor in them. 'You like the colours of your nuns,' Eleanor had said; and she had not cared enough to protest.

The serving girl brushed her dark hair and let it fall about her shoulders, saying:

'My lady said not for you the wimple or the dorelet. Your hair is too pretty to be hidden.'

Mary felt like a stranger to herself when the Countess came to her chamber to see the effect and to conduct her down to the hall.

It was clear that her aunt was pleased by the transformation.

In the hall was the Earl, who bade her welcome to the castle, and with him were his daughters Elizabeth and Joan.

Mary was glad that they were there. The boys were away from home—as was the custom with boys who always seemed to be brought up in someone else's home. But it was pleasant to meet her cousins.

The warmth of her welcome was heartening and she could not help feeling glad to have escaped from Eleanor, who would have been highly critical of her, and that would have spoilt her pleasure.

Mary was placed at the high table in between the Earl and the Countess and they talked to her about life at Pleshy and naturally the convent of the Poor Clares was mentioned.

'The nuns are the best people possible to give a girl a good education,' declared the Countess. 'Poor creatures, what sad lives they lead.'

'They are not in the least sad, my lady,' said Mary hastily. 'They serve God through the unfortunate and that brings them great happiness.'

The Countess laid her hand on that of her niece. 'Indeed they do. I am sorry for them because they will never know the joy of having children. I speak as a mother, dear child. I wonder how many of them ever regret the life they have chosen when they hear children chattering and laughing together.'

Mary was silent.

This was a special occasion, whispered her uncle. They were so delighted, he and her aunt, that she had come. He was going to lead her into the dance when they had eaten. What did she think of that? Did she like to dance?

Oh yes, she loved to dance.

And music? Did she enjoy that?

She liked to sing. She played the guitar accompanying herself.

'We must hear you,' said the Earl. 'Do you sing to your sister and her husband? It would be no use singing to the nuns, I'll warrant.'

'Oh no,' she said with a little laugh.

'This venison is to your taste, I hope,' went on the Earl. 'I'll swear you'd not taste better at the King's table. He has a fine palate, our King. Do you know he interests himself in the actual cooking of the food which is served at his table?'

'The King has very unusual tastes for a king.'

The Countess laughed. 'You are right,' she said. 'One could not imagine his father or his grandfather caring how much honey in proportion to mulberries was put into a moree.'

'Does the King care about such matters then?' asked Mary.

'Indeed he does,' replied the Earl. 'He concerns himself not only with his cooks but with his tailors. He spends hours in consultations with these fellows who are, they say, getting a grand idea of their worth. He'll be bestowing the Garter on one of them soon, some say, because he has produced some delicate recipe or a particularly magnificent cote hardie.'

There was laughter at the table. And then while the sotiltees were being served the minstrels and the mummers arrived.

It was a wonderful entertainment, more amusing than anything she had seen at Pleshy. The mummers danced and pirouetted in the most agile manner; in their grotesque masks they looked like beings from another world. Mary laughed a great deal and the Earl and Countess were delighted at her pleasure. They were determined that by the time she left Arundel she was going to have changed her mind about this wish to join the Poor Clares.

She slept soundly that night and arose feeling fresh and full of vitality the next morning. She could not help being pleased that Eleanor had been unable to accompany them, for she was realizing that Eleanor had a way of damping down her pleasure and implying that it was sinful for Mary to indulge in that of which she, Eleanor, could not have enough.

Her cousins showed her their horses and they crossed the drawbridge, ran down the incline and walked as far as the forest. How she had enjoyed standing under the trees and inhaling the scent of earth and pines. She loved the forest and longed to be there alone free of her cousins' chatter. She felt she had so much to think about. They believed they had been very bold to cross the drawbridge but said Elizabeth: 'It is all right because there are three of us.'

She felt much older than they were, though she was not really so; she supposed it was due to her upbringing with the nuns. It seemed that during the last days she had grown up suddenly; she was presented with a problem which could affect her whole life and she needed solitude to think of it. How she would love to wander alone among these beautiful trees and think of the future. She was thoughtful as they returned to the castle.

It was after dinner and the household was very quiet. Mary knew that her cousins were with their mother before she took her rest. An irresistible urge came over her to get out into the forest. She wanted to be absolutely alone and she could not feel that within the castle walls.

On impulse she put on her cloak and went to the drawbridge. It was down and there were no guards on duty. She crossed it and felt free. She ran down the incline and turned towards the fringe of the forest.

It was greatly daring. Her uncle and her aunt would be horrified if they knew she were out alone. I shall only venture into the edge, she promised herself, and shall keep the castle in sight. I must be alone to think.

The grass was green and springy under her feet. There had been much rain of late. How beautiful it was! There was a tang in the air which made her cheeks tingle but it was not really cold for January. She liked the winter; she thought the trees raising their stark branches to the sky made a more intricate and delicate pattern than could be produced with needle on silk and the evergreen pines were as resplendent now as in the height of summer. She stood listening to the call of a skylark; she filled her lungs with the sharp fresh air and gratefully smelt the scent of grass and foliage. She looked up at the grey sky and the pale wintry sun and thought the world was a beautiful place. There was so much to discover and if one were shut away in the convent one would learn so little about it. She was deep in thought as she walked through the glades, pausing every now and then to look closer at the tassels of the hazels and to see whether the blossoms were beginning to show on the ancient yews, as she inhaled the fresh air.

She began to smile, suddenly thinking of the mummers she had seen last evening. How excited she had been when her uncle had led her in the dance! It had been a great honour; she wondered why he and the Countess had taken such pains to make her feel so important. She was, after all, only just past ten years old.

Her uncle had talked about her going to Court. That would be much later of course but he had made it sound exciting. Richard would be pleased to receive her, he had said. How would she like that? It must always be a pleasure to be received by a king, she had replied.

It was so different here at Arundel from Pleshy. Was it because Eleanor always made her feel that she was destined for the convent and must never forget it for it would be sinful to turn her back on her destiny.

But was it her destiny? Since she had come to Arundel she was unsure.

She stood listening. She could hear the sound of horses' hoofs. There must be arrivals at the castle. There was nothing unusual in that. Travellers were constantly calling. They came often to Pleshy. They were never turned away unless, of course, there was some reason for doing so.

The incident had reminded her where she was and what she was doing. She was disobeying rules, which was not very good of her since she had been treated so affectionately by her aunt and uncle at the castle. Because they had behaved as though she were much older, with the honours they had bestowed on her, she had felt grown up. Perhaps it was for that reason that she had ventured into the forest.

She should return at once.

She started to walk back the way she thought she had

come, but after she had gone some little distance and expected to emerge from the forest to see the castle before her, she did not do so.

The trees hedged her in and with dismay she realized that she was not sure of the direction in which she should go. It was nothing to be alarmed at. She had not really penetrated the forest; she had just skirted the edge. She must emerge from the trees and see the castle soon.

But alas, it was not so simple. She had been so deep in thought that she had not noted any landmark which might have helped her. All the trees looked alike. She paused uncertainly and tried to work out which way to go.

She must not panic. This was a situation she had never had to face before. It was the first time she had been away from her home alone. What had she been thinking of to come into the forest? The treatment given her by her relations had made her feel she was no longer a child.

How foolish she had been and here she was alone, lost in the forest.

This was nonsense. She would find her way. She stood quite still and as she did so she thought she heard a rustling in the undergrowth.

Was someone else in this part of the forest?

Her first thought was of relief. If some woodman was there he could show her the way back to the castle. Then she thought of robbers. She heard that they abounded on the roads. During the early days of the reign of the late King there had been strict laws against them and the roads had been comparatively safe; but, when the old King had grown senile and paid more attention to his mistress Alice Perrers than to the affairs of the country, laws had become lax and the robbers multiplied. Richard was young yet and it was not known what his rule would be but it seemed clear that his laws would not be as strict as those of his grandfather in his heyday.

Her hands went to the girdle at her waist. It was not over elaborate, not to be compared with the kind Eleanor wore—but it would have great value in the eyes of some needy vagrant.

There was another sound. There was no doubt now. Someone was coming nearer. She walked on, quickening her pace. Whoever it was quickened pace also. So she was being followed.

She was now really afraid.

She started to run. Was she going in the right direction? So many trees, so many bushes, that looked alike and she had been too absorbed in her thoughts to notice landmarks.

Could she be sure that she was going the way she had come, that the trees would be less dense in a few moments and she would be able to glimpse the grey walls of the castle?

Whoever was following her was running now.

'Wait!' called a voice.

She ran on.

Someone was immediately behind her, and a hand was laid on her arm. She started violently as a voice said: 'Good day to you, my lady.'

She turned sharply. It was a boy—a few years older than herself, tawny-haired, blue-eyed and fairly tall.

'Why do you run from me?' he asked. 'You are quite breathless.'

'What do you want?' she asked and instinctively her hands went to her girdle.

He stood back a pace and bowed low. 'To serve you,' he said and there was a slightly mocking look in his eyes.

'Then show me the way to the castle.'

'You have not come far.'

'Am I on the right path?'

He shook his head. 'You will need my help.'

'You will want payment for it, I see. Never fear. Take me back to the castle and you will be rewarded.'

'How did you come to lose your way?'

'No matter, I have lost it. Are you going to show me the right path?'

'Follow me,' he said.

She was relieved for a moment. He walked ahead of her. She noticed his well shaped head and how his tawny hair curled softly; he held himself proudly. She thought he might be the son of some neighbouring squire.

After a few minutes she said: 'I do not remember coming this way.'

He turned to smile at her and there was a hint of mischief in the smile. 'Ah, but you lost your way.'

'Are you sure this is the way back to the castle?'

'I swear that I will show you the way.'

They had come to a clearing in the trees.

'I did not see this before.'

'It is a pleasant spot,' he said.

She had become very frightened. He was not leading her to the castle. It seemed rather that he was taking her away from it.

'Please show me the way at once,' she said.

'You are tired,' he answered soothingly. 'Rest awhile. Then I promise you that I will show you the way back.'

'I have no desire to rest.'

'I think you have. You are flushed with exertion and alarm. Sit for a few moments. Look, there is a pleasant spot under the trees there.'

'I have no wish to. Good day to you.'

He had thrown himself down under a tree and looked up at her smiling. She thought: How insolent he is, this son of a squire! My uncle would punish him severely for this.

She turned away and immediately asked herself which way to go.

She hesitated and she heard his voice. 'You will go farther into the forest. Better wait for me.'

She came back to him. 'If you will take me back now, I will pay you well.'

'Later,' he said. 'Later.'

He indicated the spot beside him. She hesitated for a second and seeing that she needed his help she sat down beside him.

'You must know how eager I am,' she said. 'It is not very gallant to behave as you do. You should study the manners of knighthood, even though you may not be of noble birth.'

'You ask too much of one . . . not of noble birth. You *are*, indeed. I guess that. You are a guest at the castle.'

'The Earl of Arundel is my uncle. He would be displeased if he knew of your conduct.'

'I wonder what my punishment would be. Perhaps I shall find out when you betray me.'

'I will say nothing of this if you take me back to the castle without delay. Indeed I shall see that you receive a good meal and some reward.'

'I am overcome with gratitude.'

She leaped to her feet. 'Then, show me the way back, now.'

He did not rise but lay back smiling at her lazily.

'Very soon,' he said. 'I promise you. You have not told me your name but I believe you are the Lady Mary de Bohun who is at this time visiting her aunt and uncle at Arundel.'

'How did you know this?'

'We humble folk discover these matters concerning the great ones.'

'Then as you know who I am you will realize the need not to offend me . . . or my uncle.'

'It is a great need,' he said. 'You have not asked my name.'

'It is of no importance to me.'

'That was scarcely friendly. Then I will tell you. My name is Henry.'

'Then Henry, it is time we left this place.'

'Such a pleasant place,' he murmured. 'It has been a happy adventure for me.'

'If you will not show me the way back I shall attempt to find the way myself. And rest assured I shall tell of your knavish behaviour to me. You will regret it.'

'You are not often angry are you, my lady?'

She turned away.

'But you are angry now because you are frightened. Please do not be, Lady Mary. I want you to like me.'

'I shall not do that after your behaviour. Take me back at once.'

He stood up meekly and said: 'It was only a game. Come. It is here. You will be surprised how close you were to the castle. The trees grow so thickly and the bushes so high that even in winter weather it is easy to lose the way.'

She walked beside him uncertainly. From time to time he glanced at her almost appealingly as though begging her to forgive him; and strangely enough because he was rather handsome and seemed really contrite and was after all only a boy, she found she could, particularly when she saw the castle a little way ahead.

At the edge of the wood she paused to bid him good-bye and thank him.

'You shall be rewarded,' she told him. 'I will tell my uncle.'

'I shall come to the castle for my reward,' he said.

She hesitated. Perhaps that was the best way. He could go to the kitchens and be refreshed there and be satisfied.

They came to the drawbridge. There were men-at-arms there now and they bowed both to her and her companion.

Together they passed under the portcullis and into the courtyard.

He was preparing to accompany her into the hall and she said to him: 'You must go through that alley there. You will come to the kitchens. You may tell them I sent you.'

'I prefer to enter by way of the hall.'

'But you do not understand.'

He raised his eyebrows. He was a most unusual boy. He had, she noticed now, an air of arrogance which implied that he thought himself equal to anyone.

'My uncle . . .' she began.

And at that moment her uncle came into the hall and with him was the Duke of Lancaster himself. Even at such a moment she could not help but be overawed by her guardian.

He was a tall man, commanding in appearance. His deep-set eyes were a vivid blue and his hair tawny as a lion. He had the long nose and narrow cheeks of the Plantagenets, and on his tunic was emblazoned his emblem of the lilies of France and the leopards of England.

Beside him her uncle looked insignificant.

For a moment she forgot the boy at her side and then she was afraid for him. It was one thing for him to venture into the hall of the castle but to come face to face with her uncle and the great Duke of Lancaster was another.

'It is Mary herself,' said the Earl.

She walked forward and to her astonishment so did the boy.

He stood beside the great Duke, who did not display any surprise at this strange behaviour.

Apprehensively she curtseyed, wondering how she was going to explain.

The Duke lifted her up in his arms and said: 'Why, Mary, you have grown since we last met. You have already made the acquaintance of Henry.'

Henry!

The boy was smiling at her.

'We met outside the castle, my lord father,' he said. 'So . . . we came in together.'

It was bewildering. The boy whom she had thought to be some humble squire was in fact the son of the great John of Gaunt—more noble than she was. She was overcome with shame. What had she said to him!

It was all something of a joke now. He had come to the castle with his father who had been anxious to see his ward and to discover how she was getting on at Pleshy.

The Countess said: 'When my lord Lancaster heard that you were coming here he thought it would be an easy way of assuring himself that you were well and happy. It was so much easier than going to Pleshy.' She lowered her voice. 'And you know he and his brother are not on the most amicable of terms.'

'It is a pity when there is conflict in families,' said Mary.

'But always inevitable. This young Henry of ours is a fine young sprig of the royal branch, do you not think? He was the cause of the trouble between the brothers. Knight of the Garter and already Earl of Derby! I am not surprised that his father dotes on him. He will be a good companion for you while you are with us, Mary.'

'I have my cousins.'

'Yes, but I am sure you will find Henry more amusing.'

It was true, she did.

At first she had reproached him for the way he had behaved in the forest.

'It was but a game,' he said. 'I could not resist it. I saw you as we arrived. You were just entering the forest—which was forbidden, I am sure. I came to guard you.'

'It was deceitful not to say who you were,' she retorted.

'Oh dear. I had forgotten they are going to make a nun of you, are they not?'

'*They* will not make anything of me if I do not wish it.'

'Then I'll tell you something. You are not going to be a nun.'

'How do you know?'

'Because you will never agree to shut yourself away from the world. You like it too much.'

'My future is not yet decided.'

'It will be soon,' he told her, and there was laughter in his eyes.

He wanted always to be with her.

'You neglect my cousins sorely,' she reprimanded.

'They do not mind. They are but children.'

'And how old are you?'

'Soon to be fifteen.'

It was indeed a few years older than she was, but he never seemed to notice that difference.

She could play as good a game of chess as he could. They would often be seated together in a corner of the great hall, their heads bent over the chess board. Sometimes the great Duke himself would stand by watching the game—applauding a good move. He seemed very contented to see them together.

She would sing to him, playing her guitar as accompaniment. His voice would join with hers; they were in perfect harmony.

The Countess said they must sing together for the company after supper and when they did so, she noticed the eyes of the great John of Gaunt glazed with emotion. He clearly had a great affection for his son and she could understand it for she was discovering that she had too.

The days passed too quickly. She knew that she would have to go back to Pleshy very soon and when she thought of returning to the old way of life she felt depressed. Perhaps Henry would come to see her at Pleshy; but if she became a nun they would not be able to meet very often.

They rode out together with a party but Henry always contrived that he and she escaped. She fancied that their elders realized this and were amused rather than displeased by it.

Then one day when they had escaped from the party and were riding in the forest they came to the clearing where they had sat on that first occasion.

Henry suggested that they tether the horses and sit in the same spot for a while as he had something to say to her.

'You will soon be going back to Pleshy,' he began.

She sighed. 'Alas yes. My stay here has been longer already than I thought it would be. I shall be returning soon, I am sure.'

'I too shall be leaving here with my father.'

'It has been such a happy time.'

'For us both,' said Henry. 'Mary, you will not go into a convent, will you?'

'I am unsure . . .'

He turned to her passionately, and putting his arms about her held her close to him. 'Oh Mary,' he whispered, 'you can't do that. Promise you will not.'

'Why should it mean . . . so much to you?' she asked rather breathlessly.

'Because I want to marry you.'

'To marry *me*. Oh Henry . . .'

'Does that please you?'

She looked about her at the stark branches of the trees which she loved and she thought the forest of Arundel was the most beautiful place in the world.

'You have answered,' he said. 'It does please you.'

'So much,' she said. 'I have never in my life been so happy as I have since you came.'

'Then it is settled.'

'What is settled? I shall have to go away from here and so will you.'

'We shall be married,' he said.

'Married. How can we be? I cannot marry . . . just like that.'

'Why not?'

'It would never be allowed.'

'I can tell you that my father will not forbid it and he is your guardian.'

'How can you know that?'

'He has told me.'

'So . . . you have talked with him.'

'Only because I was so eager. I felt if I could get his consent that would be all we needed.'

'And . . . he has given it.'

'He loves you. He says you have been his ward and now you will be his daughter.'

'Is this truly so?'

'It is indeed. He has been delighted by the way in which we have grown to love each other. He says he sees no reason why we should not marry . . . soon.'

'Henry, I am not yet eleven years old.'

'That is a very pleasant age. I am fourteen. You see there is not much difference between us.'

'They would never let us marry yet. We should have to wait.'

'There could be a ceremony . . . so that none could keep us apart. What say you, Mary?'

She clasped her hands together and was silent. It was too much to take in. It was not so long ago that she had sat here, lost in the forest, uncertain of the way she must go back to the castle, uncertain of her way in life too.

Henry had taken her hand and kissed it. 'You want to marry me, Mary. You know you do. Think how you have enjoyed these last days. It would be like that for the rest of our lives.'

She contemplated it and it seemed to her too wonderful to be true. Not to have to live at Pleshy; to give up her studies at the convent. How could she ever have thought she wanted to become a nun?

'Yes, Henry,' she cried. 'I do want it. I want to marry you. I want to have many children. I want to be a wife and a mother and live like this for ever.'

Henry was laughing. He embraced her fervently. He told her that he had never been so happy in his life.

'Let us go back to the castle and tell them.'

She did not want to go yet. She wanted to linger in the forest. For all he said, she feared their disapproval. Although they had seemed content to see her and Henry together and had not stopped their being alone, which in itself was strange, she still felt that her extreme youth would be stressed and while they would be kind, might let them become betrothed, that would be as far as this matter would go for the time. They might be married in say three years' time . . .

But she was wrong.

When they returned to the castle Henry took her immediately to his father.

'My lord,' he cried, 'Mary has promised to marry me.'

Mary was astonished by the expression on the Duke's handsome face. His eyes looked more fiercely blue than ever and a smile of delight spread across his face.

'But, my dear children . . . this news moves me and delights me. Nothing could please me more.'

He took Mary into his arms and held her tightly so that she felt she would suffocate against the lilies and the leopards. Then he released her and embraced Henry.

'It is what I hoped for,' he said. 'It has delighted me to see you two grow to love each other. Love is the best foundation for marriage.' He was too emotional to speak for a moment. He meant what he said. His ambitious marriage with Constanza of Castile had been undertaken for love of a crown which was love of another sort and often he had wondered whether he should not have been recklessly romantic and married Catherine Swynford, the woman he loved. Marriage for love. What a blessing. But when there was great wealth as well as love, then there could be no doubt that the marriage was an ideal one.

He smiled benignly on Mary. 'So, my child, you have decided the convent life is not for you, eh. You have chosen wisely, and most happily for this son of mine. You shall be betrothed.'

'We are anxious, my lord, that we should be married,' said Henry. 'We do not wish for a long delay.'

'You see what an impatient man you are to marry, Mary,' retorted the Duke. 'Well, it is a measure of his love for you. I tell you sincerely, nothing shall stand in the way of your wishes.' Mary could not believe she heard aright. The great man seemed as happy about the union as she and Henry were.

THE CHILD WIFE

Lancaster could not await to acquaint the Earl and Countess with the good news.

'It has worked perfectly,' cried Lancaster. 'Henry has played his part to perfection. He knew what I wanted and it seems that when he saw the pretty child he wanted the same thing himself.'

'It is a pleasure to have such a dutiful son,' replied Arundel.

'They make a charming pair,' said the Countess. 'I think Henry is a very lucky boy and I am so glad our little Mary has escaped from that sister of hers. I wonder what Thomas is going to say when he hears the news. I should love to be present when it first comes to his ears.'

'He will rant and rave,' said the Earl. 'And try to prevent it.'

'That is what we must beware of,' added Lancaster. 'I do not think it wise for Mary to return to Pleshy.'

'No indeed,' agreed the Earl. 'Eleanor would be capable of anything. She might lock the child up until she promises to go into a convent. She'll be furious—particularly as this has happened while Thomas is away.'

'He could not have refused to let Mary come to Arundel,' pointed out Lancaster.

'He would have tried to if he had known you and Henry were coming here,' said the Earl.

'He would not have thought of this . . . in view of Mary's youth.'

'Mary's youth!' mused the Countess. 'She *is* young for marriage.'

'Oh let them live together,' said Lancaster. 'They will act according to nature and that is the best way. I want to see them married and I intend that the ceremony shall take place with all speed.'

'And you want her to remain here right up to the time when it shall take place?'

'I think it best. And we should keep quiet about the proposed marriage. Then it shall take place at the Savoy. I doubt my brother—if he has returned which I hope he will not—or his wife will be among the wedding guests.'

Eleanor had begun to realize how long her sister had been away, but she was not unduly disturbed. The weather was bad and it was not easy to travel in the winter. Her aunt had given the impression that she believed a convent life would be good for Mary and if the girl came back convinced of her vocation Eleanor would be delighted.

Pregnancy was irksome to one of her vitality. It was a necessity of course if she was to breed; and she must produce sons. She hoped she would have one to show Thomas when he returned from France. Even so they would have to busy themselves in getting another.

She sat disconsolately among her women who talked continually of the baby and sometimes they would mention the Lady Mary and wonder if she missed the convent.

'Of course she does,' retorted Eleanor firmly. 'Her life is with the nuns. Dear child, she has a saintly nature. It is clear where her destiny lies.'

The ladies murmured agreement. It was always wise to agree with Eleanor and it was impossible to be in this household and not know the urgent wish of its master and mistress.

On a snowy afternoon her pains started. Everything

was in readiness and within a day the child had made its appearance.

It was a great disappointment to the countess that it should be another girl.

She lay disconsolately in her bed and listened to the wind buffeting the walls of Pleshy. How frustrated Thomas would be. But the child was healthy enough and she decided to call her Joan. Before long she would be once more pregnant she supposed and would have to go through the wearisome months of waiting and then produce . . . not another girl. No, that would be too unfortunate. But it had happened to others. Lancaster had got girls and a stillborn son before young Henry had been born at Bolingbroke.

While she was brooding a messenger arrived. It was strange that he should have come from Lancaster when the Duke had just been in her thoughts.

'A messenger from my lord of Lancaster,' she cried. 'What news from him, I wonder.'

The messenger was brought to her bedchamber and the letters were handed to her.

She did not hasten to read them, but questioned the messenger whence he had come and when she heard that he came from Arundel the first quiver of concern came to her. She sent the messenger down to the kitchens to be refreshed in the accepted manner, and broke the seals.

What she read almost made her leap from her bed, weak though she was.

The Duke was delighted to inform her that his son Henry, Earl of Derby, had fallen in love with her sister Mary. There was no one he would rather see married to his son. He had therefore given his consent to the marriage, for he could see no reason why the young people should be denied their happiness. Thomas was away but he hoped she would make all speed to his Palace of the Savoy where the marriage was to be celebrated without delay.

She could not believe this. It was impossible. It was a nightmare. She was dreaming!

Mary to be married! The child was not yet eleven years old. How could she marry at such an age! Of course it was Mary's fortune Lancaster wanted. The avaricious scheming rogue!

Mary was too young for marriage. She was going to protest. Oh, why was not Thomas here!

Yet what could Thomas do if he were here? Lancaster was Mary's guardian. Lancaster was the elder brother. It was said that Lancaster was the most powerful man in the country for poor King Richard counted for little. And he had taken advantage of the fact that Mary was away from Pleshy.

'The scheming devil!' she cried.

She was helpless. Unable to leave her bed.

They had planned this. Was Arundel in it? Thomas would never forgive them. There would be murder between those brothers one day.

She should never have let Mary go to Arundel. She should have seen what was coming. She might have known . . .

She read the letter again. Henry and Mary in love! She sneered in fury. Henry was in love indeed and so was Lancaster. In love with Mary's fortune.

That was at the root of the matter. It was Mary's money they wanted. It was Mary's money they all wanted.

'Oh Mary, you little fool,' she cried, 'why did you not go into your convent?'

Clenching and unclenching her fists she lay in her bed.

The midwife came in and shook her head. 'My lady, you need rest. You must be calm. It is necessary to your good health.'

She felt limp and exhausted.

She had gained a child—a *girl* child and lost a fortune.

Mary was bewildered. There was no time to think very much about anything but the approaching wedding. She was in a state of blissful happiness, but the rapidity with which everything was happening could not fail to make her feel somewhat bemused. She had expected betrothal but not this hurried wedding. It was not that she had any doubts about her love for Henry. She wanted to marry him; but she had naturally thought that in view of their ages they would wait for a year at least.

But no, said the Duke of Lancaster. They would have

this happy matter settled without delay. Henry wanted it. She wanted it. And the Duke wanted their happiness.

In the circumstances he thought it wise that the ceremony should take place at his Palace of the Savoy. It would be simpler than having it at Cole Harbour which he believed was an uncomfortable draughty place.

Mary confirmed that this was so. 'There is Pleshy,' she suggested.

The Duke said hastily that he thought the Savoy would be more suitable.

'It is one of our homes,' he said, 'and one particularly dear to me. After the ceremony you and Henry can go to Hertford or Leicester or perhaps Kenilworth. I think Henry will want to show you Kenilworth. I believe it to be his favourite of all our castles.'

Mary said she would be pleased to go wherever Henry wished, which made the great Duke take her hand, kiss it and declare that Henry was indeed lucky to have found such a bride.

They were wonderful days. She and Henry rode together through the forest. He told her of how he hoped to stand beside his father and bring glory back to England. He seemed to her so knowledgeable of the world. He was on intimate terms with the King. 'We're cousins,' he said, 'and of an age. Three years ago we received the Order of the Garter together. That was when the old King was alive. It was just before he died. He was a sick old man then. I remember him as little else, but people say that when he was young he was goodly to look on. Then he was a faithful husband and a strong King.'

She loved to hear of these matters, many of which she had heard discussed at Pleshy but they seemed more colourful and exciting coming from Henry. Or it may have been that as his wife she would have her part to play in them.

He talked of Alice Perrers, the loose woman of whom the old King had become enamoured. She had bewitched him and robbed him and had even started to do so before Good Queen Philippa died.

'I shall be faithful to you for ever, sweet Mary,' vowed Henry.

She swore that she would be true to him.

They were idyllic days.

But there was one small fear which had started in her mind. She had overheard women talking as women will—and all the talk at Arundel was of the coming marriage.

'Oh 'tis a wonderful marriage. The best for the little Lady Mary. Why young Henry is the cousin of the King and the grandson of great Edward and the son of the great John of Gaunt. How much higher could she go than that . . . lest it was the King himself?'

'But she is so young. Are they going to put them to bed together . . . Two children like that.'

'The Earl of Derby is not so young. He's rising fifteen. I have known boys of that age give a good account of themselves and I'll swear young Henry is no exception.'

'I was thinking of the Lady Mary.'

Talk like that disturbed her; and it was not once that she was aware of these allusions.

Henry noticed that she was disturbed and she told him why.

He was all concern. Yes, there was that side to marriage but she need not fear. He knew what must be done and she could leave it to him. 'You see, because of who I am we have to get children. We want sons.'

'I always wanted children,' she told him. 'That was one of the reasons why I hesitated about going into the convent.'

'Always remember that I saved you from that.' He laughed at her fears. 'Nay, there is nothing to fear. You will like well what must be done. I promise you that. We'll have lusty sons. How will you like that?'

She would like it very well, she told him. And she wondered why the women had tut-tutted and looked grave.

Whatever she had to do with Henry would be good, she was sure.

They sang together; they played chess; and she was fitted for the most splendid garments she had ever had. It was exhilarating until the messenger came from Pleshy with a letter from Eleanor. It was clearly written in a rage. Eleanor could not understand what had happened to her little sister whom she had always thought to be a saint in the making. How mistaken she had been for it was now disclosed that Mary was deceitful in the extreme. She had pretended to want the religious life, when all the time she was nothing more than a wanton. She had betrothed herself to Henry of Derby without consulting her sister. 'After all we have done for you, Thomas and I,' wrote Eleanor, 'you treat us like this. I am deeply wounded. I beg of you stop this folly and come back to Pleshy. Here we will talk out these matters. We will see what it means. Why do you think John of Lancaster is so eager for this match? If you had been some girl without a fortune do you think Henry of Bolingbroke would have been so eager to marry you . . . ?'

Mary paused and thought: Had I been I should never have met him in this way. It was because I was staying at Arundel with my uncle and aunt that I did.

'It is clear to me that it is your fortune which makes this marriage into the house of Lancaster so attractive to them,' went on Eleanor's letter.

And, thought Mary, it is my fortune that makes you so eager for me to go into a convent that I may resign my share for you. Oh dear! How I wish I were indeed a penniless girl!

That was foolish. Eleanor was right. John of Gaunt was pleased because of her fortune. It was different with Henry. She was sure he would have loved her whoever she was. But the marriage was welcomed because of the money. She was not so unworldly that she did not know that.

'Come back to Pleshy without delay,' commanded Eleanor. 'We will talk of this matter. We will put our heads together and decide what is best for you.'

She wrote back and asked Eleanor to come to Arundel. She was so caught up with the arrangements for the wedding that she could not travel. Eleanor would have recovered from the birth of dear little Joan now. But perhaps she would rather wait and join the celebrations at the Savoy.

Eleanor was not one to give up. Mary *must* come back. Out of gratitude she must come. The Abbess was desolate. She was sure it was wrong for Mary to marry so hastily and while she was so young. Let her return to Pleshy. Let her talk with her sister. Let her remember all that Eleanor and her brother-in-law Thomas had done for her.

Mary showed Eleanor's letters to Henry. She wanted there to be no secrets between them, she said.

Henry read the letters and said: 'There is an angry woman. Sister though she may be to you, I would not let you go near her. Why she might lock you up and starve you into submission.'

'Oh she is not such an ogre as that.'

'*I* am protecting you from now on, Mary.'

She was consoled. She was always so happy with Henry; she had even ceased to worry about the matter of the marriage bed.

A few days before they were due to leave for the Savoy, Mary's mother the Countess of Hereford arrived at Arundel.

She had of course been informed of the coming marriage of her younger daughter and she was somewhat uneasy about it.

She would have preferred Mary to have remained in her care but in accordance with the custom, as Mary was a great heiress, she must become a ward of some person of high standing. There was no one of higher standing under the King than John of Gaunt and as Eleanor was already married to his brother Thomas of Woodstock, the Countess had no alternative but to let her daughter go.

She could not of course complain about the husband selected for her. The eldest son of John of Gaunt, heir to the Lancastrian estates, a few years older than Mary, healthy, already a Knight of the Garter—there could not have been a more satisfactory match. But what concerned the Countess was the youth of her daughter.

Mary was a child, as yet unready for marriage in the Countess's view, and she should not marry until she was at least fourteen.

She embraced her daughter warmly and looked searchingly into her face.

She was certain there had been no coercion. The child looked very happy.

She sought an early opportunity of speaking with the Duke of Lancaster.

'I am happy about the marriage,' she said, 'apart from one aspect of it.'

The Duke looked haughty as though wondering what

aspect could possibly be displeasing about a marriage with *his* son.

'It is the youth of my daughter.'

'She is just eleven years old.'

'It is too young for marriage.'

'They are both young.'

'Too young, my lord. Let them be betrothed and marry . . . say in two years' time.'

Lancaster appeared to consider that although he had no intention of doing so. Wait two years? Let Thomas and his harridan of a wife get to work on the girl? They would have her packed into a convent by some devious means in no time.

'Poor Mary,' he said, 'she would be so unhappy. Wait until you see them together. They are so delighted to be in each other's company. No I could not allow that. They shall live together . . . naturally like two children . . .'

'I do not think girls of that age should have children.'

'Children! They won't have children for years. They are so innocent. You should hear them singing in harmony. They ride; they dance; they play chess. It is such a joy to see them. No, my dear Countess, they must marry. I understand a mother's feelings, but let me assure you that there is no need for the slightest apprehension.'

'I will have a talk with my daughter,' said the Countess.

John of Gaunt was uneasy. He wished the Countess had not come to Arundel but it had naturally been necessary to tell her what was planned for her daughter. She was a shrewd woman. She would understand why Eleanor was trying to force the girl into a convent. But at the same time she would do all she could to keep Mary unmarried until she reached what she would consider a suitable age.

The Countess talked to Mary.

'My dear child,' she said, 'you are very young for marriage.'

'Others have said that, my lady,' replied her daughter. 'But Henry and I love each other and are so happy together. He does not mind that I am young.'

'You must understand that there are obligations.'

'I know what you mean. It is the marriage bed, is it not?'

The Countess was a little taken aback.

'What do you know of these matters?'

'That there is nothing to fear . . . if one loves.'

She was quoting Henry. The Countess guessed that. There was no doubt that John of Gaunt was right when he said they loved each other.

'I have asked the Duke to put off the wedding. At least for a year. Then we could consider again when it should be.'

Mary looked very woebegone.

'And will he do that?'

The Countess put an arm about her daughter and held her firmly against her. She thought: No, he will not. He wants your fortune for his son. Dear child, what did she know of the way of the world?

At least she could console herself. The child was happy. So many girls in her position were forced into marriages which were distasteful to them. None could say that of Mary.

The Countess knew the determination of John of Gaunt. No matter how she protested, the marriage would take place.

She must resign herself to the fact that it was what Mary wanted.

So they were married and there was great rejoicing in John of Gaunt's Palace of the Savoy, which was to be expected as this was the marriage of his son and heir. Mary was made to feel that she was marrying into the greatest family in the land and that her marriage was even more brilliant than that of Eleanor. Eleanor was not present. She had declined the invitation from her false sister; and Thomas was still in France.

This breach created a mild sadness in the bride's heart but she did not dwell on it. Henry had made her see that Eleanor was in fact more interested in the de Bohun fortune than the happiness of her younger sister, and Mary was beginning to look to Henry and to accept what interpretation he put on all matters, and as Henry was always only too delighted to tell her and she to listen, they grew fonder of each other every day.

Now she was the Countess of Derby, and the impos-
ing man who sat at the head of the table was her new
father-in-law and there in the great hall of the Savoy
Palace tables had been set up on their trestles, for all the
nobility of the land must be present at the marriage of
John of Gaunt's son. Mary herself on the right hand of
the great Duke with Henry beside her was at the high
table. Her mother was there; so were her new sisters-in-
law Philippa and Elizabeth. Also present was a very
beautiful woman whose presence caused a few titters
among the guests. It was characteristic of the great
Duke that he should insist that his mistress not only be
present but be treated with all the deference which would
normally be bestowed on his Duchess.

Henry pressed Mary's hand and she smiled at him. It
was comforting to believe that while he was at her side
all would be well.

He selected the best parts of the food and fed them to
her and happily she munched the delicate morsels, although she was not really hungry. But the guests rev-
elled in the banquet, declared that they had rarely seen
such large boars' heads, such joints of beef and mutton,
such pestles of pork, such suckling pigs which made the
mouth water to behold. There was mallard, pheasant,
chicken, teals, woodcocks, snipes, peacocks and par-
tridges, as well as that delectable dish called the leche
which was made of pounded raw pork, eggs, sugar,
raisins and dates all mixed with spices and put in a
bladder to be boiled; and then there were those pastry
concoctions which were known as raffyolys and flam-
poyntes. Everything that could have been thought of to
make this a feast to outdo all feasts had been provided.

There would be a joust the next day but this one was
given up to feasting and indoor merriment.

The mummers trooped into the hall in their masks,
some of these so strange that they looked like spectral
figures and sent shivers of horror down the backs of the
spectators. They wore horned animals' heads and those
of goats and creatures who could never have existed
outside the imagination of the mask maker. Some of
them wore masks of beautiful women which sat oddly
on their square masculine bodies. But they were calculated to bring laughter to the lips of all who beheld them

and this they undoubtedly did although some might have been overawed.

It was wonderful to see them dance and play their scenes in mime. The company applauded with gusto and then the dancing began. Henry led out Mary and others fell in behind them. Lancaster danced with the beautiful Catherine Swynford; the company held its breath watching them and many thought—though they dared not give voice to such thoughts—that there was not a man in the kingdom now who would dare behave as John of Gaunt did. The old King had done it with his mistress Alice Perrers. It was a King's privilege he would have said; but the people did not like him for it. In some way it was different with John of Gaunt. There was true love between those two and that being so obvious was something which must command respect wherever it was.

Then John of Gaunt took Mary's hand and danced with her while Henry danced with Lady Swynford. Her new father told Mary that he regarded this as one of the happiest days of his life. He wanted her to regard it as such also.

The torches guttered and the evening was passing. It was time for Henry to lead Mary away. His father restrained the people who would have attempted to carry out some of the old customs. 'They are young and innocent,' he said. 'I would not harry them. Let nature take its course with them.'

In the great bedchamber which had been assigned to them, nature was taking its course.

Henry was advanced for his years. He was in love with his bride and because she was intelligent beyond her age it did not occur to him to consider that she might not be physically mature.

He was glad that there had been no ribald jokes; Mary would not have understood them and they might have alarmed her. As it was she was entirely his to teach as he could, he believed, so comfortably do.

Henry helped her remove the wedding garments, which jewel encrusted as they were were heavily uncomfortable, and it was a relief to be free of them.

She stood before him—a child in her simplicity. He himself took the loose nightgown and put it over her head.

Then he led her to the bridal bed; she lay down while he divested himself of his garments.

Then he joined her.

Gently with tender explanation he initiated her into the mysteries of procreation which for such as themselves, who had the continuance of great families to consider, was the primary function of marriage.

They set out for Kenilworth, for, as his father had said, Henry loved that best of all the Lancaster estates which would one day be his.

Mary was very happy journeying with Henry; he was kindly, loving and gentle and she had not believed there was so much contentment in the world. If she could but forget Eleanor she could be completely happy.

The sight of Kenilworth was breathtaking. They had travelled some way, for the castle was situated between Warwick and Coventry, being about five miles from each. It consisted of a magnificent structure of castellated buildings which owed their charm to the fact that they had been added to over the years, for Kenilworth had been nothing but a manor in the days of the first Henry, who had bestowed it on one of his nobles, and it was this noble who had begun the task of turning the manor into a castle. The keep was massive and was known as Caesar after that of the same name in the Tower of London. Kenilworth had the distinction of once belonging to Simon de Montfort and on his death it was bestowed by the King on his youngest son Edmund, Earl of Lancaster. Thus, like the Savoy, it had come to John of Gaunt through his marriage with Henry's mother, Blanche of Lancaster.

Henry told Mary that his father, who had taken a great fancy to the place since it had been in his possession, had extended it even more than those who had owned it before, and to prove this Henry pointed out to her the magnificent extension which was known as the Lancaster Building.

Kenilworth was a fairy tale palace ideally suited to a pair of young people who were realizing the joys of getting to know each other.

Mary would remember those days to the end of her life. She was completely happy and it did not occur to her in the full flush of her happiness to question its transience. She did not look to the future; if she had she would have known that a man in Henry's exalted position could not revel in the joys of newly married bliss in the castle of Kenilworth for ever.

They rode through the forest together—not hunting, for she had confessed to him that she hated to see animals killed and always hoped the deer and the boars would escape. Henry laughed at her but loved her more for her gentleness and he said that as she did not care for the hunt they would look for the signs of the spring and not for the spoor of animals.

She did not care for hawking either; she liked to watch the birds flying free. She would stand and admire Henry when he practised archery and happily applauded when he excelled those in competition with him. She thought how fine he looked when he shot at the target with his bow which was the same height as he was and his arrow was one full yard long. Their attendants played games with them. There was great hilarity over Ragman's Roll which was the preliminary to a mime. One of them would bring out a parchment roll on which were written couplets describing certain characters; and attached to these verses were strings with seals at the end. Each player must take a seal and pull the string and then play the character whose description he had picked. There were shrieks of laughter when this game was played for it always seemed that people chose the characters least like themselves. When they tired of mimes they would play Hot Cockles, in which one player was blindfolded and knelt with hands behind the back. The other players would strike those hands and the kneeling blindfolded player must guess who was the striker before being released. Mary much preferred the games of chess when she and Henry would retire to a quiet corner and pit their wits one against the other, or when Henry suggested she should bring out her guitar and they sang and played together.

They were happy days indeed as the spring passed into summer but they could not go on for ever, and one day a messenger from the Duke of Lancaster came riding to the castle with the command that Henry was to join his father.

It would only be for a short time, he told Mary. As soon as he could he would return or if that were not possible he would send for her to come to him.

She knew that she must accept this. She watched him ride away and desolation overcame her. She must try to be brave, she knew. It was what happened to all wives. Their husbands could not stay with them for ever.

It was shortly after Henry's departure that she knew she was to have a child.

She was delighted, although she overheard her women discussing the matter in private and she knew that they shook their heads and melancholy looks came into their eyes.

One of them said: 'She's too young I tell you. It's not right for one so young.'

'They say,' said another, 'that if a woman can conceive she's ripe for child bearing.'

'She's little more than a baby herself. They should have waited.'

She did not want to hear more. Such talk frightened her.

There came a day when the Earl and Countess of Buckingham were passing Kenilworth. They stayed for a night, and that was very unpleasant.

Eleanor was cold; Thomas was hotly indignant.

'By God's ears,' he said. 'I'll never like brother John again. He planned this, he did. He waited until I went away.'

'It was not so,' she cried.

'Married!' cried Eleanor. 'At your age. It shocks me deeply.'

'You were going to send me into a convent,' retorted Mary. 'I was old enough you considered to make up my mind about that.'

'How could you have been so deceitful. The nuns are heartbroken.'

'The Abbess was most concerned that I should be sure I was doing what was best.'

'I wonder you are not ashamed,' cried Eleanor. 'To go off like that and the next thing we knew was that you were betrothed!'

'It so happened that Henry was at Arundel . . .'

'So happened!' snapped Eleanor. 'It was arranged.
And why do you think it was arranged? Because you
happened to be an heiress, that's why. Do you think the
high and mighty Duke of Lancaster and his romantic son
would have been so eager to take you without your
fortune?'

'Is that why Thomas took you?' retorted Mary.

'You wicked girl! You give yourself airs. How dare
you talk to me thus. Oh I am so disappointed. After all
we did. We went to Pleshy because you were so interested in the convent there.'

Thomas shouted, 'Stop bickering. The evil is done.
Would to God I had not been out of the country at the
time. I would have taken up arms against Lancaster. I
would . . .'

He spluttered on in his rage. It was all so ridiculous,
thought Mary. He would not have dared to take up arms
against his brother over such a matter. But perhaps he
would. He was known throughout the country as a man
who acted on impulse however foolishly.

She was glad when they departed. It was very upsetting.

Occasionally Henry visited her but he was in attendance on the King and could not be with her as often as
he wished. She liked to hear about the King, whom she
suspected Henry despised a little. He was not as clever
as Henry at any of the outdoor sports; Henry would
always triumph over him.

'Does he mind?' asked Mary.

'Not he. He cares more about his books; and he will
talk of his fine clothes for hours. He is very particular
about his food. Not that he eats a great deal; but it must
be served in the most delicate manner. To tell you the
truth, Mary, he is not what one thinks of as a king.'

Henry was often wistful when he talked of the King.
Mary understood why when he said to her one day: 'Do
you know, if my father had been the first of his father's
sons, I should have been the King.'

'Would you have liked that, Henry?' she asked.

'It is not a matter of liking it,' was his reply, 'but of
accepting the fact and moulding oneself accordingly.
You see Richard was not meant to be King. If his elder
brother had lived he would have taken the crown; and

then his father died and there he was aged about nine years old, King of England.'

A faint resentment was in Henry's voice.

She did not say so, but she was glad his father had not been the eldest for then she would in due course have been Queen and she knew that would have been rather alarming.

Henry's visits were so brief and she was left much to herself. She did a great deal of needlework, played her guitar, learned new songs to sing for Henry and awaited the birth of her child with some impatience.

She heard scraps of gossip from the women. She could get a picture of what was happening in the outside world from them. She discovered that there was a murmuring of discontent throughout the country. Some said the peasants were getting too big for their boots because of the land laws which enabled them to cultivate for their own use a portion of the land belonging to the lord of the manor and to pay for it by working for him. They complained that the lord took the best of their time and their own crops were spoilt because they could not deal with them in an emergency since at such a time the lord's own lands would need all their attention. They were slaves. They were bound to the land and so were their children. But the greatest grievance of all was the poll tax which was levied on every man, woman and child over fifteen.

She heard the name of John Ball which was mentioned frequently. He had been, she gathered, a 'hedge priest' which meant that he had had no church and no home of his own, but had wandered about the countryside preaching and accepting bed and board where he could find it. He had preached to the people on village greens at one time but when he began to be noticed by people in authority these meetings had been held in woods at night.

Not only had he been preaching religion, it had been said, but he was preaching revolution, for he was urging the peasants to rise against their masters, to throw off slavery, and demand what he had called their rights.

It was not to be wondered at that a man who preached such fiery doctrines should be considered dangerous, and John Ball had been seized and put into the Archbishop's prison of Maidstone.

And now there was all this talk about the peasants' unrest; but no one took it very seriously.

Certainly not the household at Kenilworth where all were concerned with the coming birth.

It began one early evening when Mary sat with her ladies. She was playing the guitar while they stitched at their tapestry. The child was due in a few weeks and Mary was suffering acute discomfort. It was all very natural, said her women; it was the fate of all in her condition and all the inconvenience of the last months would have been worth while when her child was born.

Her pains began suddenly and they were so acute that her women took her to her bed immediately and sent for the doctors.

She was lost now in mists of pain; she had never believed there could be such agony. Vaguely she heard a voice saying: 'But she is only a child herself . . . too young . . . immature . . .'

She had lost count of time. She just lay waiting for the waves of pain to sweep over her, to subside, to flow away and then flow back. It seemed as though it would never end. She lost consciousness and when she awoke the pain had gone. She felt completely exhausted and for some time was unsure of what had happened. And when she remembered her first thoughts were for the child.

'My baby . . .' she murmured.

There was silence. She tried to struggle up but she was too tired. 'Where is my baby?' she asked shrilly.

One of her women came to the bed and knelt down. She was about to speak and then she bowed her head and covered her face with her hands.

'Tell me,' said Mary stonily.

'My lady,' said the woman, and there was a sob in her voice, 'the child was born . . . a beautiful child . . . perfect in limb . . .'

'Yes, yes. Where is it?'

'It was born dead, my lady.'

Mary sank back on her bed. She closed her eyes. All the months of waiting . . . all the hopes and plans . . . gone. The baby was born dead.

'There will be more . . . later,' went on the woman.

'You have come through, praise be to God. You are going to get strong again and then, and then . . .'

Mary was not listening. Henry! she thought. Oh Henry, I have disappointed you.

She was unable to leave her bed. She lay listless wondering where Henry was, what he was doing now. He would come to her room, she was sure. She would not be able to bear his disappointment.

She was right. As soon as the news was taken to him he got leave of the King to ride to Kenilworth.

He knelt by the bed. He took her hands and kissed them. She must not fret, he said. They would have a son in time . . .

He did a great deal to comfort her. Think how young they were, both of them. They had the whole of their lives before them. They must not fret because they had lost this child. He sat by her bed and he talked to her of the future and how happy they were going to be and in time they would have as many children as his grandfather King Edward and his grandmother Queen Philippa had had. She would see.

She began to recover, but she was still weak.

A few days after Henry arrived there was another visitor to Kenilworth. This was Mary's mother, the Countess of Hereford.

She went at once to her daughter, embraced her and then declared that she had come to nurse her. Joanna de Bohun was a woman of great strength of character; she was devoted to her daughters and in particular to Mary because she was the younger of the two. Eleanor, she believed, was able to take care of herself.

Joanna had always resented the fact that the custom of the land demanded that her daughter be removed from her care and that she should become the ward of John of Gaunt, in order, so she said, that that mighty Duke should have the prize money which went with such appointments.

She, Mary's mother, was better fitted to look after the child than anyone; and in view of what had happened she had now come to assert that right.

Mary was delighted to see her mother.

The Countess studied her daughter and hid the concern she felt. The child was too thin. What a terrible ordeal for a girl not yet twelve years of age to pass through. Some girls developed earlier than others and then early childbearing might be permissible; but Mary herself was still too childlike and delicate.

There shall be no more of this, thought the Countess grimly. If I have to fight John of Gaunt himself I'll do so.

'Dearest Mother,' said Mary. 'I am so happy to see you.'

'God bless you, my child. It is natural that when my daughter is ill her mother should be the one to look after her. You are going to be well in a week. I shall see to that.'

Mary smiled. 'We always had to obey you, my lady,' she said. 'So I must do so now.'

'Indeed you must and shall.'

Henry had come into the sick room and the Countess was aware of the manner in which Mary's face lit up at the sight of him. A fine boy, she thought, and indeed a worthy husband for a de Bohun, but they were too young . . . far too young, and there was going to be no more of this.

Henry welcomed her gallantly and was clearly delighted that she had come for he was apprehensive about his young wife's health and she liked him for it. She told him she would soon have Mary well.

'No one understands a daughter like her own mother,' she announced.

She took charge of the invalid. She had a bed brought into the room which she would occupy. She would be with Mary day and night. She made possets and special broths for her daughter which under the stern eye of her mother Mary dared not refuse.

She felt a great sense of security which she had missed in the days of Pleshy. To be here with Henry and her mother made her very happy and she began to grow away from her sorrow at the loss of the baby.

'You have your whole life before you,' said her mother. There was one matter which she had not discussed with Mary yet, but she intended to when she considered the time ripe.

She blamed herself for not being firm enough in the

first place. When she became a widow she should have refused to allow her younger daughter to be taken out of her care.

The King had given the wardship to John of Gaunt as a consolation prize for something else, and she had been obliged to let her daughter go because of the royal command. Her husband, Humphrey de Bohun, Earl of Hereford and Essex, had been one of the richest men in the country and so had a vast fortune to leave, and it was that fortune which had led to this situation when Mary might have lost her life.

She was now putting her foot down firmly and taking matters into her own hands.

She broached the subject to Henry first.

'Henry,' she said, 'I am going to talk to you very seriously. I am deeply concerned about Mary.'

He looked alarmed. 'I thought she was getting better.'

'She is. But you know, do you not, that she has come near to losing her life.'

'I know she has been very ill.'

'The plain fact is that she is too young to bear children. Her body is not yet fully formed. She needs another two years at least in which to grow up.'

Henry looked shamefaced and the Countess went on hurriedly: 'I do not blame you. It is the fault of those who put you together at such an early age.'

Henry flushed hotly. His father was a hero in his eyes.

'Oh, men do not always understand these matters,' said the Countess hastily, realizing that if she were to have her own way in this matter she must not antagonize John of Gaunt.

She believed she knew how to handle this, but she would have to be tactful; and she knew that John of Gaunt's great desire had been to get the marriage celebrated and Mary's fortune secure. That had been done and he would be prepared to postpone the begetting of children for a few years.

'What do you want me to do?' asked Henry.

'There must be no marital relations between you for at least two years. You must see the reason for this. There must not be any more children . . . yet.'

'Have you told Mary?'

'I will explain to her. She will understand. In fact I am sure she does not want to endure again what she has so recently come through. What I am going to suggest is that I take Mary back with me. I shall look after her and you will know that she is safe in her mother's care. You will be welcome at my castle whenever you wish to come on the understanding that there is to be no love-making until she is of a suitable age.'

Henry was ready to swear to agree to these terms. He had been very very anxious about Mary and had felt a terrible sense of guilt. But now she was well again and he could see that they must wait a few years before they lived together. Yes, he could do nothing but agree.

The Countess was triumphant. John of Gaunt was absent in Scotland on the King's business so he could raise no objections. Eleanor and her husband were no longer interested now that her share of the de Bohun fortune was lost to them.

She had only to tell Mary and as soon as the girl was well enough to travel they would leave.

Mary listened attentively to her mother.

'My dearest child,' said the Countess, 'I was very sad when you left me to go to your sister. It was no wish of mine, you know.'

'I do know,' said Mary fervently.

'It is so wrong when a child is taken from her rightful place just because she happens to have a fortune. Oh that fortune! I could wish that your father had been a much poorer man. Your sister coveted it . . . and so did her husband. They would have had you in a convent for the sake of it.'

'I was fortunate to meet Henry,' put in Mary. 'He does not care for my fortune.'

The Countess was silent. Did he not? She would be surprised if this were so. In any case there was one who cared deeply and that was Henry's father, John of Gaunt.

Thank God he was in Scotland and could not interfere. And would the King? He had given the wardship to his uncle John. No, she had nothing to fear from Richard. He was only a boy. If need be she would see him and explain; she was sure she could touch his pity for a mother who was concerned about her child.

'My dear,' went on the Countess, 'you know very

well that you have been very ill. There was a day when your life was despaired of. The fact, daughter, is that you are too young as yet to bear children. Henry agrees with me that you must wait for a year or so.'

'Wait . . . what do you mean?'

'You and Henry will be as betrothed . . . There will be no more marital relations between you.'

'I must ask Henry . . .'

'I have already spoken to Henry. He sees the point. He agrees with me.'

She looked relieved. Then she said in alarm: 'Do you mean I shall not *see* Henry?'

'Of course you will see Henry. He will come to Leicester to visit us. He will stay and you will sing your songs and play your guitar together. You'll pit your wits at chess. It is simply that you will be as betrothed . . . as though the actual ceremony of marriage has not yet taken place.'

She was silent. And her mother burst out: 'You shall not be submitted to that pain again. You are too young to bear children as yet. Your body is not ready for it. All I ask is for you to wait for a year . . . for two years perhaps. In fact I am going to insist.'

'As long as Henry agrees . . . and I shall see him.'

'But of course you shall. Dear child, understand all I ever want is what is best for you.'

So it was arranged and when Mary was well enough, the Countess left Kenilworth with her daughter.

THE LORD HARRY

For more than three years Mary lived with her mother during which time Henry visited her whenever it was possible for him to do so. Her mother explained to her that when one married a man who was of such high rank one must be prepared for him to have many duties outside his domestic life to claim him.

Mary was resigned. She eagerly learned how to manage a large household; she spent long hours in the still room; she studied the various herbs and spices and how to garnish dishes with them; she could brew ale to perfection; her mother allowed her to instruct the servants on those occasions when important visitors were expected and the Countess insisted that they all realized that in spite of her youth, Mary was the Countess of Hereford and wife of the son of the great John of Gaunt. Nor was she allowed to neglect the finer pursuits. She must learn the latest songs and dances which were fashionable at Court and she played the guitar and sang to guests. The finest materials were sent to the castle for her to choose which she preferred and the Countess insisted that she pay special attention to her appearance.

Those were the waiting years and Mary knew now without a doubt how wrong it would have been had she allowed herself to be forced into the convent. Henry had saved her from that and she would always be grateful to him. She was intended to be what he would make her: a wife and a mother. Providing a happy well managed home for her husband and children was her true mission in life and during those waiting years she longed for the time when she would be old enough to go to Henry.

Often she thought of him, wondering what he was doing at that time. During the day she was busy; her mother saw that she was well occupied; but at night she would lie in her bed, watching the flickering shadows on the walls, for after the fashion of the day she burned a small lamp in her bedchamber. It was a small metal cup filled with oil with a wick in it; and it was a comfort during the darkness when certain fears came to her.

She was always apprehensive lest something happened and she not be told of it. During the time when she and Henry had lived together and she had been pregnant terrible things had been happening and she had known nothing of them. The peasants had risen and the whole country had been in danger; as for Henry he had been with the King at the time in the Tower of London and had come near to losing his life. She had been—and still was—so appalled at the second near calamity that she could give little thought to the first.

It was only after the tragic birth of her stillborn child that she had heard the truth and she would never forget as long as she lived the day Henry had sat with her and told her about it.

'A man called Wat Tyler was at their head,' he had said. 'The story is that the collector who had gone to gather the poll tax had insulted his daughter and the tyler killed the tax collector and the peasants rallied round him. They marched to London eventually. They wanted to rule the country themselves; they wanted to take all the riches of the land and divide it between them. They were looting everything as they went. They have destroyed my father's palace of the Savoy.'

She had listened wide-eyed, her heart beating furiously to think that while that was happening she had been living quietly in the country expecting her baby and knowing nothing of it. And Henry had been there in London . . . with the King.

'They came into London, that seething rabble,' Henry went on. 'The King went out to meet them . . . first at Blackheath and then at Smithfield. He showed great courage—everyone said so—and it has to be remembered that he saved the day. When he was at Blackheath I was left in the Tower and the mob broke in.'

She felt sick with fear, and he had laughed at her.

'It's all over now. It came out all right. Richard talked to them . . . promised to give them what they wanted . . . not that he can . . . but he promised them and Wat Tyler was killed. They were without a leader. They broke up and disappeared . . . and afterwards the ring leaders were caught and punished.'

'And you were in the Tower,' she had murmured.

'I was lucky. Oh Mary, you nearly lost your husband on that day. They would have put an end to me because they hated my father. Everywhere you go, Mary, you hear them murmuring against him. You know all the lies they tell against him.'

'Why do they hate him so?' she had asked.

Henry had shrugged his shoulders. Then he had said, his eyes glowing with pride: 'Because he is the greatest man in England. He should have been the first-born so that he could have had the crown. He was meant to be a king.'

Mary had begged him to tell her about his lucky escape.

'It was like a miracle, Mary. There I was expecting them to burst in on me at any moment. I was thinking of you. I thought: My poor little Mary, her heart will be broken. And it would have been would it not?'

She had only been able to nod, being too full of emotion for speech.

'And then,' he had gone on, 'the door flew open and there was one of them; he had a billhook in his hand and I thought he had come to kill me. He called me "My lord" and spoke urgently and told me that he had come to conduct me to safety for my life was in great danger. He told me what to do, and I put on some rough clothes which he gave me. He had a wooden stick for me and he bade me follow him shouting abuse on the rich and so did I and we ran out of the Tower and through the streets of London shouting all the while until we came to the Wardrobe, which is the royal offices in Carter Lane, and there I joined the Queen Mother and others who had managed to escape from the Tower.'

She had only been able to cling to him and marvel with horror that while this had been happening she had been calmly sitting at her needlework with no hint of the tragedy which had nearly ruined her life.

'I shall be grateful to that man who saved you for the rest of my life,' she said fervently.

'And so shall I,' Henry had replied. 'His name is John Ferrour and he is from Southwark. He has been well rewarded. He must have done it out of love for my father for I had never heard of him. But there is no doubt that but for him there would have been the end of Henry of Bolingbroke.'

Later she had heard much of the Peasants' Revolt and the young King's bravery and everyone said that Richard would be a great king like his grandfather. The Peasants' Revolt had been Richard's triumph, so it seemed at first; but as she saw it he had won by false pretences. He had promised to give them what they wanted and what they had received was cruel death for their leaders and their grievances had remained.

Henry had tried to explain to her that there could have been no other solution. The revolution had to be stopped and Richard stopped it; and the only way it could be done was by promising them what it was impossible to give.

'We were fortunate,' said Henry. 'It could have been the end of England, the end of us all.'

But what lived on in her memory was the danger that could beset her husband; and it was impossible to know real peace except when he was with her.

She was avid for news from Court. Henry gave it on his visits and those were the highlights of her existence. When she heard visitors arriving her heart would leap with joy. Alas, often she suffered bitter disappointment. But those occasions when he came were wonderful. She longed for the time to pass that she might reach that stage when she would be considered old enough for marriage.

Henry longed for it too. That was another anxiety. What if he were to love someone else? His father was married to Constanza of Castile but everyone knew that he loved Lady Swynford. Marriage was no certainty of love.

When the young King was married there was great excitement throughout the country. It was said that Anne of Bohemia was not very beautiful and what good looks she had were marred by the hideous horned head-dress she wore; but the King liked her and very soon horned head-dresses were the fashion in the highest circles. 'You must have one,' said her mother.

Henry spent a great deal of time with his father and it was clear to Mary that to Henry no one could ever quite compare with John of Gaunt. There was a great bond between them which pleased her and she knew that Henry was very fond of Lady Swynford, who was treated by all—on pain of the Duke's displeasure—as the Duchess of Lancaster. It would not be long, said Henry, before they were together. As soon as she reached her fifteenth birthday he was going to overrule her mother's objections; and his father would help him, he knew.

Meanwhile he brought news of the outside world. The King was devoted to the Queen and she was friendly with his friend Robert de Vere, whom, some said, Richard loved more than anyone, so that it was suspected that he had inherited certain traits of character from his great great grandfather Edward the Second. But the Queen made it all very cosy and the trio were always together. It was foolish, said Henry, because Richard was paying too much attention to his favourite not only privately but in State matters and that was a great mistake.

'Richard has outgrown the glory of Blackheath and Smithfield and if he goes on like this he will have to take care,' said Henry ominously, and there was a certain gleam in his eyes which vaguely disturbed Mary.

Later he told her that John Wycliffe, who had caused so much controversy with his ideas on religion, had died of apoplexy while assisting at mass.

'But this is not the end of John Wycliffe,' prophesied Henry.

There was more trouble when John Holland, the King's half-brother, murdered the Earl of Stafford's son and was banished from the country.

'The Queen Mother is distraught,' Henry explained. 'She is trying to persuade Richard to acquit him but I don't see how he can. This will just about kill her. Her health is not good and she is getting old.'

And it did kill her for she died soon after.

But by this time Mary had reached her fifteenth birthday and one day John of Gaunt sent word that he was coming to see them.

There must be great preparations for such an important visitor and the Countess with Mary beside her ordered that beef and mutton, capon, venison with herons and swans and peacocks be made ready for the honoured guest. The smell of baking pervaded the kitchens for there must be pies and tarts of all descriptions to be worthy of such a guest and the retinue he would certainly bring with him.

Henry was to accompany him and Mary guessed what the object of this visit was. So did her mother for she watched her daughter anxiously.

'My lady,' Mary reminded the Countess, 'I have passed my fifteenth birthday and am no longer a child.'

The Countess sighed. She would have liked to keep her daughter with her a little longer.

From one of the turret windows Mary watched the arrival of the great John of Gaunt, resplendent with banners displaying the lions and the leopards. Beside the great Duke of Lancaster rode his son, Henry of Bolingbroke.

How noble they were—these Plantagenets, and how similar in looks! There could be no doubt of their origins; they bore themselves—all of them—like Kings.

The Countess was waiting to greet them, with Mary beside her. John of Gaunt took Mary in his arms, when she would have curtsied to him.

'And how fares my dear daughter?' he asked. She replied that she was well and trusted he was also.

Her mother looked on with pride as she must to contemplate this brilliant marriage of her daughter's; and the fact that Mary and Henry so clearly loved each other was great balm to her motherly heart.

Henry was watching Mary with glistening eyes and when he embraced her she sensed the joy in him; so she knew that the waiting would soon be over.

There was an air of festivity at supper that evening as the dishes which had caused such a flurry of activity in the kitchen were set before the honoured guests. In addition to the meats and pies there were dried fruits preserved in sugar—almonds, raisins and fancy march-pane with every delicacy that had ever been thought of.

'Your daughter grows apace,' said John of Gaunt to the Countess. 'And her beauty increases. She is no longer a child. Do you agree?'

The Countess reluctantly admitted that this was so; and then there could no longer be any doubt of the reason for the visit.

Mary and Henry danced together; she played the guitar and he sang with her; and while they watched them the Duke of Lancaster explained to the Countess that he was shortly leaving the country for Castile where he would try to win the crown to which he had a claim through his wife Constanza; he was leaving his son in charge of his estates.

'He is a man now,' he added.

The Countess was thoughtful. She did not greatly care for John of Gaunt; he was too formidable for comfort. Moreover she knew how ambitious he was and that he longed for a crown. He had married Constanza of Castile in the hope of being King of Castile since he could not be King of England, though he did not live with his lawful wife but with his mistress Catherine Swynford. And he had married his son to Mary because of Mary's fortune.

Now he was telling her that it was time Mary left her mother and became a wife to Henry.

It must be, she saw that.

Meanwhile Henry was explaining to Mary. 'The waiting is over,' he said. 'You are coming away with me.'

She clasped her hands together and closed her eyes; she was overcome with joy.

'Does that mean you are pleased?' asked Henry.

She nodded.

'I am nearly twenty,' he said. 'My father says it is time I had a wife. Oh, Mary, the waiting has been so long.'

'For me, also. I am sorry I was so young.'

That made him laugh.

'Listen,' he said. 'When I go from here, you will come with me. My father is going to Castile.'

'Oh Henry . . . you . . .'

'No, I am not going with him. There must be someone here to look after the estates. I shall doubtless travel with him to the coast. Perhaps you will come with us, Mary.'

She put her hand in his.

'Henry, I am so happy,' she said.

Those were busy days that followed. The great John of Gaunt must be entertained and she must prepare herself to leave with Henry. Her mother watched her with a certain sadness.

'I am pleased that you are happy in your marriage,' she said, 'but sorry that you are going away. If you are ever in need of me, you have but to send word, my child, and I shall be with you.'

Mary said solemnly: 'Was there any girl more fortunate than I? I have the best husband and the best mother in the world.'

Mary was indeed a wife and it was not long before she was expecting to become a mother. She and Henry had gone to their favourite castle in Monmouthshire and there they had spent a few ecstatic weeks during which Mary had become pregnant. Life was so wonderful if she could but forget that parting could come at any moment. Henry was deeply involved in politics and that meant uneasy living. He did not like his cousin, the King. He called him a fool in private; he said he was futile, riding for disaster.

'He lost his slipper at his coronation,' he once said, 'and if he is not careful, ere long he will lose his throne.'

Mary hated to think how deeply Henry was being embroiled. She could have wished they could have lived quietly in Monmouth Castle happily from day to day.

She was so happy when he played his recorder and she played her guitar and then sang and danced; or when they played chess with the beautiful silver chessmen which were Henry's father's gift to them, or they rode together in the forest as they had when they had first met.

But this idyllic existence could not last. Sometimes she thought—but secretly—how happy she could have been had he been the son of a humble squire. She dared not hint of her feelings for the fact that he was the son of his father was one of his proudest boasts.

As the months passed her discomfort increased; it was a difficult pregnancy as it had been with her first child. Henry was a kind and thoughtful husband, but she sensed his restlessness. She could no longer ride with him; she could not dance; and sometimes she was so tired that she could not even concentrate on a game of chess.

She was realizing that she had married a very ambitious man. It was hardly to be expected that the son of John of Gaunt would be otherwise, and while he dallied with her in the castle she sensed that his thoughts were far away. The political situation was growing rather tense; when he talked to her about it his eyes glowed and his voice trembled with excitement; she quickly understood that he would rather be at Court than with her; it saddened her and yet she understood. She was only a part of his life; she must not expect him to share her desire for this cosy domesticity; and now, pregnant as she was and often feeling ill, she could not be the lively companion he needed. She must face facts; the idyll was over; it was changing rapidly into sensible marriage. He loved her still but how could she expect the same whole-hearted devotion from him which she was prepared to give.

There came a day when his uncle—Mary's brother-in-law—Thomas of Gloucester came to the castle. Mary was apprehensive about the visit for she knew that Thomas would never forgive her for leaving Pleshy and marrying Henry. Eleanor had been very cool towards her on the few occasions when they had met.

Thomas however greeted her with a brotherly affection and when she asked after Eleanor he said she was well and so were the children. Eleanor now had a son and that seemed to have given her and her husband a great deal of pleasure. He had been named Humphrey which was a favourite name in the de Bohun family.

The boy was strong and healthy, Thomas told her with pride and he trusted she would honour them with a visit.

This was offering the olive branch without doubt and having learned something of her brother-in-law's nature when she was living at Pleshy, Mary thought that it could only mean that he had some project in mind which had made the loss of half of the de Bohun fortune seem less significant than it once had.

He and Henry spent a great deal of time alone together and she became apprehensive for she was aware of the excitement these talks had engendered in her husband.

When they were alone that night she ventured to ask him what Thomas's motive was in visiting them.

At first he had been disinclined to tell her, which was hurtful.

'He is my uncle,' he said, 'and now my father is away no doubt he feels he must keep an eye on me. He was riding this way so naturally he would call on us. Moreover he is your brother-in-law. I dare swear Eleanor wants news of you.'

'Why, Henry,' she replied, 'your uncle has not been very pleasant with your father and that means with you, since you were given the Garter in place of him and since you married me when he and my sister wanted me to go into a convent so that my part of the family inheritance should go to them, it is hardly likely that they feel much affection for us.'

Then he decided to tell her. 'That is in the past,' he said. 'They were petty differences. I can tell you that something of the utmost importance is afoot.'

Her heart seemed to miss a beat. 'What is it, Henry?'

'You know that for some time the King's behaviour has not pleased certain men in the country. His besotted attitude towards de Vere gives great offence. That man is a menace to the peace of the country. He plotted against my father. It is time the King learned that there are men in this country who will endure this state of affairs no longer.'

She said faintly: 'And you are one of those who stand against him?'

'I am in good company,' he replied.

'Who else?' she asked faintly.

'My uncle Gloucester, Arundel, Nottingham and Warwick.'

'Five of you then.'

'We are the leaders and we are well supported.'

'Oh, Henry, I am afraid of these quarrels. You could find yourself in danger.'

'My dear little Mary, these are matters which you do not understand. We have to rid the country of those men who are ruining it.'

'You mean . . . the King.'

'The King if need be.'

'But he is the true heir to the throne. The son of the Black Prince . . .'

'Unfortunately yes,' said Henry with a note of anger in his voice and she knew that he was thinking: Why was my father not the King's eldest son?

'Henry, don't do it . . .'

He laughed at her and stroked her hair.

'I shouldn't have told you,' he said. He touched her stomach lightly. 'You have other matters to think of.'

'It *is* my concern what becomes of you,' she answered.

'Have no fear then. Richard is weak. He is a fool. He resembles his great-grandfather. *He* lost his throne . . .'

She shuddered. 'And his life . . . most barbarically.'

'Richard should remember that.'

She turned to him and hid her face against him. She knew it was no use protesting, no use trying to persuade him. He was an ambitious man; and though neither of them mentioned this, he was fascinated by a golden crown.

She wanted to shout to him: 'It can never be yours. It is Richard's by right. Richard may have a son.' Oh God, send Richard a son. That would put an end to these wild ambitious dreams. But even if Richard did not have a son, there were others before John of Gaunt. There was Lionel's daughter Philippa to come before him for there was no Salic law in England and women could inherit the throne. If Richard were ever deposed and John of Gaunt took the crown then his heir was Henry. Henry could not forget it, remote possibility though it was. It was like a canker in his mind; he was becoming more and more obsessed by it and it frightened her.

Now he was joining with those four other ambitious men to stand against the King. They wanted Richard out of the way, and Richard was the rightful King.

'Now,' said Henry, 'you distress yourself. We shall show Richard that he must rule for the benefit of the people not for that of his favourites. If he is wise, he'll see that; if not, well then he should go.'

'There will be war,' she said.

'Nay,' he corrected her. 'Richard would never fight. He would give way. There is no fighting spirit in him. Sometimes I wonder whether he is the son of his father. His mother was a flighty woman. She lived with Holland before she married him, you know.'

'Oh Henry have a care. What if some servant overheard!'

'My little Mary, you are too nervous. It is your state. Never mind. Very soon we shall have our boy, eh?'

'And when shall you leave with your uncle?'

'Tomorrow. There is little time to lose.'

'And when shall you come back?'

'So much depends on Richard,' he said. 'But I shall see you are safe and well looked after. That is why I chose Monmouth for you. It is a little remote. You can forget everything here but the coming baby.'

'Do you think I should ever forget you, Henry?'

'I trust not, my love. But you are my wife and you must obey me. My commands are that you should rest quietly, be at peace, not fret, and in due course you will be delivered of our child.'

'You set me impossible tasks,' she replied. 'How can I rest quietly while I know you are involved in plots against the King.'

'Not against the King, my love. *For* the King. Everything we do shall be for his good . . . if he is wise enough to realize it.'

There was nothing more she could say. She must accept the fact that she was married to a very ambitious man who could see the crown glittering only a few steps away and if it seemed unlikely that he could ever take those steps, he was optimistic and determined to lose no opportunity which might arise.

The next day he left with his uncle Thomas.

It was impossible for her to settle comfortably. She fretted; she suffered sleepless nights; she was constantly watching for messengers who would bring dreaded bad news.

August had come; the days were hot and sultry; she

could not move from room to room without a great deal of discomfort.

'You must rest, my lady,' said her women.

Rest was no good to her, they knew. She wanted peace of mind.

Her pains had started; all through the day they continued. She was in agony. Her women were growing anxious. They were reminded of that other occasion when she had given birth to a stillborn child.

'It will break her heart if she loses this child too,' said one of them.

'And small wonder,' added another. 'She has been sick with anxiety since my lord went away.'

'She is frail for childbearing and it did her no good that she should have a child when she was so young.'

'God help us. I fear for her. Is there no sign of the child yet then?'

No sign.

Mary could think of nothing but the pain. It came and went and came again. She tried to stifle her cries.

She was glad Henry was not there.

'Please God,' she prayed, 'help me. Help me and give me a boy.'

She was unconscious when the child was born.

The midwife took it.

'A boy,' she said. 'She's got her boy. A puny little thing. No life in it.'

Then she cried out. 'Oh no. He does not breathe. He is dead. This will kill her . . .'

She laid the little naked body across her knees and began slapping its purple exterior with a vigour which alarmed those who looked on.

'This is no fault of the child . . .' said someone.

But the midwife paused suddenly, listening. Then a smile of triumph illuminated her features. 'He breathes,' she cried. 'It has worked the miracle. I have slapped life into him. A weakling . . . but a live baby. Thank God . . . for her blessed sake.'

She laid the child aside and went to look at the mother.

Mary was breathing with difficulty.

'Send a message to my lord,' she said. 'He will be waiting for it. He should come without delay. Let him be told that he has a son.'

* * *

Henry was on his way to Monmouth when he heard that his son was born. He had been determined to be close by so that he could go to Mary and see their child as soon as it arrived. He had been so preoccupied with his allies that he had had little time to brood on what was happening at Monmouth. He was in a quandary. All the time he was aware of the overwhelming ambition of his uncle Thomas. There was no affection between them; they were allies only for the sake of expediency. Henry knew that Thomas would like to see Richard deposed and himself take the crown. That was something which must be avoided at all costs. If Richard was to relinquish the crown it should not go to Gloucester. He was the youngest of the sons of Edward the Third. No. It must go to John of Gaunt because only then could it come to Henry. But John of Gaunt was out of the country trying to win the crown of Castile and if this revolt came to anything it would be Thomas of Gloucester who was on the spot. But of course Lionel's offspring should come before him. Then John of Gaunt. Then Edmund of Langley, now Duke of York. But Henry could well imagine how Thomas would dispose of their claims. Lionel's *daughter*! A girl on the throne. What they wanted was a strong man, and with John of Gaunt out of the country pursuing the crown of Castile, and Edmund Duke of York having no desire for the crown, Thomas came next.

No, never, thought Henry. Richard must not be deposed until my father is here to take the crown!

These were his thoughts as he rode towards Monmouth.

At Ross on Wye he was stopped by a ferryman, who cried out: 'Goodmorrow to you, my lord.' And recognizing the lions and leopards he added: 'And God's blessing on your bonny son.'

'Why do you say that?' asked Henry.

'Because I know you for Henry of Bolingbroke and your lady has borne you a son I have heard.'

Henry was overcome with joy. For a while he forgot the inadequacies of Richard and the devious ways of his uncle Thomas; he even forgot his own ambitions.

He threw the man a purse of gold, and not waiting to

receive his thanks shouted to his followers: 'All speed to Monmouth.'

Arriving at the castle his delight was decidedly dampened. He was shown a puny infant—a boy it was true, but only just alive.

'He'll need special care, this one, my lord,' said the midwife.

He looked at the child in dismay. This tiny scrap of red and wrinkled flesh, the son he had so longed for! It did not bawl as he would have liked to hear it. It just lay still in its nurse's arms.

'He'll need a wet nurse, my lord. My lady is in no state to feed the child.'

'My lady . . .'

He went at once to her bedside. Oh God, he thought, is this Mary? This pale, wan little creature looking so small in the big bed, her hair falling about her; her eyes sunken and yet lighting with joy at the sight of him.

'Mary,' he cried, and knelt by her bed.

'Henry,' she said quietly, 'we have the boy. You are pleased?'

He nodded. 'But you must get well.'

'I will. I will. I must. There is the boy . . . and you . . .'

'He . . . he's a fine boy,' lied Henry.

'They will not bring him to me. They say I am too tired. I must rest. But I have seen him. He is a fine boy . . . Henry.'

'A fine boy,' repeated Henry.

'He is to be called after you.'

'Then there'll be two of us.'

'He shall be Harry . . . Harry of Monmouth.'

'So be it,' said Henry.

She closed her eyes and he turned away to the midwife. 'Are the doctors here?'

'Yes, my lord, they are waiting to see you.'

He talked long with them. The Countess was exhausted. She needed rest . . . and peace. As for the child, they hoped they would keep him alive. His first need was a strong and healthy wet nurse.

Henry had one purpose now. He must save the child for if he were lost he feared that Mary would die. It was the thought of the child that was keeping her alive. The child must live.

'Find a nurse at once,' he commanded. 'There must be a strong and healthy girl near by.'

He paced up and down the room. He heard the baby whimper. He prayed for God's help; and suddenly an idea came to him.

He went down to the stables and commanded the grooms to saddle his horse. Then he rode six miles to Welsh Bicknow, the home of his friend John Montacute who was the second son of the Earl of Salisbury. A few weeks previously John's wife Margaret had given birth to a lusty baby and some instinct told him that here he would find the help he needed.

It had been an inspiration. Margaret was feeding her child. She had milk to spare.

'Will you come and help our little Harry?' begged Henry.

Of course she would. She would deem it an honour.

Within a short time Margaret Montacute was in Monmouth and young Harry was suckling contentedly at her breasts.

After that he began to thrive, although, warned the midwife, he would not be a robust child and they might have difficulty in rearing him. However, his life was temporarily saved and Mary was able to hold her precious child in her arms. A terrible fear had come to her that he was dead and when she was given proof of his existence she began to recover.

It was not a speedy recovery but she was getting better every day and as for young Harry who had shown such reluctance to accept the world, he began to grow lively with the help of Margaret Montacute's milk and gave promise of remaining in it.

Rather to the surprise of those about her Mary recovered and if Harry was not exactly brimming over with good health he survived, although his nurses insisted he was a child whose health would have to be watched.

One day there came to the castle a young woman, big-bosomed and wide-hipped, who asked that she might see the Countess of Hereford.

Mary received her and discovered that her name was

Joan Waring and that she lived in a village near Monmouth.

'My lady,' she said, 'I hear that there is a baby here in the castle who is not as strong as he should be. I love little babies. I have raised my own. They were born strong and healthy but if you would give me the chance I would like to care for this little one.'

Mary was not so surprised as might have been expected; she knew there was a great deal of talk about young Harry's birth. The midwife had boasted that she had saved his life by smacking his bottom hard and forcing him to cry so that he brought the air into his lungs. It was often found expedient to get a good strong village girl to care for a baby of high rank and as Margaret Montacute could not be expected to remain for ever as Harry's nurse, it seemed a good idea to give the woman a chance.

She was obviously eager for the task and when young Harry was brought out and she took him into her arms, he seemed to take to her immediately. He ceased whimpering and lying against her soft sturdy breasts he seemed to find comfort.

Mary decided that she would engage Joan Waring. She did so and for some reason from that moment Harry's health began to improve.

They were anxious months. Mary was not sure whether she wanted to hear the news from Court or to shut herself away from it. She lived in constant terror that some ill would befall Henry. There was trouble and he was in the thick of it.

He had linked himself with the four who were now called the Lords Appellant. They had gathered together an army and had confronted Richard, arm in arm to show their solidarity, and forced him to dismiss those ministers whom they considered to be giving him evil counsel and they had set up the Merciless Parliament who forced the King's submission.

She had waited in trepidation for something terrible to happen. Nothing did. The country appeared to have settled down; the King was on the throne and he seemed to have profited from recent events. The country had moved into a peaceful stage, and this was confirmed when Henry came to Monmouth once more.

'You see,' he told Mary, 'your fears were without foundation.'

'There might have been serious trouble. You might have been in danger,' she retorted.

'Well, you see me here, safe and well. And how fares young Harry of Monmouth?'

She was able to tell him that young Harry was faring well. She had found an excellent nurse in a village woman named Joan Waring. Harry was devoted to her and she to him.

'These village women make good nurses,' was his comment; and his joy when he beheld young Harry was obvious. The child had changed from the feeble little scrap of humanity which had filled him with such misgivings a few months earlier.

'Now,' he said, 'there is no longer the need for you to remain here in Monmouth. I am going to take you away from here to London and then, Mary, you will not be so far from me. Do you like the idea?'

She did like it very much and preparations were set in motion to leave young Harry's birthplace. They were to go to London for a while and as the Palace of the Savoy had been destroyed by the mob during the Peasants' Revolt they took up residence at Cole Harbour, one of the de Bohun mansions.

It was a cold and draughty house and Joan Waring expressed her fervent disapproval of it. The dirty streets, the noise and all those people were not good for her baby, she declared. What he wanted was some fresh country air.

As little Harry seemed to agree with this verdict it was soon decided that London was not the place to bring up the child and on Henry's suggestion they retired to Kenilworth.

By this time Mary was once more pregnant.

Kenilworth! How beautiful it was with its massive Keep and its strong stone walls. Here Mary felt secure and because Henry stayed with her for a while she was happy.

In due course the time arrived for her child to be born. Perhaps because she felt at peace if only temporarily, because Henry was with her and perhaps because she had already shown that she could bear a son, this confinement passed off with moderate ease and to the delight of both parents another boy was born to them. He was strong and lusty and they called him Thomas.

There was great rejoicing in Kenilworth when news arrived there that John of Gaunt had returned from Castile, and so eager was he to see his grandsons that he was setting out at once for the castle with his mistress Lady Swynford.

Joan Waring was determined to show off her charges at their best, at the same time declaring that there was not to be too much excitement for that would not be good for her babies—particularly the Lord Harry who was naughty enough without that. She was more concerned about him than she was about Baby Thomas. Lord Harry was what she called a Pickle and could be relied upon to make some sort of trouble no matter where he was. Moreover his delicacy persisted and she had to keep a special eye on him.

'We must see that he is not allowed to disgrace himself before his grandfather, Joan,' said Mary.

When the great man arrived accompanied by his beautiful mistress, he embraced his son and Mary warmly, studying Mary a little anxiously for he had had word of the illness which had almost ended her life at the time of Harry's birth. She looked frail still but her skin glowed with health and her eyes were bright.

'And my grandson?' cried the Duke. 'So this is young Harry, eh.'

He lifted up the child and the two regarded each other steadily until Harry's attention was caught by the lions and leopards emblazoned on his grandfather's surcoat and he clearly found them more interesting than their owner.

'He looks to me like a young fellow who will have his way,' said the Duke.

'My lord, you speak truth there,' replied Mary. 'He is the despair of his nurse.'

'Well, we do not want a boy who is afraid of his shadow, do we. So we'll not complain.'

He put down Harry who made no secret of the fact that he relished being released.

The baby was brought to him and he took the child in his arms.

'Thomas is a good baby,' said his mother. 'He smiles a great deal, cries very little and seems contented with his lot.'

'Let us hope he remains so,' said the Duke. 'You have a fine family, Mary. May God bless you and keep you and them.'

She thanked him and left him with Henry while she took Lady Swynford to the room she would share with the Duke and talked to her about the children and household matters.

Lady Swynford, having borne the Duke four children and being the mother of two by her first husband, was knowledgeable and ready to impart this knowledge and advice.

She had a friendly personality and her devotion to the Duke and his to her, made Mary warm towards her. Because she refused to consider there was anything shameful in the relationship based as it was on selfless love, there seemed to be none; and Mary was happy to welcome Lady Swynford with the respect she would have shown to Constanza Duchess of Lancaster and, she was sure, with a good deal more affection.

The two women found undoubted pleasure in each other's company. Mary could talk of her anxieties about Harry's health and his wayward nature and Catherine could imply her own anxiety for her Beaufort family, those three sons and one daughter who were the Duke's and who were illegitimate, for however much their parents loved them the stigma was there and the rest of the world would not pretend it was not.

However, they were philosophical and both happy with their lot.

Catherine could interest herself in the trivia of domesticity as deeply as Mary could. She could admire Mary's handsome popinjay in its beautiful cage and declare that, although many of the fashionable ladies possessed them, she had never seen a finer bird than Mary's. She could laugh at the antics of Mary's dogs and compliment her on the decorated collars of silk in green and white check, which she herself had had made for them. All this she could do as any woman might and yet she had a deep awareness of political matters which she could discuss with a lucidity Mary had discovered in no one else and consequently she could more clearly picture what was happening. Moreover Catherine shared Mary's fears of what their men might be led into; and they felt similarly about the futility of war and any sort of conflict. Thus they found great pleasure in each other's company.

Meanwhile the Duke was in earnest conclave with his son. He knew of course what had happened in his absence, how Henry with the other four Lords Appellant had faced the King and forced the Merciless Parliament on him.

'Dangerous,' commented the Duke. 'And your Uncle Thomas is not to be trusted.'

'Well I know that,' replied Henry, 'but our action bore fruit.'

'Do not underestimate Richard,' insisted his father. 'He acts foolishly I admit but he has flashes of wisdom. You see he has extricated himself from a very difficult position, accepts the restrictions imposed on him and now that he is not hedged in by his favourites, rules moderately well.'

'Yet it was necessary to act as he did.'

'That I do not deny. But be wary, Henry. Richard is not likely to forget you five, and he is one who bears grudges. It might well be that he will seek some revenge.'

'But he must realize that affairs run more smoothly now. He should be grateful to us.'

'Do you think a king, no matter who he was, would ever forget being confronted by five of his subjects who threaten to take his crown if he does not behave as they think fit. Nay, Henry. Walk warily. My advice to you is to stay in the country for a while. Keep out of politics. It is a course I have had to follow from time to time and always did so with advantage.'

Henry did see the point of this and decided he would try it for a while but, as he pointed out to his father, he could not be content for ever with the life of a country squire.

'There is to be a great joust at St Inglebert near Calais. Why do you not go and show them your skill? Your brother John should go with you. I doubt there are two knights in France or England who could compare with you two.'

The Duke spoke with pride. He was always trying to bring forward the Beaufort bastards, the sons of Catherine, and he liked Henry to be on good terms with his half-brothers.

'It would keep you busy for a while,' went on the Duke, 'and one can never be sure what is going to happen next. There might come a time when it would be necessary for you to take some part in shaping affairs. But this is not the time. Richard has regained some popularity since de Vere went. The people do not want trouble. Wait, Henry. Go carefully, but keep your image before the people. They like you better than they ever liked me. It would be wise for you to let it remain so.'

'You ever gave me good advice,' said Henry.

'My dear son, you are my hope. Everything I dreamed of for myself, I want for you. My affairs in Castile are settled now. Constanza's girl—and mine—has married the heir to the throne and will be Queen of the Asturias. That settles that matter. Constanza is pleased. She will not have the crown nor shall I, but our daughter will wear it. Your sister Philippa has married the King of Portugal. I feel I need no longer take an active part in State affairs. I have not achieved what I set out to, but who does? I must now live through my children. Henry, one day, who knows what will be yours . . . Be ready for it. Richard is unstable . . . the day may come . . . But I will say no more. It is unwise to dream too much. But be ready . . . It is a stormy path to greatness; so many fall through a false step. We are set fair. You have two fine sons. I am proud of you.'

'You are right in all you say, Father,' said Henry; and they were silent, both looking into the future and there were dreams of greatness in their eyes.

Before John of Gaunt's visit was over Henry had made up his mind to join the joust at St Inglebert; and by the time he left Kenilworth Mary was once more pregnant.

The two brothers set out for France and threw themselves whole-heartedly into the task of upholding English honour against the French.

They were friends, having known each other well throughout their childhood. Their father had never wished to segregate his legitimate children by Blanche of Lancaster from those who were illegitimate by Catherine Swynford. His daughter Catherine by Constanza of Castile had always lived with her mother; but the rest of the family had been together a good deal, often under the care of Lady Swynford.

John was a young man with his eye to his own advantage. He was a little younger than Henry, though not much, he being the eldest of the Beaufort boys. He was handsome, showing more than a trace or two of his Plantagenet origins and he had inherited a little of his mother's unusual beauty. He was quick, clever, and a pleasant companion; and, although he had ambitions of his own, he never for one moment forgot that Henry was the heir of Lancaster, that he had the tremendous advantage of being the legitimate son and John knew that all the blessings which his mother, brothers and sisters had enjoyed had flowed from John of Gaunt, and when that benefactor was removed—and death only would remove him—they would have to come from Henry who then would be the new Duke of Lancaster.

John had a great admiration for royalty. It had been bred in him; it was his boast that he had royal blood in his veins—even though it had been injected on the wrong side of the blanket—and therefore he doubly admired Henry, for that blood had come to him not only through his father but also through his mother.

Henry was descended from Henry the Third on both sides, for his mother and father were that king's great great grandchildren and their great grandfathers Edward the First and Edmund Duke of Lancaster had been brothers.

There was complete harmony between the brothers—John being determined to please Henry and Henry enjoying the obvious respect of his half-brother. Moreover it was not merely paternal pride when John of Gaunt had declared them to be two of the finest exponents of the joust in England and France. They had received the best possible instruction in their childhood and both being of a nature which longed to excel they had turned into truly formidable opponents for any who challenged them.

It was a glittering occasion, and a happy one, for it was such a pleasure to go into combat against the French in a *joust à Plaisance*, and it transpired that the two champions were Henry of Bolingbroke and his half-brother John Beaufort. Honour was done to them and they were cheered and fêted.

Louis de Clermont, Duke de Bourbon, who was among the knights present, was greatly impressed by their prowess and he invited them to come to his tent where he promised to entertain them royally.

Many of the French nobles were gathered there and the guests were served with special delicacies and fine wine such as the French produced better than any other nation; and during the feast Louis de Clermont talked at great length about an expedition he was going to launch.

'I have had a deputation sent to me from the rich merchants of Genoa,' he explained to Henry and John. 'It appears they are plagued by Barbary pirates who waylay their ships and rob them of their merchandise. They say the menace grows and they plead for help.'

'What do you propose to do?' asked Henry.

'It would be profitable for all those who took part,' went on Louis. 'It would be a great adventure. We should be helping to promote trade. The merchants are doing good work. But they cannot go on if this wicked piracy continues. You ask what I propose, my friend. It is to take out a band of brave and adventurous men and attack El Mahadia, the home of the corsairs. They sail from there; they have their homes there. Mahadia grows richer as Genoa grows poorer. The robbers are winning the battle against honest traders.'

'It sounds a worthy project,' said John Beaufort.

'It is, indeed it is. What I need is men who know how to handle a sword. They are desperate men, these corsairs. It would be a fine adventure. We should recapture the spoils which have been stolen from the merchants and let me tell you, the merchants would be so grateful to see the end of the corsairs that the goods would be our reward.'

'Are you inviting us to join your expedition?' asked Henry.

'I should be glad of your company,' was the answer.

John Beaufort's eyes were gleaming. The thought of that treasure was very attractive to him.

Henry was more cautious. 'Let us think about it,' he said. 'It is not a matter to be lightly decided.'

Louis de Clermont agreed. He was pleased; he felt certain that these two young men, who certainly knew how to handle a sword, would be members of his party.

When they were alone in their tent Henry and John discussed the proposition and John listened with the utmost respect to what his half-brother had to say.

'Our father thinks that I should not become embroiled in politics,' said Henry. 'It might be a good plan to go to El Mahadia, particularly if there are good profits to be made.'

John enthusiastically agreed.

'We have given a good account of ourselves at the joust,' he said. 'Why should we not do the same and reap some profit with it?'

'Then let us go,' cried Henry.

'Together,' echoed John.

'We should return to England with all speed. We shall need to equip ourselves and that will take a little time.'

'We could leave for England tomorrow.'

'Then let us do it.'

Louis de Clermont was overjoyed at their promise to join his expedition and as soon as the tide permitted they set sail for Dover.

Henry was back in England in time for the birth of his third son. He was named John. So now he and Mary had three boys and their grandfather was delighted to have this one named after him. Young Harry was three years old and showing a decidedly rebellious character. The fact that he still had a tendency to be delicate meant that he was spoilt a little by Joan Waring who rarely let him out of her sight. He was undoubtedly the king of the nursery, which was understandable on account of his seniority, but there was that about Master Harry which implied that nothing would deter him in the business of getting his own way.

Mary was disturbed when Henry told her that he was going to attack the Barbary pirates. She had been pleased for him to go to the joust at St Inglebert. He had stressed that it had been *à Plaisance* and she had thought, It is just a game really, jousting with blunted lances or those fitted with special heads which rendered them harmless. Why could they not always fight like that—if fight they must? But the Barbary pirates were different. They were desperate men. There was real danger there.

Henry tried to soothe her; he gave her an account of the jousts at St Inglebert and stressed his own success and that of his half-brother, in the hope of implying that they would know how they would defend themselves. But Mary could not be comforted and was very uneasy, although she tried to hide this.

While Henry was mustering the knights he would take with him and giving instructions to Richard Kyngeston, the man whom he called his 'treasurer of war', as to what weapons and stores would be needed, he did manage to spend a little time with his family.

He delighted in his sons and in particular in Harry. This eldest son of his was so bright, a boy to be proud of. The fact that he was constantly in some kind of mischief amused his father. Of course the child being of a quick and lively mind, had already grasped his importance. Joan Waring might scold and even deliver the occasional slap but she was always ready to follow that with a cuddle and an assurance that naughty as he was he was her very special Lord Harry.

He would climb onto his father's knee and Henry told him about the joust, and how he had tilted his lance at his opponent and thundered to meet him.

Harry listened, brown eyes alight with excitement. He was dark for a Plantagenet, but handsome none the less, with an oval-shaped face and a nose which was long and straight. He was too thin but Joan Waring had reported that he was the most lively agile child she had ever encountered and it was her opinion that he would grow out of his childhood delicacy.

'Go on. Go on!' Harry would shout if his father paused and even went so far as to thump him on the chest if he were not quick enough, which should have brought a reproof but Henry was so pleased to see his son excited that he let that pass and obeyed him.

'We scored a great victory over the French. We were

honoured throughout the country. I and your uncle John Beaufort were the heroes of the hour.'

Harry did not take his eyes from his father's face and Henry wondered how much of what he was told he understood. He had a notion that Harry just liked to be seated on his father's knee because his father was the most important person in the castle—apart from Harry himself of course—and Harry liked to be made much of by him.

His father watched him ride his little pony, on a leading rein naturally. There must be no risk to the heir of Lancaster even though he had two sturdy young brothers. Henry, like everyone else in the household, felt that there was something rather special about young Harry.

His father went down to the field to watch him ride with his riding-master. Round and round the field they went. Harry was flushed with excitement and every time he rode past his father he looked at him sharply to see whether his full attention was given to the marvellous prowess of his son.

One day Henry was standing with one or two of his men watching the riding lesson when Richard Kyngeston came out to speak to him. There had been a hold up of some of the supplies and they would not be leaving for Dover for a week.

Henry turned aside to discuss this with Kyngeston just as Harry rode by and seeing that his father's attention was not on him, Harry suddenly, by some trick which he had obviously learned, disengaged himself from the riding-master, and broke into a gallop.

The riding-master cried out in great alarm as he went after the boy, and Henry immediately forgot Kyngeston as he saw his son making straight for the hedge.

'Oh God help us,' he cried. 'The boy will be killed.'

Harry was still ahead of the riding-master. Henry started to run. The boy had reached the hedge and turning and slackening speed began to canter across the field. He was smiling triumphantly as the riding-master caught up with him.

Henry said coldly: 'You are a wicked boy.'

Harry looked defiant and still pleased with himself.

'You know you are forbidden to do that.' The boy just

regarded him rather insolently, Henry thought. 'Do you not?' he shouted.

Harry nodded.

'Answer me when I speak to you.'

Harry paused. He was a little afraid of the coldness in his father's voice and eyes.

'Yes, I know.'

'And yet you deliberately disobeyed. You defied orders. Do you know what happens to people who defy their masters?'

Harry was silent.

'So you do not know, eh. They are punished. Get down from your horse. Go to your room and wait there.'

Harry dismounted and went into the castle.

Henry was far from as calm as he seemed. He had been deeply shaken by the sight of his son in danger; that had passed and he was confronted by another danger. This boy was rebellious by nature and that rebellion had to be curbed. He must be beaten. And who would administer the punishment? Joan Waring? She would never do it. She would never be able to forget that this was her precious charge. He must not be hurt, she would say, he is too delicate. Mary? Mary would be quite incapable of inflicting a beating. He knew that he would have to do it himself. Soon the boy should have a tutor and he would have to perform these unpleasant duties—for it seemed likely that there would be the need for chastisement in the future.

He took a stout stick and went to the nursery. Harry was there sitting on Joan Waring's lap telling her a woeful story of his cruel father.

Joan was horrified and trembling with agitation.

It is time, thought Henry, that the boy was taken away from a parcel of women.

Joan stood up when he came in and Harry clung to her skirts burying his head in them.

'Leave us,' said Henry curtly to Joan.

Harry turned and glared balefully at his father as Joan gently prised his hands away from her skirt.

'No,' cried Harry. 'Don't listen to him, Joannie. Don't go.'

'Leave us at once,' commanded Henry.

Joan murmured as she passed: 'My lord, he is so young . . . and remember he is delicate.'

Harry's eyes were on the stick, and Henry felt his heart quail. He loved this boy. The child would never understand that this was no less painful to him than it was going to be to Harry himself.

'You were a wicked boy,' he said, trying to force a cold note into his voice for he was secretly full of admiration for the manner in which the child had managed the horse and it was obvious that he had been quite fearless. 'You have to learn obedience.'

'Why?' asked Harry defiantly.

'Because we all have to.'

'You don't,' he said.

'Of course I do.'

'Whom do you obey?'

'Those above me.'

'Nobody's above you . . . except the King. Do you obey the King?'

For a moment Henry thought of himself standing before Richard with the other four Lords Appellant. The boy was making him uncomfortable, instead of the other way round.

'Enough,' he said. 'Come here.'

He tried to make him lie across a stool. Harry wriggled so fiercely that there was only one thing to do and that was pick him up and put him across his knee. He felt like a foolish old man. Nevertheless he brought down the stick and it was effective to judge by Harry's yells.

He was glad he could not see his face.

Not too much, he thought, just enough to teach him a lesson. He threw down the stick and pushed Harry off his knees.

The child glared at him. There were no tears, he noticed, though the little face was scarlet with rage.

Henry said: 'That will teach you a lesson.'

The fine brown eyes were narrowed. Never had hatred been so obvious as that which Henry saw in the face of his son.

Mary was upset that Henry had been obliged to chastise Harry.

'It had to be, my dear,' Henry explained to her. 'He is too wilful. We shall have trouble with him later unless a firm hand is taken.'

'I trust you did not beat him too hard. Joan said his screams were terrible.'

'He was screaming with rage. He did not shed a tear,' he added with pride.

'He is not four years old yet.'

'He cannot learn discipline too young. I want him to go to Oxford when he is a little older. His uncle Henry Beaufort will look after him.'

'I do not want him to leave me too soon,' said Mary. 'Let me keep my babies for a while.'

'Of course, of course,' soothed Henry. 'But not too much coddling of the child. Joan pampers him.'

'She is very good with him. He is so fond of her.'

'I don't doubt it when he twists her round his little finger.'

'Oh come, she can be severe. She will slap him if he needs it.'

'He is a child who is in constant need of correction. Well, he has now had something which will remind him for some time to come.'

The following day Harry was riding round the meadow but his father did not go to watch him. Instead he spent the time with his wife and younger sons. Harry seemed to take this philosophically though when Henry went into the nursery the child eyed his father with caution, but in a moment or two he seemed to have forgotten the beating and was intent on drawing his father's attention from his brothers to himself by asking about the Barbary pirates.

Within a short time Henry said good-bye to his family and set out for the coast. Mary took Harry and Thomas up to the topmost turret to watch him go.

'I want to go too,' declared Harry. 'I want to go and fight the pirates.'

'You must wait until you're older,' replied his mother.

'I don't want to wait. I want to go now.'

'Little boys don't go and fight pirates.'

'Yes, they do.'

'Now, Harry dear, don't be silly.'

Harry stamped his foot and narrowed his eyes in the way he did when he was angry.

He snatched his hand out of hers and ran round the spiral staircase ahead of her.

He went into the bedchamber which she shared with his father. He was not allowed to go there unless especially summoned but there was no one to stop him now. His father had gone to fight Barbary pirates and had not taken him with him. He touched his buttocks. He could still feel the effects of the stick. It made him angry, not so much because it hurt his body as his pride. He hated to think that he, Lord Harry—his mother's darling, Joan's little precious mite—had to be at the mercy of a strong arm. He was not sure whether he hated his father or not. He did sometimes. At others he wanted to be like him particularly if it meant fighting the Barbary pirates.

But they wouldn't take him and they were all saying how clever his father was and they were not taking enough notice of Lord Harry.

He saw the popinjay in its cage. How pretty it was with its brightly coloured feathers. Sometimes his mother let him talk to it and put the seeds into the cage.

Harry was suddenly angry because they were all making a fuss about his father, and they wouldn't let him go and fight the pirates.

On a sudden impulse he opened the cage.

'Come out, pretty bird,' he said. 'Come and see Harry.'

The bird flew out. He watched it fluttering round the room. Then it went out through the door.

'Come back,' he called. 'Come back.'

But the popinjay took no notice. It flew on . . . down the staircase to the hall and out through the open door and away.

THE LAST FAREWELL

Henry met John Beaufort at Calais. They had received permission from the King of France to cross his country as they were bent on a mission which would benefit the merchants of France as well as those of Genoa. While they were at Calais they were joined by a knight who was on his way to Lithuania to fight with the Teutonic Knights.

'We are going to El Mahadia, the lair of the Barbary pirates,' Henry told him. 'We plan to destroy the place.'

'A worthy cause,' replied the Knight, 'but I am eager to crusade. I shall be fighting the infidel. You may return richer men but I shall have expiated my sins and have struck a blow for Christ and Christendom.'

Henry was silent. It was true. Suddenly he had made up his mind.

He sought out John and told him that he had decided not to go to El Mahadia but to join the Teutonic Knights in Lithuania.

John was astounded. 'My lord, you have come so far,' he protested. 'Can you change now?'

'I can,' said Henry, 'and I will. It is better for me to win honour in fighting what is tantamount to a crusade than to win riches from a gang of pirates.'

John's face fell. He had been looking forward to the spoils which he was sure would come his way.

Henry put his hand on his half-brother's shoulder. 'You must go on,' he said. 'One of us must. Take your men and the equipment and travel across France to Marseilles. I will return to England. I shall need different equipment for Lithuania and shall certainly not sail from Calais.'

'What shall you do then?' asked the bewildered John Beaufort.

'Return. Raise more money and set out afresh. But John, you must go. It is what our father would wish. Go with his blessing and mine and may God go with you.'

So the two brothers parted and Henry returned to England.

Mary was delighted to see him, but alarmed when she heard that the new plan was to go to Lithuania. She believed this would be even more dangerous than attacking the pirates. But at least he was home for another brief spell.

She was relieved that he was so concerned with his preparations that he could give little attention to young Harry who seemed to grow more and more wilful every day. He had blatantly admitted to setting her pet popinjay free and when she had asked him why, he said, 'He wanted to go. He did not like being in a cage.'

He showed no repentance for what he had done but when she told him that popinjays must learn to like their cages because they were unfit to live wild, he was thoughtful and she thought a little contrite.

In her heart she guessed that he had let the bird go free because he wanted to turn the attention of the household on himself. The matter of great concern to everyone at that time had been the departure of Henry and Harry had doubtless felt himself overlooked.

She did worry about Harry—but there were other things to concern herself with. For instance Henry's burning desire for adventure. Of course she had known that it would be impossible to keep him with her, that in his position he must take part in the country's affairs, but this was not the country's affairs. This was adventure for the sake of adventure, the desire to be somewhere other than in his own home. The truth was that the love that was between them and the family they were rearing was not enough for him. He sought adventure abroad.

The thought made her sad. She was foolish, she knew. Her sister Eleanor would laugh at her and tell her she did not behave like a lady of high rank but like some peasant, clinging to her husband and her family. She must keep her thoughts to herself. Moreover the prospect of more childbearing frightened her a little. The last confinement had been agonizing. Joan Waring said that she thought her husband should know how she suffered.

'There are some ladies who can bear children with ease,' said Joan, 'and there are some who cannot. My lord and lady have three fine boys. For your health's sake, my lady, that should be enough.'

She was right, Mary knew. But how could she tell Henry that?

In due course he left for Lithuania and the crusade which would wash away all his sins.

He had not been gone very long when she discovered that she was once more pregnant.

After having landed at Rixhöft Henry hastened on to Danzig at which port the main body of his force had landed with their equipment. Within ten days they had joined up with the Teutonic Knights and were soon in the thick of battle of Alt Kowno which was known later as the Battle of the Pagans.

Henry and his allies won an undoubted victory with few casualties, and immediately advanced on Vilna and laid siege to that town. It seemed as though victory would be certain but the inhabitants of Vilna were a stubborn and stoical people; they would not give way and as supplies were running out for the besiegers it was necessary to call off the attack and return to Konigsberg.

By this time the winter had come and activities must be postponed. Henry set up in quarters in the town and tried to fill in the time before fighting could be resumed.

This was not difficult, for the Teutonic Knights were delighted to have him with them; he had fought hard for their cause and they wished to show their gratitude, and they arranged that there should be good hunting in the forests and in the evenings feasting and merriment.

One day when he returned from a hunting party it was to find an English sailor waiting for him.

The man had come from England, he said, for the purpose of bringing him a message from the Lady Mary.

'My lord,' said the man, 'I am to tell you that your lady was delivered of a fine boy. She says that as the last was named for his paternal grandfather this child should be named for his maternal one. He is Humphrey.'

Henry was so delighted that he gave the messenger a purse of gold. Four boys! His father would be pleased. He had done better than he had for he only had one legitimate son. One could not really count the Beaufort boys. Harry, Thomas, John and now Humphrey. Dear Mary, she had played her part well. No man could ever have had a better wife. Mary had given him so much, a fortune, four sons and docility and admiration. She looked up to him and thought he was right in all things. He was a happy man. If only his father had been *his* father's first-born and was the son of a king instead of the grandson of one, he would be completely content with life.

As it was he had a great deal to be thankful for and now there was a birth to be celebrated.

Christmas would soon be here and on Twelfth Night he proposed that as he had accepted so much hospitality he would now entertain his hosts. There should be a banquet in the English manner with mummers, minstrels and perhaps a joust.

He threw himself into the preparations. He had a new son, he kept reminding himself. He could not stop talking about his sons. Four of them and he was young yet. He would rival his grandfather for begetting children. Edward and Philippa had had twelve, and he saw no reason why he and Mary should not equal that number.

At his feast he received the congratulations of his allies. The health of his children was drunk with special mention of the newcomer Humphrey and his eldest Harry the heir.

Rich presents were brought to him. Silks, velvets and jewels; and from one of the Teutons three bears. 'To amuse those fine boys,' said the giver of the animals.

It was a glorious occasion and Henry thought how wise he had been to indulge in such an adventure which could bring him so much pleasure while at the same time it washed away his sins.

The winter began to pass and still hostilities were not resumed. At the beginning of March he began to wonder whether they would ever be, for the Teutons had been unable to raise the money necessary to carry on the war, and it seemed as though it was going to peter out.

Henry began to consider that it was time he returned home. After all he had not intended to stay away so long, so he ordered two ships to be made by two Prussian ship-builders, and, as soon as they were ready, to be loaded that he might set out on his journey home. The three bears were caged and brought on board. It was not easy to take them with him but he could not offend the giver by leaving them behind and he smiled to himself wondering what the boys would think of them.

Then they set sail and finally they came into the port of Hull where Henry disembarked though many of the party sailed down to Boston in Lincolnshire with the baggage.

Henry had sent word ahead that he was coming home and he wished the family to be at Bolingbroke, where he would come with all speed.

Mary and the children were awaiting his arrival. John could not remember his father. Thomas was not really sure whether he could; but Harry remembered. He remembered his standing before him with a stick in his hand. Strangely enough he did not feel fear at the thought of his father's return, only a kind of stimulation as he would later when he was going into battle.

Mary's feelings, too, were mixed. In one way she longed to see Henry and she was thankful that he was safe; she wanted to hear of his adventures; but at the back of her mind was the fear that the result of his return would be another pregnancy for that seemed inevitable whenever Henry was home.

During Humphrey's birth she had suffered intensely, and Joan Waring had become even more concerned. Her relief when Mary recovered made it obvious that she had feared the consequences might have been disastrous. 'Now there shouldn't be any more, my lady,' she said. 'Four fine boys! My lord cannot ask for more than that.'

But he did, of course. He wanted to rival his grandfather. Poor Queen Philippa! Mary had never known her and she heard that she had children easily, but she had grown very fat and unable to move at the end. 'It was no sooner up from childbed with one than she was preparing for another,' one of her women had said. 'Now that's not good. A woman needs a rest . . . a good long rest between.'

She could agree with that. But when Henry came riding into the courtyard, his eyes shining with joy to see them all assembled there, when he embraced her and she felt his warm kiss on her mouth, she thought: How could I tell him? She could not. Life must take its course.

It was a joyful reunion. He must admire Baby Humphrey. He must see how John and Thomas had grown. And there was Harry too—just the same—slender to the point of thinness, with that oval face and sharp eyes that missed nothing—smooth dark hair rare among the fair curly Plantagenets.

He had changed little. He was demanding attention as clearly as though he actually asked for it. He stood there legs apart, fearing nothing but that so much attention might be given to the returning adventurer that people would forget Lord Harry.

There was great excitement when the baggage arrived and Henry unpacked the rich exotic things he had brought for them. The beautiful silks delighted all the women; he had brought a parrot for Mary.

'Something to make that popinjay of yours jealous,' he told her.

There was a brief silence while Harry looked at his mother almost challengingly. He could almost hear the whacks of the stick as it came through the air.

'He escaped from his cage,' said Mary at length.

'Silly creature!' commented Henry. 'What chance would it have outside?'

The thought of the popinjay being set upon by fierce birds . . . eagles and hawks . . . disturbed Harry even more than the memory of the stick.

He said nothing. He would never let a bird out of a cage again. His mother had explained to him what happened to cherished little birds when they fell among the wild fowl.

It had made a deep impression on him and Mary believed that he had had enough of a lesson. She would not tell Henry of the many scrapes in which their first-born had been involved. She could not bear to think of his being beaten. She believed there were other ways of teaching him.

When Henry told the children about the bears they were overcome with awe and wonder. Harry could not restrain his joy; he talked of nothing else. Their father ordered that a pit should be dug for them and there their antics could amuse the children, but there must be a keeper for them and the children must remember that they might be dangerous animals.

The thought of danger made Harry's eyes sparkle. He was very anxious for everyone to know that he was not afraid of anything. Thomas might be frightened in the dark; Harry jeered at that. When he heard the servants talking about the hare of Bolingbroke he listened intently; he frightened Thomas with his account of it and Thomas had nightmares and would awake crying out that the hare was in the room so that Joan had to take him into her bed and assure him that there was no such thing.

'There is, there is,' Thomas insisted. 'Harry says so.'

'That wicked limb of Satan,' murmured Joan. 'If the hare came for anybody it would be for him.'

Then she crossed herself for she feared she might have ill wished her precious Harry.

Harry cared nothing. He boasted that he wished the hare would come out and he'd catch it, he would. He'd catch and boil it in a pot for dinner.

'You mustn't say such things,' said Joan. 'If this hare is the shape some poor tormented soul has taken you couldn't boil it in a pot and eat it.'

'I could,' boasted Harry.

'That boy frightens the life out of me,' Joan told Mistress Mary Hervey, a newcomer to the castle whom the Countess had engaged to act as a governess to the children.

Mary Hervey said that Harry was a bold and imaginative boy, by far the most interesting child it had ever been her lot to teach, so it was clear that she too had fallen under his spell.

Mary Hervey taught the two elder boys and when they grew older the others would come under her care. Harry was a bright child, good at his lessons when he was interested in them, and she had hopes of making a scholar of him.

In the meantime he was obsessed with the bears and when they arrived, he was almost wild with excitement.

The keeper was going to teach them tricks and Harry and Thomas were allowed to watch. The bears were in a deep pit from which they could not escape. Only the keeper went down to them. Everyone else, decreed Henry, must watch them from above.

Every day for an hour Harry and Thomas were allowed to watch them. Harry would become so excited; he would shout to them. He loved all three but the smallest of them delighted him most. He longed to go down and tell this bear that one day he would rescue it from its pit and they would go travelling together. They would have the most wonderful adventures. They would go and joust with the French knights; then they would go and fight with the Teutonic knights; and they would always be together. When his enemies were surrounding him the bear would come and drive them all away; and when some wicked men tried to take the bear away and put him into a ring to be baited by wild dogs, Harry would leap into the ring, kill all the dogs and emerge triumphant with his dear dear bear.

It was galling that he was never even allowed to go into the pit.

The bear had become so much a part of his days and he half believed the adventures he had imagined were true. One afternoon when the household was quiet he slipped down to the pit. The bears were sleeping. Around the top of the pit there were iron spikes to prevent the bears getting out. It was not difficult for Harry to slip between these. Now he could scramble down to the bears.

It was not as easy as he had imagined. The slope was steep. He made his way cautiously; he slipped a little, regained his footing and continued to clamber. Now he was right down in the pit. The bears looked very big so close and he could not help feeling very small. They were asleep—all of them, even his own special bear.

What would have happened to Harry in the bear pit was never known because the keeper happened to pass by at that moment and glancing down into the pit, he could not believe his own eyes. When he had assured himself that it was indeed the Lord Harry who was down there, he was horrified. The bears were sleeping and if they were disturbed they could be bad tempered. What might happen then, he dared not think. He could not slip through the spikes as Harry had been able to, but in the pit was a hut which he used to prepare the bears' food and store other things he needed for the care of them, and this was reached by steps from the outside and into the pit. He unlocked the gate to the steps and within a short time he was in the pit. Harry was standing by the smallest of the bears and talking to it. The bear had awakened and was sniffing the child. The keeper snatched up Harry and carried him into the hut.

'How did you get down here?' he demanded.

'I got through the spikes and climbed down.'

'You have been told not to do such a thing.'

'No I have not,' said Harry. 'I have not been told not to go through the spikes and down into the pit.'

'But you knew the bears could be dangerous.'

Yes, Harry had known that, but no one had said he must not get through the spikes.

Of course he had not been told precisely that because no one had thought he would do so.

'I shall have to tell where I found you,' said the keeper.

'Why?' asked Harry.

'Because you might have been killed.'

'My bear would never have killed me. If the others had tried to he would have saved me.'

The keeper was exasperated. He would have to tell Harry's father for if there was an accident later he would be blamed. He could not risk that. The boy had to be stopped.

Mary was with Henry when the keeper asked to be seen. Harry was with him and he explained where he had found him.

'He was quite fearless, my lord. There in the bears' pit. Why, they could have turned on him.'

'Oh Harry!' cried his mother reproachfully.

But it was at his father that Harry was looking.

Henry regarded his son sternly. 'Go to your room at once,' he said.

Harry lifted his head high and gave his father that defiant look which Henry had seen before. But he obeyed and went from the room.

'He had worked his way through the spikes, my lord. He had scrambled down. He's so fond of the bears, especially the smallest one. He was talking to it when I found him. I could see he was going to touch it at any minute. My heart was in my mouth as I snatched him up.'

'You did well,' said Henry. 'Put more spikes in so that not even the smallest child can get through. I shall remember what you have done today.'

The keeper went out gratified and Mary said: 'Oh Henry, he is only a child you know.'

'What I don't know is what we are going to do with him.'

'Henry, you won't beat him too hard. He is really delicate, you know, although it's hard to believe.'

'He doesn't seem to be afraid of anything.'

'It is admirable in a way.'

Henry smiled slowly. 'You're right,' he said. 'When he looks at me in that defiant way I think he would like to kill me.'

'Oh Henry, don't say such things. You're his hero. In the games he plays it is all about what you are doing. He pretends to joust and fight the Lithuanians. And he always takes your part. He is always *you*. Poor Thomas has to be whatever Harry decides. It is just that he has unbounded energy and he does get into such mischief.'

'He is a grand boy, I'll grant you. But he needs discipline. I'll go to him.'

'Henry.' She laid her hand on his arm pleadingly.

'Rest assured,' he said softly, 'I will do what is best for him.'

Harry was waiting for him, sullen and defiant.

'Harry,' said Henry, sitting down, 'I wish to speak to you. Come here.'

Harry went. He was looking for the stick. He could not understand why his father had not brought it.

Henry drew the boy to him. 'Why are you so disobedient?' he asked.

'I was only talking to my bear.'

'You know you are not supposed to go down into the bear pit.'

Harry was silent.

'Did you know it?'

'Nobody said.'

'You knew it though, did you not?'

'I knew Thomas must not go.'

'And you thought you might?'

Harry drew himself up to his full height. 'I knew they wouldn't hurt me.'

'So you were not afraid?'

'If the others had tried to bite me we'd have fought them.'

'Who would?'

'My bear and I.'

Henry thought: It is useless. I should be proud of him. I could never have endured a weakling. He is fearless. He is a boy any father would be proud of.

'Harry,' he said, 'you know your grandfather is a very great man.'

'He's John of Gaunt, Duke of Lancaster,' said Harry promptly.

'That's right, and because he is who he is you must learn to be worthy to be his grandson. You must be bold; you must fear nothing but what is evil.'

'I'm not afraid of evil,' boasted Harry.

His father smiled. 'Harry,' he said, 'I am not going to beat you this time. It was wrong to go into the pit. You might have been mauled by the bears, perhaps even killed. You must think before you act. I like it well that you should not be afraid but you must be more thoughtful for others. Think of how sad your mother and I would be, and your brothers too, if anything happened to you.'

Harry was shocked by the thought. Then he said: 'Thomas and John wouldn't mind and Humphrey wouldn't know.'

Henry said: 'And I and your mother . . . ?'

'*You* don't like me,' said Harry. 'You don't like me when I do bad things . . . and I do a lot of bad things.'

'Harry, will you promise me one thing? I shall go away soon. I want you to look after your mother and your brothers till I come back.'

Harry looked pleased at the prospect.

'You,' said Henry, laying a hand on his shoulder, 'will be the head of the house while I am away. My son and heir. Who else should guard my home? But of course if you are going to do foolish things . . . a *little* boy might do . . . well then it is useless.'

Harry cried: 'I won't do silly things. I'll be head of the house.'

Henry drew him to him and held him fast. It was rare for him to demonstrate his affection.

Perhaps this was the way to deal with this son of his. He was thanking God for him. He was at heart very proud of Harry and would not have had him other than he was.

John of Gaunt came to Bolingbroke to see the family. This was a great occasion. The children were very much in awe of him, even Harry in spite of his pretence not to be—but they were fond of Lady Swynford who always accompanied him.

He inspected the bears and the parrot and the falcons and the dogs, and heard an account of young Harry's descent into the bear pit which amused him and which he applauded as showing a daring spirit.

There was no doubt that Harry was the one who aroused the most interest and Harry was deeply aware of this.

But the Duke's motive in visiting his son was not only to see the children.

As he told Henry, while it was wise to hold aloof from dangerous factions he must not lose the high place in the kingdom which was his right as his father's heir.

'We must have peace with France,' said the Duke. 'There will be no prosperity until we do. Richard sees this, I think, I am sure that he wishes that this claim to the crown of France had never been raised. He agrees with me that we should try to bring about some sort of settlement.'

'You mean you are proposing to take an embassy to France?'

'I mean just that,' said John of Gaunt, 'and you should be a part of it.'

Catherine Swynford talked with Mary about the proposed mission which the Duke had discussed at great length with her.

'It will take them away again,' she said, 'but at least it will be on a peaceful mission.'

Mary toyed with the idea of telling Catherine about the fears that came to her and how after each pregnancy she felt a little weaker. But somehow she could not bring herself to do so. Catherine looked so full of health although she was so much older and she had borne the Duke four children and her husband two with, it seemed, the utmost ease.

Mary felt ashamed of herself for being so weak. After all it was a woman's mission in life to be a mother.

So she said nothing and instead discussed the prospects of peace with France.

In due course the embassy left and by this time Mary was once more pregnant.

The terrible foreboding came to her. She felt ill as the months passed. I must tell Henry, she promised herself. There must be an end to this. We have four sons and now there is this other child.

That must be enough.

She had the feeling that she must get away from Bolingbroke. Perhaps a stay in pleasant Peterborough would do her good. In any case a change of scene would be beneficial. There was excitement in moving from castle to castle. After his adventure in the bear pit Harry had lost some of his devotion to the bears. He was more interested in a falcon which he had had given to him. The children would enjoy a move.

So they travelled to Peterborough.

Strangely enough Mary's health improved. The months passed quickly and there was news from France. Everywhere the English went they were treated with honour and courtesy by the French; there were tournaments and banquets at which as usual each tried to outdo the other in splendour.

Henry excelled as always at the joust and there he met those on pilgrimages to the Holy Land. It occurred to him then that that was something he would like to undertake. The truth was that he needed adventure. When he had joined with the Lords Appellant there had been plenty of that, but now that the King had settled down and the Queen was beside him to keep a steadying influence on him, life had changed in England; and there was not enough to keep a man like Henry occupied.

He fancied going on a pilgrimage and discussed it with his father, who thought it a good idea.

He had heard from Mary that she was once again pregnant. She seemed to be having a child almost every year which was very commendable. The more his family grew, the happier Henry was. Boys to stand beside him and support him in his quarrels, girls to make good alliances and bring more strength to his house. They were young yet. Mary was now twenty-two; she had years of childbearing before her. Yes, they were going to rival Edward and Philippa.

Meanwhile Mary waited in Peterborough.

She was aware of the anxious looks of Joan Waring and Mary Hervey; she knew that they whispered about her and feared the worst.

Joan was indignant. Ladies had more to do in life than bear child after child. This was for gipsies and the poor. My lord should understand this. Of course he did not know what toll these pregnancies took of the Lady Mary. When he came home there was a baby smiling—or yelling—in its cradle and his lady wife smiling as though it had all been as easy as she could have wished it to be.

It was spring and the buds were opening and the birds were going wild with joy when Mary's pains started. A cold fear took possession of her as her women helped her to bed.

'Let me come through this,' she prayed. 'What of the children if I do not? They need their mother. Oh God, let me live and let this be the last.'

It seemed as though her prayers were answered for it was an easier birth than the others; the baby was small but perfectly formed.

A little girl.

It was a change after the four boys. She marvelled at the dainty creature and in that moment she thought it was all worthwhile. She had five wonderful children. She must not complain because she had had to pay a certain price for them. The painful birth . . . the deterioration of health . . . they could be forgotten while she held her baby girl in her arms.

Would Henry be pleased? She believed so. After all they had their four boys.

She thought of a name for the child. She should be named after Henry's mother. Blanche, that was a good family name. So Blanche it should be.

The little girl thrived and Mary was delighted that she should feel so much better than she usually did after her confinements.

Henry was as delighted as Mary had known he would be. He was pleased that she should be called after his mother whom the poet Chaucer had extolled in his verses but whom Henry could not remember. He sent silks from Champagne and Flanders to decorate the font in Peterborough Cathedral and there Mary's fifth child was baptized.

Henry returned to England but almost immediately set out again. He was going to travel across Europe to the Holy Land. On the way the King wished him to call on the Queen's brother Wenceslas who was also the Holy Roman Emperor. He was to pay his respects and to let Wenceslas know how devoted Richard was to his Queen. Indeed there was no need because the devotion of the royal pair was well known throughout Europe. However, it was a friendly gesture and one which Henry was delighted to make.

From Bohemia he went to Venice, where he arranged that a ship was commissioned and when it was built and filled with the requisite stores he set out for Palestine which he reached in due course. He paid a visit to the Church of the Holy Sepulchre at the Mount of Olives and glowing with righteousness he began to journey home. He stayed for a while on the island of Cyprus where he was entertained by its King, and when he had watched the performing bears he could not resist telling the story of how his first-born had fearlessly descended into the pit to play with the bear. The boy's valour was applauded and when he was leaving, the King presented him with a leopard.

'To amuse the young Lord Harry,' was the comment, 'but tell him he must not come too close to this one.'

'Which,' replied Henry, 'would be the way in which to make him do so!'

'Oh he is a bold brave Prince, that one,' was the laughing reply and a cage was found for the leopard so that it might accompany Henry when he returned to England.

John of Gaunt sent a message to him. It was time he came back. A new situation was arising in the country. The Earl of Arundel, one of the five Lords Appellant who had faced the King with Henry, was circulating rumours about John of Gaunt, doubting his loyalty to the King.

The Duke was soon able to deal with these and so strongly had he won the King's confidence that Richard commanded Arundel to apologize to his uncle.

Richard had come to believe that John of Gaunt was his most trusted ally. He was too old now to want the crown for himself; moreover it was understood that Richard was undoubtedly the true heir to the crown and that it would be folly to attempt to shift it from his head. These were uneasy days when those about the throne must take care how they walked.

Henry returned and Mary, to her dismay, discovered that she was once more pregnant. Her spirits drooped for this time she felt really ill.

There *must* be an end to this incessant childbearing. She would *have* to tell Henry how she dreaded it. He was naturally not aware of this because he was generally if not out of the country away from the family circle. Soon after she had made this alarming discovery news was brought to the castle of the death of Henry's stepmother, Constanza of Castile. Mary had met Constanza only rarely and she had always seemed remote, for Henry's stepmother was entirely Spanish and had never fitted into the English way of life. She and her husband had rarely lived together and since they had returned from Castile after arranging the marriage of their daughter Catherine with the heir of that country, Constanza seemed even more like a stranger to them all. The Duke's wife was in all but legality Catherine Swynford and it was Catherine who interested herself in family affairs and whom the children loved. Still it was a shock as death must always be and Henry, who came back to the family for a brief spell, expressed his curiosity as to what would happen now.

The Duke was free of Constanza but could he marry Catherine Swynford? If he were not the son of a king he undoubtedly would. But he must always remember that he *was* King Edward's son. 'Of one thing we can be sure,' Mary pointed out, 'Lady Swynford will not attempt to influence him.'

'He cannot marry her,' said Henry emphatically. 'His rank is too high and she is too humble.'

Mary sighed. 'There is no woman in the country more worthy to be the Duchess of Lancaster.'

'In all ways but one,' agreed Henry. 'Her humble birth can never be forgotten.'

'Can it not?' asked Mary almost wonderingly.

Then she said that she would like to go to Leicester for a change. She wanted the new child to be born there.

A terrible tragedy had struck the King. His beloved wife, who was known throughout the country as Good Queen Anne, caught the prevailing sickness and in a few weeks was dead.

The King's grief maddened him and he was inconsolable. Anne had been his constant companion and had grown ever closer since the passing of his friend Robert de Vere. He could not contemplate life without her and was filled with rage that fate could have been so cruel as to take from him this beloved Queen.

In his uncontrollable anger he slashed the hangings in the room where she had died and declared that he never wanted to see Sheen again.

Then his morbid rage took possession of him so that he was unable to control it. He broke up the furniture in that room; he destroyed it utterly. Never could he bear to look on that room again.

There is death in the air, thought Mary.

The time was growing near. Joan Waring and Mary Hervey were growing more and more uneasy.

'There is no time between for her to recover,' grumbled Joan. 'It is a mercy my lord is away on his travels or the intervals would be even shorter I'd swear.'

'If he were here perhaps he would be aware of the toll it is taking of her.'

'Men!' snapped Joan. 'What do they know of these matters. All they think of is their own pleasure and getting children to bring them honour and glory. My lord will have to be spoken to after this one and if no one else will do it I will.'

'Better leave it to my lady.'

'She, poor soul, does nothing but submit.'

'She is a great lady.'

'The best in the land. But that won't bring her through. I fear for her, Mary. I fear for her.'

'You have always feared yet she recovers.'

'Yes, in time for the next one. It will not continue, I know that.'

'You fret too much, Joan,' Mary Hervey said. 'Blanche's was an easy birth.'

Joan said nothing. She pursed her lips to express disapproval.

The weeks passed and Mary was so tired that she spent most of her time in bed. She was glad Henry was away. She would have hated him to see her so indisposed. Thousands of women were having babies every day. And she had only five. It was not a great number. It was just that they had seemed to follow so quickly on one another.

Perhaps when this child was born, she would try to explain to Henry . . .

Summer had come. She thought of Constanza and wondered what her life had been with a husband who had made no secret of the fact that he had married her for the sake of her crown. Henry would never have been allowed to marry her, she reasoned, if it had not been for her fortune, but they had met romantically and they had been lovers. Yet he had known from the first who she was and had no doubt been advised by his father to court her.

Perhaps it was better not to probe into motives too closely. Suffice it she had been happy—completely happy in those first years before the fearsome task of bearing children had begun.

It is my weakness, she admonished herself. Other women do the same without complaint.

She thought often of the King and his grief. She had heard how he had destroyed the room at Sheen in which the Queen had died because he would never be able to bear to look at it again. And theirs had been a marriage of convenience, arranged by states, and they had never seen each other until Anne had come from Bohemia to marry him.

Poor, poor Richard. Unhappy King; who had come too young to the throne but had found a wife whom he could love and then had lost her.

But she must not brood on death. There was a life stirring within her. And she loved her children. She loved them dearly. Once they had arrived and she had recovered from the ordeal she was happy . . . until the time came to give birth again.

I am a coward, she thought. And then: But oh, if Henry only knew the pain I suffer!

Leicester was a magnificent castle situated on the right bank of the River Soar, just outside the city but close to the wall which the Romans had built when they called the town Ratae. When the name had changed she did not know but the town and the castle, which had been of great importance both to the Saxons and the Danes, had come into the possession of the House of Lancaster more than a hundred years ago and John of Gaunt had restored and beautified it in the manner he liked to employ with so many of his properties.

June was almost over and the birth was imminent. Mary lay on her bed waiting for her pains to start.

Her labour was long and arduous. All through the day and night it persisted. The pain grew more intense and never before even in her most gruelling experiences had she known such agony.

When at last the child was born she was too exhausted to ask its sex and if it were healthy in every way.

Her doctors said above everything she must rest. They gave her a soothing potion and set two women by her bedside to watch over her.

The child was a healthy girl. As soon as Joan heard

her lusty cries she was there to see her new charge. A fine girl!

'Bless you,' she murmured, 'let us hope your coming has not cost my lady too much strength.'

It seemed that it had cost a great deal, for Mary remained exhausted through the days that followed. But when the baby was brought to her and laid in her arms she was content with it.

'I have given my lord six children,' she said. 'That is a fair number—four boys and two girls—is it not?'

Her women assured her that it was.

'I am twenty-four years of age,' she said. 'How long can a woman expect to go on bearing children? Another ten years?' She smiled wanly. 'Not for me, I think. Not for me.'

Joan said quickly: 'Six is a goodly number. It is enough for any parents, no matter who they be.'

'Queen Philippa bore twelve,' she said.

'It is too many,' mumbled Joan.

'I shall call this child Philippa after that Good Queen,' said Mary.

They took the baby from her for she was so easily tired.

During the next day a lassitude came over her and she lay listlessly in her bed. She kept drifting into sleep—though it did not seem like sleep but almost as though she had escaped from the present into the past. She was in the convent and the Abbess was with her. 'You must be sure if this is the life you want, Mary.' Oh the peace of the life—lived by bells, she had always thought. Bells for nones, bells for compline . . . working in the herb garden, baking the bread, tending the poor, living in a bare cell chilled to the bone in the winter but somehow happy in the service of God.

She had turned away from it. Henry had made her turn and from the moment she had met him in the forest she had had no longer any desire to be a nun. Her future had been planned she knew. She was a pawn in the hands of the great John of Gaunt as she would have been in the hands of her sister and Eleanor's ambitious husband.

But it had come about so naturally and no matter what happened she would never want to be without her children. Beloved children. Harry the rebellious, Thomas who liked to imitate his elder brother; John who was a good boy, and little Humphrey. Then sweet Blanche and now Philippa. No, they were her life, though soon the boys would be taken away from her, but at present she had them.

She asked that Harry and Thomas be sent to her.

They came and stood by her bed, rather overawed, which was strange for Harry, but he realized there was something momentous about this occasion.

Her eyes rested on Harry—seven years old now, with more of a look of de Bohun than Plantagenet. That smooth dark hair and brown eyes and oval face, the very slender little body. He lacked the tawny lion-like looks of his paternal antecedents. The brown eyes were curious now, alert with speculation, but at the same time he was clearly disturbed to see his mother looking so unlike herself.

'Harry,' she said, 'come near the bed.' She took his hand. 'And Thomas. Come to the other side. There, I have a son on either side of me. You would guard me, would you not?'

'What against?' asked Harry. 'No one will harm you here.'

She thought: Against Death. Death is in the castle, my son. I feel him close.

She laughed and said: 'No, but I like to have you with me.'

'No enemy of my father's could come into the castle, I would stop him,' boasted Harry.

'So would I,' added Thomas.

'God bless you both, my sons. I know you would. I want you always to be friends. Will you promise that?'

The boys looked bewildered, and Mary went on. 'I know you quarrel now and then in the schoolroom. But you forget your differences after a while, don't you? And if anyone tried to harm Thomas, Harry, you would go to his rescue wouldn't you?'

'Is anybody going to hurt him?' asked Harry, his eyes sparkling.

'No, no. But I just said if . . .'

'People do not say if unless they think it may happen,' replied Harry sagely.

She thought: I must not alarm them. Harry is too sharp and Thomas is wondering what is going to happen to him.

'I just want you to remember it is my wish that you should always be friends.'

'You don't want me to give him my new falcon?' asked Harry suspiciously.

'I want it,' cried Thomas hopefully.

'No, no,' replied their mother. 'Just be good friends always . . . and never let a quarrel between you last.'

The two boys were surveying each other across the bed with intensity and Mary said quickly, 'You have a new sister.'

'We have one,' said Thomas.

'We did not really want another,' added Harry rather reproachfully. 'And you were so ill bringing her.'

'You mustn't hold that against her.'

'When will you be up?'

'Soon.'

'And shall we have a feast? And will my father come?'

'Yes, we shall and he will.'

She closed her eyes. Harry beckoned his brother and at that moment Joan came in.

'Come,' she said, 'your mother is tired.'

As she led them out Harry turned to her and said: 'I think she was trying to tell us that she is going away.'

There was a gloom in the castle and a terrible premonition of disaster.

Men and women walked about on tiptoe and spoke in whispers. The Countess was in a fever.

In the nursery the new baby thrived. A wet nurse had been found for her and it was not the baby who showed signs of her difficult entry into the world.

The question was whether a message should be sent to the Earl of Derby to tell him that the health of his Countess was causing grave anxiety and that since the birth of the Lady Philippa grave symptoms were beginning to show themselves. They hesitated, but as the days passed it was considered that he must be told.

Henry was alarmed. He came at once to Leicester.

In his heart he had known that Mary dreaded childbirth but he had looked upon it as one of the inevitable patterns of life.

Children were the very reason for marriage and he had delighted in the fact that he had six and was hoping for more.

And now Mary was ill. The after effects of childbirth, he assured himself. It was nothing. Those women about her fussed too much. They encouraged her fears.

Nevertheless he rode with all speed and when he arrived at the castle, a terrible depression came to him.

He went at once to his wife's bedchamber. The pale wan figure lying on the bed was scarcely recognizable. Her dark hair hung lank and limp about her emaciated features; only her eyes seemed the same: loving, earnest, eager to please.

'Henry, you came.'

'My love,' he said, 'what ails you?'

'It was too much, Henry . . . too much.'

'The child is well.'

'Thank God, she is a fine child. It is your poor Mary who has changed, Henry.'

'You will soon get well. We'll have six more yet, Mary. You see.'

She smiled wanly, and shook her head.

'Well,' said Henry, 'we have our six. Oh Mary, I hate to see you like this.'

'I know. I did not wish you to see me so, but they would send for you.'

'I am happy to be with you.'

'I have not disappointed you?'

'My dearest, you have made me so happy. I have never ceased to love you from the day we first met in the forest. Do you remember?'

'It is something I shall never forget. I treasure the memory . . . and I have given you six children, have I not? I did my duty as a wife . . .'

'Oh speak not of duty. It has been for love has it not?'

'Yes,' she said, 'for love. Always remember that, Henry. For love.'

He sat long by her bed and she made him talk of the past, of those days at Arundel and then the birth of Harry and how they had been so happy in the early days of their marriage.

Afterwards he had been away so much and she had seen him rarely, just often enough to become pregnant and start the exhausting business of bringing another child into the world.

But they were her beloved family and blessings had to be paid for.

After a while he saw that she was sleeping and he crept away and left her.

Soon after his arrival it became clear that she was very ill. The finest doctors in the country were at her bedside, but there was nothing they could do. She was exhausted, worn out by too much childbearing. She was small and fragile and not meant for such an arduous life.

Henry was bewildered. The stark fact faced him. It need not have happened. If she had stopped in time this would not have happened.

The progress of the fever was rapid and a few days after his arrival Henry knew that this was the end.

He knelt by her bedside, for she seemed comforted to have him close. She was at peace now. A woman with her travail over. She did not send for the children for she did not wish them to see her thus.

'It will frighten them,' she said. 'Let them remember me as I was. I am leaving them to you, Henry. You will care for them. Do not be harsh with Harry. I want him to love you. I want them all to love each other. No deadly quarrels. They must always work together. That is what I want . . .'

'It shall be,' said Henry. 'All that you ask I will do.'

'Stay with me then. It will not be long now.'

He was with her when she died.

He sat at her bedside, stunned with disbelief.

But he must rouse himself. Mary was dead. She was twenty-four years of age. Too young to die. But she was dead. It was the Year of Death—Constanza, the Queen and now Mary, and both the Queen and Mary had been struck down in the flower of their youth. He could understand his cousin's grief which had obsessed him and driven him mad for the time.

Sometimes he thought that his fate was entwined with that of his cousin. He had always thought that but for that quirk of fate he should have been in Richard's place. They had been born in the same year. They had been happily married and within a few weeks of each other they had lost their beloved partners.

He felt lost, bewildered. Although during the last years he had spent more time abroad than with her, he knew he was going to miss her sorely.

She must have a splendid funeral. Her mother would insist on that. She should be laid to rest with the de Bohuns for that was what she had wanted.

It took his mind from his desolation to plan the grand funeral she should have, just as it had Richard's when he buried his Queen.

When it was over he must give thought to his family.

The children had all been together, cared for by their loving mother. Now he must make other plans for their future. He would be with them when he could but the political situation was such that it demanded his constant attention.

He was considering very carefully what must be done for the motherless boys and girls.

THE FORGET-ME-NOT

The children were now in the charge of Mary Hervey and Joan Waring and they lived mainly at Kenilworth, and when that castle needed sweetening, they moved for a while to Tutbury. Life went on for them very much in the same way as before their mother's death, but they missed her sorely. Blanche could not remember her of course, but all the boys did, even three-year-old Humphrey. As for Harry, he was sobered for a while. He was seven and old for his years. He felt that in the absence of his father he was head of the family and his ascendancy over his brothers seemed stronger than ever.

He missed her more than Mary and Joan would have believed; and at times he was quiet and rather sad thinking of her. He remembered what she had said to him and he realized that she knew then that she was dying. He promised himself he would try to do what she wanted and in consequence took up a protective attitude towards his brothers.

In the winter of the following year he caught a chill and became so ill that everyone thought he was going to die. His father in an agony of apprehension had the best doctors sent down from London and very soon Harry was surprising them by his determination to live. His health began to improve and he would lie in his bed listening to the songs of Wilkin Walkin, the minstrel whom their father had sent to them to teach them to sing. They were fond of music because their mother had always seen that there was plenty of it in the household. There were lessons with Mary Hervey and games with his brothers; he commanded them and tolerated his sisters and so life passed during the first year after his mother's death but none knew more than Harry that it would not remain as it was.

Henry was becoming more and more preoccupied with the country's affairs. Moreover, the King had gone to Ireland to attempt to sort out the troubles there and John of Gaunt went to Aquitaine with the same purpose in mind. This threw responsibilities on Henry, for the King had made him a member of the Council which ruled during his absence; and as his father was out of the country it was Henry's task to look after the Lancastrian estates.

Richard and John of Gaunt returned to England; and that year, the second after Mary's death, two important marriages took place in England.

John of Gaunt snapped his fingers at convention and did what he had wanted to do for a long time and that was marry Catherine Swynford. There were some members of the nobility who were horrified at this, but there were many who applauded it and thought the better of John of Gaunt for making Catherine his wife.

The King was one who approved of the match. He had always liked Catherine; moreover he was completely reconciled to his uncle Lancaster and as he relied on the advice the latter gave him, he was eager to please him. So not only did he show his approval of the match by receiving Catherine as the new Duchess, but he set his seal on it and won her eternal gratitude by legitimizing her children, the Beauforts, which next to marriage with the Duke was her dearest wish.

Henry was pleased. He had always looked upon Catherine as his stepmother and the Beauforts as his brothers. Now they were legally so.

The other marriage was that of Richard himself. Dearly as he had loved Anne he wanted to please his counsellors by marrying again, but he chose Isabella, the daughter of the King of France, much to the consternation of those about him, for Isabella was a child not quite ten years old. Perfect wife as she had been, Anne had failed in one respect. She had not provided an heir to the throne. It seemed the utmost folly therefore for Richard, the main purpose of whose marriage should be the begetting of children, to marry a child who would not be ready for childbearing for some four years at the earliest.

The inference was that Richard did not greatly care for women, and he did not want to replace Anne; and that the thought of a child wife who could be brought up in English ways and make no marital demands suited him very well.

Both John of Gaunt and Henry accompanied the King to France for the royal marriage. As Duchess of Lancaster Catherine Swynford was one of the ladies who would attend the new Queen, as were Mary's sister Eleanor and the Countess of Arundel. This Countess was Philippa, daughter of the Earl of March and therefore granddaughter of John of Gaunt's elder brother Lionel. She was very conscious of her royal blood and wished everyone about her to be.

Eleanor and Philippa created a sensation by their rudeness to Catherine and although the latter behaved as though she had failed to notice their bad manners, John of Gaunt was furious and determined to make them pay at some time for the insult.

There were however matters to occupy them other than this, and Lancaster was very eager that his son should understand the significance of what was happening.

'What can this marriage of Richard's mean?' he asked. 'Obviously that there can be no heir to the throne for years. Anne could not get one either. The fault may have lain with Richard. The fact that he has chosen this marriage may be a key to the situation. But think what it means, Henry. When he dies who will follow him?'

'Lionel's heirs . . .'

John of Gaunt snapped his fingers. 'Too remote,' he said. 'You stand well in line, Henry.'

'I am the same age as Richard and he seems in good health.'

'He is unpredictable. At one time he showed signs of becoming a great King. He stood up to the rebels at

Blackheath and Smithfield. He was a hero then. But where is the hero now? He faced the rebels because he did not realize what danger he was in. He was a child then. It worked, but it might easily not have done and then instead of a heroic act it would have been judged as one of folly. I see great events looming, Henry, and I want you to be prepared when they come. No more travels. You must stay near home. You must defend our estates. You must see that when the time comes you are at hand.'

So when they returned to England Henry abandoned all thought of further travel and kept a watchful eye on what was happening about the King. There was peace with France but instead of easing the situation this seemed to aggravate it. The people were still complaining about the heavy taxes which were levied on them; and now that there was peace with France—if only temporary— for what reason did the exchequer need so much money? The answer was clear. Their King lived most extrava-gantly; he was constantly giving lavish banquets and entertainments to his friends; large sums were spent on his clothes which were bedecked with valuable jewels; the fact was that the people were expected to pay heav-ily for the upkeep of a Court which was far too luxurious to be paid for without their support.

Would Richard never learn? wondered John of Gaunt. There was trouble brewing.

Richard was aware that revolt was in the air; he knew that the leaders of it were his uncle Thomas of Gloucester, and the Earls of Arundel and Warwick. He decided to act and for once did so promptly. He invited them all to a banquet, his intention being to arrest them when they came. Gloucester and Arundel scented danger and did not appear. Warwick came and was arrested. But War-wick was of less importance than the other two and he was sent to the Tower where he remained. Arundel was lured to London and arrested on a charge of treason, and John of Gaunt, as Seneschal of England, presided at his trial and sentenced him to death with some relish as he remembered the insults he had thrown at Catherine.

There remained Gloucester, who was eventually cap-tured and sent to Calais where he died mysteriously in an inn, said to have been smothered by feather beds being pressed upon him.

John of Gaunt was very disturbed. Thomas was after all his brother. There had never been great friendship between them even when they were young but when John had arranged for his son to get the coveted Garter award by ousting Thomas he had aroused his vitriolic brother's enmity; and even more so when he had snatched Mary from his control and married her fortune to his son Henry.

Still he was a brother and, as he confided to Henry, it was interesting to note that the three who had been pursued so relentlessly by the King—Gloucester, Arundel and Warwick—were three of the five Lords Appellant who had some years before confronted the King arms linked to show solidarity and wrung concessions from him.

The other two were Thomas Mowbray and Henry himself.

'You see,' said the wise Duke of Lancaster, 'it is necessary to tread very warily. Richard does not forget what he considers to be an insult. You and Mowbray should be watchful.'

Richard however seemed to be fond of his cousin. He made him a Duke, and Henry was now Duke of Hereford and Thomas Mowbray was Duke of Norfolk, so it seemed that long-ago incident was forgotten.

When he had bestowed the honour, Richard showed his friendship towards Henry by asking about his family and condoling with him on the death of his wife.

'We share a misfortune,' he said, and went on to extol the virtues of his beloved Anne. It was true he had a little Queen of whom he was already fond. A child merely; but he was going to cherish her and bring her up to love England and to be its Queen.

'In some ways you are more fortunate than I,' said the King. 'You have your boys and girls. How many is it now? Four boys, I hear.'

'Yes, I have four and two girls.'

'And how old is your heir—young Harry of Monmouth is it not?'

'He is ten years old.'

'And bright for his age, I hear. I want to meet Harry

of Monmouth. I'll tell you what, cousin, he shall come to Court.'

'I am overwhelmed by the honour,' said Henry, trying to hide his uneasiness. 'He is now at Oxford in the care of my half-brother Henry Beaufort. He is Chancellor of the University, as you know, and it is good for Harry to be under his tuition.'

'He would learn more at Court, cousin.'

'You are too kind to the boy, my lord. He is over young to be a courtier.'

'I am determined to have him here. I hear he is something of a rogue.'

'My lord, he is but a child.'

'But able to give a good account of himself. I like the sound of young Harry of Monmouth. I will send word that he is to come to Court.'

It was clear that Richard was determined, and with a sinking heart Henry went to his father to tell him what had taken place between him and Richard.

Lancaster was at first disturbed by the news and then he said: 'It may well be that Richard wishes to show friendship. He has made you a Duke. He relies on me and has come to trust me. I think he is perhaps merely showing favour to my grandson.'

'In any case,' replied Henry. 'There is nothing we can do about it.'

Harry was not sorry to leave Oxford for the Court. The King received him with a show of affection. 'My good uncle's grandson,' he said. 'You are welcome, Harry.'

Harry responded with genuine pleasure. He liked this good looking, sumptuously attired man with the delicate hands and the pink and white skin which coloured so pleasantly when he showed excitement, with the glittering garments and delicate perfume which hung about him.

And he is the King, thought Harry; and from that moment he wanted to be a king himself.

There was so much to see at Court. He first went to Eltham where the King was at that time and he was enchanted by the place. It was very different from gloomy Tutbury and even Kenilworth suffered by comparison.

Richard, about whom everything must be elegant and in what he considered perfect taste which meant a reflection of his own delight in the combinations of colour and patterns, was amused to see how overawed his young kinsman was and for a while kept him close to him.

He showed him the rebuilding he had done at Eltham—the new bath house. 'Never neglect to bathe, Harry,' he said. 'The practice gives pleasure to yourself as well as those about you. I abhor unsavoury odours.' It was a practice the King carried out regularly. His person was always exquisite. He gave as much thought to the cut of his long-sleeved coats, the new houpelandes, his high collars, the padded shoulders of his jackets, his skin tight hose and his long pointed shoes as he did to matters of state. There was also the painted chamber and the dancing chamber—for the King loved to dance—and he had made new gardens for his recreation and alfresco entertainments.

It was a new world for Harry. He had been given a cote hardie decorated with the badge of the white hart which showed he was of the King's household; and when the Court travelled he travelled with it.

His days were full. He longed to be a knight and take part in the jousts but he was ten years old and others did not forget it if he did. He must attend his lessons with others of his age, for there were boys like himself from noble households at Court; then he must learn to ride and use his sword, practise archery so that when the time came for him to win his spurs he would be able to give a good account of himself.

It was a very different life from that he had lived under his mother's care or when he had been at Oxford. Harry absorbed what was going on around him and it excited him. Life at the King's Court was the life for him.

After he had been at Court for a week or so the King lost interest in him and he was just one of the boys who was being brought up there. He did not mind. There was enough to absorb him and he was more interested in the outdoor life than the books and music and fine clothes which the King set such store by.

The Court had moved to Windsor and the King was in good spirits. It was because the little Queen was there

Harry was told, and Richard very much enjoyed the company of the little girl.

Harry was interested in the Queen because she was about his age and he thought how wonderful it must be to be so important.

Sometimes he would see the riders going off into the forest led by the King and beside him would ride the most beautiful girl Harry had ever seen. She was vivacious and added gesticulations to her persistent chatter. Her dark long hair hung loose about her shoulders and she wore the most elegant clothes which Harry learned had been chosen by the King.

One day when he was having a dancing lesson, which he was obliged to tolerate, she came into the room to watch. There were two other girls and two boys as well as himself and his partner and they were practising the newest Court dances. He felt more awkward than ever for those sparkling dark eyes had selected him for her special attention and it did not help matters when the dancing instructor pointed out another false step he had made.

Then the little Queen ran to him and taking his hand cried: 'Come, dance with me, clumsy boy. I will show you the way.'

He was overcome with embarrassment and disliked her in spite of her beauty which excited him and made him want to keep looking at her.

'I do not wish it, Madam,' he said with a haughty bow.

'My lord,' said the instructor. 'The Queen honours you.'

Harry said: 'I am not honoured.'

She began to laugh.

'He has no grace, this one,' she said in rather halting English.

'The Queen commands you to dance with her,' said the instructor, glaring at him and trying to convey some message.

'No, no,' cried Isabella. 'I do not command. If he does not wish . . .' She lifted her shoulders and set her features in an expression of mock tragedy. She turned to one of the other boys and took his hand, as she said, 'Music, please.'

The musicians began to play. Harry refused to dance and his partner and the girl who had danced with the boy whom Isabella had chosen, danced together while Harry stood by sullenly watching.

There was no doubt that the Queen danced beautifully. She had a special grace all her own. Now and then she glanced Harry's way and caught his eyes on her. That seemed to please her.

When the dance was over, she seemed to lose interest in the incident and laughing ran out of the room but not without first throwing a mocking glance in Harry's direction.

As soon as she had gone the instructor cried at Harry: 'You are a fool. I never saw such behaviour in all my life. This could cost me my position and you your place at Court. Am I not supposed to be teaching you courtly manners as well as dancing and have I not just seen the worst display of bad manners that have ever been seen at Court? Do you realize she is the Queen?'

'I knew she was the Queen, of course,' muttered Harry.

'And you refused to dance with her when she did you the honour of selecting you!'

'She was laughing at me.'

'You refused to dance with the Queen! Rest assured, my lord, this is not the end of the matter. She will tell the King and you will be sent back to the country where you belong.'

'I do not care,' said Harry contemptuously.

But he did care. He very much enjoyed Court life. He could not bear to think of going back to the country to the care of Mary Hervey or return to Oxford to work under the stern eye of uncle Beaufort.

He kept thinking about her. She gave herself airs. Well, why shouldn't she? She was the Queen. And she was very beautiful. He had never seen anyone so beautiful. Her way of speaking was fascinating, as was her manner.

He had made her angry—although she had pretended not to be. She would tell the King and everyone said that the King denied her nothing for he loved her dearly and treated her like some precious little pet. She would only have to say I want that ill-mannered Harry of

Monmouth sent away from Court and he would be dismissed.

All through the day he kept realizing how much he enjoyed Court life. He noticed too how elegant and charming some of the women were. None of them had the style of the Queen of course, although she was only a child. But she had changed him in some way. She had made him aware of things which he had never noticed before.

He was desolate, calling himself stupid to have antagonized her. At any moment the dismissal would come. His father would be angry with him; his grandfather would despise him. What hope would he have of rising if he was going to let his silly pride govern his actions?

He should have danced with the Queen; he should have flattered her. He should have made her like him. He could see it clearly, now that it was too late.

The summons did not come, however, and in a few weeks he ceased to expect it although he did not forget the Queen and whenever he could he took the opportunity of watching her, though she never noticed him again.

Everyone at Court was talking about the combat which was to take place between the Dukes of Hereford and Norfolk and as the Duke of Hereford was the title which had recently been bestowed on Harry's father this matter was of especial interest to him.

As far as Harry could understand, Thomas Mowbray, recently created Duke of Norfolk—at the same time as Henry of Lancaster had been made Duke of Hereford—had made a suggestion to Hereford which the latter construed as treason and which he had laid before the King.

Norfolk had retaliated by declaring that he was no traitor and that Hereford was bringing the accusation to cover up his own nefarious intentions.

The outcome of the matter was that the King had agreed that the two men should meet in combat. There was a great deal of whispering at Court and Harry had what Joan Waring had called long ears. If one of these men was a traitor, it was asked, what was the point in having a combat to settle it? A traitor might be the victor and an innocent man killed. It was all very strange. But the excitement grew as the days passed. The Court had moved to Coventry, a fair city surrounded by thick walls mounted by thirty-two towers. There were twelve gates into the city and it was consequently one of the strongest fortifications in the country.

Outside the city walls there was great activity while pavilions were erected. Harry watched the work with mixed feelings for his father would be one of the chief actors in this drama which was about to be played on this glittering field and if his father were to die . . .

The thought bewildered him. He saw little of his father and he had found him stern and undemonstrative—very different from his mother who although long since dead lingered on in his memory. He would never forget the beatings his father had given him. For his own good, his mother had told him; but he had always felt that he would have been better without them, for when he felt the urge to do something which would incur punishment he never stopped to think of the consequences. That came after. In the castle they were gambling on the life or death of the Dukes of Hereford and Norfolk—for this was no *joust à Plaisance* but the culmination of a bitter quarrel, which would mean the end of one of them.

His grandfather arrived. Harry noticed with satisfaction that his pavilion, flying its pennants and lions and leopards, was almost as fine as the King's. They would be his emblem one day. His grandfather summoned him to his presence. He was a very old man and he seemed to have aged since Harry had last seen him.

'Your father will triumph over the traitor Norfolk,' he told Harry.

'Of a certainty,' replied Harry loyally.

But he could see that his grandfather was no more sure of this than he was.

'You will sit with the Duchess and myself,' said John of Gaunt. 'It is well that you will be here to see this day.'

He is afraid, thought Harry; and he is reminding me that if my father is killed I shall be my grandfather's heir. He is a very old man. It could not be long before I would be head of the House of Lancaster.

But Harry was not yet to be head of the House of

Lancaster. It was the most extraordinary gathering that had ever been.

Harry saw his father ride out. He looked magnificent on his big white horse caparisoned in green and blue velvet decorated with gold swans and antelopes. His armour, Harry had heard, had been made in Milan where the best armour was made.

Then came the Duke of Norfolk who looked almost as splendid; his colours were red and the velvet was embroidered with lions and mulberry trees.

Then the strangest thing happened. The heralds on orders from the King suddenly dashed forward shouting: 'Ho! Ho!' which meant that a halt was to be called to the proceedings.

The King disappeared from his pavilion.

'Where has he gone?' whispered Harry.

His grandfather said: 'This is a strange business. I think he is going to stop the combat.'

Harry could hear the relief in his grandfather's voice. He knew then how frightened he had been.

There was great tension in the crowd of spectators who felt they were about to witness unusual events. They had come to see a life and death struggle between two of the highest in the land, but whatever was going to happen now could be equally exciting.

Two hours passed before one of the King's advisers came out to announce to the crowd that there would be no combat. The King and his counsellors had decided the issue could not be settled in this way, and it had been agreed that since there was a doubt of the loyalty of both contestants they would be exiled from the country. Hereford would not return for ten years; Norfolk would never return.

A hushed silence fell on the crowd. Harry saw that his grandfather's face had turned a greyish colour. He gripped his seat and whispered: 'Oh God help us. Not this. Not this.'

Everyone was talking about the exiles and Harry noticed that when he appeared there was an abrupt termination of the conversation. As son of one of the leading players in the drama, care had to be taken as to what was said in his hearing.

His father was going away. He would be away for ten years. I shall be twenty when he comes back! thought Henry. Would the King send him away? Was the family in disgrace? It must be so if the King suspected his father of treachery and was sending him out of the country.

The two Dukes had been given fifteen days in which to make their preparations and leave the country. After that time they would be arrested if they remained.

A harsh sentence was the comment.

'Do you wonder?' Harry overheard someone say. 'These are the last two of the Lords Appellant. The other three are taken care of. Now exile for these two. Richard never forgets an insult. Depend upon it he has been waiting to take his revenge on these two.'

'He seemed to have trusted both Mowbray and Bolingbroke.'

'Seemed to. But Richard never forgets.'

Harry knew about the Lords Appellant. He learned such matters with absolute ease because they concerned his father and family and that meant himself.

He heard that his father was coming to say good-bye to him before he left the country and he steeled himself for the farewell.

His grandfather arrived with his father. They were both very sober.

His father embraced him and told him that he must grow quickly now. He must remember that in the absence of his father he must take his place. 'Thank God your grandfather is here to protect you,' he said.

'You will be leaving Court and coming with me,' went on the great Duke. 'Your father and I think that best. The Duchess is looking forward to welcoming you. We shall go to Leicester after we have accompanied your father to the coast.'

'Yes,' said Harry quietly.

'I think Harry is old enough to understand,' went on the Duke. 'Your father will not be allowed to come back to this country, and you must learn how to look after our interests. That is what I shall teach you. And if you are thinking that I am an old man, you are right. I am. I could die at any time and we must be prepared for that. I have seen the King and he has agreed that when I die my estates will not be confiscated. The Lancastrian inheritance will be for your father and in due course for you, Harry. You understand?'

'Yes,' repeated Harry.

'This is a sorry matter for our family but we stand together and never fear or doubt that we shall emerge triumphant in the end.'

While they were talking the King came in.

They were all startled because it was rarely that he was seen without attendants. They were there now . . . but waiting outside the room.

'You are saying good-bye to the boy,' said Richard.

His father and grandfather stood back uncertainly.

'You need have no fear for your son, cousin,' said the King.

'He will be well cared for,' said his grandfather. 'I shall take him with me when I leave.'

The King smiled slowly. 'I have grown fond of Harry. You know that don't you, boy?'

Harry murmured that his good lord had always been gracious to him.

'So much so that I cannot part with him.'

Harry heard his grandfather catch his breath and saw him put out his hand to touch a chair to steady himself.

'It is good of you to say so,' said his father, 'but in view of my sad state you will wish to be rid of him.'

'There you are wrong, cousin. I have interested myself in Harry. I like him well. In fact he interests me so much that I have decided to keep him with me.'

'He is young,' said his grandfather in a quiet voice. 'He needs to be with his family.'

'Well he is to some measure. Are you not my uncle and is he not your grandson? At Court he can be with his King and his kinsman.' The next words were ominous. 'It is what I want and I shall not change my mind. Come, Harry, say good-bye to your father. You shall be at my table this night.'

The King turned and went out of the room.

Harry looked from his white-faced father to his stricken grandfather. He understood.

He had become a hostage.

*   *   *

Harry did not see his grandfather again. Four months after his son had been exiled John of Gaunt died in Leicester Castle. He was nearly sixty years old and he had led a full and adventurous life. His great ambition had been to wear a crown and he had never achieved it, although his daughter by Constanza of Castile was now a Queen and the son Blanche of Lancaster had borne and those of Catherine Swynford would, he was sure, make their mark in the world.

But he would not see it; and he died, with his son in exile and his grandson a boy who would not be twelve years old until the summer.

His body was carried from Leicester to London and the cavalcade stopped one night to rest at St Albans where that other son, Henry Beaufort, now Bishop of Lincoln, celebrated a requiem for his father.

The name of John of Gaunt was on every lip. Now that he was dead it was forgotten that he had been the most unpopular man in the country, and only good was remembered of him.

When the King seized his estates, a number of people were shocked, for it was known that Richard had promised that the estates should go to the rightful heir even though he was an exile. Solemnly the King had promised this to John of Gaunt. It was unwise to break promises given to the dead.

'No good will come of this,' was the prophecy. 'Richard should take care.'

Henry of Bolingbroke, Duke of Hereford, exiled from his native land, arrived disconsolate in France and made up his mind that he had no alternative but to throw himself on the mercy of the King of France, hoping that since Richard had sent him away he might find some favour in that quarter.

Even this was questionable for Charles's daughter Isabella was now the wife of Richard and the two countries were at peace. All the same it would be naive to assume that there was true friendship between them and it was almost certain that the King of France would be ready to receive a notable exile from England, if only to learn what was happening in that country.

Henry was right. No sooner had he arrived in Paris

than King Charles expressed his willingness to receive him, and did so with such a show of friendship that Henry's spirits rose, especially when the King presented him with the very fine Hôtel Clisson which was to be his while he stayed in France.

He was received at Court presided over by Queen Isabeau, one of the most beautiful women he had ever seen and, if rumour was correct, one of the most evil. In spite of the outward appearance of elegance and wealth there was a distinct uneasiness throughout the Court and it was not long before Henry heard of those mental aberrations which the King suffered and which robbed him of reason. These lasted for varying periods of time— none could be sure how long—and when they ended the King would emerge remembering nothing or very little of what had happened during his periods of insanity.

Henry began to fret. Richard had, under pressure from John of Gaunt, reduced the sentence of ten years to six. But six years away from home! How could he endure that! His father was ageing, young Harry was but a boy, and exile was the most disastrous thing that could have happened. Moreover, although he had been warmly welcomed at the French Court, he knew how quickly enthusiasm for men in his position waned. He was thrown into melancholy.

One day, however, there were visitors at the Hôtel Clisson who were to cheer him considerably.

He could scarcely believe his eyes when the two men arrived asking for audience with the Duke of Hereford. He received them with caution for the elder of the men was Thomas of Canterbury and the younger the Earl of Arundel whose father had been executed for treason.

It was natural that exiles should work together against a common enemy but the first thought that struck Henry was that his father John of Gaunt as Seneschal of England had been the one to pronounce sentence on the unfortunate Earl of Arundel—and how could he guess what the Arundels' feelings would be towards the son of John of Gaunt.

It soon became clear that past grievances must be forgotten. After all, although Henry had been a member of the court which had condemned the Earl of Arundel, he himself had not actually passed the fatal sentence;

now they were all exiles from England and must join against the common enemy, Richard the King.

So Henry could draw comfort from the arrival of these two and in Paris they could discuss the fate which had overtaken them, through the misgovernment of Richard, and ponder as to what could be done about it.

The Archbishop had come from Rome where he had exhorted the Pope to request Richard to allow him to return, alas to no avail.

'One day,' he said, 'I shall return. I am the Archbishop no matter whom the King should set up in my place.'

Henry agreed. It was comforting to have Englishmen of standing to share his fate. Oh yes indeed, let bygones be bygones. They had the future to think of.

Young Thomas Fitzalan the Earl of Arundel was the only surviving son of the executed Earl. He had been only sixteen when his father had died; it was not very long ago and he remembered it vividly. How could he forget? Not only had he lost his father, but the way of life to which he had been accustomed was drastically changed.

He told Henry what had happened to him. It had made him very bitter.

'My father's estates were confiscated. I had nothing . . . nothing at all. The greatest misfortune of all was to be handed over to John Holland. Duke of Exeter now! He is greatly enriched but not through merit, simply because he is the King's half-brother. How I hate that man! He takes pleasure in humiliating those better than himself. Richard knows this and yet he goes on honouring him. He is unfit to move in noble circles. How he delighted in humiliating me. "You would call yourself my lord Earl, would you?" he said to me. "Now your father has lost his head you would take his place, eh? Have a care that you do not follow too closely in his footsteps, my young brave." Then he took off his boots, threw them at me and bade me clean them. I was treated as a servant, I tell you. I'll have my revenge on Holland one day.'

Yes, it was comforting talk, and each day the exiled Archbishop cast aside more of his grievances against the House of Lancaster. The three of them talked often and earnestly about events in England. They could do nothing as yet, but when the opportunity came they would be ready.

One day the great Duc de Berri, uncle of the King, called at the Hôtel Clisson. He was affable and showed signs of friendship towards Henry. He too talked of affairs in England. He had his spies in that country and he knew that the King's conduct was finding less and less favour with his people.

'The English have a way of chastising their kings if they do not please them, is that not so?' The Duc laughed. '*Mon Dieu,* England came very near to having a King from France in the reign of John, remember? Henry the Third, Edward the Second . . . they had their troubles. It could well be the same with Richard. And then . . . Ah, but we look too far ahead.'

Such talk created great excitement in Henry; but he had learned not to betray his feelings. At what was Berri hinting? That Richard might fall and then . . . and then . . .

His next words made his thoughts quite clear. 'You are a widower. You lost your good Countess. You are too young a man to remain unmarried eh? Particularly in view of your position. I have a daughter. Marie is a pretty girl. Well, perhaps you would consider this. If you were agreeable, I should raise no objections.'

He was decidedly agreeable. He felt exultant. Berri could only believe that Richard's throne was tottering and—oh intoxicating thought—that he, Henry of Lancaster, had a chance of attaining it. Only such a hope and a good chance of its becoming a certainty could have brought Berri to this.

Henry replied quietly, for he was determined not to appear too eager and it might be dangerous to utter a word which could be used against him, that he had not thought of remarrying as yet. He had been devoted to his countess; her death had been a great shock from which he had not yet recovered. He had four fine boys and two daughters so he need not worry at this stage about his heirs. But he appreciated the honour done to him and if the Duc de Berri would give him a little time . . .

'A little, my friend,' cried the Duc, 'but not too much.

A girl such as my daughter has many suitors as you can imagine. You will let me know your answer within the week.'

When he had left Henry considered this. Marriage into the royal house of France. Richard would be deeply disturbed and Henry would be delighted to put Richard into that state.

He discussed the matter with the Archbishop and the Earl of Arundel.

'It can only, mean one thing,' said the Archbishop. 'They know something of what is happening in England. Richard's crown is becoming more and more insecurely fixed on his head. It may well be that we shall not be long exiled from our native land.'

'Then you think I should accept this offer of Berri's daughter?'

'Undoubtedly yes.'

'I will appear to hesitate. I do not want him to think I am over eager.'

The Arundels agreed that this was the best way and they were excited guessing what events had come to the ears of the Duc de Berri.

A few days later John Montacute, Earl of Salisbury arrived in Paris. He had come on an embassy from Richard and spent a good deal of time with the King and the Duc de Berri.

He did not visit the Hôtel Clisson which was perhaps to be expected as Henry was in exile and Montacute was the King's messenger.

Henry meanwhile had decided to agree to the suggested marriage but when he called on the Duc de Berri he was told that it was impossible for him to have an audience. As the Duc had advised him that there must be no delay in agreeing to the marriage with his daughter and he must have known that this was the reason for Henry's call, this was decidedly odd.

During the weeks which followed the Duc was extremely cool to Henry whose pride forbade him to demand an explanation.

Eventually he did get one, though not from the Duc de Berri.

Berri had decided that he no longer wished to receive Henry into his family and he had come to this conclusion after the arrival from England of the Earl of Salisbury. It was obvious. Richard had heard of the suggested marriage, had determined to stop it, and had sent Salisbury to Paris for that purpose. No doubt he had given the Duc de Berri an account of the shortcomings of Henry of Bolingbroke, and done so so successfully that Berri no longer sought the alliance. It might have been that he was so impressed by Richard's prompt action that he thought it would be no easy matter to push him from his throne and if that was the case, of what use was the marriage of his daughter to a pretender to the crown of England?

Henry was despondent and was to be even more so, for the King of France himself sent for him and when he stood before him bade him be seated for he was forced to say something which was very painful to him.

'As you know,' he said, 'I have a great regard for the House of Lancaster and have been happy to welcome you at my Court. However, I have heard word from King Richard that he regards my hospitality to you as an unfriendly act towards himself. He says that he will be very disturbed unless I ask you to leave.'

'Does this mean that you *are* asking me to leave?' demanded Henry.

'I am afraid that is so.'

Following on the affair with the Duc de Berri this was indeed a blow. His hopes had been too high. Now they had come crashing to earth.

He raised his head haughtily. 'You may rest assured, sire, that I shall lose no time in leaving Paris.'

The King looked mournful but he could not hide his relief. It appeared that Richard was as firmly on his throne as ever and what hope had a poor exile of returning to his country let alone to be its King!

With his few attendants Henry rode disconsolately out of Paris. Where could he go? He did not know. It would be the same story everywhere. He would be received at first and then if he became too comfortable Richard would show his disapproval and he would have to go wandering again.

He was making his way towards Brittany. Duke John of that land was by no means young but was noted for his valour—he was known as John the Valiant—and his violent temper. His Duchess was his third wife and many years younger than he was; she was Joanna, the daughter of Charles d'Albret, King of Navarre, whose reputation was so bad that he was known as Charles the Bad. Charles was related to the royal house of France through his mother who had been the only child of Louis X. He could not of course inherit the throne because of the Salic law which prevailed in France but, as was inevitable, Charles the Bad longed to attain that crown, a desire which had led to perpetual trouble.

Henry had no wish to arrive in Brittany to be told that Richard objected to his being there, so before he entered the Duke's land he sent a messenger on to ask him if he would be welcome if he came.

When the messenger arrived, the Duke burst out almost angrily: 'Why does he think it necessary to ask? I have always been on excellent terms with the House of Lancaster. Ride back and tell him he may expect a hearty welcome.'

Henry was overjoyed to receive the news. It solved his problem for the time being. Even so he could not rid himself of his melancholy. Am I always going to be an exile wandering over the face of Europe, never sure of my reception, knowing that I have vast estates in England which I can never see? he asked himself.

The Duke of Brittany determined to live up to his promise and rode out to meet him. This was a great honour and Henry expressed his deep appreciation of it.

The Duke was very old but he still retained a certain vitality. Not for nothing had he been called the Valiant, and Henry returned his greeting with a warmth to match the Duke's. And then he was aware of a very beautiful woman who rode beside the Duke.

She was young; she glowed with health and she was smiling at him.

'My Duchess would give you as warm a welcome as I give you myself,' the Duke told him.

'Welcome to Brittany,' said the Duchess. 'We shall do our best to make you happy while you stay with us.'

The old Duke looked at his glowing young wife with doting tenderness and Henry was charmed not only by his welcome but by the fascinating Duchess Joanna; and during the weeks that followed, when banquets and jousts were given in his honour, he did not have to pretend that he was enjoying his stay in Brittany and this was not only because for a man in his position it was good to have a sanctuary. It was something more. He found the society of the Duchess Joanna very delightful indeed.

Joanna was a woman of great strength of character. Perhaps a childhood such as hers had helped to develop this. Because of her father's recklessness and his attempts to claim the throne of France the family had lived in constant danger.

Her grandmother, daughter and only child of Louis X, had married the Count of Evreux and through him had come the kingdom of Navarre which her father Charles had inherited. But what was the kingdom of Navarre when but for this Salic law he would have been the King of France. Charles had married Joanna, the daughter of King John of France, and to them were born two boys, Charles and Pierre, and the girl who was Joanna.

The children had had a stormy childhood, all three having spent some time as hostages for their father's behavior. They had been held by the regents of France, the Ducs de Berri and Burgundy; and they had been in great peril when their reckless father made an attempt to poison their captors. This was foiled and Charles' agent was discovered and put to death. Charles himself, however, escaped punishment. It seemed possible then that the retaliation demanded would be the death of the hostages but the Ducs had no wish to be revenged on children. All the same they had been in a desperate situation.

When Joanna was sixteen she had been married to the old Duke of Brittany. The Ducs of Berri and Burgundy had thought this advisable for their great dread at that time had been that the Duke might make an alliance with England and this seemed a good use to which they could put their hostage. So Joanna was duly presented to the old Duke who immediately fell victim to her youthful charms. Joanna was not displeased. It was comforting to be made to feel so important as she was and to have gifts showered on her and fine jewel-encrusted clothes to wear. She was determined to enjoy being Duchess of Brittany and if it meant taking the old Duke as well, as long as he continued to dote on her she could endure that.

Then it had seemed that Joanna was settled, her future secure. The old Duke was more and more devoted and whenever he was parted from his bride he was restive and eager to return to her.

Her father was pleased by the match but he had no intention of paying the enormous dowry which he had promised. 'The old Duke is so infatuated by my daughter he won't miss a few pieces of gold,' he reasoned. And he was right, for the Duke was indeed so delighted with his marriage that he made light of the missing dowry.

Charles seemed almost disappointed. He so much enjoyed a quarrel and the last thing he wanted was a peaceful existence. He had for some years been suffering from a distressing complaint which stiffened his limbs and gave him considerable pain and the only way in which he could take his mind from his suffering was to create alarming situations that caused others stress.

Being amused by the Duke's devotion to his daughter, he thought it would be fun to prod the self-confidence of the uxorious husband.

There was one knight at his Court of whom Duke John had once been particularly fond. This was Oliver de Clisson, a great nobleman who had brought honour to Brittany through his chivalry and bravery both on the battlefield and in the jousts. He was of tall stature and exceedingly handsome in spite of the fact that he had lost an eye in battle in the Duke's cause. At that time there was a certain restraint between the Duke and Clisson which was due to the Duke's tendency towards friendship with England, while Clisson felt that it was better for Brittany to support France. Recently Clisson had been to Paris to discuss plans for a possible invasion of England should the opportunity arise and the Duke was displeased that he had done this.

It seemed to his wicked father-in-law, Charles the Bad, that now was the opportunity to play an amusing game. The Duke of Brittany was turning from Clisson on political issues, so Charles thought he would introduce an element of mystery and romance into the situation.

It was easy. He talked of his daughter to the Duke and there was no subject which pleased the Duke more.

'It delights me,' said Charles, 'to see your fondness for the girl. She is handsome, would you say?'

'I would indeed,' replied the complacent husband. 'I would go farther. I'd say you would not find a more handsome lady if you searched the whole breadth of France aye and of England too.'

'It is good to see a man so pleased with his marriage. I hope it may remain so. Aye, that is my earnest prayer.'

'I thank you,' said the Duke. 'I intend to see that it does remain so.'

'It is always well to hope,' replied Charles with a hint of warning in his voice which startled the Duke, as it was meant to.

'Why do you speak so?'

'Well, my friend, she is young and lusty I'll warrant. She is of my family and I know what we are. You are a fine man for your age . . . for your *age,* my lord Duke.'

Now the Duke was beginning to be really alarmed. 'You know something. What are you trying to tell me?' he demanded.

'Well, perhaps I should say nothing . . . It is just out of friendship . . .'

The Duke, who could lose his temper, began to do so now. 'Tell me what you know!' he cried and he faced the King of Navarre with an expression which clearly indicated he would do him some mischief if he did not speak quickly.

'I hasten to say my daughter is entirely innocent.'

'What!' screamed the Duke.

'But there is no doubt in my mind how Clisson feels towards her. He is a bold fellow. He is capable of anything. Why he might even try to abduct her. It's clear to see what a passion he has for her.'

The Duke was so furious that he could have struck the King down there and then.

Charles moved away with a helpless shrug of the shoulders. It was no use blaming him for the misdemeanours of the subjects of the dukedom. Perhaps he had been wrong to betray Clisson. He had thought in his friendship . . .

'You did right to tell me,' snapped the Duke; and Charles left him with his anger.

He was determined to curb his rage. He wanted to plan calmly. Clisson was already out of favour because of his policies and the fact that there had once been great accord between them only strengthened the Duke's anger.

He invited Clisson with two great friends of his, Laval and Beaumanoir, to dine with him at the Château de la Motte. They came unsuspecting and after the meal, at which the Duke had impressed them all with his affability, he told them that he wanted to show them some alteration he had made to the palace for the pleasure of his bride.

They expressed great interest.

'I particularly wish to show you the tower,' he said and when they reached a narrow spiral staircase he let Clisson go ahead. The Duke was immediately behind and he paused to point out some delicate piece of tracery on the wall to Laval and Beaumanoir.

As he did so there was a shout from above. Guards had emerged to seize and fetter Clisson.

Both Laval and Beaumanoir were immediately aware that they had walked into a trap. 'For God's sake, my lord Duke,' cried Laval, 'do not use violence against Clisson.'

'*You* would do well to go to your home while you are safe,' retorted the Duke.

Beaumanoir protested: 'What are you doing to Clisson? He is your guest.'

'Do you wish to be like him?' demanded the Duke.

'He is a great man,' was Beaumanoir's answer. 'I should be honoured to be like him.'

The Duke drew a dagger and held it to his face. 'Then,' he cried venomously, 'I must put out one of your eyes.'

Beaumanoir drew back in alarm. He and Laval saw that they were caught. If they attempted to rescue Clisson, they would find themselves the Duke's prisoners also. All the same Beaumanoir stood firmly and demanded to know on what grounds Clisson was arrested.

In a burst of fury the Duke shouted for guards to

come and take Beaumanoir, which they did. Meanwhile Laval slipped quickly away and out of the castle.

The Duke went to his private apartments and, still enraged, sent for the Sieur Bazvalen, a man who had served him well through the years and whose loyalty was without question.

'Bazvalen, my good friend,' he said, 'I want Clisson to die at once, and I want you to see that this is done.'

Bazvalen drew back in horror. He knew Clisson well. This demand was too much to ask. He was no murderer. He had killed men in battle, it was true, but this was different.

'My lord . . .' he began.

But the Duke waved his hand imperiously. 'Let him be taken to a dungeon. Kill him, I care not by what means, and then open the trap door and let his body go into the moat.'

Bazvalen could see that it was no use arguing with the Duke in his present mood or he would find himself in danger, but he was determined not to have the death of Clisson on his conscience, so he went to Clisson and warned him of what he had been ordered to do and planned that he would return to the Duke and tell him that Clisson was dead and his body in the moat. In the meantime they would plan some means of getting Clisson out of the castle.

But when Bazvalen reported to the Duke he was overcome by remorse. His anger faded and he realized that he had condemned Clisson without proving his guilt. 'You are without blame, Bazvalen,' he cried. 'You but obeyed orders. The sin is on my conscience. I have murdered Clisson.'

He would not eat. He would never sleep in peace again, he said, and when he declared that he would give anything to have another chance, Bazvalen could hold back the truth no longer and confessed that he had been unable to murder Clisson who still lived. The Duke then threw his arms about Bazvalen's neck. 'My good good servant,' he cried, 'you knew me better than I knew myself.'

The Duke's anger had faded but he was always one to seek an advantage. His mischievous father-in-law had made evil suggestions which might be false but Clisson had been working with the French and therefore he could not be released until certain conditions had been filled. The Duke demanded the surrender of several towns which were in Clisson's possession as well as a hundred thousand florins.

Clisson, delighted to escape with his life, was only too pleased to pay what was demanded and so bring about his release.

Joanna was annoyed when she heard that her husband had suspected Clisson of wishing to be her lover, especially as she was now pregnant, a fact which made her even more attractive in the eyes of the Duke. She was cool to him and when he humbly asked the cause of her displeasure, she cried:

'You have suspected me of infidelity with Clisson. This has made me very disturbed at a time when you should do everything for my comfort.'

He was beside himself with grief. 'Never for one moment did I doubt you, my love,' he assured her. 'I know you to be perfect . . . in every way perfect. You are my very reason for living. Without you I would die tomorrow and gladly. And the thought of that . . . that . . . monster . . .'

'You think I would be attracted by a one eyed varlet . . .'

'They say he is very attractive to women . . .'

'So you would compare me with . . . *women.*'

'Never! Never! You stand above them all. I will give anything . . . anything I have . . .'

Joanna smiled at him. It was good to render him humble.

'I know it . . .' she answered. 'But I beg of you do not again insult me by linking me with such as Clisson. I am the Duchess of Brittany. My great grandfather was the King of France.'

'My love . . . how can I win your forgiveness?'

She smiled sweetly. 'I know it is all the measure of your love for me,' she told him.

She knew too that now there would be even richer presents than before.

Her child was born soon after that, a daughter who died after a few weeks. The Duke was desolate. He wondered whether the Clisson affair was responsible.

Charles the Bad, the cause of the trouble, suffered a further bout of his painful illness. One of his doctors produced a remedy which gave him a little relief. Bandages were soaked in a solution of wine and sulphur and it was the task of one of his servants to wrap his limbs in them and sew the bandages together to keep them secure. When this was done he looked as though his body was wrapped in a shroud.

One night when a new man was sewing the bandages, which was a difficult task for Charles disliked being trussed up, he became even more irritable than usual for the man fumbled and the more Charles roared the more nervous he became. 'I am like a pig being trussed up for the roasting spit!' he cried in fury. Little did he realize the aptness of his simile. The servant became more and more clumsy and when he came to sever the thread he found he had mislaid the knife he needed to cut it. Charles was growing exasperated and in desperation the servant picked up a lighted candle to burn the thread and so release the needle. The effect was instantaneous and disastrous. The wine ignited and very soon Charles was wrapped in a cocoon of fire. He screamed in agony as servants rushed in. He was rolled in his bed and smothered with heavy bed coverings, and in time the fire was put out, but not before Charles was so badly burned that it seemed unlikely that he would survive. He died a few days later.

It cannot be said that he was greatly mourned and when his son, Charles, became the King of Navarre there was general rejoicing for Charles had not been known as the Bad for nothing; and his son, another Charles, having shared his sister's harsh childhood showed every sign of being the exact opposite of his father.

Joanna, who had become pregnant immediately after the death of her first child, gave birth to a son who was baptized Pierre and this birth, to the delight of the parents, was quickly followed by the arrival of a girl child, little Marie.

The Duke was beside himself with joy. He thought Joanna more wonderful than ever. Not only was she young and beautiful but she was fertile too and for a man of his age that meant a good deal. He could scarcely tear himself away from her and no sooner was one child born than she was pregnant with another. There followed after Pierre—who since he was the heir had become known as John—Marie, Arthur, Gilles, Richard, Blanche and Margaret. Eight children in all, counting little Joanna who had died soon after her birth.

This was the happy state of affairs when Henry arrived at the Court of Brittany.

There the Duke was determined to show his pleasure in his guest. One thing he wished to do was to stress his contempt not only for the King of England but for the King of France as well.

He delighted too in Henry's admiration for the Duchess.

Joanna was very different from little Mary de Bohun and perhaps for that reason Henry found her attractive. Her conversation was lively; she was a woman of strong character; in truth she was the main reason for making his stay in Brittany so delightful.

If she had been a widow, he being a widower they would have made a perfect match. They were neither of them too old, nor were they immature, and they both had a largish family. Her intelligence on the state of affairs in Europe, and that included England, was remarkable. Henry could see that she advised the Duke with a wisdom which the Duke himself did not possess.

Yes, Joanna was an admirable woman.

He did not exactly mention his feelings to Joanna, but she was a very sensible and sensitive woman and she was aware of them; and she saw no reason to hide the fact that she found Henry attractive. There was nothing she liked better than to sit alone with him and talk. Not entirely alone of course, that would have been indiscreet and there was nothing indiscreet about Joanna. There would be attendants but Joanna could always see that they were not too close.

She told him about the affair of Clisson. It was a cautionary tale. The Duke had a fiery temper and he was capable of very rash acts when it took possession of him.

Joanna liked to hear about his children and his accounts of them seemed to be dominated by the amusing and very lively Lord Harry. He was concerned about Harry who was at the Court of King Richard. 'I wished my father to take him,' said Henry, 'but the King would not let him go.'

That made him fearful, he admitted. The boy was in truth a hostage.

To her he could explain how he felt shut out from his country. It was sad to be an exile even when one was offered such hospitality as that which he had received in Brittany.

'It will not always be so,' she soothed. 'I have a notion that Richard will not long remain on his throne. And then . . .'

'And then . . . yes . . . ?'

'Well, you will no longer be an exile, will you? You will go away from us, and it would not surprise me if . . . But I talk too much.'

'Sometimes it is good to talk of one's dreams,' said Henry.

'They can be dangerous.' She looked at him with glowing eyes. 'Who can be sure of what will happen? You may be a King ere long, Henry of Lancaster.'

He said almost breathlessly, 'There is a possibility.'

'And I . . . What shall I be? My husband is not in good health you know.'

They were both silent. They felt the air was heavy with suggestion.

'I think about it,' she said. 'He was an old man when I married him. He had had two wives and outlived them. I was given to him. There was no choice for me. But he has always been good to me.'

'You have made him very happy.'

'I have borne him children and he has always treated me with great care and affection.'

'So should he do.'

'But he cannot live long, I know.'

His hand had placed itself over hers.

'Who knows what the future may hold?' he said.

It was almost like a declaration.

She spoke in a louder voice, saying: 'This son of yours, this Harry, he needs a wife.'

'He will have one ere long.'

'What of my daughter? That would link our families in a way which would be very agreeable to me.'

'My son . . . your daughter . . . Yes. It would be . . . a beginning.'

She looked at him intently, her eyes sparkling. Yes, there was indeed an understanding between them.

The Duke was agreeable that their daughter Marie should be betrothed to Harry of Monmouth, for as he confided to Joanna when they were alone he was certain that there was deep dissatisfaction in England with the reigning King.

'Richard will be off the throne before long. You will see, my dear. And then . . . it is up to Lancaster.'

'There is another before him. Mortimer . . .'

The Duke snapped his fingers. 'A strong arm and a steady head will decide. I think Henry is the one with those.'

He pressed her arm. 'We have done well to make him our friend. We will strengthen our alliance by betrothing our girl to the young Lord Harry. She shall have a dowry of one hundred and fifty thousand francs.'

Preparations went ahead. The nuptials were to be celebrated in the Castle of Brest which should be a gift to the bride and bridegroom. It was doubtful whether Harry would be allowed to come to France. Indeed it was most unlikely since he had not been allowed to go to his grandfather. However, the marriage could take place by proxy.

While these preparations were in progress there was a message from the King of France who wished for an immediate meeting with the Duke of Brittany concerning a matter of importance to them both. Duke John was now somewhat infirm; he did not want to become involved in trouble, and he could not disobey the King's summons unless he wanted to create a dangerous incident.

So he went. He was soon back. The King of France did not approve of Marie's marriage to Harry. He had another bridegroom for her. He had offered the heir of Alençon, and to marry this noble prince the Duke would not be asked for nearly such a large dowry as the English were asking.

'I could do nothing but accept,' said the Duke morosely,

thereby proclaiming that he felt his age sadly for earlier he would never have allowed anyone to force him into such a situation.

It was about this time that a messenger arrived in Brittany from the Duchess of Lancaster. The Duke had died, and Henry had now inherited the title and estates; he was head of the House of Lancaster and one of the richest men in England.

'How this must make you chafe against exile,' said Joanna.

But it was not long before there was another messenger. The King had waived aside the promise he had made to John of Gaunt and had confiscated the Lancaster estates.

'It is treachery!' cried Henry when he heard. 'I will never accept this.'

Richard was a cheat and a liar. He was unworthy to govern. He had given his solemn oath that the estates should come to Henry of Lancaster on his father's death. That was a promise John of Gaunt had insisted on.

Henry talked the matter over with Joanna and the Duke of Brittany, as well as with the Arundels who had been his close companions in exile.

They were tense days that followed.

Was Henry going to lose his inheritance? There was only one way of regaining it and that would be by going to England and wresting it from Richard. He grew excited at the prospect for he guessed that it would be more than the Lancaster estates which he would take from Richard. It was clear to him that those about him were expecting him to make some decision. He had been given an opportunity. Richard had broken his word. Why should Henry be expected to keep to his? He knew that the time was drawing near when he must return to England to claim his estates.

The Duke was full of advice. He was too old to campaign for himself now but he could be interested in enterprises such as this one.

'Richard will be on the alert,' he said. 'He will be wondering what you will do. Put up a pretence. Make believe that you are so engaged on your rounds of pleasure that you have no energy for a fight.'

'That makes sense,' said Joanna; and Henry agreed.

* But the excitement grew. Day and night he thought of little else.

The Duke, prompted by Joanna, said he would do what he could to raise an army. Henry was thoughtful. Attractive as that proposition was, he decided against it.

It would be folly to take a foreign army onto English soil. He knew his fellow countrymen. They would rise up against the foreigner. No. If what he heard was true—and both he and the Arundels had their spies in England and messengers were constantly travelling to and fro—Richard was growing increasingly unpopular. He, Henry, would return to England, yes, but he would go on the pretext of regaining his rights. There should be no hint that it was the crown he sought. He would land quietly in England.

'No one must know that I am coming,' he said and the Arundels agreed with him.

It was Joanna who suggested that they should pretend to plan a visit to Spain. Let them travel to Paris and let it be known that they were there; and when they left they should go a few miles south, and then turn and go with all speed to Boulogne. The Duke of Brittany would put the necessary ships at their disposal and they could slip quietly across the Channel.

It appeared that the ruse was effective for soon they heard that Roger Mortimer, Earl of March, who was looking after affairs in Ireland, had been killed near Kells in the county of Kilkenny. Richard himself decided that he must go out there to continue the struggle, which he certainly would not have done if he had had an inkling of Henry's plans. Roger Mortimer—grandson of Lionel Duke of Clarence, son of Edward the Third and Philippa, elder brother of John of Gaunt—had been named heir to the throne in the event of Richard's having no children. So before he set out for Ireland Richard named Edmund, Roger's son, as his successor. Edmund, however, was a boy of eight and the people would not want a child as their king. They had had a taste of that when Richard came to the throne. Edmund was an obstacle, for of course he did come before the son of John of Gaunt, but Henry was sure that Edmund's youth was against him and that if it were proved that the people had had enough of Richard, they would look to the son of Gaunt, none other than Henry of Bolingbroke, Duke of Hereford, head of the House of Lancaster.

It was a comforting thought.

Joanna showed a little sadness at the parting although he knew that she was eager for him to win a crown. There was a far away look in her eyes which he thought he understood.

They took a last walk together in the small garden within the precincts of the castle.

'I have been so happy in Brittany,' said Henry, 'that I almost forgot my reason for being here.'

'I am glad you came to us,' she told him.

'How can I repay you for your goodness to me?' he asked.

'Perhaps,' she said, 'by not forgetting us.'

He stooped and picked a little blue flower and held it in the palm of his hands.

'Do you know what it is?' he asked.

'It is called *myosotis arvensis,*' she answered.

'It is beautiful, is it not? When I see it I shall think of you. I shall have it embroidered on my emblem, and henceforth it shall be known as the forget-me-not.'

A few days later he left the court of Brittany. He found an opportunity of giving Joanna the little blue flower which she pressed between the pages of a book and often she looked at it in the months to come . . .

Harry was becoming increasingly conscious of his somewhat invidious position at Court. He was closely related to the King but everyone knew that his father was in exile and that his presence at Court was regarded as a safeguard for his father's good behaviour. It was not very pleasant for one of Harry's disposition to be a captive.

He knew very well that if he asked permission to visit his brothers and sisters or his step-grandmother or his Beaufort relations, permission would not be granted. No. The King wanted Harry where he could seize him at a moment's notice if the need should arise.

Richard was always affable with Harry. He really did like the boy. He was amused by Harry—who was so different from himself. Harry was impatient with such preoccupations as dress and jewels and epicurean meals. He chafed against life at Court. He wanted adventure.

Moreover he was anxious about his father, particularly since his grandfather had died.

His cousin Humphrey was at Court. He was not in a very happy position either. They were very closely related for Humphrey's father had been the Duke of Gloucester who had been smothered by feather beds in a sleazy Calais inn (doubtless on the King's orders) and the Duke was the brother of Harry's grandfather, John of Gaunt, and as his mother was Eleanor de Bohun, sister of Henry's mother, it was a double relationship.

It had been brought home to both boys that their safety was somewhat precarious, for the fate of their fathers was a constant warning to them that anything could happen at any moment.

They kept their ears open for news and talked in secret. Henry was sure that his father would come back to England now that the King had confiscated the Lancaster estates.

'When he does,' he said, 'there will be many who will help him regain them. The nobles do not like one of their kind to suffer such forfeiture because they say if it can happen to one it can happen to others.'

'He will have to take care,' said Humphrey.

'My father was always one to take care. He was not reckless like yours.'

Humphrey was silent thinking of that terrible day when he had heard that his father had been taken. It had been unbelievable. Thomas of Gloucester had always been a blustering reckless man, certain of his power to succeed. He would never forget how his forthright mother, who had never seemed to be at a loss before, suddenly collapsed and became a sad, silent woman. She had been so sure of herself; she had believed so completely that her husband would achieve all his ambitions and that she would rise with him; and then suddenly it was all finished. His father had been taken away. How had he died? What did it feel like to have two or three strong men pressing a feather bed down upon you until you were gasping for breath . . . and then could breathe no more?

He must not think of these things. He must be like

Harry, who laughed a great deal and followed the serving wenches with lustful eyes and even allowed himself to comment on the charms—or lack of them—of the ladies of the Court.

Now they were playing with the cards that fascinated them both. These had been invented a few years before for the amusement of the King of France, and were becoming very fashionable in England. Many people at Court played with them and with their kings, queens, jacks and aces, they seemed suited to Court life.

Harry was smiling at the fanlike array in his hands and looking slyly across at Humphrey. One never knew what cards Harry held, thought Humphrey. He put on a face to bemuse one.

But before the game began one of the King's attendants came to them to tell them that their presence was required in the royal chamber, so they laid down their cards and went at once to obey the King's command.

Richard was lounging in his chair rather informally with his favourite greyhound, Math, at his feet. The dog watched the boys suspiciously as they approached.

Harry had tried to entice the dog to come to him but Math gave him nothing but disdain. It was almost as though he was saying, I am the King's dog, I will accept none but a King as my master.

'Ah, my cousins,' said Richard, smiling at them, 'I have news for you.'

He watched them with narrowed eyes. Harry was going to be a wild fellow, he could see that. He would be everything that he, Richard, was not. Yet he liked the boy. It gratified him to keep him at Court and within calling distance. That was how it was going to remain.

These two boys were both sons of men whom he had hated—closely related to him though they were. Humphrey was now Duke of Gloucester and Richard had hated his father more than anyone. He had been one of the uncles who had made his life so fraught with irritation when he was very young. He had liked John of Gaunt, Harry's grandfather, once the old man had accepted his age and given up his fruitless struggle for a crown of some sort. But Harry's father, Henry of Bolingbroke, he would always be suspicious of.

He would never forget those five Lords Appellant

standing before him arms linked to show that they came together and were against him. No, he had determined on revenge from the moment they had stood there. And he had it. Gloucester dead, smothered by feathers, Arundel beheaded, Warwick in prison, Norfolk and Hereford exiled. So they should remain. And if Hereford decided to make trouble he had young Harry in his grasp. Harry the hostage.

'You will be wondering why I sent for you,' he said. 'Is that so?'

'My lord, you have guessed aright,' replied Harry. There was just a trace of insolence in the young voice but the smile was disarming. One could never be sure with Harry.

' 'Twas no great conundrum,' said the King shortly. 'You are to prepare to leave for Ireland.'

'Ireland, my lord!' cried Harry.

'I said Ireland,' replied the King. 'The death of the Earl of March has made it necessary for me to take an army there. You will be with us.'

The boys heard the news with mixed feelings. They liked the thought of adventure—but Ireland! They would rather have gone to France. Harry's father was in France. Suppose . . .

The King was saying, 'You will wish to make some preparations, I do not doubt. You will be instructed when we are to leave.'

Math watched them sleepily while they bowed and retired.

'To Ireland,' murmured Humphrey. 'I wonder why we are going.'

'Because the King will not let me out of his sight. I am a hostage for my father's good conduct towards him. That is why *I* am going.'

'But why am I?'

'Because he does not wish to make the fact of my going too pointed. If we both go . . . well then we are part of the Court retinue. I see it clearly, cousin Humphrey.'

'Yes,' said Humphrey, 'so do I. I wonder how long you will go on being a hostage?'

Harry was thoughtful. He knew the King had confiscated his father's estates.

He thought such an event might make a difference.

*   *   *

The two boys enjoyed the excitement of making the journey to Ireland. The boisterous sea crossing which so many found distressing did not affect them. They paced the decks in the drizzling rain and felt that they were really men now going into battle.

'Of course it is only the Irish,' said Harry disconsolately. 'I wish it were the French.'

Ireland was a disappointment. There seemed to be little but miles of bog land which could be treacherous; there were stark mountains, sullen people who lived very poorly, and above all rain, perpetual rain.

Richard at the head of his armies looked very splendid indeed and he created a certain wonder among the Irish which was not without its effect. Harry noticed this. Richard had no real qualities as a leader but he had an aura of royalty which served him in a certain way. Harry had often heard of the manner in which he had faced the rebellious peasants at Blackheath and Smithfield and he understood why he had been able to quell them. He was extraordinarily handsome; so fair and light-skinned with an almost ethereal air. He was the man to ride out among his subjects and win them with his charm; but he was not the King to lead them into battle. If there was no real fighting Richard's campaign might be successful. If there was it would fail. Harry was learning a good deal about leadership. One day he would have his own men and he would know how to lead them then.

The army grew more and more disgruntled. There was nothing more calculated to sap the spirits of soldiers than inaction and perpetual rain. They were homesick; they hated Ireland. There was no real fighting to excite them and no booty in this poverty-stricken land to make their journey worth while.

Back home in England Edmund of Langley, Duke of York, was acting as Regent. Although he was the son of Edward III he was quite without ambition and asked only for a quiet and peaceful life. Perhaps that was why Richard had appointed him as Regent. The King had chosen four men to help him: William Scrope, Earl of Wiltshire, Sir William Bagot, Sir John Bushby and Sir Henry Green. He could not have chosen four more unpopular men. Young as he was, Harry was amazed at the carelessness of the King.

It was a wretched campaign made even more so by the weather. The high seas made it impossible for stores to cross the water so lines of communication were cut off. The men were weary of the struggle, and although the Irish could not put up an army they had other ways of harassing the invaders. They destroyed even the little there would have been to leave behind them as they fled from the enemy and by the time Richard reached Dublin his army had one thought and that was to get back to their firesides as quickly as possible. They had had enough of senseless wars which brought them no profit.

There were messengers awaiting Richard in Dublin and the news they brought was catastrophic. Henry of Lancaster had landed in England; he had come to regain his inheritance, and men were rallying to his banner.

Richard had always been afraid of his cousin. He saw then that he had made two major mistakes, first by exiling Henry and then by confiscating the Lancaster estates.

It was too late now to turn back.

He had two alternatives: to stay in Ireland and conduct a campaign against Henry from that country or to return and face him. He must, of course, return to England, but there would necessarily be some delay. He sent John Montacute, Earl of Salisbury back to England immediately to raise the people of Wales against Lancaster. He would follow at the earliest possible moment when he had made some arrangements here in Ireland.

Then he remembered Harry of Monmouth, son of the invader, who was in his hands.

He should be able to turn that to advantage.

He laughed aloud at the thought. The son and heir of the enemy in his hands!

He sent for young Harry, who came, a little truculently, having heard the news of his father's landing of course. He had to admire the boy. He was in a dangerous position and he knew it.

'So you are the son of a traitor, eh?' said Richard.

'No, my lord, indeed I am not. My father is no traitor.'

'Have you heard that he has landed in England although I have put him in exile?'

'He comes to regain his estates I doubt not,' said

Harry. 'Those which you promised my grandfather should not be forfeit.'

'You make bold, my young bantam. I hold you my prisoner, you know.'

'I know I have been and still am a hostage.'

'For your father's good behaviour.'

'Then I have nothing to fear for my father does not act as a traitor. He comes but to take the estates which are his by right of inheritance.'

'You will have to learn to curb your tongue, Harry.'

'And lie . . . as others do.'

Richard flushed. 'You're a young fool,' he said.

'Better that than a knave,' retorted Harry.

Richard cried: 'Get out of my sight, or I'll have that saucy tongue of yours cut out.'

Inwardly Harry quailed at the thought, but he showed no fear. He bowed and retired.

Richard buried his face in his hands. A thousand curses on Henry Bolingbroke! What a fool he had been to let that man live, to have sent him abroad to plot with his enemies, to have taken his estates. He had brought this on himself.

Young Harry knew it. He was a shrewd, clever boy. Richard hated violence. That was why he was so loth to go to war. Why could not people all enjoy the things that he did—music, literature, art, good food in moderation, fine wines, sweet perfumes, rich clothes, sparkling jewels, a clean and beautiful body . . . ? They thought him unkingly because he cared for these things. And now Lancaster was forcing a war on him; and Harry, his son, was defiant, almost insolent because he knew in his heart that to harm him would be loathsome to Richard who abhorred violence. What to do with Harry?

He summoned two of his guards. 'Let the Lord Harry of Monmouth be taken to the castle of Trim and with him his cousin Gloucester. There they shall remain until I have settled this matter with the traitor Lancaster.'

So the two boys were sent to Trim Castle, there to fret away the days playing chess and games they contrived with their playing cards, while they waited for news from England.

*   *   *

Henry had decided to make for that part of the country which he expected would be most loyal to him, so instead of landing at Dover or Folkestone as he would have been expected to, he set a northerly course and finally arrived at Bridlington. He was amazed at the numbers who flocked to his banner. They were welcoming him because they were tired of Richard. He made his own castle of Pickering his temporary headquarters and from there he marched to Doncaster, his following growing more numerous every day.

At Doncaster he was joined by the Earl of Westmorland, and Henry Percy, Earl of Northumberland with his son Sir Henry Percy known as Hotspur. The Percys were a powerful family who helped to keep watch on the Scottish border for any trouble which might flare up. They were like kings of the northern provinces. With them they had brought the Lords of Greystock and Willoughby, a formidable force.

The Earl of Northumberland called together a council which he asked Henry to attend and when they were all assembled, he said, 'It is important to know what your intentions are, and why you have returned to England.'

Henry replied promptly that his intentions were to regain his estates which had been unjustly forfeited. He had no other intentions.

The company was relieved. They implied that they had no desire to take part in a campaign to take the crown from Richard and put it on his cousin's head. But being men of property themselves they had very strong views about the seizure of estates. The King had acted foolishly in breaking his promise to John of Gaunt and they agreed that there had been only one course open to Henry of Lancaster. He must come to England and take back what was his.

So these powerful earls of the North joined with Henry of Lancaster in a righteous course.

The next week saw the complete débâcle. Richard's followers deserted him one by one, and they flocked to Henry's banner. The King was at first bewildered, then resigned. What he had always feared had come to pass. The people were tired of him; they no longer loved the bright and handsome boy they had cheered so wildly at

Blackheath and Smithfield. They had had enough of him and they thought that Henry of Lancaster would serve them better.

When Richard was left with but six loyal men he knew that it was only a matter of days before he was captured. He wandered from castle to castle until he came to Conway and there he rested for he had no heart to continue the futile struggle.

His old enemy Archbishop Arundel came to him there and extracted from him a promise to give up the crown.

He did so, almost with alacrity. He was tired of the crown, tired of his life. He did regret though that he was parted from his little Queen.

The young Isabella had brought him what he had lacked in his life since the death of Queen Anne. He wanted to love and be loved; and this exquisite little girl who adored him and whom he could regard as a beloved child—wife though she was to him—had supplied that.

Poor sweet Isabella, what would become of her now!

As for Henry, he had succeeded beyond his wildest expectations.

He had seen that Richard must give up the throne from his own desire to do so. Henry did not want trouble which would be inevitable if Richard were forced to abdicate. Henry wanted to be persuaded to take that which his hands had itched to grasp for many years.

Richard was obstinate at first when the irrevocable step had to be taken but eventually he gave in.

There was a new King on the throne. Henry of Bolingbroke, Duke of Lancaster had become King Henry the Fourth of England.

THE PRINCE AND THE
VIRGIN WIDOW

Harry was becoming very restless in Trim Castle, for
on the orders of the King, a close watch was kept on
him and Humphrey. They were not allowed to ride out
which was a hardship scarcely to be endured. They
played games until they were tired of them; Harry made
all sorts of plans for escape which Humphrey dismissed
as impossible. Harry knew this too but it helped a little
to plan.

Then one day when they sat idly in a corner of the
room they shared, they heard the sound of footsteps
coming up the steep spiral staircase; the footsteps stopped
at their door and they heard the clanking of keys as the
door was being unlocked.

Two of the guards came into the room. They were
looking at Harry and there was a distinct change in their
demeanour. Not that they had been cruel. Richard would
never have wanted that. But now there was respect in
the bow they gave in Harry's direction and then in
Humphrey's.

'Great news, my lord,' said the guard, looking straight
at Harry, who was beginning to feel a little light-headed
with the possibility which had occurred to him.

'Yes, yes,' cried Harry, impatient and imperious.

'We have a new King, God save him. King Henry IV of England.'

'My . . . my father!' gasped Harry.

'Your noble father, my lord, God save him.'

'Then Richard . . .'

'Has abdicated, my lord. He knew himself to be beaten.'

Harry smiled to himself. This was the biggest thing that had ever happened. Yesterday he had been Harry of Monmouth, son of an exile, a hostage in the hands of the King. Today he was Prince Harry, heir to the throne.

He wanted to go home. He wanted to share in the triumph. This was the end of this dull and pointless life. A wild exultation took hold of him. Everyone was showing respect, even Humphrey. Heir to the throne. The words kept ringing in his ears.

'What news of my father the King?' he asked.

'Orders, my lord, that you and Duke Humphrey are to leave at once for England,' was the answer.

'Come Humphrey,' cried Harry. 'Let us lose no time.'

Nor did they. They would leave at once. There would be a ship waiting for them. His father had seen to that. He wanted his heir with him with all speed. He would be made the Prince of Wales, that was certain. A glorious life lay before him.

Humphrey was more cautious and very thoughtful.

Poor old Humphrey, it would make little difference to him. He was already the Duke of Gloucester and he could not go much higher than that. Still, he would have the distinction of having shared exile with the Prince of Wales.

When they were alone Humphrey said: 'Harry, don't hope for too much.'

'What do you mean? Hope for too much! I'm heir to the throne, am I not?'

'It must be very insecure as yet.'

'Insecure! Depend upon it, my father had made it very secure.'

'For one thing young Edmund Mortimer is the true heir.'

'That's not a serious claim.'

'You have to see things as they are, Harry. Edmund is

descended from Lionel who was older than your grand-father.'

'I know. I know. But he's only a child.'

'Age makes no difference.'

'Oh yes it does. My father has the people behind him. He is the one they want. They want no more child kings.'

'Not even if they are the rightful heirs?'

'Enough, Humphrey. Remember . . .'

'To whom I speak. The heir to the tottering throne. Don't hope for too much, Harry.'

'Will you stop it or . . . or . . .'

'You'll send me to the Tower and have me lay my head on the block? You'll be a vindictive king, Harry, but you won't last long if you don't look the truth right in the face and accept it for what it is.'

Harry seized him and the two of them wrestled together on the floor of the chamber as they loved to do. Harry often scored in these bouts although he was several years younger than Humphrey.

The tussle ended up in laughter as it always did and Harry cried: 'What are we doing, wasting our time? Come, we must return to the scene of action with all speed. I am no longer a hostage, Humphrey. Think of that.'

'I can think of nothing but how glad I am to leave this damp unfriendly land.'

'Come, then, let us make ready. To England.'

Within a few days they left Ireland. The crossing was rough and during it Humphrey became ill. Harry chaffed him and told him he was a poor sailor and commented that it was a mercy they were not going into battle. Humphrey smiled wanly and said he could never remember feeling so strange.

'You'll be well again as soon as you set foot on dry land,' Harry promised him.

But this was not so and the crossing was so rough that it seemed at one time that they would never make it. It was a great relief when they were able to land in Anglesey. Oddly enough Humphrey was no better and it soon became clear that his malady had nothing to do with the sea.

He was in a fever and wandering in his mind. They

had come to an inn which was nearest to the spot where they had landed and Harry had thought that after a brief rest there Humphrey would be himself again.

Humphrey was rambling about his father. He thought he was himself in an inn in Calais instead of Anglesey and that what had been done to his father would be done to him.

'Nonsense,' cried Harry. 'I'm here with you, Humphrey. We're in Wales . . . soon we shall be with my father. We are not Richard's prisoners any more.'

Humphrey was soothed but he did not improve. In fact he was growing worse and a cold fear suddenly touched Harry.

Was this some sort of a plague which had attacked his companion?

He should ride on. His father was impatiently awaiting him, but he was not going to leave Humphrey.

That was to prove a sad homecoming for Harry in spite of the glory which awaited him. Within a few days of their landing Humphrey had died of the mysterious illness which had attacked him so suddenly.

When the Duchess of Gloucester heard of the death of her only son she was overcome with melancholy.

It was difficult to recognize in this grief-stricken lady the forceful Eleanor de Bohun who had once been so pleased with herself when she had married Thomas of Woodstock, and together they had planned to get their hands on the entire fortune left by her father.

Then she had had dreams of greatness. Becoming royal through marriage with one of the sons of Edward the Third she had been so proud. And when her son had been born and he had been given that good old de Bohun name of Humphrey she had doted on him.

Her only son! Her Humphrey! She had known what it meant to love something other than riches and power when he had been born, although she had never ceased to value those things and wanted them for Humphrey.

When her husband had been murdered that had been the end of her ambition for him and she had turned her thoughts more and more to this precious son.

He had accompanied his cousin Harry to Ireland at

the command of Richard but it had not occurred to her that any harm could come to her son.

And now this news had shattered her. She had been robbed of that which was the meaning of life to her. She had three daughters; but it had been on Humphrey that her love and devotion was centred.

She went about Pleshy silent-footed and mournful. Her attendants watched her anxiously.

'She will die of a broken heart,' they said.

She would sit in the window seat and look out across the country to where the grey walls of the convent rose and she thought of those days long before Humphrey's birth when her sister Mary was here and had made her journeys to and from the convent. How they had urged her to take up the life of the nun. And she might have done so had it not been for that meeting with Henry Bolingbroke—contrived of course by John of Gaunt. They had wanted Mary's fortune . . . well so had she.

How different everything would have been if Mary had entered the convent. Harry of Monmouth would never have been born.

'Oh Humphrey,' she mourned, 'never to see you again. Humphrey, my son, my boy . . .'

She was tired in body and in mind. She had nothing now to live for.

Then she saw again the grey walls of the convent and it seemed to her that they offered peace. Could it be that she, Eleanor Duchess of Gloucester, who for years before had tried so hard to persuade her sister to enter that convent, should now be considering ending her own life there?

It was strange what peace the thought brought her. She could almost hear her own arguments with which she had bombarded Mary. The quiet. The peace. The life lived to a pattern of service to others.

There was comfort in it.

It was ironical that the Duchess, who had thought the convent life so suitable for her sister, should now want to embrace it herself.

As the days passed the more firm became the decision and finally she took the step.

She did not live long. She found that she must mourn

her son within the convent walls as bitterly as she had in the castle.

She died very soon after entering the convent. Of a broken heart, it was said.

Harry realized that Humphrey had been right when he had talked about the insecurity of the new King's position; and none was more aware of this than Henry himself.

He was delighted to receive his son and to see that he was in good health, though somewhat melancholy still owing to the sudden death of his cousin.

There were other matters with which to concern themselves, Henry reminded his son, and because Harry was next in importance to himself he discussed matters candidly with him.

'Do not imagine,' said the new King, 'that we are as safe on the throne as if it had come to us through straight inheritance. Richard has been crowned King. He still lives. The people have shown they have had enough of him and he has agreed to abdicate, but it is a dangerous position.'

'Richard's reign is over,' cried Harry. 'Should we concern ourselves with him?'

'Of a certainty we should, my son. I tell you this, I shall not rest easy while he lives. There is Edmund de Mortimer—that child. He does not add to my peace of mind. Harry, we must tread with the greatest care. You give yourself airs. Do not do so. Behave with modesty. Let it be as it was before.'

'Did I ever behave with modesty?' asked Harry grinning.

'This is a serious matter. So much will depend on the next few weeks. I have not won the crown by conquest, for there has been scarcely any fighting. It is rather by election.'

'Is that not a good thing?'

'Yes, but I want to make it firm. I want now and in the years to come people to say of me, "There is a true King and ruler". If we do not take care we shall have risings. There will be those ready to support Richard . . . till he dies . . . Edmund de Mortimer's adherents . . .'

''Twould be safer if we could prove in some way that you were the rightful heir.'

'Well, there is the story you know, that Henry the Third's eldest son was not Edward who became the First of that name, but Edmund, Earl of Lancaster, he whom they called Crouchback, and from whom we are directly descended. But because of the latter's weakness they substituted Edward the second son for the first-born and so he was brought up as the heir.'

'Will any believe that, my lord?'

'I think very few would, but it would save a great deal of trouble if they could be persuaded to.'

'Why do you not claim the throne because you have won it?'

'Claim it is mine through conquest! A dangerous situation, Harry. Someone one day might be taking it from me . . . claiming it by conquest. Chief Justice Thyrnynge has warned me against that. But perhaps I could be said to have a greater claim because I am descended on both sides of the family from Henry the Third. You see that king was my father's great great grandfather and my mother's great great grandfather also. Edmund de Mortimer could not claim that.'

'My lord,' said Harry, 'as I see it, you have the power; you have the riches; you have the crown in your hands. That makes you King. All you must concern yourself with is keeping that crown, until it comes to me and rest assured, my lord, that when it does I shall clamp it to my head with bars of iron.'

Henry could not help smiling at his son. As soon as he possibly could he would create him Prince of Wales.

The new King rode through the teeming rain from the Tower on the traditional journey to Westminster for the next day would be that of his coronation.

The water streamed down his face, soaking his fine clothes but he laughed at it and so did the crowds of people who had come out in spite of the weather to welcome him.

With him rode his four sons, Harry who was to be created Prince of Wales within the next few days, just past his twelfth birthday, Thomas who was ten, John nine, and Humphrey eight. The sight of the boys warmed the people's hearts. Here was a man to rule them and he was strong and clever, the son of wily John of Gaunt, and already he had given proof that he could provide strong heirs to the throne. Young Harry's affable smiles and manner towards the crowd delighted all; and now everything would be different from the reign of Richard when they had been taxed to pay for his fine friends and general extravagances and he had shown them quite clearly that he was either unable or disinclined to produce an heir.

Harry thought the most magical sound in the world was that of the people's cheers and the words 'God Save the King'. It was particularly exhilarating to think that this would one day be happening to him.

He was almost sorry to reach the dry comfort of Westminster Palace where they would lodge for the night in preparation for the next day's event.

His father had said: 'I shall be uneasy until the coronation is over. When a man is crowned King people are less inclined to topple him from his throne.'

Harry was beginning to think that his father worried too much and was not going to be uneasy merely till the coronation was over but would go on being so for ever. He should forget how the crown had come to him. He must put the image of an imprisoned Richard and the child Edmund Mortimer out of his mind. Richard had been deposed and nobody wanted a child on the throne.

Harry awoke early on coronation day.

In his own chamber the King prayed that nothing would go wrong. It did not occur to Harry that anything could.

Fortunately the rain had stopped. The people had been in the streets since early morning and had assembled in their thousands around the Palace and the Abbey.

There were wild cheers when the procession emerged led by Henry Percy, Earl of Northumberland carrying in his hand the sword of Lancaster which Henry had said should always be preserved, as he had carried it when he landed in England. Northumberland was Constable of England and it was for this reason that he took such a prominent part in the coronation; moreover he reckoned that he and his son Hotspur had made it possible for Henry to gain the throne by offering their support when he arrived, without any army or the means to conduct a campaign the object of which at that time had been merely the regaining of the Lancaster estates.

Harry was entranced to play an important part in such a spectacle. It was his task to carry the curtana, that sword without a point which was always carried at coronations as a symbol of mercy.

He walked immediately behind his father who, dressed entirely in white, walked beneath a blue silk canopy which was carried by the barons of the Cinque Ports.

It was one of the most impressive ceremonies ever seen and if all the time Henry was uneasy wondering whether at the last moment some would protest that the country had a King already and this man who was being crowned was an impostor, he did not show it.

Nothing of the sort happened. It appeared that the country was well satisfied with its new King. But Henry's uneasiness continued all through the splendid banquet that followed and when Sir Thomas Dymoke, the traditional challenger, rode into the hall to demand that if any man present did not accept Henry as the rightful King of England he must enter into single combat with Sir Thomas, Henry himself answered.

'If the need arises, Sir Thomas,' he said in a clear voice, 'I will myself take this office from you.'

It was well spoken though it betrayed a departure from tradition—as indeed was this occasion. It was rare that a King was crowned while a crowned King lived and there was one other closer to the throne.

A moment's silence followed and then the cheering burst out.

There was no doubt that Henry the Fourth was King of England by will of the people.

A few days later Harry was created Prince of Wales.

It was inevitable that there should be some voices of dissent. Henry was wary; and when there was a plan to seize and kill him and his family and put Richard back on the throne he took firm action. He crushed the revolt but it was absolutely necessary that Richard must die. At Pontefract Castle Henry put him under the care of Sir Thomas Swynford, the son of Catherine the Duchess of Lancaster. Thomas had risen in the world and he owed his advancement to his mother's connection with the house of Lancaster. If Henry failed Thomas's fortunes would wane. Thomas was a man whom he could trust, he was a shrewd man who knew where his own advantage lay; he was aware that there would be rebellions and risings as long as Richard lived. It was up to Thomas to see that Richard did not live.

Nor did he. He died in Pontefract. Some said he had been starved to death; Thomas Swynford's story was that he had refused to eat. There was rumour that he had been attacked and had died defending himself. But the story which worried Henry most was that he was not dead at all and that a priest who bore a striking resemblance to him had taken his place in the castle while Richard escaped.

That was a story which must be denied at once. Richard must be shown to be dead, and Henry acted with his usual promptness. The late King must be accorded a burial worthy of his rank, he declared. True he had become merely Sir Richard of Bordeaux, but he had once been a king; and he was after all first cousin to the reigning monarch.

Henry gave orders that Richard's body should be placed on a litter and covered with black cloth. There should be a canopy over the litter of the same black cloth. Four horses should be harnessed to the carriage-litter and they also must be caparisoned in black. Grooms should ride the horses which drew the litter and four knights should follow it on its journey. Their demeanour must match their garments of mourning for it must be seen that all due respect was paid to the late King. His face should be exposed so that all might see who the dead man was that there might be no more tiresome rumours about his not being dead. In all the towns and villages through which the cortège passed the litter was to be left in the market square or some such public place where all might see it and satisfy themselves that it was indeed Richard who lay there.

In due course it arrived in London and it proceeded at a slow pace through the streets until it came to Cheapside and there it rested for two hours.

Twenty thousand men and women came to see it and

gaze mournfully at the dead face which was all that could be seen of the King.

When the funeral litter left Cheapside it travelled to Langley and there Richard was buried.

Harry of Monmouth, Prince of Wales, was riding out to Havering Bower. He was in good spirits. Life was turning out to be very interesting indeed. Who would have believed it could have changed so quickly! It seemed only a week or so ago that he and Humphrey had been playing and fighting together, captives in Trim Castle, and his father had been an exile with little hope of returning to England for years. He did not wish to think too much of Trim Castle for that brought back thoughts of Humphrey which made him sad. If only Humphrey had been here now, how he would have enjoyed boasting to him. But Humphrey was dead and Harry was Prince of Wales with a King for a father.

It was too exciting a prospect for him to entertain melancholy for long.

And he was almost a man. He chuckled too, contemplating his mission.

His father had come straight to the point in his customary manner.

'Harry, you're growing up. Moreover you are the Prince of Wales. It is time we considered a marriage for you.'

Marriage! The thought excited Harry. He had already shown a certain fondness for women—and so far his attentions had been mainly for serving girls. They liked him and were ready to accept his attention with a giggle and a rather patronizing air which reminded him that he was 'only a boy'.

Marriage would be different.

'Well, you will soon be thirteen and not over young for your years,' went on his father. 'I think there need be little delay. I see no reason why the marriage should not take place as soon as we have arranged all that will be necessary.'

'Who is to be my bride?' asked Harry.

His father smiled at him. 'One you have already met and I believe are inclined to admire. She is of the highest birth—in fact a queen. What do you think of that?' As

Harry looked puzzled, his father went on: 'Why, young Isabella of course.'

'Richard's Queen!'

'A widow now—a virgin widow. Just about your age, Harry.'

'Isabella!'

'Ah, I see the idea does not displease you.'

'She is the prettiest girl I ever saw.'

'That is exactly what you should say about your future wife.'

'When shall I marry her?'

'Not quite so much haste, please. She is the daughter of the King of France. I don't want to let her go for he is sure to demand her dowry back, so it seems an excellent solution for you to marry her. In due time she should be reigning Queen of England again.'

'I think she will like that.'

'What is most important at the moment, Harry, is that she should like you.'

'Oh she will like me,' boasted Harry. 'I will go and see her.'

His father had thought that would be an excellent idea. Isabella was an imperious young person and as she had been far too much indulged by her late husband, she would need a certain amount of wooing, reasoned the King. He wanted the marriage to be acceptable to her.

Harry had no doubt whatsoever that he was carrying good news to Isabella and he arrived at Havering in good spirits.

When she heard who had come to see her Isabella was at first amazed and then angry. She was in a state of great melancholy mourning Richard. From the moment she had seen him she had loved him; he was so beautiful with his golden hair, blue eyes and delicate skin. He had always been so exquisitely dressed and perfumed and he had been as delighted with her as she was with him. She had been longing for the day when she would be old enough to live with him as his wife and now here she was nearly twelve years old and reaching that goal, and they had killed him.

She was certain they had killed him. She did not believe that he had starved himself to death. He had talked so glowingly of what their life would be together when she was grown up. He would never have killed himself. After all she was his wife and even if they robbed him of his crown and called him Sir Richard of Bordeaux instead of what he really was, King Richard, she was still his wife.

And now he was dead and she was alone and she did not know what would become of her—yet in her grief she did not care.

'I shall not see this braggart Harry,' she said. 'Why should he come here to see me?'

Her maids, Simonette and Marianne, whom she had brought with her from France and whom Richard had indulgently allowed her to keep, fluttered round her, one brushing her long dark hair and the other putting on her shoes.

'It is important, my lady,' said Simonette. 'He is the Prince of Wales now, this Harry.'

'He is not the Prince of Wales,' cried Isabella. 'There is no Prince of Wales. He is the son of the usurper.'

'Hush, hush, my lady,' warned Marianne. 'People listen. They say the King is very harsh with those who go against him.'

'Let him be harsh with me. Let him kill me as he has killed my dear Richard. My father will come and fight him and perhaps kill him which would please me much, I tell you.'

The two chambermaids shook their heads and looked sadly at each other. It was hardly likely that the King of France would come to England to rescue his daughter. He was at this time in one of his lost periods, which meant that he was kept shut away from the world, until his affliction left him and he was sane again.

The little Queen had been so indulged by her husband that she believed that the whole world would be ready to grant her whims.

'She has much to learn, that one,' was Simonette's comment to Marianne.

Isabella could not refuse to see the Prince of Wales and now she did not want to because her hatred for his father—and that hatred extended to him—was so overpowering that she wanted to give vent to it.

She was dressed all in white for mourning and with her cheeks ablaze and her eyes alight with passion she made a very pretty picture and Harry's heart leaped with pleasure at the sight of her. She was indeed the loveliest creature he had ever met. The daughter of the King of France, a Queen already! What luck that she was worthy of him.

He bowed in his best manner while she regarded him with haughty disdain.

'Well met, my lady,' he said. 'It is long since I have known such pleasure as this meeting between us gives me.'

She remained silent. Wait till she knows, thought Harry. Pretty little Isabella, she is a prisoner here. She must have been wondering what will happen to her. I have come to rescue her. How she will love me when she knows.

'I have a matter of the greatest importance to discuss with you,' he went on.

She said coolly: 'I do not know what you and I could have to discuss.'

'You will, sweet lady. You will. Such good news I bring to you that I will withhold it no longer. Is there somewhere where we could be quiet that we may talk?'

'State your business here and now, my lord,' said Isabella. 'You have a long journey back to Westminster.'

Her manner made Harry laugh. Of course, she still thought of herself as the Queen. She had forgotten that Richard was dead, that he had been dethroned. Still, she still bore the title of Queen and she was the daughter of the King of France, madman though he might be.

'I shall go back with good news for my father, I doubt not. Come sit with me and I will tell you why I have come.'

With reluctance she allowed him to conduct her to the window seat.

Then he took her hand and said, 'Isabella, my father has created me Prince of Wales. That means I am heir to the throne. You never reigned with Richard. How would you like to do so one day with me?'

She refused to believe the implication.

'I do not understand, my lord,' she said. 'I know that the true King is dead and that there is a usurper on the throne. You mean that if the true King's loyal subjects do not displace this usurper you will one day be King.'

'There is no usurper. My father reigns by the will of the people because Richard proved himself unable to do so. My father is the descendant of Kings on both sides of his family. England will be happier under him than it ever was under Richard. My father, King Henry, has given his consent to our match and I come here to give you this good news.'

'*Our* . . . match!'

'Isabella, my beautiful little Isabella, I love you. I want you to be my wife . . . my Queen one day. My father . . .'

She had sprung to her feet; her hands were clenched at her sides, her eyes stony.

'You . . . the son of my husband's murderer . . . You dare to come here and say this to me!'

'Isabella, you are mistaken. Richard was not murdered. He chose to die. He knew he was useless and he gave up the throne of his own free will. You were his bride . . . his child bride . . . you were never his wife in anything but name.'

'Please do not speak of him. I do not wish to hear his name on your lips. Your father is a murderer, Harry of Monmouth. You have killed my husband. You make your crime worse by suggesting that I would marry you.' Her voice had risen. 'I hate you, Harry of Monmouth. I hate you. I hate you.'

'Well,' said Harry with a grin, 'that need not prevent your marrying me.'

'Go away. Never let me see you again.'

'Now that is asking too much. A wife must see her husband now and then you know. How else are they going to get the heirs the country will expect of them?'

She tried to push past him but he held her fast.

'You are like a wild cat,' he said. 'I must tame you.'

'I shall send to my father,' she cried. 'I will tell him how you insult me. He will make war on you.'

'Sweet Isabella, dear child. Kings do not make war because of naughty little daughters. Your father will welcome this match as mine does. Come Isabella, I am a fine fellow really, and I am ready to prove it to you.'

'Let me alone. Go away. Never talk to me like this again.'

With that she gave him a push which sent him back to

the window seat and she ran as fast as she could up the stairs to her bedchamber.

Harry looked after her ruefully. She would get used to the idea.

In her bedchamber Isabella found the Duchess of Ireland whom Richard had put in charge of her. The Duchess, who had been Eleanor Holland before she married Roger de Mortimer, had little cause to love the new self-styled King, for her son was Edmund de Mortimer whom many said was the true heir to the throne. The Duchess was still mourning the death of her husband who had died of his wounds in Ireland just before Richard had begun his campaign there.

Isabella turned the lock in the door and stood against it facing the Duchess.

'What do you think he has dared say?' she demanded. 'This . . . this boy . . . who calls himself the Prince of Wales. He says his father wishes me to marry him.'

'Oh, my child!' There was a bitter twist to the Duchess's lips. 'He wastes little time, does he, this Henry of Lancaster.'

'Eleanor, I refuse. I told him I hated him. I will never . . . never marry him. Oh why did they kill Richard? I love Richard . . . I'll always love him. Being dead doesn't make any difference.'

'My dear lady, he is only a boy obeying his father.'

'I hate him. He's just as bad as his father. I hate them both. I won't marry him. I'll run away. I'll go to my father. Eleanor, I want to send messengers to him at once . . .'

The Duchess stroked Isabella's hair.

Poor child, she thought, she is just a counter in a game to them all . . . to be moved this way and that as pleases them best.

Whatever the young Queen felt about her unwelcome visitor he could not be churlishly refused hospitality. He was after all the son of the King and must be treated as such. Everyone at Havering knew that his or her present position was precarious and that Isabella would not remain long at Havering. It had been believed that she would most likely return to France but the arrival of the

Prince of Wales presented a new and exciting possibility for it was quickly learned what his purpose was in coming.

When Isabella recovered from the shock of Harry's proposal she was a little calmer and her attitude towards him was one of cold disdain.

At first this amused him. He would not have cared for an easy conquest; and the more aloof Isabella became the more he decided that he wanted to marry her.

He contrived to be with her as often as possible but as she was determined to avoid him he was not always successful.

In exasperation she tried to explain to him. 'I will never marry you,' she said. 'I have been married once. I loved my husband, the true King, and I shall never love anyone else.'

Harry tried to reason with her. 'That is nonsense,' he insisted. 'Richard was never your husband. He was like an indulgent father and you were his little pet . . . like one of his dogs.'

'I hate you, Monmouth Harry,' she murmured.

'You were never a wife to him. You don't know what it means to be a wife.'

'And you would teach me what it means?'

His eyes glowed in anticipation. 'That would I do right gladly.'

'You never will.'

'Come, give me your promise.'

'I will promise you one thing: I will never be your wife.'

'I am not one who easily gives up.'

'It takes two to make a bargain like this.'

'Not always,' he answered. 'In fact royal marriages are arranged for us. My father is very willing. What if your father is too?'

She was cold with horror. She escaped from him as soon as she could and seeking out the Duchess she told her that she was sending a message to her father without delay. He must save her from the odious Harry and his murdering father.

The message was sent to France and at the same time an embassy arrived from Henry proposing the marriage of his son to Isabella. Charles the King of France was at the time suffering from one of his bouts of madness and his brother, Louis of Orléans, received the message. He certainly did not wish for the marriage. For one thing Henry was scarcely firm on the throne. There would be all kinds of murmurings against him, he was sure; moreover Louis had a son and it seemed to him that Isabella would be a very suitable bride for young Charles of Angoulême who was a year or so younger than she was.

Louis was pleased that Isabella had no wish for the match with Harry although of course if it had been expedient her feelings would not have been of paramount importance.

Louis's reply to Henry was that the King was at the moment suffering from one of his bouts of illness and it was impossible for the King's eldest daughter to be given away without consulting the King. Therefore no answer could be given at this time.

When Isabella heard she was grateful for a little respite; she believed that her father who had always been affectionate to her would listen to her pleas.

For some weeks after that Isabella lived quietly undisturbed by the visits of her would-be suitor. His father had decided that as Isabella felt so strongly about the marriage it was better to leave it for a while. In a few months it would be considered that she had reached a marriageable age and then it might be possible to perform the ceremony in spite of her objections. As yet it was too soon and Richard's death too recent.

The King of France came out of his madness as he had done on other occasions and as soon as his mental aberrations ceased he was quite normal again. His first thought was for his daughter and when he heard what was proposed for her and knew of her abhorrence for the match he decided to send the Count d'Albret with an embassy to England to see Henry and Isabella and discover what should be done. Isabella had gone to England with a magnificent dowry. If she returned to France that must come back with her and the King, like Louis of Orléans, felt that Henry's hold on the crown might not be very secure.

Isabella meanwhile had continued in some trepidation at Havering. Harry paid another visit during which she had remained cool towards him and avoided him as much as possible. He was however unabashed because he had thought that Isabella would relent in time, but he was beginning to realize that what he had at first regarded as an amusing game was a more serious matter which might end in defeat for him, for Isabella truly hated him, and was amazingly loyal to Richard. There was no doubt that she was a person of determination and unless the French were very eager for the match it might well not take place.

When the Count d'Albret arrived in England and presented himself, King Henry entertained him lavishly at Eltham. The Count said that he wished to see the young Queen, to which Henry replied: 'You will find her in a melancholy state. She mourns the late King. I should not wish you to speak of him when you see her.'

'How can that be avoided, my lord?'

'If she mentions him you must indeed answer, but I insist though that you must not introduce the subject, nor must you discuss his abdication and death with her. I would need your oath on this.'

The Count replied that he had not come here to talk of what was past. It was the future with which he was concerned, and he gave his promise.

The King then sent one of his guards to Isabella to extract the same promise from her. 'The King is allowing the Count d'Albret to visit you,' she was told, 'on condition that you do not mention the late King to him.'

Isabella was aghast. 'How can I not speak of something that is in my thoughts night and day?'

The guard replied: 'Unless you give this promise the Count will not see you. He has given his promise to the King.'

Isabella was silent for a moment. She was a prisoner of the men she hated. There was nothing for her here—nothing but memories of her beloved Richard. She must go home. It was the only place where she could find peace of mind and escape from the odious attentions of Henry and his son.

She gave her promise.

The Count arrived at Havering, where he was received by Isabella in the company of the Duchess of Ireland and a few other ladies.

Isabella plied the visitor with questions about her parents. Her father was well now, she was told; and so were Dauphin Louis and his two younger brothers and her sister.

'I long to see them,' said Isabella, her tone meaningful.

'It seems, my lady, that you will do so ere long,' was the answer.

It was an implication that the King was not eager to let his daughter marry into England.

The embassy returned to France but not until it had been made clear to Henry that there should be no marriage. The King of France wished to receive his daughter back at his Court. He would, of course, require that the jewels she had brought to England should be returned to France. She was young yet but at some time it might be necessary to provide another dowry for her. Charles wanted his daughter's valuable jewellery.

Henry was not very pleased by the turn of events but he wanted no trouble with France. Isabella was young. It might be better for her to return to France and a marriage between her and Harry could well be arranged at a later date. But what of the jewellery which must go with her? Henry had distributed that between the members of his family. He could only promise to return it and informed the French that he had commanded his children to send it to him. He intimated to them that he had not told the French that the jewellery would be returned but only that he had commanded it to be; and they were not to hurry to send it to him. In the meantime certain other items were put together—silver drinking cups and dishes and tapestries which she had brought with her—and these could be sent in her baggage. Now there was no doubt that Isabella was going to return to France.

It was a beautiful May morning when she set out on her way to Dover accompanied by the Duchess of Ireland and the Countesses of Hereford and March, Lady Mowbray and a few others of slightly lower rank. Isabella looked with some emotion at the countryside which was at its most beautiful now, alive with the promise of summer. The fields were so green and the banks blue and white with germander speedwell and ground-ivy, stitchwort and meadow-sweet. As she passed woods she caught a glimpse of misty bluebells waving under trees and she thought of the first day she had set foot on this land. She remembered her trepidation, her homesickness . . . and then her first sight of Richard.

She must not go on thinking of him. But how could she help it, and she knew she would never be happy again.

Henry had determined that she should be treated with the utmost honour and she was met on the way by the Bishops of Durham and Hereford and the Earl of Somerset, who was the King's half-brother, one of the Beaufort sons of John of Gaunt and Catherine Swynford.

Isabella was insensible of the honour. She was bemused. She did not want to stay in England, nor did she wish to go to France. All she wanted was to go back in time to the day when she had first come and seen Richard. I would protect him, she thought angrily and illogically. I would never have allowed him to be murdered. I should have been with him. But it was all such nonsense. He was dead and she was alone, floating in limbo not wanting to look forward, hating to stay where she was; all she could do was look back to the bliss she had shared with Richard.

At Hackney she was met by Prince Thomas, Harry's brother, who was a year younger than he was and loathed by her because he was the son of his father. But at least he did not pester her as his brother did. She received him coldly.

The Lord Mayor and the aldermen had come out of London to greet her and to guard her as she rode into the city. They did not forget that she was Queen and they were gracious to her and reminded her of the tumultuous welcome she had received when she had entered this city with Richard, but she despised them all. They had stood by and allowed Richard to be murdered; they had accepted the usurper and called him King.

She was lodged in the Tower of London and there she stayed for a few days before making the journey to the coast, and it was late June before she set out. In due course she reached Dover; and when she had crossed the Channel in the company of Sir Thomas Percy, a member of that family which had played such a big part in putting Henry on the throne, she was escorted to the little town of Leulinghen which was in between Boulogne and Calais and there she was ceremoniously handed over to the Count St Pol to be conducted to her father's Court.

When she reached Paris her family awaited her. Her parents embraced her warmly while her brothers and little sister regarded her with frank appraisal.

Her father she noticed at once was different from the man she remembered. He looked haggard, which she supposed was natural after the illness he had undergone. But he was kind and calm and showed no sign of the mental stresses he must have suffered. Her mother too was different. Her beauty was breathtaking. Isabella had never seen anyone more beautiful. It was a glittering beauty, which made it impossible for people to stop looking at her. Her brothers and sister were just children, not so experienced of the world as she was. Had they been to England; had they been married and widowed and almost forced into hideous union with someone they hated! No, they were young, innocent, unmarked by time.

She soon discovered that there was something strange going on. She was aware of covert looks; of the manner in which her mother and the King's brother, Louis of Orléans, looked at each other. She was aware of many watching eyes; and it soon became clear to her that an adulterous intrigue was going on between her mother and her uncle.

Louis of Orléans was affable. He gave himself the airs of a King. Isabella recoiled because she could not stop thinking of her poor father with his bouts of madness and how her mother and her uncle were deceiving him and the aura of intrigue which surrounded the Court.

Her uncle Louis was very much aware of her, she knew. He was planning something. So was her mother. And she felt afraid.

Uncle Louis said to her one day soon after her return: 'How good it is to have you with us, sweet child. We are going to keep you with us. We shall find a husband worthy of you, never fear.'

She wanted to shout: 'It is what I do fear. I had one husband. I shall never forget him. I want no more.'

Then she began to wonder whether she would be any happier in France than in England. She longed to be a child again, with the belief that everything was good and beautiful and made for her pleasure. How sad that she must grow up and learn the truth. She had wanted to leave the English scene because to her it was stained red with the blood of her husband and had become hateful because of the blatant usurpation of the throne. And now she was in France and because she was older, more experienced, she could feel tragedy here, as intense as that which she had suffered in England.

What would become of her poor father who for long periods of time lost his sanity? What were her mother and Uncle Louis planning together? When would they force her to marry the man of their choice? Could she be any happier in France than she had been in England? But how could she be happy anywhere now that Richard was dead.

HOTSPUR

It had quickly become clear to the King that though he had won his crown with comparative ease, he was going to find it a more difficult task to hold it.

Richard's mysterious death and the knowledge that the priest Maudelyn had borne an almost uncanny resemblance to him made a good foundation for rumour. Henry feared that for years to come there would be those who declared Richard still lived and the body they had seen paraded through the streets had been that of the priest. Another cause of concern was the existence of Edmund Mortimer whose claim came before that of Henry. None knew more than he that the crown which had been put on his head with such ready hands was very precariously balanced there.

The first real trouble came from Wales and there he discovered a formidable enemy in a man called Owain ab Gruffydd, lord of Glyndyvrdwy, or as he was becoming known throughout England, Owen Glendower.

Owen had been a student of English law at Westminster and at one time was squire to the Earl of Arundel who had estates in Wales. When Arundel took sides with Henry of Lancaster Owen was with him, although Wales in general supported Richard and there was murmuring throughout that country when Harry was created Prince of Wales.

The trouble really started when Owen quarrelled with Reginald Lord Grey of Ruthin over certain lands which they both claimed, and Owen came to Westminster for the case between them to be tried. There he was treated with a certain amount of contempt but he managed to get the case brought before the King and Parliament. 'The man is bent on getting what he calls justice,' the King was told. Henry impatiently waved the matter on one side. 'What care we for these barefooted scrubs,' he cried contemptuously. The King's words were reported to Owen, who went fuming back to Wales.

Henry had made an enemy for life.

When a Scottish expedition was planned Owen should have been a member of it, but out of revenge Grey of Ruthin failed to deliver the summons until it was too late for Glendower to comply, and, as he did not join the expedition, Grey denounced him as a traitor. This was too much for a man like Owen to tolerate and if he could not get satisfaction at Westminster over the matter of his lands, what justice could he hope for now. He decided to take the law into his own hands. He made war against Grey, plundered his lands, killed some members of his household and declared publicly that the Welsh would never receive justice, that they were treated with contempt by the English, and if any Welshman would march under his banner they would do something about it.

Henry heard the news with dismay and at first thought this was but a local rising but he was soon to learn his mistake. The Welsh were on the march. The cry was Liberty and Independence. Not only did the inhabitants of Wales rally to Owen Glendower's banner, but Welshmen in England left their homes to travel to Wales.

It was necessary to put an end to this rebellion and Henry marched in person to the Welsh border. Owen Glendower might have rallied a great force but it would not stand out long against the trained bands of English archers. There he was wrong, for Owen Glendower was too cunning to meet Henry's army in a confrontation. Instead he and his men retreated to the mountains where it was impossible to follow them. They knew every rock and crevice.

Those mountains were impassable and had defeated others before Henry. They provided the perfect stronghold. Moreover the weather was treacherous and the Welsh had their successes, the chief of which was the capture of Lord Grey and Sir Edmund Mortimer, the uncle and guardian of the young Earl of March whom so many believed had more right to the throne than Henry. It was simply not possible to bring the conflict to a speedy end. The Welsh could not be conquered as easily as that and what could have been settled by law—if Owen Glendower had been treated with justice—developed into a war which neither side could bring to a satisfactory conclusion.

Henry left a company in Wales and went to Oxford where he saw his son.

Harry had been sent to study under his uncle, Henry Beaufort, who was Chancellor of the University, but he was tired of Queen's College and chafed against his youth; therefore when he heard what his father had to say he was delighted.

Harry noticed his father had lost some of his healthy colour. Being a King had its responsibilities, that was obvious, but Henry was clearly delighted with his son's appearance. Harry had grown and he was a picture of glowing health.

When they had embraced Henry said: 'I have come to talk to you very seriously, Harry. I think it is time you gave up Oxford. There is work for you to do.'

Harry's eyes shone at the prospect. 'Right gladly will I leave Oxford,' he said. 'I am no scholar, my lord, and nothing will make me one. I want to fight beside you.'

'That is exactly what I want you to do, Harry.' The King touched his forehead in a weary gesture. 'There is so much trouble everywhere. The Welsh . . . the Scots. And can we ever trust the French?'

'It is no time for me to be poring over books in college,' agreed Harry.

'That is a view we share, my son. The truth is I need you. Would to God you were a little older.'

'I am fifteen now, Father.'

'Fifteen. God's truth, Harry, you look three years older.'

Harry beamed with pleasure. 'Where would you have me go?'

'To the Welsh border. Perhaps later to Scotland. You have to learn, Harry. You have to learn fast.'

'Never fear, my lord. I have learned much already.'

'You have to learn how to defend us. We have to hold what we have. My God, Harry, we shall have to hold on to it firmly.'

'I have always known it. I shall be ready, never fear. I shall leave at once.'

The King held up his hand. 'Not quite so fast. Remember you are the heir to the throne. I will speak to the Chancellor. He will understand. You will have to do with what education you have. Your task now is to learn to be a soldier.'

'I am ready, my lord,' said Harry.

Yes, he was. And a son to be proud of. I thank God for him, thought Henry. Would he were older.

He hesitated. Should he tell Harry of the strange malady which he feared might be threatening him? He decided not. He did not want to show him the discoloration of his skin and thanked God that he could so far hide it. It came and went and when it was there a terrible lassitude came over him.

He hoped it was not some dreaded disease.

Harry must be prepared.

When Harry arrived in North Wales he was greeted by Sir Henry Percy, known as Hotspur and a man some twenty years his senior with one of the most formidable reputations in the country. He had in fact been born in the same year as those two Kings, Henry the reigning one and Richard the dead one, and his attitude towards young Harry was inclined to be paternal. A great soldier himself, Hotspur recognized those qualities in Harry; but Harry had much to learn. No matter, he would learn.

Hotspur's home was in the North. His father was the great Earl of Northumberland and his family looked upon themselves as the lords of the North and of no less importance than the King. They were very much aware that it had been their power which had put Henry on the throne; and they were determined that Henry should remember it.

Harry recognized Hotspur's qualities and was ready to learn from him. This was the life for him. He was born to be a soldier. He won immediate popularity with the men, his manners were free and easy, and while he retained a certain dignity he could talk with them on equal terms; he had an affability which his father lacked, yet at the same time there was in him that which suggested it would be unwise to take advantage of his nature or his youth. Hotspur recognized in him the gift of leadership; and this pleased him.

There was another man who was attracted by the character of the Prince and Harry himself could not help liking this man; consequently they would often find themselves in each other's company. They made a somewhat incongruous pair—Harry the young Prince fifteen years old and Sir John Oldcastle who was thirty years his senior—the fresh young boy and the cynical old warrior had no sooner met than they were friends.

They would sit together while Sir John talked of his adventures, of which he had had many. His conversation was racy and illuminating and it gave Harry a fresh glimpse into soldiering.

'It is not all glory, my Prince,' Sir John told him. 'There's blood too . . . plenty of it. No use being squeamish in war, my young lord. You've got to get in first and skewer the guts of your enemy before he gets yours. Always be one step ahead . . . that's war. But there's another side to it.' Sir John nudged Harry. 'Oh yes, my little lordling, there's another side to it. Spoils . . . there's wine and good meat and there's something better still. Can you guess what it is? It's women.'

Harry was already very interested in women and Sir John knew it.

'I can see you're another such as myself,' he commented comfortably. 'I couldn't get along without them . . . nor will you. Well,'tis a good and noble sport . . . pleasuring here and pleasuring there and always with an eye for the next one. Always on the look out. There'll be all sorts to your taste, I don't doubt. The dark and the fair . . . and not forgetting the redheads. I knew a redhead once . . . the best I ever knew. Warm-natured, redheads are. You'll know that one day, my lord, for you're like old John Oldcastle, you've got a warm and loving nature. And it's the sort that'll not be wasted.'

Harry greatly enjoyed these conversations. They were in contrast with his association with Henry Percy. Percy was very much the great nobleman, as proud of his name as a king might be. In fact, Harry thought, Hotspur looked upon himself as a king. He expected to rule; he could endure no interference. He had once said the Northumberlands were the Kings of the North and no King of England could rule without them. If anyone failed to show the respect he considered his due, Hotspur's fury could be roused. The men went in fear of him while at the same time respecting him for the excellent leader he was.

Harry found that he could work well with Hotspur and learn from him, because in Harry there was a certain military instinct which he recognized, and so did Hotspur and Oldcastle. The Prince could enjoy the company of these men and draw enlightenment from both of them. From Hotspur he learned how to conduct a campaign while Oldcastle made him see the needs of the men and to understand how to treat them.

Thus Harry applied himself to learning the art of war with more enthusiasm than he had been able to give to his studies at Oxford.

Hotspur had been appointed Constable of the castles of Chester, Flint, Conway and Caernarvon; he was also justiciary of Cheshire and Sheriff of Flintshire in addition to all his commitments in Northumberland which were his natural heritage. He wanted to settle the Welsh troubles as quickly as possible so that he could return to his native country and he applied his energies to this; however even such an energetic warrior as Hotspur could not be everywhere at once and one day—it was a Good Friday—he was dismayed to learn that Conway Castle, one of the strongest fortresses in his care, had been captured by Rhys and Gwilym ab Tudor.

Hotspur immediately called a conference over which Harry presided as he was, in name, the head of the English in Wales, although none knew better than Harry that this was but a title.

'We must immediately regain this stronghold,' declared Hotspur. 'It is too important a place to be let go lightly.

I suggest, my lord . . .' he had turned in deference to Harry . . . 'that we send an armed force to surround the castle. When we have regained it we will show leniency and promise there shall be no recriminations. It is my firm opinion that this is the way to deal with the matter.'

'My lord Percy, you are right,' agreed Harry. 'Let us act in this way, and the sooner we get Conway back into our hands, the better.'

'Then the matter is agreed,' said Hotspur. 'It remains now to put this plan into action.'

Sir John Oldcastle told Harry that Hotspur was right. 'Now there is a man,' he commented, 'who will invariably be right in his judgments, but he's got flaws. But then, my lord, you'll say and who hasn't got flaws? Which one of us, eh? And you'll be right. But Percy is hot in the head as well as the spurs and though his judgment in battle is heaven-sent there's the devil at his elbow reminding him when he's not getting all that a Percy should. He'd never forget a slight, our Hotspur, and to get even he'd risk his head. That's not calm judgment, is it, for where's the sense in avenging a slight if it costs your head to do it? You can't enjoy your pride if you have no head to do it with.'

'We'll take Conway in a week, I'll warrant,' cried Harry.

'And I'll not be one to deny it, my young bantam. Why with you there to crow us to victory and Percy to spur us on, it's in our hands before we start.'

Oldcastle was right. Within a very short time they had regained the castle; and they put into action their plan to show leniency to those who had given way to the Welsh.

While they were congratulating themselves on their success they received a despatch from the King.

He rejoiced that the castle had been regained but considered that it should never have been lost in the first place. Moreover he did not believe in showing leniency to those who had so easily given over the castle to the enemy. 'If men are to be rewarded for betraying us when we, at some cost, have recovered what was lost, they will take this easy course when besieged again,' was his comment.

Hotspur was angry. He could not endure criticism. He had planned the operation with great care and considerable skill. The suggestion that his negligence had lost them the castle in the first place was unfair. Moreover he was reminded that he had not received money from the King which was due to him and in order to carry out the recent operation he had been obliged to provide much of the expenses himself.

Anger smouldered in Hotspur's mind and Harry was disturbed by this resentment which he knew Hotspur bore towards his father. He wished that he could explain to the King what a great commander Hotspur was and how in his opinion it was unwise to cast criticism on what, had the King been present, he must have seen to be a very skilful operation.

John Oldcastle talked to Harry about the matter and he talked recklessly and as Harry knew this he liked him the more for it, because it showed that there was trust between them.

'Hotspur is falling out of love with your royal father and falling fast, my young Prince,' was his comment.

'I want to tell my father what a great leader he is. He's the best we have, you know, Sir John. My father cannot afford to offend such as Hotspur.'

'Your father cannot afford these wars but he makes them, my lord.'

'He has to. But he does not have to make an enemy of Hotspur. He should send the money that Hotspur has spent on these campaigns. The soldiers on the Scottish border have not been paid either.'

'Ah, war, war . . . matters of state.' Oldcastle put his face close to the Prince's. 'A notion occurs to me. Your father is a wily man. He likes not the power of the Percys, I'll warrant. No great king wants little kings in his kingdom. Wise kings find a means to curb the power of those little rulers. And your father is a wise king, methinks.'

'Do you mean, old fellow, that he's trying to curb the Percys' power?'

'Why not? Why not? And how better than by making them pay for his wars, eh? Now that's what one would expect from a clever king.'

Oldcastle gave the Prince a sharp nudge in the ribs. Harry nodded. He liked to think that his father was shrewd and wily. All the same he did not believe that a fine soldier like Hotspur should be so exploited.

Hotspur meanwhile nursed his grievances.

He was growing more and more disillusioned with the King and tired of waging war on the Welsh. He wanted to be back with his own people in Northumberland. That was his land and he wanted to be with his father and defend it. The quarrel with the Welsh was the King's quarrel and if the King could not appreciate what was done for him, then why should Henry Percy bother to do it.

There was another matter. Sir Edmund Mortimer had been captured by the Welsh and Hotspur wanted to bring about his release. He had a sentimental reason for this. Sir Edmund was the brother of Hotspur's wife and he knew she was anxious about him. He wanted to go to tell her that he had brought about her brother's release. Sir Edmund was a very important prisoner. He was the uncle and guardian of the Earl of March who many said was the true heir to the throne.

Hotspur therefore wished to treat with the Welsh for the return of Mortimer, and to Hotspur's fury the King would have none of it.

Hotspur raged.

'Was not Mortimer taken in the King's business?' he raged. And then he cried: 'No, of a surety Henry of Bolingbroke does not want the return of Mortimer for the Mortimers stand closer to the throne than he does himself!'

When Harry heard what had been said he was apprehensive. Hotspur was placing himself on the other side, for the rift between him and the King was growing fast.

Hotspur declared that he would no longer stay in Wales. He had done everything possible but his services had never been understood or appreciated and he had had enough of Wales.

He was going back to the stronghold of Northumberland.

Before he left he received a message to the effect that a high ranking Welshman wished to speak with him and if he would receive him they might come to some terms amicable to them both. Percy agreed and a tall man wrapped in a cloak which was concealing his identity was brought into his tent.

Percy was ready. He was in armour and prepared for treachery. Great was his surprise when his visitor revealed himself as Owen Glendower.

'I come in peace,' said Glendower. 'Put away your sword, my lord. You see I am unarmed.'

Percy saw this and laid down his sword.

'Why have you come to me?' asked Percy. 'What do you want to say?'

'That we are fighting a senseless war. There will never be peace if you English wish to subdue Wales. The mountains are our allies. Give me back the lands which have been taken from me and there could be peace. There can be no satisfactory ending to this war.'

Percy was silent. What Glendower was saying was true. They could never completely subdue the Welsh and even if they did so for a time there would always be outbreaks of trouble.

He himself was weary of the Welsh war; he had made up his mind to leave and in a few days he would be gone.

'I can put your proposal to the King,' said Percy.

'The King?' cried Glendower. 'The usurper you mean. The man who calls himself King.'

Percy was taken aback and said nothing; but he was not ill pleased to hear the venom in Glendower's voice. He himself was feeling more and more antagonistic towards Henry Bolingbroke.

'There is talk that Richard did not die, that he was not murdered at the usurper's command.'

'He is dead. I feel certain of it,' said Hotspur. 'If he were not Henry would never have tried to marry young Harry to Richard's Queen. He would not want a string of bastards calling themselves heirs to the Lancastrian estates.'

'Then if Richard is dead, the Earl of March is the true King.'

'There is some truth in that.'

'It may well be that if Henry will not return the land which has been taken from me, if he does not make peace with Wales, we shall work to put him from his throne and set up the rightful king in his place.' Owen looked intently at Hotspur. 'It might well be that some in England will be of like mind and join us.'

Hotspur was thoughtful. Then he said: 'There is one matter which is close to my heart. You have as your prisoner my brother-in-law, Sir Edmund Mortimer. Henry has refused to discuss his ransom. I want him released.'

Owen smiled slowly. 'Are you sure my lord that he wishes to be released?'

Hotspur stared in astonishment, and Owen continued: 'He has fallen in love with my daughter Catherine. I see no reason to oppose the match. I do not think he will want to take up arms against his father-in-law. And naturally he would like to see his nephew in his rightful place on the throne.'

Hotspur was astounded.

He saw that Henry was going to have a very difficult task in holding the crown and he was not displeased. Serve him right. If he did not appreciate the Northumberlands he should be deposed. Moreover the new King would be his nephew through marriage and that seemed a fairly bright prospect.

Of course Henry would not relinquish the crown with ease. But this was an interesting situation to go home to brood on.

He said: 'I will put your proposals for the return of your land and the truce before the King. But I hold little hope of his accepting.'

'Nor do I,' replied Owen. 'But if he does not, we shall know how to act, eh, my good lord?'

Hotspur was silent. He said good-bye to Owen Glendower and was very thoughtful as he made his way to Northumberland.

Fuming against Hotspur, Henry arrived at Worcester. There he was joined by Harry and he learned about the difficulties of making war in Wales.

'The country is against us,' Harry explained. 'The Welsh know every hill and valley, and we don't.'

Henry, however, was not sure of this and he was determined to show the Welsh that they could not flout him; but, when others joined their voices with that of

Harry and insisted that to attack in the mountains was a hazardous proposition, he had to listen.

It was at this time that a Welshman appeared at the camp, asking for an audience with the King and assuring the guards that he came in peace. They examined him to ascertain that he carried no weapons and Henry agreed to see him.

His name he said was Llywelyn ap Gruffydd. He welcomed the English, he said. His two sons were fighting with the rebels and he wanted them back. If Henry would restore his sons to him he would undertake to show him and his army the way through the mountain passes and conduct him to the Welsh camp.

Henry accepted his offer and in due course set out with Llywelyn ap Gruffydd riding between him and Harry. Under the guidance of the Welshman they penetrated far into the Welsh mountains but one morning they awoke to find that their guide was missing. Then they realized what a trick had been played on them. They were nowhere near Glendower's army; they had come several hard days' marches into difficult country where there were no provisions and now must find their way out.

Henry was furious. He was finding it difficult to feed his army and they could find nothing in this poverty-stricken land to help them. He must find his way back to a town where his men could eat and rest in comfort.

His fury was increased when he heard that Llywelyn was boasting about how he had deceived the English and the Welsh made matters worse by writing ballads about the incident.

Henry made his way back to the town of Llandovery, vowing vengeance on Llywelyn ap Gruffydd. 'If I can lay my hands on him he will not live long to regret. I pray God he will not keep this man from me.'

God answered his prayers for one day Llywelyn ventured into a tavern in the town and was recognized by some of Henry's soldiers as he was singing the ballad of Henry's discomfiture for the entertainment of the rest of the company.

In a short while he was standing before Henry . . .

The last months had wrought a change in the King. Before the crown had been his he had been a calm man, who prided himself on his shrewd judgements. Now, with so many threats to his position and an almost overpowering responsibility beside a gnawing anxiety that there was something wrong with his health, he had become vindictive. He would spare no one in his determination to hold the crown; and he wanted to make an example of all those who were his enemies.

With savage pleasure he condemned the Welsh joker to the barbaric death of hanging, drawing and quartering and he commanded that his sons sit beside him while they witnessed the terrible sentence being carried out.

Harry was disturbed by it. The man should be punished, yes, but the sentence was too harsh. Llywelyn was a brave man and if he had worked against the English it was natural for him to do so, because they were the enemies of his country.

However he could not remonstrate while his father was in this mood; but he did marvel at the change in him and he wondered whether he was as happy with his crown as he had been without it.

After the execution they left Llandovery and made for the Cistercian Abbey of Strata Florida which contained the tombs of several Welsh Princes. The King ordered his men to sack the place.

A lesson, said Henry, to all those who oppose me.

He sent for his son and looked at him intently. Perhaps sooner than he realizes, he thought, the crown will pass to him.

No one must know of his fears of what was happening to him. He had signs of a dread disease. Could he have caught it in the Holy Land, in Famagusta perhaps, Venice, Corfu . . . some hot and arid land where unheard of diseases flourished? So far he could keep his affliction secret. None could see the eruptions on his skin because by good fortune they were where they could be hidden by his clothes; and he could forget them when they did not plague him with their burning irritation. But sometimes he feared what they meant and he wondered whether it would grow worse.

He must hold the crown until Harry grew up and Harry must do that quickly. He had never thought that it would be so difficult to hold; and he could not have foreseen how determined he would be to cling to it.

'Harry,' he said, 'the news is not good. Northumberland with Hotspur are on the march against us. They are joining with the Welsh.'

'That is impossible. Hotspur fought the Welsh.'

'His brother-in-law has married Glendower's daughter. You know what this means. Northumberland and Glendower are joining forces against us.'

'On what grounds?'

'Read this,' said Henry.

It was a document which had been prepared by the Percys to present not only to the King but to all leading noblemen in the country. It was a call to arms. They wanted Henry deposed because as they set out he had:

Sworn to them at Doncaster when he returned to England that he wished nothing more than to restore his inheritance and that of his wife. Yet he had imprisoned Richard his sovereign and compelled him to resign the crown and had himself taken on the style and authority of kingship.

He had sworn that as long as Richard should live he should enjoy every royal prerogative and yet he had caused that Prince, in the castle of Pontefract, after fifteen days to die of hunger, thirst and cold and thus be murdered.

Because of Richard's death he had kept possession of the crown which belonged to the young Earl of March, who was the next and direct heir.

He had sworn to govern according to law and had not done so. He had refused to permit the liberation of Sir Edmund de Mortimer who had been taken when fighting for him and he had looked on the Percys as traitors because they had negotiated with Glendower. Because of this we defy thee and we intend to prove it by force of arms and Almighty God.

When Harry finished reading the document he looked at his father in dismay.

'So they come against us! The Northumberlands . . . and Glendower . . .'

'And the French have sent a company to harass me.'

'You may trust the French to seize every opportunity,' cried Harry.

'Never fear, my son. We shall defeat them.'

'Aye,' cried Harry. 'That we shall do.'

All the same he wished that the enemy was not Hotspur.

It was a long march of two hundred and fifty miles from Northumberland to Shrewsbury—Hotspur's men were eager to fight but they were tired and hungry; and they needed rest first.

The battle would be for Shrewsbury, for if he took that town Henry could block Hotspur's passage to Wales.

Hotspur thought of young Harry for whom he had cherished a certain affection. A boy of fifteen, but one who showed promise. He hoped the boy would come to no harm this day. Would you were with me, Harry of Monmouth, he thought. You'd be a better ally than your sly father, I doubt not.

But naturally the boy would be beside his father. How could it be otherwise?

The two armies faced each other. Hotspur saw a priest break from the ranks and come riding towards him. He was Thomas Prestbury, the Abbot of Shrewsbury, and he had a message for Hotspur. It was this: Let him put himself at Henry's mercy and the battle should be called off.

Hotspur sent his uncle, Thomas Percy, Earl of Worcester, back to the King with his reply.

Henry said: 'Come, Worcester, do you want innocent blood to be shed this day?'

'We seek justice, my lord,' replied Worcester.

'Put yourself on my grace.'

'I trust not in your grace,' was the answer.

'Then go to it,' cried Henry. 'I pray God that you may have to answer for the blood that is spilt this day, and not I.'

Shortly after that encounter the battle began. A strong discharge of arrows came from both sides. It was a fierce fight. An arrow struck Harry in the face but he went on fighting.

'St George! St George!' cried Harry. The blood was streaming down his face but he ignored it. Excitement gripped him. Men were falling all about him and he was in the thick of the fight.

Hotspur was determined on victory. He wanted to slay the King with his own hands and with thirty or so of his most valiant knights he rode full tilt into the company about Henry. But the King and his men were a match for them and they were driven back.

It seemed then that the victory was going to Hotspur. Shouts for him filled the air. Harry stood firm. This was battle and he knew he was meant for it. He could scarcely feel the wound on his face.

He rallied his men about him and all forgot that he was but fifteen years old.

Hotspur was certain of victory. He was going to dethrone Henry. He was going to see the rightful heir on the throne; he was going to avenge Richard's death.

'Hotspur!' shouted the triumphant voices about him.

Then it happened. Flushed with imminent victory as he was, he did not see the arrow until it struck him. It pierced his brain and he fell from his horse—a dead man.

He did not hear the triumphant cry from the King's forces.

Hotspur was dead and his death decided the day.

It was the end of the battle and triumph for Henry.

The Duke of Brittany was dying. The Duchess Joanna nursed him herself but as she did so she could not prevent her thoughts straying to Henry of Lancaster and wondering how he was faring in England.

She had pressed the little blue flower he had given her. Forget-me-not. That was what he had called it and she never would forget him.

He had on several occasions indicated the warmth of his feelings towards her and implied that had she not been the wife of the Duke there might have been a match between them. He was King now. Well, she was the daughter of a King and her mother had been the daughter of the King of France. There could be no question of her worthiness to become Queen of England.

News came now and then to Brittany of what was happening overseas. She knew that Henry had not married again. His time had been taken up first with seizing the throne and then holding it; and this she believed he was doing now.

There had been rumours about Richard's death. Some said he had been murdered. One version was that men had entered his cell and killed him. Another was that he had been starved to death. But the murderer in both cases had been named as Henry, for though, it was said, he may not have done the deed himself, he would have ordered others to do it.

It would have been necessary, argued Joanna.

She wondered whether he ever thought of her or whether his mind was completely taken up with the stirring events about him.

Suppose he sent for her, would she have been able to go to him? It would not be possible at this stage. She was forgetting her young son, now the Duke of Brittany and a minor. She could not leave him.

She feared Clisson; she knew that he had a very ambitious daughter, the wife of the Count of Penthievres, who believed that through him she had a greater claim to the throne of Brittany than Joanna's son.

Clisson was an honourable man, and although the rival claimant to the throne had married his daughter he had regarded the late Duke as the true heir to Brittany. Joanna believed she could treat with him.

In this she was proved right. She would promise concessions to Clisson; she would remain Regent and with his help rule the Duchy until her son was in a position to do so. The Duke of Burgundy, who was Joanna's uncle, and the King of France were to have guardianship of the Duchy and the young members of the family until they came of age.

Joanna had in fact shown great shrewdness in bringing about this reconciliation for the power, wealth and popularity of Clisson if used against her could have robbed her son of his inheritance.

But once Clisson had given his word and signed the treaty he was as strong a supporter of the little Duke as Joanna could wish, which was proved when his daughter Marguerite, who had wanted the Dukedom for her husband, went to her father in a state of great agitation and asked him why he worked against his own family.

'So much could depend on you,' she said. 'You could give us Brittany. It is my children's inheritance.'

'You ask too much,' Clisson had replied. 'The Duke of Burgundy is coming here. It may be he will take the children with him to the French Court. He is one of their guardians now.'

'Father,' cried the ambitious Marguerite, 'there is still time to remove them.'

'Remove them?' he answered. 'Are you mad?'

'You could have them killed. If they were no more, our path would be clear.'

Clisson was so overcome with horror that he cried out: 'What a wicked woman you are! You ask me to kill these innocent children. I would rather kill you.' And so great was his disgust that momentarily he meant it and drew his sword.

She, seeing the purpose in his eyes, turned and fled and in doing so fell headlong down a flight of stairs. She was always to remember that encounter for she broke her thigh bone, which never healed properly and made her lame for the rest of her life.

The Duke of Burgundy arrived in Brittany and twelve-year-old Pierre, who was now called John, was invested with the ducal habit, circlet and sword and in the same ceremony his younger brothers Arthur and Jules were knighted.

Now that her son had been proclaimed Duke and he had the powerful Duke of Burgundy and King of France as his guardians, and Oliver Clisson had sworn to uphold him, Joanna felt herself to be free.

If Henry were to send for her she could go to him; but the Pope would never agree to the marriage, she knew, and how bring it about without that approval?

The fact was that the papal schism now existed and England supported Boniface who was called the anti-pope by those who gave their allegiance to Benedict as Brittany did.

But Joanna was not of a nature to accept obstacles.

Henry had not yet suggested marriage and only he and she were aware of the feelings they had aroused in each other. She hit on a plan to ask the Pope's permission to marry anyone of her choice within the fourth degree of consanguinity. She had not very long been widowed;

she was quite young so it seemed reasonable to predict that she might wish to marry again. So carefully was her plea to the Pope worded that he saw no reason why he should not give his consent and this he did, having no notion at all that the bridegroom she had in mind was that King whom Benedict would call a rebel.

Joanna was amused by her own cleverness.

When she sent word to Henry to tell him what she had done, he responded with alacrity. Let them be married by proxy without delay. Joanna then sent one of her squires, a certain Antoine Riczi, to England and there in the Palace of Eltham the proxy marriage took place.

It was impossible to keep secret for long such an event as the marriage of the King of England and the widowed Duchess of Brittany, and the Papal Court at Avignon heard word and immediately sent word to Joanna that in being a party to this marriage she had committed a deadly sin. She had promised to live in matrimony with a supporter of Boniface.

Joanna however was not going to allow such a decree to stop her marrying the man of her choice and when she made this clear Benedict, realizing that he might lose her support, gave his permission for her to live with Henry as long as she did not swerve in her allegiance to himself, the true Pope. It might well be that she could turn her husband from the error of his ways and bring him back into the fold.

Joanna herself was delighted with this show of friendship, clever woman to have got the better of the Pope.

The Duke of Burgundy had arrived in France with rich gifts for the Duchess and her family. She had shown by her forceful acts that she was a woman to be reckoned with and it was disconcerting to contemplate that she was going to be allied with that old enemy Henry of England.

Joanna herself was delighted with this show of friendship and she felt that she could with a good conscience leave her sons in the guardianship of the powerful Duke of Burgundy.

She said good-bye to her sons and watched their departure to the Court of France knowing that the King of France would keep the peace of Brittany and preserve the Duchy for her son. Her two daughters, Blanche and Marguerite, should travel with her to England.

It was a rough crossing and at one time Joanna thought she would never see England; the intention had been to land at Southampton, but so strong was the gale that their vessel was blown along the coast. They were lucky to be able to land at Falmouth.

At the head of her party she rode inland and at Winchester she had the pleasure of seeing Henry who, when he heard that she had landed at Falmouth, came to meet her with all speed.

It was a moment of great joy for her when they were face to face.

He took her hand and kissed it.

'It seems long since we last met,' he said.

She answered: 'But I kept the flower you gave me. Do you remember?'

'You may be sure I do. Forget me not was its message.'

'Then all is as it was . . .'

'And shall be as long as we two live.'

They rode side by side into the city; and the next day their marriage was solemnized in the Church of St Swithin with great pomp and ceremony.

Henry was determined to honour his bride.

The old Earl of Northumberland was stricken with grief when he heard of the death of his son. Hotspur had been a great name; he was his father's favourite son and his defeat and death must plunge the house of Northumberland into deep and bitter mourning.

But not for long. The old Earl cried out for vengeance. He was going to get it and he would not rest until he had driven Henry of Lancaster from the throne he had no right to possess.

He was still in touch with Owen Glendower. The Mortimers were with them. They had a right to the throne. Their cause was just. Together they would go on fighting and to hell with the usurpers.

The power of the Percys was great; they were more than border barons; they were the border kings. 'We have been defending that border at our own expense for years,' declared the Earl. 'Are we going on doing it for the benefit of Henry of Lancaster?'

Northumberland was stricken with furious grief when he heard that his son's body, which had been given decent burial at Whitchurch, had been dug up on the King's orders. That it had been taken in a rough cart to Shrewsbury, and had been salted to prevent decomposition and set up between two millstones close to the pillory so that all might see to what end proud Hotspur had come.

'He is too great an enemy to rest in obscurity,' said Henry. 'I want all the world to see what he has come to because he defied his King.'

Hotspur's head was cut off and the rest of his body cut into quarters and sent for prominent display to Newcastle, Chester, Bristol and London. As for the head he wanted that placed in York on the city's northern gate so that it was turned towards that part of the country over which for so long he had been a ruler.

The old Earl was mad with grief. He lived only for revenge. When he received a command from the King that if he came to York they would talk and settle their grievances he had no alternative but to accept the invitation. Henry knew that he would have to pass through the northern gate on which was the head of his son.

As Northumberland rode into York and saw that grisly relic he was filled with an all-consuming hatred against the King. 'A thousand curses on Bolingbroke,' he muttered.

He was soon to realize that he had been a fool to come. Henry had no intention of making terms with him as yet. He told the old man that several of his castles would be confiscated and he himself confined near Coventry until his case could be tried by his peers.

This was utter humiliation. And there was more to come. But it was no use allowing his pride to stand in the way of his purpose. He had to make a show of humility if he were going to save his life, and he intended to save it if only for the purpose of taking his revenge on Bolingbroke. It was finally decided that as he had not actually been in battle he could not be judged guilty of treason so would merely be fined; and if he swore to serve the King faithfully in future he might return to Northumberland.

Henry was a man who did not keep his promises; Northumberland would be the same.

Yes, he would agree to anything. But when he returned to Northumberland he would plot the downfall of the man who called himself the King.

Northumberland was determined. He was in communication with Owen Glendower; he had made a pact with the Scots, who now that he was against the English had a shared interest.

Henry was aware of this. He should have destroyed Northumberland when he had a chance. He might have known that the Earl would never forget nor forgive what Henry had done to the valiant Hotspur.

Henry marched north. It was winter and there had not been in living memory such a harsh one. The snow lay thick on the ground and in the northern part of the country particularly this would be known for years to come as the winter of frost and ice.

It was not the weather for fighting battles, but Northumberland was determined. He had to regain what had been taken from him and turn the usurper from the throne.

Henry had no alternative but to go into battle. This he did. His numbers were superior; his men were better equipped. The battle was brief and decisive and Northumberland fell from his horse when an arrow struck him, wounding him fatally.

Henry was triumphant.

That must be an end to rebellion in the north. Men must understand what happened when they came against the King.

They had come to a small place called Green Hammerton and there it was decided they would stop for the night.

The King and his close attendants were lodged at a manor house while his company found lodging in the town and, cold as it was, some set up tents.

Henry was wet and cold; his limbs felt stiff and he wanted mulled wine, hot food and a bed on which to rest.

He removed some of his clothes and the wine was brought to him. Suddenly he threw the goblet from him screaming. 'What have you done? Who is the traitor? Who has thrown fire over me?'

Those about him recoiled in horror, for his face had grown a deep purple and they could see pustules appearing on his skin. He must have contracted some dreadful disease.

'What is this?' cried Henry. 'What is this?' He put his hands to his face. 'Why do you look at me like that? What has happened to me?'

'My lord,' said one of the attendants, 'we should send at once for your physician.'

Henry lay back on his bed. He touched the horror of his face. He knew it was the same which had been appearing on his body. Now he could hide it no longer.

There was one word which kept coming to his mind. Leprosy! He had seen it on his travels. Oh God, he prayed, let this pass from me. Anything I will endure . . . Take my crown from me . . . Do anything . . . but do not afflict me with this. Richard's death can be laid at my door, I know it. But it was for the good of the country. No, Lord, for the good of myself. Take this from me . . . and ask anything of me . . . and I will do it. I will bear it . . . but not . . . leprosy . . .

He could not leave his chamber. He could not be seen like this. He wondered what would become of him, of the country. Harry was too young yet. He kept praying incoherently. He touched his face. He knew that he looked hideous.

The doctors came. They gave him potions and unguents, and in a few days' time the terrible pustules had almost disappeared. His face was still discoloured and the surface of his skin rough; but he could at least emerge.

The success of defeating Northumberland had become bitter. He turned his attention now to Glendower. Harry was on the Welsh front. Henry thanked God that his son was becoming a great soldier. He was doing good work in Wales and had already brought about the defection of several important noblemen who had been supporting Glendower.

Harry was successful in regaining Harlech and in capturing Glendower's daughter and her Mortimer children after Sir Edmund had died in the siege.

The battle left Glendower without an army. He escaped but was still free to roam in his mountains and attempt to gather a force. Henry, however, was confident that this would never amount to much more than an occasional skirmish. They would have to be watchful, nothing more.

The success was due to the brilliant leadership of young Harry. He was a son to be proud of. He was growing up. He was old enough in experience if not in years to command an army.

Henry could have felt more at peace than he had since he took the throne if it had not been that he was constantly on the watch for the greatest enemy of all, of whose identity he was not sure but which he greatly feared could be that dread disease leprosy.

Harry must marry. The sooner the better. He must get sons to follow him. The Lancastrian side of the Plantagenet tree must be strengthened.

Isabella of France was still unmarried. It might well be that after all this time the child had got over her obsession with Richard. She might be ready to consider a match—or her family might which was more to the point. And why should her bridegroom not be the once rejected Harry of Monmouth?

ISABELLA AT THE COURT OF FRANCE

WHEN Isabella had returned to France she had quickly realized that something was very wrong at her father's Court, and gradually she began to understand what it was.

Her father had bouts of madness. People did not at first talk about this to her. She just heard that he had attacks. These attacks could last for months and when they were in progress he would be shut up in the Hôtel St Pol, that Paris residence where she had spent much of her childhood. When he recovered her father was just as she had always remembered him, kindly and seeming in full possession of his senses, but she detected a wariness in both him and the people around him and she knew they were watching for the madness to break out again.

There was her mother—beautiful, and forceful so that she seemed to be the real ruler of France, with Uncle Louis of course.

Louis Duc d'Orléans, her father's brother, had been appointed by the King to be Regent during his bouts of madness. The Queen who had great influence with the King had advised this and sometimes it seemed to Isabella that her mother and her uncle wanted her father to fall into madness, for when he did Uncle Louis behaved as though he were the King and it was obvious to everyone—even young Isabella—that Isabeau acted as though Louis was not only the King on the throne but in her bed as well. The fact was that this adulterous intrigue between Queen Isabeau and Duc Louis of Orléans was becoming a scandal not only throughout France but beyond.

Then there was her father's uncle the Duke of Burgundy, a serious-minded man, who deplored what was happening and made no secret of this.

It was a very unhealthy state of affairs and Isabella yearned as much as ever for the happy days at Windsor when Richard had ridden out to see her and they had been so happy together.

'I shall never be happy again,' she mourned.

She did however enjoy being reunited with her family. There were her three brothers and three sisters; for recently a new baby girl had been born. She was named Katherine.

The little girls were lodged at the Hôtel St Pol and no one bothered very much about them. When the King was ill he would be taken to a part of the Hôtel and shut in there with a few attendants. Isabella would often lie awake and listen for the strange sounds which came from her father's apartments. She did what she could to look after the little girls for their nurses were not always careful and when Isabella told her mother this, the Queen said they should be dismissed but did nothing about it. She was too busy with her own affairs which mainly consisted of entertaining and being entertained by the Duc d'Orléans. Isabella thought the Duc the most handsome man she had ever seen and that her mother was the most beautiful woman. It seemed inevitable that they should be lovers. She wondered whether her father knew. Everyone else seemed to, so perhaps he did too.

It was a strange life for one who had been a Queen of England; she clung to her memories of her life with Richard. Isabella would hold little Katherine in her lap and the others would cluster round her while she told them stories of her life at the English Court; and always Richard would appear in these stories, the knight in shining armour.

Isabella kept her ears open and discovered much of

what was happening at her father's Court. As soon as Uncle Louis had the power he had levied a tax on the clergy as well as the people, which made them very angry. Some said: 'We will not endure the rule of this profligate young man and his shameless concubine any longer.'

And the shameless concubine was Isabella's mother!

Oh, it was a very unhealthy state of affairs.

It was difficult not to like Uncle Louis—who besides being handsome, was always good-tempered and generous; he was amusing and there was always laughter where he was; his clothes were exquisite and he was notorious for his extravagance. He always treated Isabella as though he were very fond of her and when she had first come to France he had professed himself to be very angry at the manner in which Richard had been treated. It had given her great comfort at that time to hear Richard's praises sung and the usurper King of England vilified. 'He and his son Harry, I hate them both,' she said. 'And they tried to marry me to Harry. I would have none of him.'

Uncle Louis said, Indeed not! She was far too beautiful and too important. What, a daughter of the King of France to marry the son of an impostor! True he held the title of King at this time, but how long would that last?

'I will go and fight him on your behalf,' he declared.

'How can you, Uncle Louis?'

'By challenging him, my dear. He has plundered you of your dowry and he has murdered your husband. I shall challenge him to face me in the lists.'

'You would not do this, Uncle,' she breathed.

'I would indeed, my dear. I shall send a challenge to him without delay.'

In the flamboyant grandiose manner in which Louis of Orléans did everything he sent his challenge.

Her mother was delighted.

'How like him!' she said. 'He is a very gallant gentleman.' Then she added: 'Henry will not accept, I promise you.' But she was really promising herself. The last thing she wanted her lover to do was fight in a combat which could end in death.

She was right. Henry treated the challenge with scorn.

'I know of no precedent which gives the example of a crowned King going into the lists to fight a duel with a subject,' was his cold reply. 'No matter how high the rank of that subject.'

This made Louis fume and fret. Queen Isabeau was with him when he received the reply and she sent for her daughter that she might realize what a gallant champion her uncle was.

'I shall answer this!' cried Louis. 'I shall shame him.'

He sat down and wrote with Queen Isabeau standing over him, watching, applauding and stroking his neck as he wrote.

'How could you allow the Queen of England to return to her country desolate with the loss of her lord, robbed of her dowry and everything she carried with her at the time of her marriage? Those who seek to gain honour should espouse her cause. Are not noble knights bound to defend the rights of widows and virgins of virtuous life such as my niece was known to lead? It is for this reason that I challenge you.' He added with sarcasm: 'I must thank you for the care you have taken of me by refusing this combat which is more than you did for the health and the life of your royal and rightful King Richard.'

'That,' cried the Duc, 'will upset him. I understand there is one thing that never fails to and that is to refer to the murder of Richard in Pontefract Castle. I'll swear the deed will haunt him for the rest of his life. Yet if he had never committed it, how could he have become King of England?'

The note did sting Henry into reply.

Louis laughed over it with Isabeau as he read it aloud. Most indignantly did Henry deny that he had had a hand in Richard's death. 'God knows how and by whom my cousin—whom may God absolve—met his death, but if you are hinting that that death was brought about by me then you lie and will lie foully whenever you say so.'

Nothing more was done about the matter and the months passed. It seemed to Isabella that there was a perpetual tension as though trouble was ready to burst out at any moment. Her mother and Uncle Louis were quite blatant in their relationship; her father was overcome with melancholy; her father's uncle, the Duke of Burgundy, was constantly urging the King to do something, threatening that if he did not he would lose his crown. Did he want to find himself in the position of the dead Richard of England? he demanded. Isabella wanted to protest. It was no fault of Richard, she wanted to cry out. It was due to the wicked ambitious men around him. But no one would listen to her, of course. She was afraid of the Duke's son, who was known as John the Fearless, Count of Nevers. He was a man of violence, not caring what he said and of whom he said it. He always seemed to be at the centre of some cause and vowing vengeance on someone. She was glad when he was not at Court.

The Duke of Burgundy was for ever trying to persuade the King to take the Regency out of the hands of his brother of Orléans during those periods when he was unable to govern himself. The King wavered, but Isabeau always managed to persuade him. She was a siren who could conduct her smouldering love affair with Louis of Orléans in her husband's presence and somehow delude him.

Isabella would never forget the day the Augustine monk came to the Court to preach. He was named James Legrand and noted for his writings, and the directness of his sermons, and the subject of his sermon was the corruption of power and licentiousness. It was clearly aimed at the Court.

During the sermon the King rose from his seat and went and sat closer to the preacher, being immediately opposite him so that he could watch him while he spoke and not miss a word.

'The King your father,' said Legrand, 'likewise taxed his people but he did so to build fortresses to defend his country. He saved his treasure and made himself the most powerful of kings. Now nothing of this kind is done. The nobility in this day spend the money on entertainments; they live in debauchery; they wear dresses with ornamental fringes and big cuffs.' He turned to the Queen and thundered: 'This is the shame of the court, oh Queen. If you do not believe me, dress as a peasant and go into the city and mingle with the people that you may listen to what they say.'

The Queen was incensed. She said that the preacher should be arrested. Let him rot in a dungeon and see what brave words he would have to utter then; but for once the King would have his own way.

'Nay,' he said. 'The man speaks some sense. It is true what he says of my father. I would I were more like him.'

The Duke of Burgundy was beside his nephew. 'Take warning,' he said. 'During your illnesses the country is being led to ruin. Your brother is too feckless, too frivolous. His morals are not of the highest standard. His wife frets about him. He has a good wife in Violante Visconti and how does he treat her? He is notoriously unfaithful to her. She is an unhappy woman. Sire, you must take from him the power to govern when you are stricken. There are others more suitable to the task.'

'You mean yourself, uncle.'

'I am of a more sober age, nephew. You will find there are many who support me.'

The King had been so impressed by the sermon and the fact that it was true there were many to support the Duke of Burgundy that he gave way. He knew in his heart it was the right thing to do although he could not allow himself to believe what was so blatantly obvious and that was that his brother was his wife's lover.

When the Queen knew that power had been passed to Burgundy she was furious. So was Louis. They both disliked Burgundy who they knew would keep a firm hold on the reins once he had them in his grasp. Life was not going to be as amusing as it had been.

'A plague on Burgundy!' cried Louis of Orléans, but what was the use of words. It was a fact that under Burgundy a new rule of law and order was imposed. The great Duke set an example to the country by his exemplary family life. He surrounded himself with men of his own kind, whose great desire was to preserve the country, and the people were beginning to see what a difference a good ruler could make. There were no longer the bacchanalian feasts in which the Queen had loved to indulge at the expense of the State. Burgundy could not stop the intrigue between herself and Louis of Orléans, but he could mend so much that was wrong and he had the people behind him.

Isabella was now seventeen years old. The day she had known Richard was lost to her was a long time ago but for her it was as fresh as ever. Never, she told herself, would she love anyone but Richard. He would always be there in her thoughts to stand between her and whoever they married her to; and they would marry her. She would not be allowed to live long in her single state.

Matters came to a head when an embassy came from England. It contained surprising news. It was secret it seemed, but Henry of England stated that if the King of France would give him the hand of his daughter Isabella for his son Harry, Prince of Wales, he himself would abdicate in favour of his son.

This was astounding. Henry abdicate? Why? The rumours of the terrible disease which had taken possession of him must be true.

Could he really be suffering from leprosy? It was the disease which had finished that great Scottish warrior, Robert the Bruce, years ago. Afflicted by it a man must become so unsightly to society that he had no alternative but to hide himself away.

Isabella Queen of England again! It was a glittering prospect.

It was necessary to convey the information to Isabella. There was a tradition that a woman who had once been married for reasons of state should be given a modicum of choice in her second marriage. Moreover Burgundy was not sure—nor were his advisers—that this match with England was the best possible at this time. If Henry were indeed incapable of ruling and was ready to be supplanted by his son, was that not an admission of weakness? If he wanted a marriage with France could that mean that he was seeking peace or at least a truce, because he feared his grasp was weakening? One country did not fight another when there was a marriage alliance between them.

The French were uncertain.

When the proposition was put to Isabella she was vehement in her denunciations of it.

'I will never go there. I will never live among the murderers of my husband. Anything . . . anything but that.'

'Anything?' said the Duc d'Orléans. 'Dear niece, it is necessary that you marry, you know.'

'I know it,' she replied. 'But I will not marry Harry of Monmouth.'

Since Isabella was so determined and the council was so unsure, it seemed a good way out to let Isabella decide, but none knew better than she that had it been expedient to her country for her to marry Harry of Monmouth she would have been forced to do so.

It was then that her Uncle Louis spoke to her about his son Charles of Angoulême.

'He loves you dearly,' said Louis. 'It is a wish very close to my heart . . . and to your mother's . . . that you two should marry.'

'I do not think my mother cares very much what becomes of me,' said Isabella.

'Oh my dear dear child,' cried Louis, attempting to show deep concern, 'you must not say that. She cares for you so much . . . you and your brothers and sisters.'

'I have not noticed it, sir,' replied Isabella coolly. 'My sisters are in need of new clothes. Their food is not of the best. I am told that the money is not available to feed and clothe them in a manner due to their rank. My mother of course needs it for her ornamental fringes and big cuffs.'

Louis laughed. 'You have been listening to the ramblings of that miserable preacher. If I had my way he would be thrust into an oubliette and left there.'

'I doubt that not,' replied Isabella. 'But know this. I have no wish to marry.'

'Oh come, dear child. You are not meant to waste the years. Why, you are a beauty. You will be like your mother one day.'

'I pray not.'

'She is the most beautiful woman in France.'

Isabella was silent. A terrible fear gripped her. They would pretend for a while that they wanted her consent and when she refused it they would force her. She knew their methods.

The possibility of a match was forgotten temporarily for the great rejoicing of Orléans and the Queen, the Duke of Burgundy fell ill. Within a short time he was dead. The new Duke of Burgundy was his son John the Fearless, Count of Nevers.

The whole of France waited in trepidation for what would happen next.

Louis was more anxious than ever now to bring about the marriage of his son and Isabella and the Queen told her daughter firmly that there must be no more delay.

'Do you want us to send you to England?' she demanded. 'That is what will happen in time, depend upon it, if you delay much longer. There are some who believe it would be good to bring about a truce with England and they would do it with this marriage. The new Duke of Burgundy is against pursuing the war. You can guess what he has in mind. There is your cousin Charles. I know he is younger than you, but that will give you a chance to mould him in the way you want him to go. Come, Isabella, do not be foolish. Marry Charles. It is what I want for you and so does your Uncle Louis.'

'And what of my father? Does he want it?'

'Your poor father alas is in one of his twilight phases. He does not know what he wants. But when he is in good mind he would agree that this is right for you. Think, child, it will keep you with us. Do you want to go to a foreign land? Do you want to be sent back to the son of your first husband's murderer? I hear rumours of the life young Harry leads. Roystering in taverns . . . choosing the lowest companions. Not the sort of husband who would suit your sensitive nature and your refined tastes. If they wanted to find you a man as different from Richard as they could they would choose no better.'

So it went on and finally she agreed.

There was great rejoicing and her mother, delighted that her daughter had promised to marry the son of her lover, set about preparing the most lavish entertainments. They were cousins of course—first cousins at that—but never mind. The Pope would not dare to raise any objection and the dispensation was a foregone conclusion. Banquets and jousting, dancing, players . . . everything that could be devised was included. The Queen excelled at arranging such occasions; and Louis of course was beside her. It was the best thing that had happened since Burgundy had ousted him from his position as Regent.

Only the prospective bride was unhappy. She sat

mournfully through the festivities and she could only think of Richard.

She had little feeling for the boy to whom they were marrying her, but he seemed bewildered and she tried to comfort him as well as she could.

'You need not worry,' she told him. 'It will be all right.'

He clung to her hand reassured; but she could only turn away to hide the tears which she could not hold back.

So she became the Countess of Angoulême and was no longer Richard's sorrowing widow.

The wedding did not arouse a great deal of interest throughout the country. People were more concerned with the scandalous behaviour of the Queen and her paramour and the growing tension between the Duke of Burgundy and Louis of Orléans.

There was a certain relief when Burgundy showed that he was seeking to placate Orléans. In the streets of Paris they said if these two could forget their differences, it would be to the advantage of France; and Burgundy, in order to show that the fault did not lie with him, invited Orléans to dine with him.

It was a dark November evening before the day fixed for the meeting between Orléans and Burgundy. Louis had dined with the Queen and he was in very high spirits. It was eight o'clock. He would join the Queen later but now he was returning to his apartments.

He was accompanied by two of his squires riding on one horse and by four menservants who carried torches. The Duke was singing as they walked along. As they came into the Vieille Rue du Temple, a band of armed men sprang out and surrounded the party.

Luckily for the squires their horse took fright and bolted with them on its back; the servants dropped their torches and closed in round the Duke, who cried out: 'What is this? I am the Duc d'Orléans. What do you want of me?'

One of the assailants cried out: 'You are just the one we want. Ready friends.'

The man who had spoken struck at the Duke with an axe and another came at him with a sword. Louis fell fainting to the ground.

One of his servants attempted to defend him and was struck down but managed to crawl away; the others, seeing it was useless to try to defend themselves escaped into a nearby shop.

By this time windows were flung open for many had heard the commotion and the shouts of the assassins.

'Murder!' screamed a woman from the window of a cobbler's shop.

'Hold your tongue, strumpet,' shouted one of the murderers and shot an arrow in her direction at which she immediately disappeared from sight.

'Out with all lights,' cried the leader of the band.

Then the murderers ran. By this time people had been wakened and were coming fearfully down onto the street; and now that the murderers had gone they came to look at that night's work.

The Duc d'Orléans was dead. His body had been hacked and mutilated till there was no sign left of the handsome philanderer.

The Queen was in despair; so was Orléans' wife, Violante. There was no doubt that they loved the Duke dearly.

'Find his murderers,' cried the Queen. 'I swear I will take revenge of them.'

The Duke of Burgundy joined his voice with the Queen's.

'There was never a more wicked murder in the whole of the kingdom of France,' he declared.

The Provost of Paris, Sieur de Tignouville, was sent for. Nothing must be spared in the hunt for the murderers, he was told.

'My lord,' was his reply, 'if I may be granted permission to make my enquiries in the hostels of the King's servants and those of the Princes, I will discover the criminals.'

The answer was that whatever help the Provost needed was to be given to him. He was to have free entry into every palace, hotel, shop or house in Paris.

'Then,' cried Tignouville, 'I think I shall be able to give you the murderers.'

The Duke of Burgundy showed obvious signs of stress at this pronouncement and the Duc de Berri, his uncle, noticed this.

He drew him aside for a terrible suspicion had come to him.

'You know something I believe, John,' he said.

Burgundy could see that there was no point in denying that he was the instigator of the murder.

He answered: 'Orléans was bringing dishonour to the King's bed. He was a menace to the nation. Yes, it was I who hired the assassins to kill him.'

'Oh my God,' cried the Duc de Berri. 'Now I have lost both my nephews. Louis murdered and you John his murderer.

'You should not go back to the council,' added Berri.

'Nor will I,' said Burgundy. 'My wish is that none shall be accused of murdering the Duc d'Orléans, for it was I and none other who caused what has been done.'

With that he walked out, leaped onto his horse and taking only six of his attendants with him galloped away across the frontier to Flanders.

When it was known that he had escaped there was great indignation and a hundred of Orléans' men gave chase but they were too late and could not catch up with him.

The affair had shaken the Court. People talked of nothing else. There was nothing that could be done to bring Burgundy to justice; and people were beginning to say that Orléans had deserved his death. He had dishonoured his brother; he had made no secret of his adulterous relationship with the Queen, he had imposed taxes on the people, his rule had nearly brought the country to ruin, whereas everyone knew that Burgundy was a strong man. Fierce he might be, ruthless, violent; but his father's rule had been good and he showed signs of his father's strength.

Violante Visconti, widow of Orléans, was determined that his murderer should not go unpunished. In spite of his infidelities she had loved the Duc passionately, and she was eager to avenge him. She arrived in Paris with her children. The weather was bitterly cold—the worst Paris had experienced for several years. Nevertheless she came because the King was in the midst of one of his lucid periods and she believed that she would get justice from him.

She came to the Hôtel St Pol, where the King was in

residence, and she forced her way into the room where he was sitting with his council. There she threw herself onto her knees and demanded that her husband's murderers be brought to justice.

The King promised her that everything should be done. 'We regard the deed done to our brother as done to ourself,' he told Violante.

Isabella, unhappy in her own unsatisfactory marriage, did her best to comfort Violante. She knew what it meant to have a husband done to death.

'We have much in common,' she said sadly. 'I feel for you.'

There were rumours in the town. Burgundy had no intention of remaining outside France. True he had murdered the Duc d'Orléans but he had done it for France. Everyone knew that he was ruining the country. Burgundy was building himself up as the saviour of France. The King beset on all sides immediately lapsed into madness.

Paris waited for what would happen next. It soon came. A monk arrived with a message from the Duke of Burgundy to the King. Poor Charles, his mind being in a clouded state, was unable to receive the monk; but his son the little Dauphin who was now aged twelve, sat at the head of the council and listened to what the monk had to say.

The burden of his discourse was that it was lawful, honourable and meritorious to slay or cause to be slain, a traitor to his country—especially when that traitor holds greater power than the King. Was this not what had happened in the case of the Duc d'Orléans, whose object had been to set aside the King and his sons and take the crown himself? Far from blaming the Duke of Burgundy, the King and the country should applaud what he had caused to be done.

The poor little Dauphin was bewildered. So was the council. There was some truth in this. Orléans, the extravagant libertine, had no gift for government. The country had prospered temporarily under the old Duke of Burgundy. Was his son right in what he had done?

While the monk continued to lay before the Dauphin and the council the case for Burgundy, the King recovered and was able to preside and listen to the arguments put forth. It was true, he thought, that Orléans had almost brought the country to ruin; it was true also that the old Duke of Burgundy had saved it. All he wanted was peace and there never would be if he did not agree that what Burgundy had done was good for France. Orléans had been a traitor to him. The King knew of his liaison with the Queen.

A letter was brought to him from the monk who implored him to sign it.

'My lord,' he pleaded, 'a stroke of the pen from you and this matter will be settled.'

The King read the letter:

> 'It is our will and pleasure that our cousin of Burgundy abide in peace with us and our successors in respect of the aforesaid deed and all that hath followed it, and that by us and our successors our people and officers no hindrance on account of that may be offered to the Duke and his.'

'Just your name, sire,' begged the monk, 'and this highly dangerous matter is at an end.'

Charles was tired of strife. He did not know from one day to the next when an attack was coming on.

He signed.

'Tell the Duke of Burgundy that I will receive him,' he said.

The Duke did not need a second invitation. He came at once to the King.

Charles received him cordially but somewhat mournfully.

'I can cancel the penalty,' he told him, 'but not the resentment. It will be for you, Monsieur le Duc, to defend yourself from attacks which it seems likely will come.'

'Sire,' replied the Duke, 'if I am in favour with you I fear no man living.'

The Queen was dismayed. The King would not listen to her. She had lost her lover. She was distraught and she wondered what would happen to her.

Isabella, deeply concerned by all that was going on around her, caught up in a marriage which had not been of her seeking, found time to visit her little sisters who were lodged in the Hôtel St Pol and were often neglected.

She arrived one day to find they had gone. The servants, distressed and weeping, told her that the Queen had come and taken them away.

'Where has she taken them to?' cried Isabella.

No one could say. This was particularly strange because the Queen had never shown much interest in the children.

Later it was discovered that she was hiding in Melun and had all the royal children with her. The King had lapsed into one of his mad periods and the Duke of Burgundy seized the reins of government and showed by his strength of purpose that he was capable of the task.

After a few months a revolt in Flanders demanded Burgundy's presence, so he left France and rode off to settle the trouble in Flanders.

No sooner had he gone than the Queen came back to Paris with the Dauphin, and the latter was very warmly received by the Parisians. It was clear that the people were with him. The widowed Duchess of Orléans then began to plead with the Dauphin to bring her husband's murderer to justice and the Dauphin was advised to tell her that he would consider the matter, but before he had time to do this news came that Burgundy had subdued the rebels in Flanders and was on his way back to Paris. The Queen with the Dauphin and all the members of the royal family set out for Tours so that when Burgundy returned he found no one there to greet him.

He was wise enough to know that he could not rule as King; what he wanted was the Dauphin to be his figurehead; so he immediately set out for Tours in an attempt to make peace between the two factions. At this time Violante died—some said of a broken heart so much had she loved her faithless husband; but with her no longer begging for revenge and with the Queen realizing that it was to her advantage to make a pact with Burgundy, peace was made between the parties.

Isabella had watched all that was going on with disgust and sadness.

She did not dislike her young husband, and she was now going to have a child. She wondered whether that would change her feelings and whether she might be happy again.

If only it were Richard's child, how happy she would be! So many years had passed. Was it nine since she had last seen him? She remembered how he had picked her up and held her fast and begged her never to stop loving him.

As if she could!

He had not known what lay ahead then—a cold and dismal cell in Pontefract Castle, death . . .

And she a child then, to be left alone . . . to face life without him.

From the Court of that scheming murderer and the blustering hateful Harry she had come to her home to find her father mad, her mother a wanton and to be plunged into another drama of murder and revenge.

But soon she would have a child. It must make a difference.

Charles, her young husband, had grown up considerably in the last few months; he was delighted that they were to have a child; he could not do enough for her. She was beginning to care for him.

As she lay on her bed, heavy with child, she sometimes asked herself if she could be happy again. Perhaps. When she had the child and she and Charles had become absorbed by it. Who knew? Perhaps the future would chase away those figures of the past. Perhaps she would cease to mourn for Richard and accept the fact that he was lost to her for ever.

She had gone to Blois, home of the Orléans family of which she was now a member. There was something formidable about this massive château with its thick stone walls rising from the rock on which it was built. It looked impregnable standing high over the town, supported by its mighty buttresses. Isabella could not forget that here such a short time ago Violante Visconti had died, of a broken heart, they said; and on her deathbed she had implored her three sons and daughters to avenge the death of their father. There had been one other child she sent for—the bastard son of her husband and a woman called Marietta d'Enghien; she saw in this boy of six the making of a warrior. 'You will avenge your father, little bastard of Orléans,' it was reported she had said; and he had sworn he would.

Was she wise to have come to Blois, the scene of so much unhappiness? But then what place was not so haunted?

Charles came to her. He did not seem so young now. She herself was twenty-one—not so very much older than he was yet she felt old in experience.

He talked of the child. He wanted a boy who would become a future Duc d'Orléans. She wondered how often he thought of his murdered father. He never spoke of him. Like her he was looking forward; there was only sadness in looking back.

The thought of the child was always with her. It will be a new life, she thought. And she shut out the memory of the violent happenings about her. Her mother did not come to see her. She was too involved in her intrigues. She must not brood on what might be to come. She had had enough of trouble and wanted peace.

September had come. She had carried the child through the hottest months; now she was grateful that the weather was a little cooler.

Her pains started early in the morning. Her labour was long and arduous. She was only half aware of the figures round her bed. There was nothing now but the agony.

She fell into unconsciousness . . . and when at last she heard the cry of a child, she was not sure where she was. She was riding in the country. It was England and Richard was coming to meet her. They were looking at each other, in a kind of bewilderment. He was the most beautiful creature she had ever seen with his golden hair waving in the breeze and his blue eyes alight with admiration for her and a faint flush on his delicate skin. And for him she was the most beautiful little girl in the world. She could hear his voice telling her so.

'Oh Richard . . . Richard . . . dear Richard . . . I am coming to you now . . .'

How had she known? It was some premonition. She had a new life to lead but she was not going to start it. Her happiness had been Richard. There was nothing that could replace that.

They put the child in her arms. A little girl.

Charles, Duc d'Orléans since the murder of his father, was kneeling at her bedside. She could see his anxious eyes. She put out her hand and touched his face. It was wet with tears.

Why did he weep? But she knew.

She was twenty-one years old. It was young to die. But she was ready.

Within a few days after the birth of her child Isabella was dead.

PRINCE HAL

The Queen of England was thoughtful as her women dressed her. She was beautiful, everyone had agreed with that; but she had to grow accustomed to the fact that the people did not like her. She was not very sure that they liked the King himself. They called her the Foreigner and some whispered of him: Usurper. Coming to the throne as he had would naturally mean that there would always be some to raise their voices against him.

Her hair hung in thick curls; and her close-fitting gown accentuated the excellence of her figure. She did not look as if she had had several children. Her women placed the tall Syrian cap on her head. It became her. She would have changed the fashion if it had not done so; she herself arranged the transparent veil.

Life had not been quite what she had expected in England. She supposed that after her arranged marriage to the ageing Duke of Brittany it had seemed romantic when Henry of Lancaster had come to the Court—an exile needing comfort and help, and with a throne to win. And a far off lover . . . that had been very romantic. Both of them waiting on fate. And when fate had worked in their favour it had seemed like a miracle.

Well, the reality was somehow different.

Kings and Queens could not expect life to run smoothly for them. They were neither of them in their first flush of youth; she was thirty-three years old, Henry four years older; both had known other marriages—fruitful ones. She had her daughters here with her. More important perhaps was the existence of her sons, and their interests, closely allied with France, might not always be the same as those of Henry.

Henry's daughter Blanche was married to Louis, son and heir of the Duke of Bavaria and Elector Palatine of the Rhine. The child had already left England when Joanna arrived. His second daughter, Philippa, would soon be departing for her marriage with Eric of Sweden, and Joanna's own daughters would have to marry sooner or later.

There were too many cares in their lives for romance.

She was fortunate in having been able to form a friendly relationship with the Prince of Wales and she had been greeted warmly by other members of the family.

There was one in particular. She smiled at the thought of him. Joanna liked admiration—who does not?—and coming from such a person as the royal Duke of York it was very welcome.

Henry was deeply immersed in the affairs of the country. He had a great deal to occupy and worry him, and he was often morose. There was a reason for this which she had soon discovered.

It had alarmed her.

She remembered the scene in their bedchamber when he dismissed the servants and would not allow them to assist in his disrobing.

He had had to confess to her for she might easily discover his affliction for herself.

'Joanna,' he said, 'a terrible misfortune has come upon me.'

His face had turned grey as he talked to her and that made more noticeable the marks on his skin which she had thought till then were due to cold winds or sitting too close to the fire, and that they would pass with the aid of balmy weather and unguents.

'I am afflicted by a disease. I know not what it is. I had thought it would pass. But it does not. It affects my skin and at times I feel as though I have been doused in fire. The irritation is sometimes unbearable. Once it showed itself on my face . . .' He touched his wrinkled skin. 'It disappeared . . . or almost did. But I dread its return and it never goes completely away.'

She had looked at the marks on his body with growing uneasiness and tried to comfort him. She would consult the keeper of her stillroom. She believed there were ointments which could cure such afflictions.

But she was disturbed and so was Henry.

This man with the fear of a horrible disease which was advancing on him was very different from the romantic lover who had given her a forget-me-not to remember him by.

She had found unguents but they had no effect on him. A terrible thought kept occurring to her. Could it be leprosy?

As she mused one of her women thrust a paper into her hands.

'The Duke of York himself gave it to me,' whispered the woman. 'He would have me swear to deliver it to no one but you.'

'Oh, he becomes too foolish,' said Joanna.

'And reckless, too, my lady,' giggled the woman. ''Tis to be hoped this does not come to the King's ears.'

Joanna gave the woman a sharp push. 'There is no need to fear that,' she said sharply. 'I may show it to the King myself. There is nothing wrong, my good woman, in writing a verse to a lady of the Court, which is what the Duke has done. In the Courts of Provence and such places it was the natural order of the day.'

'Yes, my lady,' said the woman quietly.

Joanna looked at the paper.

It was verses, as she had expected it would be, and from that foolish young man. She must warn him. It was gallant of him to find her so beautiful that he sighed for her love, but he must remember that she was the wife of the King and such writing could be dangerous.

She would warn him when next she saw him, not to write so to her again.

She left her women and went to join the King. They would sit side by side in the royal box and watch the jousts. Young Harry would give a good account of himself she doubted not and the people would shout for him. There was something about the boy which won cheers wherever he went.

Henry's face was grey beneath the velvet cap looped up at the side with a fleur de lys. His furred velvet mantle hung loosely on him. Joanna dared not ask him whether more spots had appeared on his skin. She could see a redness on his neck and she wondered what would happen when his face began to be really disfigured.

'I see you looking in good health,' he said.

She smiled warmly and heartily wished she could say the same for him.

'Have you seen Harry?' he asked.

'No, but I look forward to his performance. I am sure he will be the champion.'

'No doubt of it. The boy gives me cause for alarm, Joanna.'

'Has he been in further trouble?'

'I hear stories. They think they ought to tell me. I know he will be the champion. I know that he can lead an army. But there is more to kingship than that.'

'He can win the applause of the people,' Joanna reminded him. 'They love him.'

'The people love today and hate tomorrow,' said the King ruefully. 'Not that they have ever shown much adulation for me. I always had my enemies. I came to the throne through a back door you might say. That is never good for a king.'

'You came because the people wanted you. They were tired of Richard. And you were the next . . .'

'There was the young Earl of March, remember.'

'A boy! They wanted you, Henry. You were King by election. You have done well for them.'

'They do not like me. Perhaps they will like Harry better . . . that is if he mends his ways.'

'What have you heard now?'

'That he visits the taverns of London. That he spends hours in the company of low people. That he throws off his royalty and is one of them. It will not serve him well, Joanna.'

'Have you spoken to him?'

'I have in the past. There is an insolence about him. He is the Prince of Wales. He has the people with him.

He implies that he does not need me. I believe he would be ready to take the throne from me.'

'Never. He is high spirited, that is all. He chafes against the bonds of royalty. Give him time. He will be a great king when the time comes . . . and I pray he will be a sober old greybeard by that time.'

'You bring me comfort, Joanna,' he said. 'But there is one other matter which causes me concern . . . and were I to believe what is whispered it would bring me greater unhappiness than I suffer from the bad habits of my son.'

'What is that?' asked Joanna in surprise.

'It concerns you . . . and my cousin of York.'

Joanna flushed slightly. 'Oh you have been listening to tales. He is a foolish young man.'

'And you are a beautiful young woman.'

'Not so young. But this is nonsense. He fancies himself as a poet and I am a good target for his verse.'

'He sends them to you?'

'Yes, he does.'

'And you?'

'I read them and tell him he has much to learn.'

'Of what matters?'

'Of how to write verse for one; and of me for another.'

'I like it not,' said Henry.

'My dear husband, trust me. I loved you when I was the wife of the Duke of Brittany but I did not tell you so. Never a word of what we felt for each other passed between us. I am a woman who respects her marriage vows and even if I felt a tenderness towards this man—which I hasten to tell you I do not—there would never be anything but friendship between us.'

'I believe you,' said the King. 'But I do not trust him. There was a time when he was ready to support Richard against me. I might have lost my crown. Oddly enough he saved it for me. He was one of the conspirators who planned to rescue Richard and set him on the throne. He was then Rutland for his father was alive and he had not yet acquired the title of York, and suddenly he was afraid and confided in his father. My good uncle of York saw at once what must be done. I was informed by both father and son of what was afoot and so the plot did not succeed.'

'So you may well owe your throne to him.'

'I may well do that but all the same I do not care for a man who changes coats so easily.'

'Then you must believe that he is not a strong enough man for you to waste your thoughts on. I swear to you that nothing has passed between us but that which you know of.'

'I believe you.'

'Then you must not pay attention to such trivialities.'

'Nothing that touches you can be trivial to me.'

'I know it,' she said, with her voice soft and tender. 'May God smile on you. May he preserve you in peace and happiness for as long as we both shall live.'

He was moved. He had not been wrong when he had taken her as his second wife. That she lacked Mary's meekness did not disturb him. Mary had not been meant to be a Queen.

He was satisfied with his marriage. It was one of the few aspects of his life which was satisfactory and he was not going to have it even faintly tarnished by his amorous cousin. He would be watchful of him and at the first opportunity he would know how to deal with him.

They went out together to take their places at the joust which was being performed in the Queen's honour. They acknowledged the rapturous greetings of the company and sat at the balcony where all could see them. The Queen was beautiful and in his royal velvet Henry himself made an impressive figure. From the distance it was not possible to see clearly the havoc the disease was causing to his skin.

The opportunity came. York was a reckless young man; the kind who would be embroiled in some plot or other if he were given the chance. It might be why he was a close friend of the Prince of Wales.

After the death of Richard and the fact that people no longer could believe the story that he lived—for if he had Henry would never have been so eager to marry his son to Richard's queen Isabella—the greatest bogey in Henry's life was the young Earl of March. The older he grew the more likelihood there would be of discontented men rallying round him and stating his claim to the throne.

That was why when news came of the plot to rescue the young Earl of March and his younger brother from Windsor, where they were kept under the eyes of the King's guards, and the Duke of York was proved to be involved in it, Henry was able to act justifiably and none could attribute his action to a jealousy regarding the Queen.

It was a plot worthy of York, thought Henry grimly. He was involved with his sister Lady de Despencer who was not a woman of the highest character and they had bribed a blacksmith to make a set of keys to enable them to open the doors of the apartment where the young captives were kept.

There was a period of great consternation when Henry learned that the two boys had been taken from Windsor. Henry visualized armies in the name of the Earl of March coming against him. Henry imagined that many would flock to their banner simply because they disliked him. His infrequent public appearances did not endear him to the people; how could he tell them of the terrible anxieties he suffered and that sometimes his face was so inflamed that he could not venture out? They did not like his foreign Queen either. Sometimes he thought how popular he and Mary used to be when he was plain Bolingbroke, or Derby or Hereford. It was only when he had become Henry the King that the people had begun to dislike him.

York was no brilliant strategist and it was inevitable that any plot in which he was involved should fail. And so did this one.

After cleverly getting the boys out of Windsor he carelessly allowed their destination to be discovered, and it was not long before the two boys were sent back to Windsor and York was the King's prisoner. Then the story came out. The blacksmith lost his life; it would have been unwise to allow York to suffer the same fate and make a martyr of him; he was sent to Pevensey Castle for safe keeping.

Henry had had his revenge. He had wanted York removed for he did not like the thought of a handsome young man writing verses to Joanna. Now was his chance. He could dismiss York from Court and no one could say he had not good reason for doing so, and Joanna would no longer be able to compare smooth-skinned York with her husband who grew more ill-favoured every day.

Joanna made no attempt to plead for him, which gratified Henry, and he was convinced that York meant nothing to her. York was one of those men who would always involve himself in dangerous situations in which he had little chance of achieving his goal.

There remained the matter of the Earl of March. The older he grew the more of a problem he would be.

Henry sent for Harry. When his son arrived Henry's feelings fluctuated between pride and irritation. There was no question of his not being a fine specimen of manhood; all sign of that childhood weakness which had caused such anxiety to his mother had disappeared. He was less Plantagenet than de Bohun, but looks were the only characteristics he had inherited from his mother. Her gentle meekness, her main characteristic, was completely lacking in young Harry. He was dark, with thick smooth hair; his nose was long and straight, his face oval; his teeth were outstandingly white and well shaped and he had a cleft in his chin. He had a glowing complexion which indicated extreme good health; there was a reddish tinge in his brown eyes which could be sleepily good-humoured or fierce when he was angry. Yes, he was a son to be proud of, with his lean body, above normal height, his limbs well formed and his bearing already that of a King. There was a vitality in him which seemed to be fighting to get out. It was a pity he wasted his energies in low taverns surrounded by men of similar tastes.

'I do not need to ask if you are in good health,' said Henry.

Harry thought: I cannot say the same for you, old man.

'I am well as I trust you are, my lord.'

Henry waved his hands. 'You see me in sorry state. More and more responsibility will be put onto your shoulders, Harry.'

Harry stood up very straight, smiling, confident of his ability to carry it.

'I would there were not these reports of you . . . carousing in low taverns.'

'It is my way of meeting the people.'

'You can do that satisfactorily at my Court.'

'Which I do,' said Harry. 'But I would meet all sorts. What do most courtiers know of the villeins, water men, merchants and such like?'

'What do they want to know of them?'

'What they are thinking. That they are loyal subjects. We could depend on such as them to keep us on our thrones.'

'You have not yet a throne, Harry.'

'No, sir. But I am the heir to one.'

'Take care.'

'But it is what I do constantly, my lord.'

'You are acquiring a reputation for low living.'

'And for high living, my lord. I am living my life to the full.'

'You give me cause for anxiety, my son.'

'My lord, you give *me* cause for anxiety. You are not in good health.'

The King was silent.

'Father,' said Harry, 'you may rely on me to stand beside you, to be your deputy, to take on those duties which you feel yourself unable to carry out.'

My God, thought Henry, his fingers itch to take the crown!

He said coldly: 'I have no duties in low taverns.'

'Why,' laughed Harry, 'it is my way of passing the time. Give me my tasks and I will carry them out to your satisfaction.'

'I am going to put the Earl of March and his brother into your keeping.'

Harry's eyes shone with pleasure.

'Rest assured I shall keep them safe from interfering relations and their accommodating blacksmiths.'

'See to it. And Harry . . . you have noticed this affliction of mine?'

Harry nodded.

'And others?'

'They do not speak to me of it.'

'There will come a time when I fear it will be the undoing of me. But it is a slow process.'

Harry was silent.

'There should be amity between us two, my son. I would have you remember your position.'

'I could never forget it, my lord.'

'Our claim to the crown could be contested.'

'Could and is,' said Harry.

'This matter of young March . . .'

'Ah, we have our enemies.'

'Surrounding us, my son. That is why we must stand together.'

'And take great care.'

'York is safe at Pevensey.'

'He should not be kept long under restraint. He will become a martyr. Men will speak of him and perhaps say he had right on his side.'

'What would you do then. Free him?'

'After a while, yes. And restore his estates to him.'

'As a reward for playing traitor?'

'He is of our family. He had worked for us. He saved us remember when he was with the plotters at Windsor. But for him it might well be that you and I should not be here now discussing how to safeguard the crown. We shall get good service from him yet. He is a man governed by his emotions. Let him fret a while in prison. Then I will speak for him and guarantee his good behaviour. He will be a good servant to me then, I'll promise you. He is one who will remember a service.'

'Methinks you would already govern this realm.'

'Think on it,' said Harry with a smile. Then he bowed low and said: 'At your service, my lord and father. Together we shall hold the crown against all who might come against us.'

After he had left Henry was thoughtful, and his apprehension and pride were stronger than ever.

Harry was right, they must not be vindictive to the Duke of York. The people might even say that he was jealous because of the Duke's admiration of the Queen.

Four months after the Duke of York had been sent to Pevensey, he was released and his goods and lands restored to him.

Harry appeared to have judged correctly. The Duke was grateful. Henry believed that if there was another attempt to snatch the crown, York would be beside him and his son.

*　　*　　*

Two men swaggered over the cobbles of East Cheap and entered the Boar's Head. They were an incongruous pair—one rotund, the other slender; and there was such a difference in their ages that they might have been father and son.

They sprawled together at a bench and called for wine. The girl who brought it, her hair hanging lankly over the tawdry ribbons of her none too clean gown, laid her hand on the young man's shoulder and gave him an inviting smile.

He squeezed her thigh. 'Some other time,' he said with a wink at his companion. 'Tonight mayhap.'

'Nay,' said the older man with a rumbling laugh, 'have naught to do with these callow youths, lass. Take a man like me . . . a man who has travelled far and wide . . . in the French wars . . . in the German wars . . . and in any wars you can name.'

'Listen not to him,' said the younger one. 'He is old and incapable.'

'You two!' said the woman with a flounce of her skirts. 'If I know aught it'll be talk and talk. That's what you do best, mark my words.'

With this she left with a twirl of her musty skirts.

The older man sat back on the bench and surveyed the younger.

'You effect a good disguise, my lord,' he said. 'I'd find good sport in standing on this bench and shouting to them all: Behold your Prince.'

'I don't doubt you would,' replied Harry. 'Would they believe you?'

'A right good scandal it would make.'

'Bless you, John, there are scandals enough about me.'

'What's for tonight?'

'A little bit of robbery methinks.'

'What have you in mind then?'

'There are some about me who suspect my fondness for this place. I heard them whispering about the Boar's Head in East Cheap. We'll surprise him, they said. That'll be good sport. *I want* to surprise them.'

'You bring good custom to the Boar's Head, my lord. The landlord should be pleased with you.'

'His harlot of a daughter does not seem to be. God's ear, John, I think she prefers you.'

'Ah, there is a lot to be said for a man of experience.'

'There's more to be said for youth.'

'Well you, my lord, are in good way of combining the two. But take care with the poxy wenches.'

'Away dull care,' cried Harry. 'Care is for courts. Bawdry for the Boar's Head, trickery for taverns . . . What say you, John, to this? Here we meet the people. We hear what they think of the King and his son. The King who filched Richard's crown. The Prince who is itching to take it. The King who is mean and grasping. The Prince who wastes their money on debauchery. By God, I would it were true, John; I would I had it to waste on debauchery.'

'You manage debauchery at a low price,' replied Oldcastle.

' 'Tis to be had at all prices and cheaper here in the Boar's Head than at Court.'

'Tell me, what is this plan?'

'Tonight we lurk in the streets. We play the footpad on these fine gentlemen from Court. We take their money. 'Twill be a new game. A good one too.'

'Are you short of money again?'

'Not of the kind they will have on their persons.'

'They could harm you.'

'God bless you, John, am I going to curb my inclinations because I am afraid of being hurt? Would you say, "Do not go into battle my lord, you may be hurt?" Look at this scar here on my forehead. Battle honours, John. An arrow at Shrewsbury where we slew brave Hotspur. Enough of your caution. Out into the streets. We'll lurk there and we will catch them on their way to the tavern.'

'It seems a good sport,' said Oldcastle.

Harry drew something from under his cloak. 'Masks, John. They must not know it is a game.'

' 'Tis easier for you to disguise yourself than it is for me to do so. My bulk betrays me.'

'Why John, there are thousands of bulky men and where in England is a figure as neat and slender as mine. They look at me, no matter how I'm clad and say: "There goes noble Harry." '

'Nay. I shall be the better known.'

'Would you start a quarrel now then, fat man?'

'I would and I will it, boy.'

Harry laughed. 'No time for private wars, old fellow. Come . . .'

'Are you going then, fair sirs?' It was the landlord's daughter.

Harry took her by the shoulder and gave her a hearty kiss on the mouth.

'I'll be back, sweetheart,' he said.

They came out into the streets. The flickering tallow candle in the tavern had given little light but it was some seconds before their eyes were adjusted to the gloom.

They picked their way carefully over the uneven ground avoiding the kennel in the middle of the road which would be overflowing with refuse, yet keeping from the walls in case someone threw out something which was even more obnoxious.

Harry loved the adventure of the streets by night. At any moment some cutthroat might spring out on them, or they might be accosted by some prostitute whom they would know must be hard pressed since she had wandered out in the darkness. To Harry it was excitement. He liked the streets by day with their lively activity; he liked to mingle with apprentices and pretend to be one of them; he liked to bargain with the stallholders and talk of the iniquities of the tax laws; he liked to buy a ballad of a ballad singer and take it into the tavern and try it out; he would exchange banter with a milkmaid and parley with a madam who was trying to sell him one of her girls from the country. Sometimes he joined in fights when he could always give a good account of himself. 'What do you lack?' he would shout at the apprentices. He would stand and watch the craftsmen at work in their open shops. He would startle a beggar by the size of his contribution and then slink away quickly while the beggar called a blessing on him. He loved it all—the filth, the squalor and the grandeur of the London streets. It was a delight to mingle with these people, to know how they thought, how they acted; he liked their pride and that certain dignity which was as ingrained in them as it was in the highest nobility.

It was men such as these merchants and their apprentices who would stand beside him against his enemies, he believed. He did not want them there because they feared not to join him; he wanted to understand them, to talk with them, to have them work for him and give him loyalty not because it was treason not to, but because they wanted to.

He wanted to know the people he would one day rule. That was one reason why he mingled with them. The other was that he enjoyed the sport of it. He liked to spend a night with a woman who thought he was a young apprentice and who had no idea that briefly she enjoyed the privilege of sharing her bed with the Prince of Wales.

It was adventure that appealed to his youth and high spirits; and because there was danger in it, he liked it the better.

'Hist,' said John Oldcastle. 'I hear revellers.'

' 'Tis they,' whispered Harry. 'I know their voices. Let's take them from behind.'

They crouched by the wall. Three young men came by, courtiers in their velvet. One held a pomander, sniffing it purposefully.

Harry laughed inwardly. He heard one say: 'Methinks the Prince has little taste.'

'He'll have a surprise when he sees us,' said another.

'Now!' whispered Harry.

They had caught two of the young men from behind. The one with the pomander dropped it and cried out: 'Help. We are set upon. Thieves.'

Harry laughed. It showed how little he knew of the London streets. Such a cry was enough to set everyone bolting their doors.

There was a scuffle. They were after all three to two. Harry was agile but not agile enough. He caught a strong blow in the ribs which left him breathless, but he was quick to respond and sent his opponent down to the ground.

He then tackled the gentleman with the pomander, who was easy prey.

'Their purses,' he whispered to Oldcastle. And in a few seconds they were running through the dark streets with three purses in their possession.

Harry leaned against a wall and burst out laughing.

'Tomorrow,' he said, 'they will tell a fine tale.'

They did not go back to the tavern that night.

The next day Harry enquired how his friends had received their bruises and expressed deep concern when they told him they had been set upon in East Cheap by a pack of ruffians.

'The streets are unsafe by night,' said Harry with a show of concern.

Oldcastle added: ''Tis unsafe to wander in them unarmed. Did you have nothing to defend yourself?'

'My good sir, try to defend yourself when set on by a gang.'

'Were there many of them?' asked Harry solemnly.

'I'd say we were outnumbered three to one.'

'No chance against so many,' muttered Oldcastle.

'A plague on them, they had our purses.'

'And you cannot afford the loss, I'll swear,' said Harry. 'Who of us can? I'll be generous. You're good fellows and brave. I'll swear you gave a good account of yourself. You will allow me to reimburse you.'

The three adventurers declared themselves reluctant to rob the Prince.

'Come, come. You have been robbed.'

Harry was almost hysterical with suppressed mirth as he handed back their own money.

When they were alone Sir John said: 'I believe you gave more to one of them than the other two.'

'You know why. He was the one who hit me in the ribs. I thought he should be rewarded for showing more fight than the others.'

They had enjoyed the adventure so much that they decided to repeat it. Secrecy was a necessity.

'It's dangerous,' said Sir John. 'Who knows, someone of them may get the better of us.'

'That's why it is exciting, you old buffoon.'

Sometimes there was some rough fighting, but the more the attacked fought back the better Harry liked it.

It was his favourite game until someone detected that he was the instigator. From then on the game had lost its savour.

But there were always ways of amusing themselves in the taverns and the streets of London.

*   *   *

Harry had a servant of whom he was somewhat fond. He knew the fellow for a rogue but he was a merry one; and his unscrupulous behaviour amused the Prince. One day it occurred to him that he had not seen Bardolph for a few days and he asked where he was.

'My lord,' was the answer, 'he has been arrested.'

'Arrested for what cause?'

'Some felony, my lord. It was of a certainty that he would be caught one day.'

'Why was I not told? Is he not my servant?'

''Twas an offence which brought him before the Chief Justice, my lord.'

'Before Gascoigne! Why he stands a chance of hanging then. I won't lose Bardolph to a hangman, that I swear.'

'My lord, he comes up for trial this day.'

'Then I shall leave at once for the courts.'

He was as good as his word and impetuously he rode out. At the King's Bench sat Sir William Gascoigne—a man in his late fifties, dignified, deeply aware of the importance of his office and known throughout the country for his incorruptible determination to administer justice to high and low alike.

There was a commotion in court as Harry appeared and the judge called for order.

Harry went forward. He had seen his servant Bardolph.

'There stands my servant,' he said. 'I wish him to be released at once. If he has done aught which deserves punishment it is for me to administer it.'

The judge surveyed the heated face of the young Prince calmly.

'You are wrong, my lord. This man's crime is one against society and it comes within my jurisdiction.'

'You forget, my lord judge, to whom you speak.'

'I speak in the name of the King,' replied Sir William Gascoigne, 'and I order you, his subject, to leave the court.'

Harry was furious. He drew his sword and advanced on the judge, who sat still calmly watching him. There was a hushed silence. Many thought they were about to witness the murder of the Chief Justice by the Prince of Wales.

Then Sir William spoke. 'Sir,' he said, 'remember I

keep here the place of your sovereign lord and father to whom you owe double obedience. I charge you in his name, desist from your wilfulness and unlawful conduct. From henceforth, I beg of you, give a good example to those who in the future shall be your subjects. For your contempt and disobedience of the King's Bench you will go to prison where I shall commit you, and remain there until the pleasure of your father the King shall be known.'

Harry was startled into silence. All he had to do was thrust his sword through the heart of this judge who had gone so far as to commit him, the Prince of Wales, to prison, yet he hesitated.

His anger faded suddenly as he began to see this incident clearly through the eyes of a bystander. If a King was going to maintain justice his courts must not be held in contempt. No one, whatever his rank, should burst in and demand the release of a prisoner. That way lay anarchy and as one who was going to wear the crown, his first duty was to maintain the laws of the land.

He laid down his sword and bowing to the judge he said: 'You are right. You must do with me as you will. I ask your pardon and that of the court.'

Sir William was clearly impressed by the wisdom of the Prince. His voice was gentle as he said: 'You will wait here in this court until I know the will of the King. Messengers shall go to him with all speed. In the meantime we will continue with the business of the court.'

The King was in his bedchamber when the messenger arrived. He was in a melancholy mood; he was looking truth straight in the face and he believed he was not going to live very long. Nor did he want to with this terrible affliction which had come to him. That was not all. There was another ailment—or perhaps the two were connected. At times he would go into a swoon or it might be a trance and be unaware of where he was or what was going on about him. One night his attendants had thought he was dead.

In his heart he wondered whether it was a retribution, a punishment for taking the crown. He was haunted by memories of Richard and he often dreamed of his cousin starving and freezing to death in his cell at Pontefract.

A crown, he thought, what men will do for it. And when they get it, what joy does it bring them?

His father had longed for it and died a frustrated man; his grandfather had rightfully inherited it and had worn it nobly—at least until his last days. And he . . . Joyfully had he grasped it but it had weighed him down with trouble ever since it had been his.

Soon it would be Harry's turn—Harry with his wild life and his fondness for low companions, profligates like himself. What would become of the country?

And now a messenger to see him. He roused himself. Not ill news he trusted.

'My lord,' said the messenger, 'I come from the King's Bench.'

He then related what had happened.

Henry listening, smiled slowly to himself. Yes, he thought, it is good news.

Then he lifted his eyes and said: 'Oh merciful God, I thank you for a judge who feared not to administer justice and a son who can nobly submit to it.'

He felt better than he had for a long time. It might well be that Harry would reform his ways. He could so easily have slain the judge, have caused havoc in the court. But he had submitted to justice.

It was a sign from heaven. His sins were forgiven. He might, after all his fears, be leaving England a worthy King.

He immediately sent his compliments and thanks to Sir William Gascoigne. He applauded his action. His son should be released. He was pleased that he had realized in time that justice must stand supreme in England.

Bardolph received a short term of imprisonment which fitted his crime and the Prince left the court on the best of terms with the judge; and the matter was said to be over.

But men talked of it and they marvelled at the Prince's behaviour. They were beginning to realize that in spite of his frivolous and reckless way of life there was within him a streak of seriousness.

The incident in the courts had without doubt had its sobering influence on Harry; and it seemed that his mood communicated itself to his crony John Oldcastle.

One day as they sat together in one of their favourite taverns, Oldcastle said to Harry: 'I have been disturbed for some time and meaning to talk to you.'

'You, disturbed? What ails you, John? Not some pox, I hope.'

'You never thought of me as a religious man, my Prince.'

'You have never shown me much evidence of your piety.'

'I think a lot, you know; and since my marriage . . .'

'Ah, the lady Cobham is having her effect on you, I see.'

'Like you, my Prince, I was always deeply affected by the ladies.'

'They render you frivolous, amorous, reckless yes . . . but this lady makes you *think*. What strange alchemy has she to bring about this wondrous feat?'

'She is my wife, my lord.'

'I know it well and through her you have discarded the comparatively humble Sir John Oldcastle and become Lord Cobham.'

'Should you blame me? One day you will discard the comparatively humble title of Prince of Wales and become King of England. But enough of banter. What think you of the Lollards, Hal?'

'Lollards? In truth I have thought little of them. My grandfather supported their leader Wycliffe for a while and I think little came of it.'

'Mayhap not through him, but they are a rising power. There is much that is good in them.'

'I like their name. Lollards, what means it, John?'

'Some say it comes from the German word *lollen,* to sing.'

'They have a habit of singing hymns, I believe.'

'A good habit to sing of what one believes. But I have also heard, now I come to remember, that they have been named from a good English word. Loller—an idler.'

'Well, what is in a name? It is what they stand for which is important. They are a dangerous group, John. I remember Archbishop Arundel's saying that they were behind the Peasants' Revolt.'

'Some say the peasant had good reason to revolt.'

'You always loved a discourse. God's truth, I believe

you take a view with which you know I will not agree just to bait me.'

'Mayhap,' agreed John. 'It makes a good pastime.'

Harry was watching one of the serving women.

'I can think of a better at this moment,' he said.

John sighed and the subject was dropped, but he brought it up again at their next meeting.

'The Lollards believe that no human law not founded on the scriptures ought to be obeyed.'

'There are crimes not mentioned in the scriptures.'

'Is it right,' persisted John, 'that popes, cardinals, prelates and the like should live in luxury while the people who struggle day and night to feed themselves and their families should pay them rich dues?'

'John, you talk like a preacher.'

'I feel deeply on this matter.'

'You do indeed, I see. John, you alarm me. You know my father does not think kindly of the Lollards.'

'I think in his heart he may . . . as his father did. But when he came to the throne he promised Archbishop Arundel to persecute them and this he did . . . for the sake of Arundel's support.'

'What's come over you, John? You should not talk thus of the King.'

'To you, I speak without thought.'

'It is a dangerous habit, old fellow. Do you remember a man named William Sawtre?'

'Would I forget the first martyr to this cause? He was a poor curate and they made an example of him. He said he would not worship the cross but only Christ that suffered on it. He would rather worship a man who was truly contrite than the piece of wood which was all the cross was. The bread used in the sacrament remained bread whatever a priest mumbled over it. He was burned to death as a heretic. The first to be so treated. His death was a dark blot on our history.'

The Prince was looking in astonishment at his friend.

'What has come over you? You've changed, John.'

'Nay, I am the same. As you are, my Prince. We frivol away the hours but when we are quiet we think of other things. As it is with you, it is with me. I look ahead, Hal. We shall not spend our lives roystering in taverns. We have other work to do.'

'I know what mine is. I thought yours was to serve me.'

'So it is, lord King-to-be. But not in taverns.'

'You've put me in a sober mood, John. I fear the wenches will be disappointed.'

'Cast off your gloom. I humbly ask pardon for creating it.'

'Nay, John, nay. You have put me in the mood for serious thought. Let us leave this place. I have no stomach for it now. One thing I would say to you. Have a care. Do not become embroiled in sects and reforming companies. They could bring you to disaster.'

'I am not of a nature to fear what may come to me . . . even as you are. Would this close friendship—with which you honour me—have existed if we had not been two of a kind? I shall do what I think right . . . as you will always. It is the nature of us.'

'Then take care, John. I am not sure that I like the serious thinker half as much as my lewd old roystering rogue.'

The King lay in his bed. His face was distorted by the hideous pustules which stood out all over it; his body was shrunken and there was a stiffness in his hands and feet so that he feared he was losing the use of them.

He dared not show himself. He relied on his closest friends and his sons. Thomas was his favourite and he wished that he had been the eldest, although there were times when he recognized a certain strength in Harry which the others did not possess, and then he would feel that the realm would be safe in his hands. Thomas was milder than Harry although he too had been involved in riotous conflict in East Cheap, which created something of a scandal. John, who was by far the most sober of the family, had been involved but that was only because he was accompanying his brother. Even young Humphrey was developing a taste for the night life of London. They were a wild brood, his sons. Odd to think that gentle little Mary had produced them.

At least he had something to be thankful for. He had produced sons—wild though they might be; and both his marriages had been happy ones. He could not have chosen better than Joanna, except for the fact that her family—by the nature of their geographical position—were inclined towards France. But there were internal difficulties in that country now—with Burgundy and the mad King and the wanton Queen. Fortunately, thought Henry, for they were causing little concern to England now; and he had no great wish to go to war, unlike Harry who was straining at the leash. Harry was ambitious. He wanted not only the crown of England but the crown of France.

Peace, thought Henry, that is what I long for now. Would to God I were well enough to go on a pilgrimage. God knows I have sins enough to wash away. There had been a prophecy made years ago that he would die in Jerusalem. There seemed little likelihood of that now, unless his health improved and he abdicated in favour of Harry. But if he were granted the miracle of good health, he would not dream of leaving the country.

The people loved Harry. He had noticed it when they were together. All the cheers were for Harry. He had that certain quality which drew men to him. A Plantagenet quality although he had the looks of a de Bohun. His father had never had it, for all his strength and power; Edward the King had had it, so had the Black Prince.

He felt angry because it had been denied him.

They never liked me, he thought. If I said I would abdicate tomorrow they would cheer themselves hoarse for Harry.

And what of me? He would tell me what I must do. He would remind me a hundred times a day that he was the King.

'Never will I give up, my son,' he murmured. 'Death's is the only hand which will place the crown on your head.'

Harry was hand in glove with his Beaufort relations. Trust them to go where the pastures looked greenest. It was an indication that they thought there was not much time left to him.

They had supported him whole-heartedly at one time. Of course they had. Their fortunes were firmly tied up with those of the House of Lancaster. His half-brothers—result of his father's abiding passion for Catherine Swynford. Clever men all of them. And now they veered to Harry. They were going to uphold him, even if it meant going against the King—for the old King was not long for this world.

'The King is dead!' they would cry. 'Long live the King.'

He was sad; he was in pain. He had committed a great sin in compassing the crown and it had brought him nothing but bitterness.

Harry liked to discuss his plans with John, who was his favourite brother, and his uncles Henry and Thomas Beaufort. Henry had been made Bishop of Winchester and Thomas, Duke of Exeter and Chancellor of England; they had been specially favoured as the sons of John of Gaunt and they had inherited a good deal of their father's shrewdness.

Their elder brother John Beaufort, Earl of Somerset, was dead and there had been a rift in the family when the King's son Thomas had married Somerset's widow for when Thomas had demanded her estates Henry Beaufort had refused to give them up.

In the quarrel, the Prince had taken sides and was in favour of his uncle rather than his brother and this had, of course, made a great coolness between them, and Thomas, knowing that their father was not on the best of terms with the Prince of Wales, did his best to turn the King still more away from the heir to the throne.

It was an uneasy situation. It brought Harry closer to the Beauforts who as Bishop and Chancellor were powerful men; and as everyone knew now of the King's fearsome disease which often kept him out of sight for long periods, an uneasy tension was growing up in Court circles. It was working towards a rift and it seemed that before long there would be a King's circle and one made up of the Prince's supporters.

At this time a new conflict had arisen in France.

After the death of Isabella in childbed her husband Charles of Angoulême, who had become the Duc d' Orléans when his father had been murdered, married again. This time his bride was the daughter of the very powerful and warlike Count of Armagnac. Charles of Orléans was of a gentle nature, a lover of the arts, thoughtful, with a hatred of war, but he was in the hands of his forceful father-in-law who wanted to establish the power of the House of Orléans which meant destroying that of Burgundy.

Civil war in France was something which England could not fail to be pleased about. It was always so much better to let an enemy destroy itself than to waste one's own strength doing it.

The Burgundians sent to England to ask Henry for his help and offered in payment for it a bride for the Prince of Wales, Anne, the Duke's daughter.

Harry had no desire for the match, but he did think that a force should be sent to the Burgundians. Let Frenchman fight Frenchman. That was a good plan. There would be fewer in the field when he went over there to fight for the crown of France, which he fully intended to do when he was safe on the throne of England.

Henry considered the matter. He was feeling very ill. Peace, that is what we want, he thought. It is unwise for us to embroil ourselves in the affairs of another nation.

'Nonsense!' cried Harry. 'It will be to our advantage.'

'I am against it,' declared Henry. 'There shall be no force sent to Burgundy's aid.'

It seemed that that settled the matter; but on the day he made that statement the King suffered another attack, which was even worse than those which had preceded it. His face became an unsightly mass of horrible pustules which stood out all over it and when he touched his skin and felt them he fainted and had the appearance of a dead man.

The doctors came and said that he could not last long, but a few days later he recovered and even his face was slightly less unsightly.

He must remain in his chamber, though. He could not show himself to the people or even the Court. Only those in his immediate circle should see him. The Queen ministered to him; she was gentle and reassuring, though it was hard to recognize in this poor maimed shrivelled creature in the bed the romantic Plantagenet who had come to Brittany an exile from his own country.

Harry took over the reins of government and the first thing he did was send men and arms to the Duke of Burgundy.

As a result of his actions the Orléans faction was defeated and it was victory for Burgundy.

*   *   *

The King did not die. In a few weeks he had recovered sufficiently to resume his duties. The first thing he discovered was that his son had gone against his wishes and sent troops to Burgundy.

He was incensed. He immediately sent for the Prince and demanded to know why he thought he could act in a manner opposed to his father—and his King's—wishes.

Harry replied that clearly the side to support was that of Burgundy. They had won, had they not? Who knew, they might be of help to him if he went into France at any time.

'Your fingers itch to lay hold of the crown, Harry,' said the King.

'I but think of the future.'

'And I am such an old and feeble man that I no longer warrant obedience.'

'You are the King and must be obeyed.'

'Until you think me dead. You have to wait awhile yet, my son, before that crown is yours.'

'My thoughts were not on the crown, only on what I believed to be best for England.'

'And King Henry . . . the Fifth, eh?'

'You are mistaken. I rejoice in your recovery.'

'You rejoice! Look at me . . . if you can bear it. What have I become? This accursed sickness has taken hold of me, but God and all his saints, Harry, there is life in me yet and while there is I shall be King.'

Harry bowed his head.

The King dismissed his son. He had made up his mind; he was going to show Harry and his council that there was only one King in England and that was himself.

He had decided, he told them, to send aid to the Armagnacs. He was going to support Orléans against Burgundy; and to show his good faith, he was going to send his son to France with troops and supplies.

He sent for Prince Thomas, his favourite. Would to God he had been the elder, he thought; and yet he knew in his heart that this second son lacked that quality of leadership which Harry had inherited from his great ancestors. In a moment of clarity he thought: Is it possible to be jealous of one's own son? And he wondered if great Edward the Third had ever been jealous of the

Black Prince. Never! He had let the battle honours fall
to him rather than accept them himself. But the Black
Prince and his father had worked hand in hand. It was
not the same with him and Harry; they were pulling
different ways.

Thomas came to him. Henry faced him, with his back
to the light. It was a habit of his now to stand in the
shadows; people knew this and had cultivated a habit of
looking at him as little as possible which they knew was
what he wanted.

'Thomas,' said Henry, 'I am sending a force of eight
thousand men to France to assist the Orleanists.'

Thomas was aghast.

'I thought we were on the side of Burgundy.'

'Your brother is,' answered the King wryly. 'That
does not necessarily mean that I am. But the side I
favour is the one this country will support.'

Thomas smiled slyly. Another piece of contention between father and heir. That amused him. Harry really
was a little too sure of himself.

'Thomas, I want to know, whom do you think we
should support. Orléans or Burgundy?'

'My lord, if you support the Orleanists then so must
we all.'

'Except your brother.'

'His support would be of little use without that of you,
Father.'

'I believe that to be true. Your brother saw fit to act
against my wishes while I was indisposed. Now I am
better I propose to act against his. What say you to
leading the force into France?'

Thomas was clearly delighted.

'I shall not wish you to go merely as Prince Thomas,
my son. I have decided to bestow a Dukedom on you.
What say you to the Duke of Clarence?'

Thomas fell on his knees declaring that he would
serve his father with his life.

He almost forgot and tried to take his father's hand to
kiss it. Then he remembered that his father's hands were
always kept out of sight. There was a rumour that his
fingers and toes had started to drop off. He did not
know whether this was so for he was never allowed to
see them.

He stumbled to his feet. He could not embrace his father. He could do no more than reiterate his willingness to serve him.

Harry knew that his father was wrong to support the Orleanists, particularly after he had given aid to Burgundy.

'He is right,' reasoned Harry with Oldcastle, 'to blame me for acting against his wishes. I knew what they were and I should have remembered that he was the King. But he is even more wrong than I to send aid to the Armagnacs just out of pique towards me. A King should never allow personal feelings to interfere with affairs of state.'

'Ah, you'll be a wise King, Harry, when you become one.'

'My father would not agree with you.'

'He might well.'

'He does not like me, John.'

'It may be that he sees in you what he would have liked to be himself.'

'He has been a virtuous man. Faithful to his Queens, and well served by them. He has at least been fortunate in his marriages. It is this accursed disease which has taken hold of him and warped his nature. He thinks it is some affliction sent to him as a punishment for his sins.'

'Yet he is a man who has tried to rule his country well.'

'But he would say he had to step over Richard's dead body to do it.'

John was thoughtful. 'He broke his word to the Lollards.'

'You are obsessed by the Lollards. I could almost fancy you are one yourself.'

'I am, my lord.'

Harry stared at him. '*You* have become serious, John,' he said. 'I have noticed a change in you.'

'Yes, I am one of them, my Prince. What will you do now? You'll not own me as your friend.'

'The Lollards cannot rob me of a friend,' said the Prince. 'But have a care, John. The Church does not like you and the Church has great power.'

'The Church is afraid of us. And that brings us back to

where we started. It may be that your father is a little afraid of you.'

'There's more to you, old man, than I ever thought.'

'There's more to me, my young bantam, than most people think.'

They were unusually silent; both busy with their thoughts of themselves and each other.

It was Oldcastle who brought home to the Prince that there was an element of danger in his position. 'There are some who are planning to destroy you,' he said. 'They know that the King favours your brother of Clarence. His action over Burgundy has set them thinking. Watch out, my young Prince.'

'I am watchful,' said Harry. 'They shall not get the better of me.'

'The King is sick and near to death. You may depend upon it there are some who believe that no favour will come to you through them.'

Harry was aware of this and when he heard the rumour that he had taken money intended for the garrison of Calais and used it for his own purposes, he realized how serious was the threat against him.

His enemies had a good foundation on which to work. All knew of his way of life in the past. Was a frequenter of low taverns, a man who spent his time with strumpets and gamblers, fit to be King of England?

'They are right,' reasoned Harry, 'but that is not the whole truth. I am that wastrel. But I am something else besides; and I have always known that one day I must say good-bye to my former self and become a King and by God's very being I swear that when I do I shall be a King whose fame will stand nobly beside that of my greatest ancestors.'

But he had been foolish perhaps. He had followed a certain bent. He had mixed with low company. But I know them better than my father ever could. I shall know the men I rule and those I take into battle with me. My youth mayhap has not been so misspent as it would appear to be.

Now he must throw off his light ways. He must think clearly. He must take action against his enemies. He must not alienate his father too completely. The King was too wise, too shrewd, not to see the qualities in his eldest son. He was bemused now—bewitched one might say—by this loathsome affliction which had taken hold of him; his strength was ebbing away; moreover he was persecuted by another shadow as great as that of this disfiguring disease. Guilt. The older he grew, the nearer to death, the more he remembered what he had done to Richard. There was the ghost who walked with him, who slept in his bed at nights. It was his cousin Richard.

Harry must put an end to his father's enmity. He must remind him that he was his eldest son; he must let the country know that there was no thought in the King's mind to set him aside.

It was New Year's Day and the Court was at Westminster. Henry appeared briefly and then he was draped in a cloak which exposed only his face. He seated himself at one end of the great hall, apart from the rest of the company. The Queen sat beside him and around them were a very few of their closest associates.

Suddenly the Prince entered the hall with a few of his attendants. Everyone present was startled because he was dressed in his student's gown with the needle and thread which was presented to students every year, sticking in his collar. In this simple garment he would have been immediately recognizable even by those who did not know him as a person of quality. He held himself with pride, and leaving his attendants clustered round the fire in the middle of the hall he approached the dais on which his father sat.

Harry knelt before the King who stared at him in amazement, wondering what prank this might be, when Harry unsheathed the dagger he wore at his waist and presented it to the King.

'What means this, my son?' asked the King.

'I have been accused of disloyalty to you, my lord father. My enemies tell you I have used for my own pleasure funds which should uphold the port of Calais. My enemies slander me, which does not grieve me greatly in itself. All men worth their salt are slandered by those who fear their own weakness. But that I should be accused of disloyalty and a lack of affection towards my King and my own father, that I will not endure. My lord, if you believe these calumnies directed against me, plunge this dagger into my heart.'

'Take back your dagger,' said the King. 'Do you think I would kill my own son?'

'He would wish you to do the deed, my lord, if you could believe for one moment these lies which are told about him.'

The King handed the dagger back to Harry.

'Put it in your belt,' he said. ''Tis where it belongs.'

'So you believe me to be your good son and loyal subject.'

'I will believe it,' said the King, 'until it is proved otherwise.'

'And this matter of the Calais funds?'

'We will dismiss it.'

'Nay,' said Harry. 'I would have my innocence proved.'

'Then proved it must be.'

'Father, I mean that I would rather you killed me than believe I am other than your loving son and subject.'

'Rise, my son. Let there be no more conflict between us. You are my heir. My first-born. We know it cannot be long before I depart this life. Let us, for the love of God, be good friends for that little time.'

'Amen,' said Harry.

He was well pleased; he had discountenanced his enemies.

Christmas was celebrated at Eltham in Kent, one of the King's favourite palaces with its thick walls and buttresses. Many tragedies had been played out in it. And now he had come here to spend his Christmas and with him was Joanna, one of the few people he allowed to come near him.

She knew the worst. Poor Joanna, who had come to England from the gardens of forget-me-nots and found life had turned out to be very different from what they had imagined it would be when they had walked together in those gardens, not speaking of their hopes and being so happy when they materialized, until they found that life was cruel.

The cherished crown was an empty bauble bringing him nothing but care and disappointment; his once splendid body was betraying him.

He was a sick and sad old man.

In the great hall the revelries persisted. There must be revelries for Christmas even though the King could not honour the company with his presence. Down there they would be playing their games; they would choose the King for the night; the mummers would divert them and there would be laughter and song.

Joanna watched him mournfully.

'You should be with the company, my dear,' he said.

'I should be with you.'

'Poor Joanna, it has been a sad life we have had together.'

'That is not true,' she protested. 'It has been a good life.'

'A good life! I did not know you were deceitful, wife. Look at this body of mine . . . made hideous . . . loathsome . . . I wonder you can look at it.'

'It is yours,' she answered soberly, 'and it is my wish to care for you, to soothe your ills and be all that I promised to be.'

'You have done that,' he said. 'I have been blessed in you as I was in little Mary. I doubt she was happy . . . any more than you. She died of bearing children . . . one after the other. Why did I not see it was too much for her? And you, Joanna, what have you had from life? Two husbands, one an old man when you went to him and the other a man persecuted by this horrible sickness.'

'Let us make the most of what we have, Henry.'

'Wise Joanna. For what else can we do?'

She soothed him as best she could. She tried not to show the aversion the sight of him must arouse in her. She was fearful because she had heard it whispered that his state had been brought about through witchcraft; and because she was a foreigner whom they had never liked there were some who declared she was the witch.

Henry did not know this. He must never know.

She must do her best to help him live through the months ahead of them. There could not be many left to him.

It was Lent. The King felt weaker. He had summoned Parliament in February and right at the last moment had been too unwell to attend.

He asked the lords to remain in London, which did not please them as they must do so at their own expense.

But they should be there. He felt their presence was needed.

March had come, and fierce blustering winds swept through the streets.

It was customary for the King to make a pilgrimage to the shrine of Edward the Confessor at the back of the high altar in the church.

Joanna tried to dissuade him.

'It is too cold,' she said, 'and you are so unwell.'

'It is expected of me,' the King reminded her.

'People must understand,' she said.

But he would not listen.

It was a slow and painful journey to the Abbey, but he reached the shrine and even as he did so he fell swooning to the ground.

His attendants picked him up and it was suggested that he be carried to the nearest room and one where a fire was burning. A pallet of straw should be brought and when this was done, he was laid down before the fire in the Jerusalem chamber.

'Let us send for the Prince of Wales with all haste,' said the Archbishop.

The King lay breathing with difficulty and he seemed to be dying when Harry arrived.

He knelt by his father's side. The King looked at him with glazed eyes and murmured his name.

'Father, I am come,' said Harry.

'Where am I?' asked the King.

'You are in the Jerusalem chamber in the Abbey,' Harry told him.

The King smiled faintly. 'They told me I would die in Jerusalem,' he said. 'Send in the crown.'

It was brought and laid beside him on a cushion made of cloth of gold.

The King seemed satisfied.

He closed his eyes.

Those about him watched him closely.

'It is the end,' said one.

'He is no longer with us,' said another.

Harry knelt at his father's side and looked at that face made hideous by the disease from which he had suffered.

Joanna knelt at his other side. She raised her eyes and looked across her husband at Harry.

He is the King now, she thought.

Harry said: 'It is all over,' and one of the attendants placed a silk towel across the King's face.

'It is for you to take the crown, my lord,' said one of Harry's followers.

He picked it up and even as he did so the King moved as though aware of what was happening.

The towel was removed from his face and Henry opened his eyes and looked straight at his son who was standing beside him with the crown in his hands.

'What right have you to it, my son,' he said, 'seeing that I had none?'

Harry answered promptly: 'Sire, as you have held it and kept it by the sword, so will I hold it and keep it as long as I shall live.'

'I am not yet dead,' he said. 'They would have sent me off before I am ready. But my time is near. Do as you will but now recommend me to God and pray that He will have mercy on my soul.'

The King took the sacrament and closed his eyes; but even now he lingered on.

'Harry,' he said, 'come close to me. This is our last farewell. I love you well. I am proud of you. Always deserve that pride, my son. Look at me now. I was once strong as you are now. Think, in the midst of your glory and prosperity, of the kingdom to which I go and whither you must come. Love the Lord God and fear him. Be not too fond of ease but engage rather in the things of God and in those pleasures and sports which have in them nothing of the foulness of vice. Pay my debts and may God give you his blessing, laden with all good things that you may live blessed for ever and ever.'

Harry was deeply moved. He promised his father that he would endeavour to be all that he would wish him to be.

The King smiled and lay back.

This time there was no doubt that he was dead.

Harry had become King Henry the Fifth.

OLDCASTLE

The night was stormy. There were few people in the streets but those who were might have seen a cloaked figure hurrying along towards the Abbey. None would have guessed that it was the King of a few hours. Purposefully he strode, ducking his head against the wind until he came to the doors of the Abbey.

He entered and as he did so a monk came towards him.

'I would speak with you, brother. I would confess my sins and ask absolution,' said Henry.

'My lord!' cried the monk, for there was no mistaking the authoritative tones of the new King. 'At this hour . . .'

'Enough of the hour. I have urgent work. Come. Take me to the confessional.'

'Follow me,' said the monk.

So Henry followed and there in the confessional he went down on his knees and burying his face in his hands he said: 'I have lived a life of dissipation. I have been a diligent follower of idle practices. I swear by God and all his saints that from this day I shall alter my course.'

'The Lord will hear your resolution, my son,' said the

holy man. 'You are young. You have years ahead to make recompense for past follies.'

'I must tell you of the heinous sins I have committed. I have been wicked, profligate, a frequenter of low taverns and an associate of robbers and prostitutes. I have been a slave to vice. I have turned my back on virtues. I have caused great anxiety to my father. I have been wanton in my ways . . .'

'Repent,' said the monk. 'Truly repent. You are young yet. You have a lifetime before you.'

'I have lived on this earth for twenty-six years, Father, and I have committed more sins than the average man commits in three score years.'

'Take heart, my son. You have opportunities ahead of you. Devote your life to the service of your country. Eschew your fleshly desires. Put on the mantle of a King and a virtuous King and the barren willow will be converted into a fruitful olive.'

'Give me your blessing and let me confess to you that you may know all.'

There were a few seconds of silence and then the King began to talk of those nights he had spent in the lowest taverns of East Cheap, of the orgies in which he had played a major part. He wished to conceal nothing. The holy man must know how low he had sunk.

The monk listened and at the end of the King's recital, he said: 'Go your way. Your sins will be washed away by the good deeds you will perform.'

But the King was not yet satisfied.

'My father died in great remorse,' he said. 'And I who have inherited his crown must share that remorse. He believed at the end that he had no right to the crown, that he had taken it from Richard and that he would have to pay for this action. Richard's death . . .'

'That is a heavy sin to lie on any conscience,' interrupted the monk. 'If the King your father murdered his predecessor . . . he cannot hope to enter the kingdom of heaven.'

'He did not murder Richard by his own hand. He did not mean him to die, mayhap. But Richard died at the hands of those who served my father. If he did not actually kill him, he believed he shared that guilt. It hung heavily on his conscience.'

'And you, my lord, you knew nothing of this?'

'I was recently returned from Ireland. The crown passed into my father's hand while I was in that country. I knew nothing of Richard's death save that it had to be for the safety of my father.'

'Twill not be laid at your door, my son. Ease your conscience by giving Richard a royal burial.'

'I will have him laid in this Abbey. It is his rightful place.'

'Go in peace, my son. Change your ways. Throw off the cloak of vice and wrap yourself round with that of virtue. Serve your people well, for in that way you will best serve God.'

When the King came out into the night he felt uplifted. Harry the dissolute Prince had been replaced by Henry the resolute King.

The Coronation was to be on Passion Sunday, the ninth of April in that year 1413.

The King was already beginning to astound all those about him by his serious demeanour.

Many said it would not last. They would soon have Harry filling the Court with his dissolute companions. This dedicated role was one which was new to him but they had to admit that he played it with skill.

He had not seen his drinking companions for days; and they had left Court on his suggestion. He was in close touch with his uncles the Beauforts, and gave Henry Beaufort back the Chancellorship from which he had resigned on being nominated to the Bishopric of Winchester. The Earl of Arundel had been a great favourite with his father but Henry did not share his father's devotion to the man, although he realized that the head of such a powerful family must not be offended. He was appointed Treasurer. Henry did public penance for his father's sins and everyone knew that what he really had in mind was the compassing of the crown for he had had Richard's body removed from Langley and buried in Westminster Abbey; and he announced that on coronation day he intended to grant a general pardon to all prisoners except those who had been imprisoned for murder or rape.

It was a good beginning but most people were cautious as yet. Harry the Prince had had too lurid a reputation to be able to cast it off with a few good deeds. He announced that he would found three religious houses at Richmond, one for Carthusian, one for Celestine monks, the other for Bregentine nuns; and in these prayers were to be offered by day and night for the repose of his father's soul.

The weather was unseasonably cold. It had been a harsh winter and persisted so through to the spring, but on coronation day people thronged the streets in spite of the bitter winds. After the traditional ceremony in the Abbey, Henry came out into the streets and by this time the snow was falling fast and the strong winds were making it into a blizzard.

A snow storm in April! Surely such a rare phenomenon that it must be a sign from Heaven.

As Henry battled his way back to the palace for the coronation banquet, it was said that this was God's way of telling England that the King had put off the ardours of his youth. He was being chastened by the bleak snow. A good omen. But there were also those who looked upon the storm as a warning of evil to come.

In any case there could be no doubt that Henry had become a new man.

Thomas Arundel, Archbishop of Canterbury, sought an audience with the King.

The last time the King had seen his Archbishop was at the coronation when Arundel had placed the crown on his head. Now Arundel had a serious matter to discuss and Henry guessed its nature.

Arundel had been an enemy of the movement which was sweeping across the country and known as the Lollards. The aim of this community was, in fact, the complete disendowment of the Church; an object which might have seemed worthy of nothing but derision at one time but had in recent years proved itself to be a menace.

These Lollards were the followers of John Wycliffe; they were reformers and their interests were not only confined to the reformation of the Church. It was believed that Lollardry was at the root of the Peasants' Revolt and they had brought disaster very close to the crown. Therefore it was a movement which must be closely watched and since he had come to the throne no one was more aware of this than Henry.

His father had never enjoyed security and he had yet to learn how firm his own hold was. When one had come there by what some might call a devious route and a debatable claim, one had to take care.

The King received the Archbishop with a show of friendship but a certain lack of warmth. He did not greatly care for the old man, but he must be approaching sixty, thought Henry, and could not last much longer.

'My lord,' said the Archbishop, 'I have come to you about a very serious matter. The Lollards are about to rise and it is time that we took action against them.'

'The Lollards!' cried the King. 'We keep them in check do we not? We know how to deal with them if they become too saucy.'

'They have become more than saucy, my lord. They have become a menace.'

Henry studied his Archbishop intently. Always alert for the rights of the Church, he thought. Always watchful lest some privileges be filched by the State. Henry believed that the State must come first. The Archbishop would not agree. There was always this conflict between the two parties.

Arundel had had a stormy career. He had been banished by Richard; and because Richard had been his enemy, Henry the Fourth had been his friend. Arundel regretted the passing of the fourth Henry and was going to be very wary of the Fifth of that name. And rightly so, thought the new King.

No need to worry. He was an old man. I shall soon be appointing my own archbishop.

'My lord, the Lollards conspire against the crown when they would attack the Church.'

Henry raised his eyebrows.

'Lollardry was behind the Peasants' Revolt, my lord,' said the Archbishop. 'Make no mistake about that. This is a villeins' charter. They would try to make you their puppet or set up one in your place.'

'We have had the Lollards with us for several years. Tell me, my lord Archbishop, why are you excited about them now?'

'Because, my lord, they have a new leader. A man of some wealth and the power to lead. They are gathering together under his leadership. They will be marching on London if we do not take some action.'

'Cannot you take this leader and put him in the Tower that he may be judged of his treason?'

'It can be done, my lord, but in view of who this man is, I thought it best to bring the matter first to your notice and ask what you would have done.'

'But if this man is the leader of a band of rebels who plan to revolt against the crown . . . why do you hesitate?'

'It is Lord Cobham, my lord, who was at some time Sir John Oldcastle. He is known to be a man whom you held in some regard. Before he is arrested we would know your will.'

'Oldcastle!' cried the King. A slow smile touched his lips. You old rogue, he thought. What are you up to now? 'So he has become a reformer, eh?' Henry was thoughtful for a while. He was not entirely surprised. Old John had loved to discuss, and at times he had leaned towards, those views which were held by the Lollards. It was difficult to imagine him completely serious. He would never give up his lazy lecherous life for a cause surely.

'It appears to be since his marriage to Lady Cobham my lord.'

The King nodded. 'She is an heiress, is she not?'

'The granddaughter of old Lord Cobham who died some years ago. She now owns Cobham Manor and Cowling Castle.'

'What sort of a woman is she?'

'She is about thirty. Oldcastle is her fourth husband.'

'A much married lady. One of firm opinions I imagine, and of course by his marriage to her John Oldcastle acquires the title. He will like that.'

'There is much Lollardry in the district in which he and his wife now live. It has increased of late. I have heard that the reason is that Lord Cobham is a forceful leader and knows how to recruit men to his cause.'

'He would do that,' agreed Henry. 'I never knew a man more persuasive in his arguments.'

'It is proposed that he be arrested and questioned.'

Henry nodded. 'I will talk to him,' he said. 'I will

show him what a dangerous position he places himself in. It is true he was a friend of mine. It would please me to advise him.'

The Archbishop nodded and when he had retired the King sent to Cobham Manor with a command that his old friend visit him without delay.

They faced each other—those two who had been the roystering companions intent on savouring adventures, outdoing each other in their recklessness, boastfully declaring that they would stop at nothing—however offensive to conventional society.

There is a change in him, thought the King. He is as rotund as ever; he still has the merry twinkle in his eyes; but there is a new seriousness, a purpose; one might even say fanaticism.

'Well John,' said Henry, 'you may have guessed why I have sent for you.'

'It is because you have missed my merry company and wish to make use of it again.'

'Of a truth I have missed it but there is little time in my life now for such merriment as that which you and I indulged in. You have become over serious, John.'

'My lord, you have become a King and I detect something of a change in you.'

'I have to speak to you seriously.'

'You have been in conference with my lord Archbishop I'll swear.'

'Then you know of this grievance against you.'

'I'll warrant that my lord Archbishop knowing of a certain fondness between you and me will have your permission first before he proceeds to clap me into the Tower.'

'John, you have to stop this nonsense.'

'Nonsense! My lord, you have failed to understand. As well might I ask you to give up your crown.'

'Now it is you who talk nonsense. You have not only joined the Lollards but have become their leader and because you are yourself . . . with a strength of persuasion which I know is powerful . . . and because you have now married Lady Cobham and make use of her wealth and her title you have provided a rallying point.

You are in danger, old man. As one who has been your friend, I am warning you.'

'Your words fall on stony ground, my dear lord.'

'Then I intend to cultivate that ground and make it fertile. John, you must listen to me.'

'I had hoped to make *you* listen to me.'

'Come, would you turn me into a Lollard?'

'We do not stand against the King, my lord. We have our eyes on the Church.'

'What could a band of rebels . . . peasants for the most part . . . do against the Church?'

'We want to reform it. You must agree that Christ and his apostles did not wrap themselves in fine garments. They did not live in palaces. They went about humbly and in poverty to do good. A Church which holds landed possessions, collects tithes and takes money from peasants who are starving and can ill afford to pay for burials and baptizing cannot be doing the work Christ intended on this Earth.'

'I have no doubt that your intentions are good, John. We have the Church and we have always had the Church. I cannot have my Archbishop roaming the countryside and sleeping under hedges when he cannot beg a bed, living on the scraps thrown to him by some farmer's wife. Let us be reasonable, John. I fear for you. They will arrest you. They will question you. God's ears, old man, can you not see what fate could be in store for you? Have you forgotten William Sawtre?'

'I have not forgotten him. Nor will many. He was the first man to be burned to death for his religious opinions. Acts like that do not deter. They strengthen purpose.'

'They should be a lesson to you.'

'They are indeed, my lord, a lesson that a man's soul is his dearest possession and that cannot be destroyed by fire.'

'I had rather see my former lewd companion than this earnest reformer.'

'Then you do wrong,' answered Oldcastle seriously. 'I rejoice to see a King where once was a reckless boy. Do you remember, Hal—forgive the familiarity but my mind goes back to the days when we were boon companions, for I speak of those days. Dost remember a humble tailor of the diocese of Worcester? His name was John Badby?'

The King turned away shaking his head impatiently, but he did so to hide the fact that he was moved. Yes, he did remember John Badby. He had thought of him often during the months that had followed that day. He had smelt the acrid smell, heard the groans of agony. It was something he preferred to forget.

But John Oldcastle was not going to let him forget.

'They took him . . . a humble tailor,' went on John. 'Why choose such a man as an example? By God's teeth, he was a brave fellow. What was his crime? It was the denial of transubstantiation. What did he say: "If every consecration of the altar be the body of the Lord then there must be twenty thousand gods in England." He said he believed in only one God in England. They tried him in St Paul's. They showed him the sacrament and asked him what it was. He said it was hallowed bread but not God's body. And for that they took him out to Smithfield. You have forgotten this man, my lord. Who should remember a humble tailor? But if that humble tailor becomes a saint . . .'

'This foolish man's martyrdom is beside the point.'

'Oh no. No. It is very much to the point. And I never forget your part in it, my noble King. You cannot forget that you came riding by and I was with you; and you saw this man tied to the stake. They were lighting the faggots at his feet. And you stopped to watch. I sensed in you, my lord, a melancholy that a man should be persecuted for his religious beliefs. You were always one to flout convention, were you not? Those visits to the tavern were partly because you wanted to go, partly because eyebrows would be raised and people would say: "The Prince is wild. He is a reckless profligate." That made you laugh, snap your fingers at the old greybeards. But you stopped by Badby's stake and you paused to think. The flames licked his legs and the pain was intense. He cried out "Mercy". And you, my lord, what said you? "Remove the fire," you said. "Give him a chance to repent." So the fire was removed and you and the tailor looked into each other's eyes. "Swear that you were wrong," you said. "Declare that you were misled. Do that and you shall go in peace." But, my lord, Badby did not ask for mercy from mankind but from God; he called out not that the fire should be removed but that God would take him speedily into Heaven. He would not renounce his beliefs, so he was thrown back into the fire. His end, pray God, came quickly. That was Badby and methinks a man who continued to plague your thoughts for many a month to come.'

'I remember it. He was a brave man.'

'He died for his beliefs. There are many of us in this land, lord King, who would do the same.'

The King burst into laughter. 'Not you, old fellow,' he said. 'Not you. You're more likely to die from the tremors of Venus or the fumes of strong drink.'

'It is a strange and wondrous thing, my lord, that as you have changed, so have I. Does that not show in some mysterious way, that you and I walk close together.'

'You'll forget your Lollards, John?'

'Will you forget your crown?'

'Never.'

'Then why should I forget?'

'Because yours, you old buffoon, could be a martyr's crown if you persist in your follies.'

'Then I would no more cast that aside than you would your crown of gold.'

'Listen to me, John, I speak in all seriousness now. Give up these follies. Go back to your Cobham Manor. You have a new wife. Do your duty by her.'

'Rest assured, lord King, that I will do what I believe to be my duty.'

Henry realized with dismay that it was no use trying to persuade his friend to act with discretion. John Oldcastle seemed as determined now to snap his fingers at danger as he had ever been.

To his sorrow within a few weeks he heard that Lord Cobham had been arrested and sent to the Tower.

The King called on his stepmother at Windsor. To show his friendship for her on his father's death he had given her licence to live at his royal castles of Windsor, Wallingford, Berkhamsted and Hertford and Joanna had been pleased to accept this invitation, for she was eager to live on good terms with the new young King.

She was reconciled to the death of her husband. None could have wished him to live and suffer such a loathsome disease which had clearly grown worse as the months passed. It was heart-breaking to consider him as he had been when they had first fallen in love with each other; and it seemed like a cruel trick of fate that she should have been married to an old man and then when she was able to make her own choice it should have fallen on one who was quickly to develop into an invalid.

She believed that what happened had been too much for Henry. He had been haunted throughout his life by the ghost of Richard. She was sure that had he come to the throne through rightful inheritance everything would have been quite different.

Now, because she had been here so long and it had become home to her, she wished to stay in England. There would be a home for her in Brittany where her son was the reigning Duke but she feared her welcome there might be a cool one. Moreover she had rich estates in England; she had always enjoyed accumulating wealth and as the wife of King Henry the Fourth she had found opportunities of doing this. But she wished to stay; and therefore she must remain on the best of terms with her stepson.

She welcomed him into her apartments.

He had come, he said, to assure himself that she was comfortably settled; but it was more than that, she knew. He wanted her to do something for him; and she must of course, if it were possible.

It was not long before he came to the point.

'My great-grandfather Edward the Third was convinced that the crown of France rightly belonged to him. I share that view.'

She waited.

'Moreover,' he went on, 'I intend to win it.'

She said quietly: 'You will resume the war with France?'

'I shall win my crown.' He spoke with quiet determination. She remembered that his father had said that his eldest son thought like a soldier and acted like a soldier; and that when he came to the throne war would be his chief preoccupation like his ancestor whom men had called Richard the Lionheart.

She said: 'Your great-grandfather won many victories as did his son, the Black Prince, but they never won the crown of France for England.'

'They did not continue long enough. Edward grew old and tired of the war. The Black Prince died in the prime of his youth. I would never give up. I would go in and win and that is what I intend to do.'

'Can you . . . raise the men . . . the money.'

'With God's help, I can and will.'

Joanna felt uneasy. She hoped he was not going to ask her to help him. She loved her possessions. Her chief joy now was adding to them, counting them, gloating over them. She would not want to see that wealth which she had taken such pleasure in garnering dissipated in war.

'You are planning . . .' she began.

'I was even before my father died,' he replied. 'I want to succeed, my lady, where others have failed. And make no mistake, I shall do so. I shall have the French on their knees, I promise you. Their King is mad. The Dauphin is not as fine a fellow as he believes himself to be. Indeed, my lady, I am planning. And indeed I shall take war into France. Now I want you to help me. I trust you are willing to do that.'

'If I could it would be my pleasure, but I am a weak woman . . .'

Joanna was silent. Her son, the Duke of Brittany, was married to the daughter of the King of France, and there would naturally be a strong influence there in favour of France. She felt uneasy.

'Your eldest son must be persuaded that my quarrel is just,' said Henry. 'I doubt not he will listen to his mother. Your son Arthur naturally owes his allegiance to me.'

That was true. She had prevailed on her husband to bestow the title of Earl of Richmond on Arthur and this he had done. It would be Arthur's duty to range himself on the side of Henry. It was the eldest for whom she feared.

'It is a pity your son was married into France,' he said.

She nodded. The marriage was arranged when she had come to England and for the reason that the King of

France had wanted to make sure of the allegiance of Brittany.

'Arthur of course will be your man,' she said. 'The Duke . . . well, that is another matter.'

Henry realized that it would be difficult for the Duke to fight against his father-in-law. On the other hand his mother was the Queen of England.

'I shall rely on your powers of persuasion,' he said.

Joanna promised to do her best and they parted amicably.

But after he had gone Joanna gave way to the gloomy mood which his coming had brought. Wars, she thought. Is it going to start again? How foolish it is. He will never gain the throne of France. It will mean bloodshed, loss of treasure and rifts between the families. She could not believe that her eldest son would ever fight on the side of the English against France.

Henry rode away thoughtful also. He must have Brittany with him, and surely the fact that the mother of the Duke was his stepmother must carry some weight. Joanna was a clever woman. She would know how to persuade. And it was to her interests, too. Look what she had done since she had been in England. She had always been well treated, even though the people did not like her. She was very comfortable in England; he had heard it said that she was a very wealthy woman—in fact one of the most wealthy in England. Like his father, she had never been over extravagant.

He was going to need money to finance his war.

He would think about that later.

When he arrived back in Westminster it was to learn that Lord Cobham had escaped from the Tower.

Christmas had come and the Court was at Eltham. Henry was fond of Eltham, and came to it often to escape the activity which there always seemed to be at Westminster. It was a secure fortress surrounded by a moat and a thick greystone external wall.

There were revelries at Christmas but his thoughts were mainly of the campaign he planned to take into France. He knew that those about him marvelled at the change which had come over him. Not long ago he would have been in the thick of the revels, drinking,

singing and watching the women, wondering which one
he would select for his night companion.

A crown had changed that. He had to think of marriage.
He was twenty-six, not exactly a boy. Few kings remained bachelors so long. There had been many marriages suggested for him but after the manner of so many
of such negotiations they had come to nothing. He must
think seriously now of taking a wife.

Strangely enough he often thought of little Isabella of
Valois, Richard's widow. He had been obsessed by that
child. He had never seen anyone to equal her for beauty—
but perhaps her image had grown more beauteous as
time passed as was often the case. She had died, poor
child, after they married her to Orléans. What a fascinating little creature she had been with her fierce loyalty
towards ineffectual Richard who had never been her
husband in more than name.

Well, there must be an end to these prevarications. A
wife . . . but first the crown of France.

He sat at the high table in the great banqueting hall,
above him the high-pitched roof with its hammer beams,
carved pendants and braces held on corbels of hewn
stone. Up in the minstrels' gallery the musicians were
playing their tunes. A great fire burned in the centre of
the room. Soon the mummers would arrive and enchant
the company with their performance.

It was just like so many Christmases he remembered.
The cooks had excelled themselves with the great joints
of savoury meats and pies and fish garnished with fennel,
mint and parsley—conger, ling, hake, mackerel, flounders,
soles and dories. It mattered not the season as the cooks
could salt anything to preserve it that they might serve it
any time they wished to do so. Cooks vied with each
other and the royal cooks must make each banquet
better than the last. Capons, fowls, swans, peacock,
bitterns adorned the tables, to the delight of those who
enjoyed strong-flavoured birds.

There was no lack of food and most of them thought
Henry would be rendered almost incapable of staggering
to bed so heartily would they partake of all the delicacies and so freely would they refresh themselves with
the wines, beer and the mead produced by the good
cellarers of Eltham.

The banquet was over, the minstrels were playing; the mummers had arrived and repleted with rich food and strong drink the guests roused themselves from the soporific state to watch and applaud.

The dancing had begun and as the King was wondering which of the ladies to select he felt a tug on his sleeve.

He turned sharply. One of the mummers wearing the head of a goat was standing at his elbow.

'My lord,' said the goat-headed mummer in a whisper, and there was an urgency in his tone.

'What means this?' said the King but he kept his voice low.

'Leave at once for Westminster, my lord. There is a plot to seize you and your brothers this night. To kill you and set up a new rule.'

'Is this a joke? By God, I like not such jokes . . .'

'My lord, my lord. I have been sent to tell you. The Lollards are planning to destroy you. They intend to do what they tried to do in King Richard's day.'

'Who has sent you to me?'

'One whom you know well. A friend who loves you and who does not wish harm to befall you.'

He knew at once. This was John's doing. Was it a joke? The kind of joke they had enjoyed playing on each other. No, John had grown serious, even as he had. And there was one thing he knew and that was that the Lollards were a force and one to be reckoned with.

'They plan to strike in the early morning, my lord. Retire to your chambers now. Let them believe that you are weary of the revels and have State matters to attend to. Summon your brothers . . . and then my lord . . . fly with them for your life.'

Henry hesitated.

Could this be true? He had an instinct for such matters and he believed it could be. He was no longer the reckless youth courting danger. He had a country to govern, a war to win.

He said: 'Methinks you come from my old friend and comrade John Oldcastle. Is that so?'

'I have sworn not to betray the source of my coming, my lord.'

'I could make you talk.'

'There is little time, my lord.'

'I'll trust you then. Go from me now. People watch. They think we are exchanging badinage.'

The mummer slipped away. Henry yawned. He said: 'Continue to revel. I will retire.' He signed to his brothers. 'Come with me to my chambers. I have matters of which I must speak to you.'

They left the great hall and when they had gone the guests again whispered together of the change in the King. In the old days he would have been in the thick of the revels; he would have been watching some of the women and testing them out as to which pleased him. Now it was retirement to talk State matters with his brothers.

They would have been surprised had they watched the scene which was taking place with Henry and his brothers.

'Prepare to leave at once,' he said. 'We are going with all speed to Westminster.'

The warning had been timely.

When the King arrived at Westminster early the following morning he was greeted with the news that something unusual was going on in the streets of London. All during the previous day those streets had been crowded, but not with Londoners. It seemed that men from all over the country were gathering there.

'Send one or two men out to discover what they do there,' was his order. 'Do not put them under guards for questioning. But mingle with them. Drink with them in the taverns and make discreet enquiries.'

This was done and it was not long before the same information was gleaned from several sources.

They had been drawn into London from the countryside with promise of great rewards. Who had made these promises? It was Lord Cobham who was behind it. He was a very rich lord and he was going to reform the Church and make living easy for the poor.

Has it come to this, John? thought Henry. War between you and me.

'We must arm ourselves,' said the King. 'I see full well that this may be a repetition of what happened in Richard's time. It is the same ragged army but if there are enough of them they could be formidable.'

'My lord,' said the Archbishop Arundel, 'it is this man Oldcastle who calls himself Cobham. He has some notion that he is fighting for the right.'

'He is an old man,' said the King. 'I knew him once. He is one who will espouse a cause and give it all he has to give. I fear this is what he does now.'

'It is a pity he was ever allowed to escape from the Tower.'

Henry nodded. He remembered his pleasure when he heard that John was free.

John, you fool, he thought. Why did you not go back to the country and live in peace? Will you never learn your lesson?

Of course he wouldn't. He was a fighter. He was ready for any adventure—now as then.

Stay out of this John, thought the King. I want no confrontation between us two. I like not that we should be fighting on different sides. Once we undertook all our adventures together. Let us remember that now. Stop this nonsense while there is still time.

There was more news. One of his spies reported that the Lollards were gathering in St Giles's Fields and that they were preparing to march. Their first plan was to destroy the monasteries of Westminster, St Albans and St Paul as well as all the friars' houses in London.

The King was restive. Some action must be taken. He remembered how Richard had saved the day by making promises, promises which had not been kept it was true. But the poor simple peasants had not believed that that would be the outcome. They had trusted the King.

'I will send out a proclamation,' he said, 'that all persons who have preached heretical doctrines and even those who have plotted against my life shall be pardoned.'

His advisers were silent. They questioned the wisdom of this but Henry was firm.

'So they are gathering in St Giles's Fields, are they? Well, I will go to meet them. And I shall take a strong company with me.'

'My lord,' said one, 'the apprentices are gathering in the streets.'

'Then when we pass through the city gates on the way to the Fields, see that the gates are closed and let no one in or out save those known to be our friends.'

'It shall be done, my lord,' was the answer; and so the King with his guards rode out to the Fields of St Giles's.

This was a good move for the apprentices, always eager to join any movement which could mean trouble, were preparing to march, and gathering with them were the beggars and criminals ever eager to loot and pillage other people's goods and houses. Many of the countrymen who had come to London to answer the call of Lord Cobham mistook the King's camp for that of their friends and were immediately captured. The result was chaos and the rebelling army quickly realized that they could not hope for success against the King's disciplined soldiers.

They took the only action possible. They fled.

The King returned to London. He had quelled the revolt with greater ease than Richard had dispersed the band of peasants who came against him. This was not, of course, on the same scale; but such risings could be dangerous.

He eagerly awaited news of the prisoners who had been taken. There were many of them.

'Is Lord Cobham among them?' he asked.

'No, my lord. It would seem that he got away . . . if indeed he were there. He is the one we want, my lord. He might attempt again what he has failed to do this time.'

'He is a slippery fellow, this Oldcastle.'

'We should bring him to the Tower and this time make sure he gets his deserts.'

'We should,' agreed the King, 'but I doubt he will be easy to hold. He escaped before.'

'His fate will be quickly decided this time. He is a heretic as well as a traitor to you, my lord.'

The King half closed his eyes. There were so many memories of John. How had they come to this? They should have been friends for life.

'Yes,' said Henry firmly, 'his fate will be decided quickly.'

And what would it be? The axe, the rope? The heretic's death?

Henry could not shut out of his mind the thought of John Badby. The hideous smell of scorching flesh.

Oh John, you fool, he thought.

When he heard that Lord Cobham had escaped from the Fields (if he had been there) and had gone into hiding he was filled with relief.

Stay in hiding, you old idiot, he thought. And for the love of God, come to your senses!

AGINCOURT

Henry burned with ambition. All the energies which had gone into his night adventures were now concentrated on one aim. That was to win the crown of France.

He called together his council and told them that negotiations with the French must begin without delay. He laid claim to the crown of France. It was without doubt his. They might maintain the Salic law in France but England took no account of it; and through Isabella of France the mother of his great-grandfather Edward the Third the crown must come to him.

His brothers the Dukes of Gloucester and Bedford stood firmly beside him; so did his uncle the Duke of Exeter and his cousin the Duke of York.

The leading nobles were assembled too with the Archbishop of Canterbury.

Poor old Arundel, he looked as though he was not long for this world. He had lived through many hazards, had suffered exile and seen his brother the Earl executed as traitor to King Richard. A long life during which the King believed the Archbishop had tried to live by his principles. He loved extravagance of course; and he whole-heartedly supported the pomp and grandeur of the Church and was therefore naturally an arch enemy of the Lollards.

And now here he was to give his assurance that Henry's claim to the throne of France was no false one.

'We have already made our feelings on that matter clear to the French,' said Henry.

'And, my lord,' his uncle Exeter reminded him, 'they laugh at us.'

'Let them laugh while they may. I promise you all that we shall be the ones who are laughing when the crown is set upon my head.'

'There will be many a battle before that happy day,' pointed out his uncle.

Henry laid his hand on his shoulder. 'You think this the dream of a wild youth,' he said. 'I know your mind, Uncle. But think, my great-grandfather had this dream too and he was not a wild youth. He was a warrior before whom all men bent the knee.'

'It is said, my lord, that he was urged into the endeavour by a rash vow he took on a heron.'

'But heron or no heron, he made every effort to seize the crown of France.'

'And did not succeed, my lord.'

'He had ill luck. He grew old and his great son, the Black Prince, was stricken by ill health. I am young. I shall not cease until I have succeeded.'

'Charles the Sixth will never willingly give up his crown.'

'Well, that is something we understand. Poor mad old man. He is beset on all sides. Burgundy would be with us.'

'It is not likely that a King of France will give up his crown without a struggle. Moreover there is the Dauphin.'

The King snapped his fingers. 'Louis is a braggart and a very pretty one, I believe. He will make sure his linen is well scented before he goes into battle. He would be wise to accept our latest terms: Charles to remain in nominal possession of the throne until his death. That is very fair, very reasonable. England to be no longer the vassal of France for the provinces of Normandy, Maine, Anjou and Aquitaine. The ransom for King John who was captured by the Black Prince and kept prisoner here in London for a while has never been paid. Is it asking much that this should now be honoured? The King of France shall give his youngest daughter Katherine to be my Queen and she shall bring with her a dowry of two million crowns.'

'They will never agree to those terms,' said Exeter.

'But they fear us,' insisted the King. 'Yes, they fear us. It is the crown I want and by God's help I will attain it . . .'

The purpose of this meeting was to receive the French ambassadors and these were brought in that Henry might tell them his will before all assembled.

He spoke clearly and witheringly: 'I little esteem your French money,' he said, 'and less so your power and strength. I know full well my rights to the crown which has been usurped. The usurper, your master, may have loving subjects who will rally to his cause. I thank God I am not unstored with the same. And I tell you this, before a year has passed I shall make the highest crown of your country stoop before me and the proudest mitre to have his humiliation. In the meantime tell this to the usurper your master, that within three months I shall enter France as into mine own true and lawful patrimony, acquiring the same not with bray of words but with deeds of men and dint of sword by the aid of God in whom I put my trust and confidence. You may depart safely to your own country where I trust sooner to visit you than you shall have cause to bid me welcome.'

The Frenchmen looked astounded by this speech; but they bowed and took their leave.

When they had gone all eyes were on the King.

'Bold words, my lord,' said Bedford.

'Bold deeds should be preceded by bold words, brother. You will see that I meant every one of them. We shall now make our preparations.'

'Charles will be shivering in his shoes,' said Exeter. 'I wonder what the Dauphin will have to say.'

The Dauphin's reply came within a few weeks.

The King was in his ante-chamber with his brothers and counsellors when the ambassadors from France arrived. They brought with them a barrel which was carried in and placed at the King's feet.

'What is this?' asked the King.

'The Dauphin's gift to you, my lord.'

The King laughed. Did the foolish fop think he could placate the King of England with gifts!

'He has sent these treasures to you, my lord, with the assurance that they will please you mightily. He knows your nature and he applied this knowledge when selecting a treasure which would be considered most suited to your taste.'

'We should not be affected by it were it ever so much to our liking,' said the King. 'But let us see what my lord Dauphin knows of my tastes.'

He was smiling when the barrel was opened. There was a gasp of astonishment when the King put in his hand and brought out a tennis ball.

'God's truth,' he cried. 'The barrel is full of them.'

The ambassadors lowered their heads to hide their smiles.

'Our master believed these would please you, my lord,' said one. 'His message is that he is sure you will use them with more skill than you could bring to sword and lance.'

Henry was silent for a few moments. His face was a deeper shade of pink than usual.

Then he said in a loud clear voice: 'Go tell your master that when I have set my rackets against these balls I shall drive them so hard that they will batter open the gates of Paris.'

'So be it,' cried those standing by; and the ambassadors retired discomfited.

'My lord Dauphin has spoken,' said the King. 'Now we shall lose no more time. Let us prepare to carry the war into France.'

Henry threw himself fervently into making ready to leave. The people were with him. He was popular. He was young; he was handsome; he had shown in his youth that he was no saint; he was a man of the people.

'We'll go with Harry,' they said.

The rich men of the country rallied round. They brought him gifts which could be converted into money; the poor could only bring themselves which they did to join his army. They were all excited by the expedition into France. They had no doubt of its success and they talked of the spoils that would come their way. France was a rich country. It was not like making war on Wales or Scotland or Ireland. There would be rich profits for those who went foraging with Harry of England.

All the greatest nobles in the land pledged themselves to serve with their followers for a year. Henry announced that for their services they would be paid, for a Duke thirteen shillings and fourpence a day; for an Earl six shillings and eightpence; for a baron or baronet three shillings and fourpence, a knight two shillings, an esquire one shilling, and an archer sixpence. Any prisoners taken were to belong to their captors and to them would go the ransom demanded when it was paid. There were clearly pickings to be had.

With the expedition the King was taking his physician, Nicholas Colnet, and his surgeon, Thomas Morstede, and they were to be paid twelve pence a day and be given a guard of three archers.

The army was growing in strength; there were six thousand men at arms and twenty-four thousand archers.

During these preparations Thomas Arundel, Archbishop of Canterbury, had a stroke. He was unable to speak. It was said of him that this was God's punishment for having tied up the word of God in the mouths of preachers.

'Poor old man,' said Henry. 'He will not be sorry to go.'

But he had no time to grieve for his Archbishop. His thoughts were with his army. Henry Chicheley was appointed in Arundel's place and Henry was pleased with his new Archbishop for he was a man who gave wholehearted support to the prosecution of the war.

Henry, determined to make sure that no important detail should be missed, himself proceeded to Southampton to watch the loading of stores.

The expedition was ready to leave within a few days when a plot was revealed to him. It was the intention of the plotters to take over the country while he was away and set up in his place the Earl of March—whom many people believed to be the true heir to the throne.

One of the servants of Richard Earl of Cambridge was discovered with letters from his master to Lord Henry Scrope of Mersham.

When the King read these letters he was filled not

only with rage but with horror because Henry Scrope
had been one of his closest companions since his acces-
sion to the throne. He had trusted him with missions
abroad; only recently he had travelled with Henry
Chicheley before the latter had become Archbishop, on
a very confidential mission to the Duke of Burgundy.

'Whom can one trust!' cried Henry. And to discover
such duplicity just as he was about to set out for France
was unnerving. Who will betray me next? he wondered.
Is it safe to leave my kingdom when those I believed to
be my truest friends are in truth my enemies?

This was the shadow which had pursued his father.
Always he had feared that someone would try to set up
the Earl of March in his place or discover that Richard
still lived. He himself would refuse to be haunted by
such fears. He would soon add the crown of France to
that of England and no one was going to deny his rights.

He could see how Scrope had been drawn into this—
Scrope and Cambridge! Scrope had married Cambridge's
stepmother as his second wife; and Cambridge was married to the sister of the Earl of March. Cambridge,
himself royal being the second son of Edmund Langley
who was a son of Edward the Third, would reckon his
son to be in line for the throne. These marriages . . .
these royal lines . . . they gave people ideas!

Prompt action was needed to deal with the matter.
Conspiracies were always dangerous but one could not
have come at a worse time than this.

He sent for Scrope. Good honest Scrope; so he had
thought—and all the time a traitor to him!

'Ah, Henry,' he said. 'I am glad you came so promptly.'

'My lord, I am always at your service.'

'Except,' replied the King, 'when you serve my
enemies.'

He was watching his one-time friend closely, hoping
to detect in his face a sign of innocence.

But Scrope had flushed scarlet and Henry saw the
fear leap into his eyes.

'Charming letters your friend Cambridge writes to you,'
said Henry.

'I understand you not, my lord.'

'Enough, traitor. I have read the correspondence between you two. So you would put March on the throne,

eh? But first you must rid yourselves of me. Who was to be the assassin? You, mayhap. You have gained yourself easy access to me with your false protestations of friendship.'

Scrope was silent.

'Tell me the truth,' thundered the King, 'for by God's own truth I swear I will have it from you.'

'There is a conspiracy, my lord.'

'That is already clear to me. And you are involved in it.'

'For the purpose of discovering when the conspirators meant to strike.'

'Oh come, Scrope, you will have to do better than that. My kinsman Cambridge, eh? He wants his wife's brother on the throne. And if he should die, well then Anne of Cambridge has a son who could well take the crown, is that it? Is Cambridge's plan to set up March and then have another little conspiracy; remove March and set up Cambridge's boy in his place?'

'My lord, the plan was to make the Earl of March the King. Though there are some who say that Richard still lives.'

'Not that old story again!'

'Few believe it.' Scrope seemed anxious to talk as though by so doing he could convince the King that he had joined the conspiracy only to betray it in due course.

Henry listened with scornful lips and a sadness in his heart. It hurt him to see Scrope flounder, betraying his fellow traitors in an attempt to save himself.

He called to his guards and cried: 'Take him away. Keep him your prisoner. If he escapes you will answer to me.'

Scrope was dragged away still protesting his innocence.

His brothers came to him for they had heard that Scrope was arrested. He told them what he had discovered. They were horrified.

'I shall act promptly,' said Henry. 'This is no time for delay. They shall have a trial today and if they are found guilty shall be despatched immediately.'

'They should be made an example of. The traitor's death should be accorded them.'

'I want them out of my way,' said the King. 'That will

be enough. God is on our side for had this not been discovered now we could have lost our throne.'

The facts were soon brought to light. The plan was to assert the claims of York against those of Lancaster. Henry was to be assassinated and the the Earl of March set on the throne. A man had appeared in Scotland calling himself Thomas of Trumpyngton who declared he was in fact King Richard who had escaped from Pontefract. It seemed pretty clear that he was a madman who was not the first to be obsessed by this idea but the conspirators promised to test his claim. Anything which would help in the fight to rid the country of Henry would be considered. But the main idea was to put the Earl of March on the throne. They planned to conduct the Earl to the Welsh border, where they could be sure of support, and proclaim him King. The Percys could be relied on to hold the north against Henry.

It was indeed a well laid plot; and, said Henry, there was only one way to act.

He was convinced that his cousin the Earl of March was innocent. He was merely to be used as the figure-head but there was no doubt whatever of the guilt of Cambridge, Scrope and Thomas Grey of Heton.

They were condemned and deprived of their heads without delay.

The conspiracy had been brought to a satisfactory conclusion.

Now for France.

On a hot August day Henry set out for France with six thousand men at arms and twenty-four thousand archers. They travelled in fifteen hundred vessels.

He immediately attacked Harfleur. The town was ill equipped to stand out against him; and the governor in desperation sent messengers to the King of France tell-ing him that unless he sent relief within a month he would have no alternative but to surrender.

No help came and Harfleur, to Henry's jubilation, fell into English hands.

'This is a good beginning,' cried Henry, 'an omen. I shall fortify this town and make it into another Calais. Then we shall have two ports of entrance to France.'

He set about consolidating his position. He wanted

the inhabitants of Harfleur to leave the town to his men and he ordered them to take as much baggage as they could carry after they had sworn on God's name that they would not take part in the war, and surrender themselves to the governor of Calais.

'My lord, do you think they will obey that order?' asked his brother Bedford.

'It matters little if they do not, brother. I wish to be rid of them and populate this town with English men and women.'

It was a resounding initial success, but alas it was soon seen to be less glorious than had at first been believed for an epidemic of dysentery soon appeared among the soldiers and within a matter of days two thousand of them were dead. That was not all, for if he had not taken some action more would have died. He saw that there was only one course to be taken and that was to send back to England those who were growing too weak to be of use.

Thus it seemed that success was turning to disaster for the army was by this time only half the strength it had been when it set out.

'We must return to England,' said Bedford. 'We must raise more men.'

But Henry shook his head. 'Return to England with only the capture of Harfleur to our credit! Nay, good brother, that will not do. The people of England have given me their men and their treasure. I will not return without something more than Harfleur to offer them. They would say I was overtimid and no man shall ever have reason to call me that.'

'Then where next?'

Henry was thoughtful for a while. Then he said: 'I intend to march through Normandy, Picardy and Artois on my way to Calais. This is my fair land of France and it is fitting that I should see more of it.'

'My lord,' cried Bedford aghast. 'We have lost so many men and many of those who remain have been weakened by illness. You will have to leave a garrison in Harfleur. How many will you take on this march?'

'There will be some six thousand.'

'Six thousand, my lord, against the French army!'

'It may be that we shall not meet the French army.'

'They will resent the capture of Harfleur. What if they come against us? And what food shall we be able to commandeer during this march of . . . why it must be some hundred and fifty miles.'

'All you say may well be true, brother, but I shall not return to England without a victory to present to my people and that victory must be as joyful in their eyes as those of Crécy and Poitiers.'

Bedford shook his head. He thought his brother was courting disaster. But there was no gainsaying the orders of the King and the march began.

They went through Fécamp to Argues, Criel, Eu and St Valéry until they reached the Somme. Now the French were on the march.

It was the twenty-fourth of October and the enemy were encamped in the villages of Ruisseauville and Agincourt.

No lodging could be found for Henry and he slept in a hut. In the morning he released the prisoners he had brought with him, exacting a promise from them that if they were caught up in battle they should return and surrender themselves.

'If I am defeated,' he said, 'then you are released. If not, you will return to me.'

He laughed to himself. How many would obey him? He could not say, but he could not afford to have enemies in his camp. Some might have executed them. It was not Henry's way. He prided himself on his justice. He was hard but not deliberately cruel.

Now there could be no putting off the battle. The enemies were face to face and the next day must see the start of hostilities.

There was great confidence in the French camp because they so greatly outnumbered the English. The French knew what had happened at Harfleur. The English had won that victory but at what cost. Their army, so the French understood, was decimated by dysentery.

It rained heavily during that long night and as they listened to it rattling on their tents the French were confidently gambling on how many prisoners they would take in the battle and boasting that they would go for those who would bring in the highest ransoms. They were certain of victory. It was not possible, they reasoned, for such a decimated band of men, exhausted by a long march and sickness, to stand up against them. Harry of England was a braggart who boasted of his claim to the throne of France. It would be their pleasure on the following day to teach him a lesson.

Henry, strangely enough, was filled with a quiet confidence. He forbade any to speak of the smallness of his army. The men must not be reminded of it, he told his generals. He must imbue them with this sense of certain victory which he himself felt.

In the quiet of the night he walked about the camp. He talked with his men, without proclaiming his identity. But they knew him; and with the rain glistening on his face and soaking his cloak they were aware of some divine power within him and they forgot their fears and knew—as well as he did—that he could not fail.

The King heard mass at dawn. Then he was dressed in his cote d'armes on which were the arms of both France and England. On his basinet he wore his crown that all might know who he was when he led his men in battle. He mounted his small grey horse and summoned his men from their quarters and when they were drawn up he addressed them. He told them that their cause was just, that they would succeed with God's help and God would not deny that help to those whose cause was right. They were going to show the French that no army in the world could stand up against English bowmen. They were going in to win. This spot was called Agincourt and in years to come its name should be celebrated, because it was one which should stand beside that of Crécy and Poitiers.

Such was his conviction and so did he glow with this shining confidence which seemed imbued with a touch of divinity that his men believed him. They ceased to think of the opposing number of Frenchmen who must be fresher and doubtless better equipped than they were. They only knew that they would follow Harry of England to victory.

Henry himself led the main host of the army; the Duke of York was in the vanguard and the rear was commanded by Lord Camoys. Each of the archers carried a billhook, a hatchet and a hammer and a stake sharp at both ends in order to defend himself against a cavalry charge.

The French stood firm as the English advanced, and from the archers came a shower of arrows which wrought fearful havoc among the French forces. The French cavalry attempted to attack but they could not stand up against the streams of arrows and it was brought home to them that the reputation of the invincibility of English archers was well founded. The horses were unable to advance because as they approached the English held the pointed stakes before them and the French horses, maddened by the wounds they had received from the arrows, ran amok and it was quite impossible for their riders to control them.

The battle raged for three hours. A wild fury had seized the English. The manner in which the archers had repulsed the cavalry even after they had shot all their arrows seemed a miracle. They were certain that God was on their side and they knew that with His help they could not fail.

It was victory for the English archers. As at Crécy and Poitiers they were invincible.

The French losses were enormous, those of the English minimal. This resounding and miraculous success was due to the archers, but it owed a great deal to the military genius of the King.

He it was who had chosen that the battle should be fought on that spot where the French could not use all their forces but were obliged to attack in one space which considerably reduced the advantage of numbers.

So the field was won, and men were saying that never had there been a battle so glorious, never one won against such desperate odds.

The French were defeated, the English gloriously victorious and the name of Harry of England would live for ever as the greatest warrior of them all.

Coeur de Lion, two great Edwards, the Black Prince himself—Henry towered above them.

So it was back to Calais and across to England.

There his loyal subjects awaited their hero. All over the country there was rejoicing. Bonfires were lighted. Pageants were enacted; and when the King arrived in his capital city he was going to be given such a welcome as no king had ever enjoyed before.

Profligate Prince Hal had become great Harry of England.

DEATH AT LOLLARDS' GALLOWS

There was one, however, who could not rejoice whole-heartedly in the great victory, for she greatly feared what the consequences might be.

Ever since Henry had visited Joanna and implied that he expected her to influence her son to fight for the English, she had been very uneasy.

Until this time she had been content with her life in England. At first she had been very happy with Henry but when that fearful disease had grown worse and he had been so horribly disfigured her feelings towards him had begun to change. When he had died it had been a kind of release and had enabled her to settle down to a new life.

She had taken up her quarters at Havering and there had started to enjoy a life of peaceful seclusion. She had amassed great wealth and her thrifty nature, which had fitted in well with that of her husband, had delighted in the growth of her possessions. She wanted nothing changed; she was content enough to live in the shadows. The last thing she wanted was to be drawn away from her quiet luxurious life to join in any controversy and especially one with her stepson, the King.

And now Agincourt! An unprecedented and unexpected victory for Henry.

She knew that her eldest son, the Duke of Brittany, had remained uncomfortably neutral. It was the only action he could have taken, for since his wife was the daughter of the King of France his allegiance must lie with that King. It was different with Arthur. He had been created Earl of Richmond by Joanna's husband and owed his allegiance to England.

Yet he had fought with France.

That would have been a wise action . . . if the French had won; and everyone had expected the French to win.

So at Havering Joanna waited in trepidation for the outcome. That Henry's attitude towards her would change, she felt certain. He would blame her for not using enough force in persuading her sons. But what could she do? It was years since she had seen them and even if she had, she would never have been able to influence them to that extent. To have supported the English would have seemed to them like suicide.

It was all very well to be wise after the event.

She was in a state of great nervousness and she sent for two men whom she kept in her household to advise her and predict the future. Petronel Brocart had come to England with her and she had found Roger Colles in Salisbury. She regarded them as her two wise men; they foretold the future and read the stars and before taking any action she always consulted them.

The household was considerably in awe of them; they lived in complete comfort for there was no one who would dare offend them for fear of bringing down their wrath and being illwished.

She sent for them and told them that she wanted to consult them; she was fearful of the future, she told them. They had not foreseen the outcome of the battle of Agincourt.

Petronel Brocart replied that he had foreseen it but had not trusted what he saw and put it down to being a dream and not true foresight. The odds were so overwhelmingly against the English that it could only have been a last minute miracle, decided on in one moment by the powers either of good or evil—it remained to be seen which.

Joanna accepted the explanation and told them that she felt herself to be . . . if not in danger, in an uneasy position because of her family in France.

Brocart made sure that he was kept up to date with the latest events which often meant he was able to prophesy a certainty; he kept messengers, whom he paid handsomely, and their duty was to give him the latest information as to what was happening at the Court of Brittany.

Therefore he had news for the Queen; and it was not pleasant news.

'It does not surprise me,' said Brocart, 'that you feel this lack of ease. There is ill news coming to you, my lady.'

Joanna glanced pleadingly from Colles to Brocart.

'Pray tell me the worst. My son . . .'

'The Duke is well,' replied Colles. 'He did not take part in the fighting but wisely remained neutral.'

'Your daughter's husband, the Duc d'Alençon, has been killed,' said Brocart.

Joanna put her hand to her fast beating heart; she could tell from the expression of these two men that there was more to come.

'Your brother Charles of Navarre was wounded in the battle.'

'He has since died of his wounds,' added Colles.

'And my son . . . Arthur?' asked Joanna faintly.

'He is Henry's prisoner.'

'Oh my God, what will become of him?'

'He will remain in England at the King's pleasure, my lady.'

'And shall I see my son?'

'Ere long, my lady.'

'It grieves us to give you such news, dear lady.'

'I know it,' replied Joanna, 'but I must also know the truth. Do not hesitate. Is there anything more I should know?'

'We have told you all, my lady.'

Joanna wanted nothing so much as to shut herself away with her grief.

She had pleaded with the King. He must allow her to see her son. She knew that he had broken the allegiance which as Earl of Richmond he owed to England. But she was his mother and she had not seen him for eleven years when as a boy he had come to England. Perhaps she had been wrong to remind the King of that occasion for it was when he had received the investiture of Earl of Richmond.

The King replied that her son was a traitor. He had been found with England's enemy and had been taken in battle. He could not expect to be received in honour in England; he was a prisoner, a danger to England, and Henry could see no reason why he should be treated otherwise even though his mother had been a Queen of England.

Joanna longed to see him. She greatly feared that he might be sentenced to death. Henry was severe but he was not wantonly cruel. He would understand Arthur's difficulties living as he was in Brittany at his brother's court with his brother's wife the daughter of the King of France. True, he had sworn allegiance to England, but he was young and Henry would not wish to be too harsh. Moreover Joanna was a clever woman; he had always liked her and did not want to inflict undue suffering upon her. It was unthinkable that he should release Arthur of course, but he saw no reason why there might not be a meeting between mother and son.

Arthur was to come, under guard, to Havering after which he would be taken back to the Tower of London. When she heard that he would soon be with her Joanna was overcome by emotion and she sent for her confessor, a Franciscan friar named John Randolf, and asked him to pray with her that she might prepare herself for the meeting.

'I must try not to weep,' she said. 'Oh, it is a sad state of affairs when children are lost to their mothers at an early age.'

'Compose yourself, my lady,' advised John Randolf. 'Prayer will be a solace to you. I would suggest Madam that it is unwise to rely so much on those charlatans, Brocart and Colles. They can bring no good to you.'

'They foresaw that my son would be a prisoner. They warned me in advance.'

'It is dabbling in evil powers, my lady, and will do you no good with God and his saints.'

Joanna was silent. She knew that John Randolf disliked the sorcerers, as they did him. They were suspicious of each other and jealous of the influence every one of them held with her.

But this was no time to consider rivalries.

Arthur was coming and she must be prepared for him, so she knelt with Randolf and together they asked for God's blessing and that the King's heart might be softened towards Arthur.

He was on his way. Soon he would be with her. She was trembling with excitement.

She said to one of her ladies, 'Do sit in my chair so that when he comes in he will think you are his mother. I will watch him for a while before I reveal myself.'

'He will know you for the Queen, my lady, by your very bearing.'

'Nay,' said Joanna, 'we shall do it this way.'

And so she was seated on a footstool at the feet of her lady attendant when her son entered. He was handsome, young, all that she could have wished him to be . . . except that he was a prisoner. The guards were standing at the door to remind her of that sad fact.

He approached her lady-in-waiting and knelt at her feet. Joanna watched sadly.

'My mother,' said Arthur, 'this is a sad meeting. But I rejoice to see you.'

They embraced.

'I will present you to my ladies,' said the substitute Queen, but at that moment Joanna could sustain her rôle no longer.

'My son, my son,' she cried, 'do you not know me?'

Arthur looked in astonishment from the lady-in-waiting to the Queen.

'Yes,' said Joanna, 'I am your mother.'

'I see it now,' cried Arthur.

'I had to wait awhile,' said Joanna. 'My heart was too full.'

They embraced warmly, then looked at each other searchingly. 'You were but a boy when you went away,' said Joanna.

'Oh, Mother, so much has happened since then.'

'I was so proud of you, my Earl of Richmond.'

'Alas, Mother.'

'Henry will treat you well. I would I could keep you here with me.'

'I come as a prisoner, my lady.'

Joanna nodded.

'Come, tell me of home. Tell me of your brother and your sister . . . She has lost her husband.'

'Agincourt was disastrous for us.'

'And such a victory here. They are still having their pageants and their revelries, their thanksgiving services. The bells are ringing all over the country.'

'One King's victory must be another's defeat, Mother.'

'And you were on the wrong side.'

'It seemed so impossible that the English could triumph.'

'Nothing is certain in war,' said Joanna. 'Now we must make the best of what is left to us. It will not be long, I feel sure.'

She was right.

That day Arthur was taken back to his prison in the Tower. The brief reunion was over.

The King kept Christmas at Lambeth.

He was restive. He had won a brilliant victory at Agincourt but all it had brought him was Harfleur. He was no nearer to the crown of France than his predecessors had been.

After Agincourt it would have been the utmost folly to have marched to Paris. Wretched and defeated as it was, what was left of the French army could have stopped him. If the French were in a sad state so were the English. Many of his soldiers were suffering from dysentery. They had fought magnificently but they were in no shape to endure another battle for a while. Good general that he was he had seen there was only one thing he could do and that was return home and get together more men and more stores before he began another campaign.

He could be proud of the achievement. The French had suffered a shattering defeat and they would be demoralized. No more barrels of tennis balls would be sent by the arrogant Dauphin. It was good to contemplate what his feelings must be at this time. It was a glorious moment, there was no doubt about that, but he must not be blinded by his success.

He needed men restored to health; he needed supplies; and raising an army was a costly matter.

But Agincourt had made Englishmen proud again. They had a King whom they could admire. It was like the days of great Edward all over again. The people loved a King who was a great soldier and could bring conquests to the honour of the country and spoils of course to add to its riches.

Celebrations there must be to remind the people what he had brought them; before they were asked to provide money for more conquests they must be allowed to celebrate those which had been won. But the King was impatient. Agincourt had been a revelation. He could almost feel the crown of France on his head.

So at Christmas while he feasted and joked with his friends and danced and watched the mummers, his thoughts were of war. Plans were forming in his mind. He must go on. It would be foolish not to follow up the victory while the French were in such a low state and the English intoxicated by victory.

The new Archbishop Chicheley was growing fanatical about the Lollards and was pursuing them relentlessly. The King often thought of John Oldcastle and wondered where he was hiding himself. How much more satisfactory it would be if he were to come and fight with his King. There were few better soldiers.

If he would come back and fight with me, thought the King, all this Lollardry would be forgotten.

But John did not come. He remained in hiding, no doubt plotting. He was as fixed in his determination to uphold the Lollards as Henry was to gain the crown of France.

Henry must raise money and continue. He was wasting time here.

The people were with him. They wanted more conquests. They were looking forward to prosperity and the end of the war with France and their King firmly established on that throne.

They were living now in the euphoria of great victory. Life seemed more prosperous. It was not, but it seemed so and thought Henry with a certain amount of cynicism, one that was as good as the truth until they woke up to reality. He had ordered that the streets of Holborn be paved. This had never been done before and the Lord Mayor of London, Sir Henry Burton, had brought in improvements to the streets of London by hanging lanthorns which were kept burning throughout the night.

The people were grateful. They loved their King.

But it was the eternal cry of Money. Money to pay the soldiers, money to pay for the arrows and all the weapons of war. Money for the food they would need. Money! Money!

The King rode to Havering to see his stepmother. She greeted him with affection and he talked to her of his plans.

She listened, feigning an enthusiasm which she could not feel. Her family were on the opposing side. It was an irritation between them. How could he boast to her of the glories of Agincourt when that battle had brought disaster for so many members of her family?

The affection he had hitherto felt towards her was tinged with a mild dislike.

She had come to England as his father's second wife and grown rich here. He had heard it said that she was one of the richest women in the country, but like many rich people who had taken delight in garnering their wealth, she was rather loth to part with it.

'My son visited me here,' she said.

'I know,' he answered. 'I gave orders that he should be allowed to do so.'

'Thank you, my lord. It was good of you. Your goodness makes me venture to ask if I might see him again.'

'My lady, he is a prisoner. He is your son but he is also a traitor. We cannot allow traitors to roam freely about our land. That would be folly, you must realize.'

She was silent.

'I intend to carry on the war in France until I have brought it to a satisfactory conclusion,' he went on. 'I should be there now . . . but first I have to build up stores, equipment, pay my soldiers and so much more.'

'War is a costly business in treasure and more tragically in blood,' said Joanna sombrely.

'So we have seen, Madam,' said the King. 'But my

cause is just and I am determined on victory. I need money.'

Her eyes strayed round the chamber. She lived well. She liked luxury. She was indeed a very rich woman.

'I am relying on those who love me and a just cause to come forward with their offerings,' he said.

She nodded.

'I have always looked upon you as a friend.'

'I will ask my treasurer what can be supplied,' she said cautiously; she was already making plans to have the finest of her treasures placed in great chests and hidden in the vaults. 'I have given much to the poor,' she went on. 'I am not as rich as I once was.'

You lie, he thought. My God, the woman is on the side of the French. She is all ready to turn traitor, as her son was.

He took his leave shortly. He was in a resentful mood. She amassed wealth under my father, he thought, and she will not give up to me what I so desperately need.

As he rode away he said to his brother Bedford: 'I do not trust the Queen.'

Bedford replied: 'I was talking to John Randolf her confessor. He says she is in constant private talk with those two sorcerers Colles and Brocart. He does not like them nor their influence with the Queen.'

'Does he think she practises their evil arts?'

'It is strange how she has become so rich.'

The King frowned. 'It might be that there is some sorcery in it,' he replied.

He felt a sudden surge of anger against her. She had won her wealth through dabbling in dark arts then; and she was very reluctant to part with a penny of it.

His thoughts were occupied with how he could raise money.

When he returned to London he had decided to pawn his crown and jewels. His uncle, the Bishop of Winchester, would advance him one hundred thousand marks for them; and he would sell a part of the royal jewels to the City of London for ten thousand pounds.

In the month of July two years after the battle of Agincourt Henry was ready to sail to France again. He left with twenty-six thousand men on board a fleet of one thousand five hundred ships.

He took among other strategic places, Caen and Falaise. But the war was not yet won.

John Oldcastle with his band of faithful followers had for four years been wandering in the Welsh mountains. During the summer they lived out of doors and would sit round a camp fire when darkness fell and talk of the days when they would establish their faith throughout England and bring a better life to many poor people. With the coming of winter there must be an end to this life which had an appeal for all of them; then they must find shelter by night in any inn or wayside cottage where someone would give them a place to lie down. All the day John was trying to recruit men to his banner; but it was amazing how difficult it was to arouse enthusiasm for battle even amongst the Welsh who like the Irish and Scots were usually ready to attack the English.

He heard news of Agincourt and it pleased him to know that Henry had won renown throughout the country.

Great Harry they called him affectionately and there was grudging admiration even from his enemies.

John smiled, recalling the braggart youth sprawling on his tavern chair drinking, eyeing the women, singing tavern songs. Those had been good days; but they could not have gone on for ever. Neither he nor Henry were of a kind to spend all their lives in riotous living, seeking their excitement in tavern brawls.

Somehow he had always known that there was more to both of them than that. Harry had found it in the quest for a crown; as soon as he had taken that alluring object in his hands, he had changed. As for John, he had changed too. His had been a yearning for spiritual matters. How strange that religion should have become the whole meaning of life to him.

He talked to his followers and all who would listen. He had always been an eloquent talker. That was what had attracted Henry to him. Then he had used his quick wits to provoke laughter. It was different now.

All that mattered to him was that he should make men understand what was in his mind. There must be reforms in Church. Men must worship God, not the trappings of ceremony. All the money which was poured into maintaining the splendours of the Church should be used to improve the life of the villeins, he believed. He wanted a simple religion; he wanted spiritual humility and peace for men and a more dignified physical existence.

As poor Sawtre had said, the cross was a piece of wood. Yes, a better piece of wood than others of its kind because Christ had died on it. But it was not to be worshipped as such. Salvation came not through the cross but from Christ who died on it.

He had come to Wales after being surprised in a house in St Albans. He had sought shelter of a villein there who greatly admired him and was ready to risk his life by giving him a bed in his house. His was a personality which could not be hidden. In time people were coming to the villein's house just to hear him talk. So in due course as seemed inevitable he was betrayed and the Abbot of St Albans sent his servants to surround the house; but he had his friends and an hour before the servants came he was riding towards Wales.

It was a lesson and brought home to him the realization of how easily he could be captured.

There in the Welsh Marches among the hills which lay between the Severn and the Vyrnwy he had found his refuge. But he would have to emerge when the spring came. It was not his intention merely to keep hidden from his enemies. He must rally friends to his cause.

He had found the perfect hide-out and decided that he would make this his refuge. It should be the place to which he returned if he were pursued; he believed he would always find shelter there. There was an inn nearby which was owned by ardent supporters, people on whom he could rely. He was safe here to work out his plans. Moel-y-sant offered beauty as well as security; it became known as Cobham's garden.

He had always been reckless; he could not change his entire nature in so short a time. He trusted the innkeeper and his wife and family; he had forgotten that servants came and went and he might not find the same loyalty among them. He had forgotten that there was a possibility that he might be traced to this spot and there might be a plan to capture him.

Lord Charlton, on whose estate John was sheltering, in due course learned that he was there. A reward was offered for the capture of Oldcastle who, because of his connections and eloquence, was considered a great menace not only to the Church but to society; and Charlton thought it could do him no harm—on the contrary much good—if he delivered Oldcastle to his enemies.

He therefore began to plan. He placed one of his servants in the inn which he suspected Oldcastle frequented. The spy soon confirmed the truth of this and one night when John was seated in the inn parlour discoursing to his friends and disciples, there was a shout of 'The inn is surrounded'. And then the armed men of Charlton's retinue burst in.

John stood up dashing his tankard to the floor, but he realized that he was trapped. However he was not going to be taken without a fight, and a battle ensued.

John was big and strong and it was not easy to take him; but while he was struggling with an assailant, one of the serving girls who had become friendly with Charlton's spy picked up a stool and threw it with such force against John that it broke his leg, thus rendering him helpless and he fell to the ground—a prey to his enemies.

It was the end. What could he do, being unable to stand? He was seized in triumph and carried off to Welshpool Castle, the home of Charlton, who was overcome with delight by the capture.

The first thing he did was to send a messenger to the Court. The King was in France and the Regent was his brother the Duke of Bedford.

Charlton received a delighted reply from Bedford. Let Oldcastle be brought at once to London without delay.

The injuries which he had received in the fight, chief of which was his broken leg, made it impossible for him to ride, but Bedford was in no mood to delay. It occurred to him that if the King were to hear of his old friend's predicament he might out of sentimental feeling find some way of pardoning him. If, reasoned Bedford, Oldcastle had not been allowed to escape from the Tower—and sometimes Bedford wondered whether Henry had connived in that facile escape—they would have been spared a great deal of trouble.

No, bring Oldcastle to London. Let him be speedily tried and sentenced to the heretic's death.

'Send him at once,' he ordered. 'Even if he has to travel in a whirlicote.'

So John was placed in a horse-litter and brought to London.

'Let there be no delay,' said Bedford. 'This man should be tried at once.'

John knew that this was the end. There could be no escape now. If he could but see the King, if they could indulge in a discussion such as they had so much enjoyed in the old days, he would have been able, he was sure, to make Henry understand.

But Henry was abroad in France bent on winning his crown. And John was here in London, in the hands of his enemy.

He was immediately brought before his judges and condemned to die the heretic's death.

He held his head high; he faced his judges and cried: 'Though you judge my body which is a wretched thing, yet I am certain and sure that you can do no harm to my soul, no more than Satan could upon the soul of Job. He who created that will, of His infinite mercy and promise, save it. Of this I have no doubt. I will stand by my beliefs to the very death by the grace of my eternal God.'

The very same day he was taken by hurdle to St Giles's Fields to what was now known as the Lollards' Gallows. He saw the fire being laid below the chains in which they would hang him; and he knew then that his last hours had come.

A multitude had gathered to see him die. He had many supporters but none who there in St Giles's would dare to come forward and claim him as a friend. The acrid smell of smoke, the writhing agony of sufferers, set them shuddering. He was a great man, John Oldcastle called Lord Cobham; he was ready to die for his beliefs. But there would be few who would want to share the martyr's crown.

He addressed the spectators as he was being put in chains.

'Good Christian people,' he said, 'beware of these men, for they will beguile you and lead you blindly into hell with themselves. Christ says plainly unto you: "If one blind man leadeth another, they are like both to fall into a ditch." ' He was now hanging horizontally above the flames which were rising to lick his body.

'Lord God Eternal,' he cried, 'I beseech Thee of Thy great mercy's sake to forgive my enemies if it be Thy will.'

There was a hush on the crowd. They heard his cry as the flames reached him.

Then the smoke hid him from view.

A CHARGE OF WITCHCRAFT

Henry was determined to complete the conquest of France and what he needed more than anything was money.

He was obsessed by the thought of attaining the crown and was convinced that it was his by right and he would let nothing stand in the way of attaining it. He was certain that if his great-grandfather Edward the Third had carried on with the fight after Poitiers he would have won it. He had given up too soon; he had become lethargic, obsessed by lust; and the Black Prince, who would have won it, had become ill and died.

He, Henry, was the chosen one.

It was agreed now that he was a great warrior—to rank with William the Conqueror and Richard Coeur de Lion. Such men were all-soldier. They allowed nothing to come between them and their objective. Henry was not cruel for the sake of cruelty but if it was necessary to the outcome of a battle he would kill without mercy. He was a soldier first; everything was subordinated to his cause. He never sought to evade any duty; he should share hardship with his men; he made it clear to them that even though he was their King and leader he was one of them, ready to suffer cold or die with them. He had the power to make them follow him. He was good to them; he was proud of his image; he knew that his men would follow him to the jaws of death if he commanded them to do so.

With such an army and such a leader, he knew he could not fail.

When he heard how Oldcastle had died he was over-come with grief but then he grew angry. John had been a fool. Why had he given up the glorious life of a soldier to campaign for his Lollard views? John, becoming spiritual, a reformer! It was nonsense. He should have been with him at Harfleur and Agincourt.

And now he was dead . . . and had died in such a way. Foolish John!

There was no time to regret the fat old martyr. God rest his soul, said Henry; and was glad that he had been out of England when it had happened.

How could he have passed judgment on the old buffoon? Yet it was a just sentence. John had been a self-confessed heretic and so it was right that he should die the heretic's death.

But it was over now. No looking back. No remem-brance of old tavern days and the tricks they had played. John had gone his way and the King had gone his.

And there was a crown to be won.

Money! Money! He needed money. He had left Bed-ford to govern England. He could trust his brother. Bedford was a fine soldier, loyal too. Almost the man his brother the King was, he had heard it said, but not quite.

No, not quite. But a brother to be grateful for.

'You must find me money,' he had told Bedford.

And Bedford had said: 'Our stepmother is a very rich woman. She does not help as she should.'

'Ah, our stepmother. Her heart is in France.'

'By God,' Bedford had cried. 'Then she would be a traitor to our lord the King. I'll find a means, brother.'

Bedford would find a means. He had rid the country of Oldcastle. It was right of course. The old fellow was a heretic and he had earned the heretic's death.

Yes, Bedford was a good brother. He would look after affairs in England while Henry was winning France.

He could trust Bedford.

* * *

There was something wrong in the Queen's household at Havering Bower. Servants of the Duke of Bedford had arrived the previous day and Joanna had presumed that this meant their master was on the way to see her.

She was always apprehensive now. Arthur was still a prisoner though they had moved him from the Tower to Fotheringay Castle and she hoped he was in less rigorous confinement there. Whenever members of the King's or Regent's household visited her she feared what reason they had for coming.

She knew that the King was in France and she guessed that he would be constantly urging Bedford to find him money. Perhaps she should have offered more to the King when he had come to her. That would not have helped. He would still have wanted more.

Roger Colles and Petronel Brocart had warned her that she should be extra watchful for she was passing into a dangerous period. She did not need to be told that. She was aware of it more every day. The longer this war continued and the more success Henry had in France the more dangerous her position would become.

Colles and Brocart were in constant attendance on her and although their prognostications were becoming more and more gloomy she wanted to hear them. There was dissension between them and John Randolf. There always had been but it seemed to have deepened of late. She had never really liked John Randolf; there was an air of self righteousness about the man which had not appealed to her; she would have dismissed him from his post but for the growing apprehension all round her. This did not seem the time.

She sent for John Randolf.

Her servants returned with the information that he was closeted with the men from the Duke of Bedford and had been so for some hours.

This made her very uneasy.

She sat with her women and they worked together on the tapestry they were making. They were more silent than usual. They were aware that something extraordinary was going on.

'My Lord Bedford will be here this day, I believe,' she said.

'Yes, my lady,' was the answer. 'They are preparing for him in the kitchens.'

'Where is Randolf? I would speak with him.'

'He is talking to the men from London.'

'What! Still talking.'

'Yes, my lady. None knows of what they speak. They have been closeted these last two hours and there are guards outside the door.'

'Of what could they be speaking to Randolf?'

Everyone was silent. They bent their heads over their work. What does it mean? the Queen asked herself apprehensively.

They were startled by a clatter in the courtyard. One of the women dropped her work and ran to the window.

'What do you see?' asked the Queen, still sitting with her needle in her hand.

'Some are leaving.'

'Bedford's men?' asked the Queen with evident relief in her voice.

'No . . . no . . . my lady. It is . . . Yes, it is. Randolf. He and two others are riding out of the courtyard.'

Joanna put down her work and with the others went to the window.

She saw John Randolf riding out of the castle with two men.

'They are taking the road to London,' said one of the women.

Joanna stared. Why? What could it mean?

She was soon to discover.

Later that day the Duke of Bedford arrived. Joanna went down to the courtyard to meet him. He was very like his brother the King and was said to be Henry's most loyal and fervent supporter. He was more highly coloured than Henry, with a prominent arched nose, well marked chin and slightly receding brow. He was a man who would not shirk his duty; and like his brother did not practise cruelty for its sake yet had no compunction in taking a severe action for the furtherance of a cause which he believed to be right.

A good meal was served and during it Joanna sat beside her guest and he talked to her of the war and the glories of Agincourt, of the King's valour and the genius he was displaying in the conduct of the war. He regretted that he was not with his brother in France; but the King had assigned to him the task of keeping law and order in England during his absence and that was a task which he was pursuing to the utmost of his capabilities.

'We shall let nothing . . . but nothing . . . stand in our way, my lady, no matter what has to be done it shall be done.'

Ominous words perhaps.

She was right.

As soon as the meal was over he said he had matters of which he wished to speak with her, and she took him to an ante-chamber and began by asking him: 'Where is my confessor?'

'He has gone to London.'

'I did not give him permission to go.'

'No, my lady. He went on my command which is the King's.'

'For what reason?'

'This is a painful subject and I would rather speak to you of it than let others do it. You are my stepmother and there has always been amity between ourselves.'

'And still is I trust,' she said.

Bedford was silent, and she looked at him in alarm. 'Pray tell me without more delay what this means,' she said.

'That I will. You have two sorcerers in your employ, my lady. Their names I learn are Roger Colles and Petronel Brocart.'

'These men are my servants. I would not call them sorcerers.'

'What then, my lady?'

'They are men with a knowledge of the stars . . . they predict the future.'

'And on occasions *arrange* the future.'

'I do not understand what you mean, my lord.'

'It should be clear. You wish for some event to take place and . . . these men arrange it.'

'How could that be! The future is in God's hands.'

'But it can often be helped by certain methods.'

'You are talking in riddles.'

'Forgive me. Your confessor has told us much. He

says that these two men at your command work with the powers of evil.'

'The man is a fool and a liar.'

'My lady, he is a Minorite Friar.'

'I would say he is a liar were he the Archbishop of Canterbury. He has always been of a jealous nature. He hated the friendship I showed for the astrologers.'

'He says they were with you when the late King suffered from his illness.'

'Oh God help me,' murmured the Queen.

'My father's disease was a loathsome one. Many said it had witchcraft in it.'

'I was with your father. I nursed him. He loved me till the end.'

'That does not prove that you had no hand in illwishing him.'

'This is nonsense. What good has his death brought me? It was better for me when he lived. He would never have allowed me to be treated as I am being now.'

'If you were guilty of what some say you are, he would have wished you to answer for your sins.'

Joanna covered her face with her hands. 'I loved the King,' she murmured. 'I nursed him through his sickness. He wanted me near him all the time.'

Bedford was silent.

'He suffered greatly,' she went on. 'Not only with the pain but the fearful disfigurement.'

'What was the disease which overtook my father?' said Bedford. 'It was said at the time that it was brought on through evil influences.'

'That is a lie. Your father would have been the first to declare it so. He knew that I loved him, that I could tend him better than anyone.'

'So we thought then, Madam.'

'Of what else have you come here to accuse me?' she demanded.

'Of practising witchcraft, of working against the King.'

'Working against the King! How could I do that? He is my friend. He has always been my friend.'

'You did not show much friendship when you gave so niggardly to him in his need to pursue the war in France.'

'I gave what I had to give.'

'My father left you rich. You are said to be one of the richest women in the country.'

Now she saw it all. It was her money they sought. What a fool she had been not to have given the King what he wanted when he had come to see her. His brother was his lieutenant. Extortion was their plan. She felt a faint relief. If it was her money they wanted, they might spare her life.

Of course they would. They dared not take that. Henry could not afford to offend the Duke of Brittany nor the royal House of France to that extent. To make war was one thing but to murder members of the family another.

'So you will believe the word of a treacherous priest against mine, my lord?' she asked.

'We shall investigate, of course. In the meantime I have decided to put you under guard.'

'Here in Havering?'

'No, you will go to Pevensey Castle. There Sir John Pelham will be your host.'

'You mean my jailer?'

'He will take good care of you and treat you as your rank requires.'

'But I shall be his prisoner.'

'And if you are guilty, my lady, your goods will be confiscated to the crown.'

'Ah,' she said, 'I understand. They will be of some help to the King in pursuing the war in France.'

Bedford was silent.

She was resigned. She knew her stepsons. They could make themselves believe that they were acting justly and all they cared about really was bringing money into the exchequer. She should have known better.

'There is one request I have to make,' she said. 'My son Arthur is in Fotheringay. He is Henry's prisoner as I shall be. Could we share our imprisonment?'

Bedford looked horrified.

She saw the thoughts chasing each other through his mind. Two of them in one castle! What plots they might fabricate.

'You will go to Pevensey,' he said stonily. 'And now, my lady, you will wish to prepare. You leave tomorrow.'

He bowed and left her. She looked about her. Soon this place where she had lived during her widowhood would be a memory. She thought then of Colles and Brocart. Perhaps they should try to escape to France. Would it be wiser for them to go or stay? If they were caught something might be proved against them, innocent as they were. Yet if they fled that would be taken as an assumption of their guilt. She must warn them and leave them to make the decision.

The next day she left for Pevensey. When she was arriving at the castle she was treated by Sir John Pelham with the respect due to her rank, so she could not therefore complain of her reception.

If only she could have been with Arthur at Fotheringay she would have been almost content for it soon became clear that no case was to be brought against her. Colles and Brocart had not been questioned even. But her wealth had been confiscated.

Bedford had achieved his purpose. Her immense fortune was now in the hands of the King.

She would remain his prisoner, awaiting his pleasure.

KATHERINE DE VALOIS

Katherine de Valois, Princess of France, was wondering
what her fate was to be. Would she indeed be the bride
of the King of England? It had seemed so once, but now
she was not so sure. Nothing had ever been very sure in
her life.

Her seventeen years had been turbulent ones. Sometimes she wondered how she had lived through them.
Her father was mad—not all the time, it was true, but no
one could be sure when he would lapse into that dismal
state. Her mother was a schemer—a Jezebel they called
her and perhaps not without cause. She had dominated
Katherine's childhood and the little girl had been terri-
fied of her while she was filled with great depth of
feeling—an admiration for her flamboyant beauty, an
awe of her vitality, and a realization of her power which
at times seemed evil. The Queen was like a goddess who
ruled the lives of her children—sometimes malignant,
sometimes benign and to whom they must offer complete submission.

Isabeau of Bavaria was reckoned to be the most beautiful woman in France and as she was married to a man
who, even though he was the King, was now and then
little more than an imbecile, perhaps it was not surpris-

ing that she, forceful woman that she was, should take over the reins of government and try to rule France.

Katherine could only rejoice in her passing out of childhood. At least now she was able to understand what was happening around her and practise some self preservation. There had been wretched days when she was very young and she and her brothers and sisters had never known from one day to the next what was going to happen to them. They had longed for the days when their father came out of what he called 'his darkness'. He was kind and affectionate and when he had emerged from that darkness everything would change miraculously. But they soon began to realize that they could never be sure when the shadows were going to claim him again.

She had been very young when Uncle Louis of Orléans was murdered in the streets of Paris, but she had been aware that some terrible disaster had occurred. At the time she and her brothers and sisters had been in the Palace of St Pol where they had not had enough to eat. She had not understood at the time why life had changed so suddenly. From luxury to this abject poverty had seemed to her just the normal way of life. Later of course she knew that her father was in one of his lost periods and that her mother and Uncle Louis of Orléans were lovers and ruled the kingdom, for her mother had persuaded the King that his brother should be Regent during his lapses. With her sisters and Louis the Dauphin and the two younger brothers she had lived as best she could with the help of one or two lower servants. The others had all left because their wages had not been paid.

For a long time no one had come to see them. Strange days they had been—but not altogether unhappy. It was amazing how quickly children could adjust themselves to a way of life. They had often been hungry but she could remember now the sheer joy of holding a cup of hot soup in her hands and the ecstatic moment when it touched her lips. Soup never tasted like that nowadays. They had all been dirty; they had lice in their hair and on their bodies; they would laugh as they caught them and vie with each other, boasting when theirs was the bigger catch. It was like a dream, looking back.

As she grew older, she understood what it all meant.

Her mother took the revenues from the household exchequer so that she could live voluptuously with her lover. Uncle Orléans was no better. This would have gone on if their father had not one day walked out of his apartments at St Pol, blinking his eyes as though he had awakened from a dream—his madness gone and ready to rule again.

The children had been hustled out of the Palace and out of Paris. They had quickly been pursued and brought back but not before they had been cleaned, clothed and fed; and soon after that Uncle Louis of Orléans had been murdered in the streets while he was leaving the Queen's lodgings. This murder had been committed at the instigation of Katherine's great-uncle, the Duke of Burgundy, who had decided to put an end to the rule of Orléans.

Her mother was imprisoned at Tours and Katherine and her sister Marie were sent to the convent of Poissy, there to be educated and brought up in a manner fitting for princesses.

It was a complete turn about—from the wild adventures of the world outside convent walls to the well ordered life inside. There were lessons, prayers—endless prayers—living sedately, thinking sometimes of the wild days at St Pol when she was hungry and lousy but for some reason she was not unhappy.

Marie declared herself to be disillusioned with the world. It was when she was thinking of their mother that she said this. Marie was becoming more and more drawn towards the convent life. Katherine never would be.

Her sister Isabella had returned from England where she had been the Queen until the people had deposed her husband. She had seen a little of Isabella, but her eldest sister was so withdrawn and melancholy that Katherine had not thought very much about her.

Then she had married the son of Uncle Orléans and when he had been murdered Isabella became the new Duchess. Poor Isabella, she had not been happy. Once she had come to the convent to see her sisters and she had told them that her happiness lay in England in the tomb of her first husband, Richard. She had died when her baby was born. Poor Isabella!

'What a sad life,' said Marie. 'One would be happier dedicated to the service of God.'

Marie was growing more and more remote every day. When she heard that Henry the King of England wanted to marry her she said she would never marry anyone. That had decided her. She wanted her father to understand that she longed for the peace of the convent and that marriage had no charms for her.

Of course Princesses must do what they were bid. But their father was a kind man. It was to be hoped that Marie was not forced into marriage during one of his dark spells by their mother who had emerged from her captivity and was making her presence at Court felt again.

'He wanted Isabella,' said Marie. 'I have heard that he was in love with her when he was only the son of the Duke of Hereford, that was before his father took the throne from Richard. Isabella would have none of him. She would have none of any but Richard.'

'But she took Charles of Orléans.'

'Yes, because she was forced to. I heard she cried all through the ceremony.'

'Poor poor Isabella!'

'She is dead now. How much better to give one's life to God.'

The news of the terrible defeat at Agincourt eventually came to the convent.

Katherine, who was now fourteen years old, realized the implication of this. The English were victorious. They would overrun France and her father might even lose his crown for that was what Henry of England was fighting for.

It was terrifying, for what hope had her father of holding off the enemy when his country was beset by internal strife. Ever since the murder of Orléans there had been a feud between Orléans and Burgundy; and in the centre of it was her poor father with his unstable mind and a wife who was renowned for her rapacity and her adulterous intrigues.

She was not altogether surprised when messengers arrived at the convent.

It was not Marie they had come for, but Katherine.

'Your presence is required at Court, my lady,' was the command.

Marie embraced her warmly, but Katherine was aware of her sister's relief.

'It will be marriage for you,' Marie said. 'This means that I am to be allowed to stay here. I shall thank God for this blessing and, dear sister, I shall pray for you.'

So Katherine rode out to her father's Court. She had realized that the sequestered life of the convent was not for her.

She was received by her father and she clung to him for she was so happy to see that his eyes were clear and that there was no madness in them.

'Dear little daughter,' he said, stroking her hair. 'How well you look, and how beautiful you have grown. You seem happy and that rejoices me. Be happy while you can, dear child. Sad things are happening to France.'

'Dear lord father, nothing could bring me more happiness than to see you well.'

'Pray God that I stay so until such time as I see you happily settled.'

'It is some marriage you have in mind for me.'

'Yes, child, with the King of England.'

'Henry. The one who asked for Isabella . . . and Marie . . .'

'He wants a Princess of France.'

'And I am the only one available.'

'Dear child, it will be a brilliant marriage. Think, my love, you will be a queen.'

'Isabella was a queen. It did not make her very happy.'

'Ah, this is different. She was married to Richard . . . a weakling.'

'She loved him dearly.'

'It was no true marriage. She was but a child. She saw him rarely and he treated her like a pet daughter. Henry is different. There is one who is seated firmly on his throne. You will admire him, grow to love him and become the mother of kings.'

'Oh no, Father. Let me be here for a while just as your daughter.'

'It seems that you will,' said the King grimly, 'for the terms he asks are excessive and we cannot meet them.'

She sighed with relief.

'You know that we were defeated at Agincourt,' went on the King. 'It was a disastrous defeat. We had superior forces . . . but they were too much for us. With a small army decimated by dysentery and disease yet he came with his archers and our losses were great, his small. It seems he is another such as his great-grandfather and the Black Prince. If so, with France in its present state we cannot stand against them. He makes great demands and one of these is your hand. If it is not granted he says he will come and take what he wants. A strange way of wooing, I told him, to come to you covered by the blood of your countrymen.'

'And what said he to that?'

'His answer was that he is a soldier with a soldier's way and he doubted not when you became his bride you would become used to his ways.'

She put her hand in her father's. 'I am afraid,' she said.

Her father looked very sad and she went on: 'But I must do my duty and I promise you, Father, that if it is necessary to marry this man, I will do it willingly for France.'

'My good child,' said the King and seemed about to burst into tears.

She wanted to tell him that the prospect was not entirely displeasing to her. She wanted to experience marriage and she wanted her husband to be a strong man, a man who knew what he wanted, who would not be cursed by the grim shadow of madness. The victor of Agincourt, the man who claimed he would conquer and subdue France—yes, he seemed a worthy husband for a princess.

It was a sad time. Negotiations had failed. Henry demanded too much. Louis the Dauphin who had been so full of health and had tauntingly sent Henry the tennis balls, had died suddenly. He had never recovered from the shame of Agincourt, it was said. He had been so certain that he was going to bring Henry as his prisoner to Paris—or at least his head on a pike. After the outcome he had been plunged into melancholy, and one day his attendants went into his apartment and found him dead. Of a broken heart, they said.

Prince Jean had become Dauphin and, when after a few months he was stricken by some mysterious disease which killed him within days, people began to say that there was a blight on France. This was a sign. The King mad, two of his sons dying within a short time of each other; the English triumphantly ranging all over the country. What could it mean?

There was a new Dauphin, Charles. The Queen was accused of poisoning her sons; the King had lapsed into madness; there was plague and famine in Paris.

What will happen next? Katherine asked herself.

The first thing that happened was the arrival of the Queen in Paris. She came at once to Katherine.

She was still so beautiful that Katherine could not help gazing at her in admiration. The Queen embraced her daughter and there were tears in her magnificent eyes.

'My dearest child,' she cried. Her dearest child—whom she had left to starve in the Palace of St Pol, in whose welfare she had shown no interest until this moment! Katherine was taken aback but she felt the old fascination creeping over her and she remembered how as a child she had hidden in cramped positions hoping for a chance to get a glimpse of the glorious goddess.

'Why are you here, my lady? I had thought you were at Tours.'

'I have escaped. Yes, I have left my prison at Tours. I am needed here and my great concern is your future . . . and that of France. For they are one and the same. You can save France, Katherine.'

'How so?'

'You are beautiful. You take after me, dear child.'

'Oh no, no. I could never be like you.'

'Perhaps not. Still you have beauty and that is always a good thing to have. I'll swear that when he sees you he will find you irresistible. He was a wild young man in his youth. Always fond of women. Oh yes, he will find he must have you. It is our way out of this dismal state which would never have happened if I had not been shut away . . . if Louis had never died . . . Never mind, Katherine. You and I are going to save France.'

'How, my lady?'

'First I want a picture painted of you. I want him to
see that lovely face . . . it is just the shape of mine; the
large dark eyes. Yes, it will mean a good deal when he
sees your portrait.'

'I wish I was not to be handed to him as part of a
treaty.'

The Queen sighed. 'It is something we of royal blood
must be reconciled to, Katherine. Think, you will be
Queen of England and there will be an end to these
senseless wars.'

'What if they send you back to Tours?'

'I have a strong ally,' she said. 'Burgundy is with me
now.'

Burgundy! Orléans! It mattered not to her which it
was. What she wanted was alliance with the one who
could bring her power.

Rouen was about to fall into his hands. He could not
fail. France was crumbling. This was the time to press
home his advantages.

Poor mad Charles would have to give in; it was a
stroke of good fortune for Henry that Dauphin Louis
had died—although he had hoped to get even with him
for that tennis ball insult. And then Jean. Such events
were invaluable for striking terror into a nation.

They saw God's displeased hand in this.

God was on the side of England. It had been obvious
at Agincourt when a small English army had been so
completely victorious.

While he was in camp before Rouen calculating that
before another day had passed the town would be his,
messengers arrived from the Court of France.

They had something for him. A portrait.

Eagerly he scanned it. She was young and beautiful
and she had a look of Isabella. Isabella had been his first
love and he had never quite forgotten her. Perhaps she
was not as beautiful as he had imagined her; but he
remembered first seeing her and most of all he remembered her devotion to Richard. He wanted someone like
that, someone to love him, to adore him, to remain
faithful throughout his life.

Katherine of France looked very like her sister. The

same dark eyes, the oval-shaped face, the masses of dark hair and the resolute set of the lips.

I'll have her, he thought. Before long she shall be my wife.

Rouen had fallen; the King was at Melun. Something had to be done.

A meeting was arranged between the Queen and her daughter with Henry. It was to take place at Pontoise.

On the banks of the river tents and pavilions had been set up. They were as elegant as the French could make them—in blue and green velvet ornamented with gold. It was a brilliant occasion and in the royal barge richly decorated with the fleur de lys Katherine came with her mother and the Duke of Burgundy. Her father was unable to accompany them because of another spell of madness.

Katherine was led into the most richly decorated of the pavilions and very soon there were shouts to proclaim the arrival of the King of England.

Henry was accompanied by his two brothers, Clarence and Gloucester, and a thousand men at arms and as he stepped into the tent Katherine's eyes were fixed on him and her heart beat fast with excitement.

Henry came forward and first bowed to the Queen and then kissed her. Then he turned to Katherine. Her lips parted; and she was smiling; and he was smiling at her. He laid his hands on her shoulders and kissed her lips.

It was unceremonious but she was delighted; and so was he.

She wished that they were alone and she could talk to him.

But this was not the time.

She was seated between her mother and the Duke of Burgundy and Henry sat opposite with a brother on either side of him. She was gratified to notice that during the whole of the proceedings Henry did not take his eyes from her.

The conference was over all too soon for Katherine and when it had broken up no definite arrangements had been made.

There must be another conference, said her mother.

'It is clear to me that the King has fallen in love with my daughter,' she added with pride.

But Henry's passion was not so great that he was going to give away any of his demands. They were excessive.

'We are not yet beaten,' said Burgundy.

There was another meeting at Pontoise. 'This time,' said the Queen, 'Katherine shall not go with us.'

Henry was clearly disappointed but as adamant as ever and the conference ended in deadlock.

Henry was sure that they must meet his demands. 'We will wait a few days,' he said to his brother. 'They will give way.'

He was disconcerted when he saw the pavilions being removed, which was a sign that the French had nothing more to say.

He sought one more interview with the Duke of Burgundy.

'I tell you this,' he cried, 'we will have the daughter of the King of France or we will drive the King out of his country . . . and you too, my lord of Burgundy.'

'You may threaten to do so,' was the cool reply, 'but before you have succeeded in driving me out of my country you will be very exhausted.'

Katherine felt deflated. She was sure he had wanted her. And yet he had let her go.

Perhaps she would never see him again.

The war continued. Henry was almost at the gates of Paris. There was nothing for the French to do but sue for peace.

Messages from Burgundy and the Queen of France were delivered to Henry's camp. Would he agree to another meeting?

His answer was: No. I trust none of you except the Princess Katherine. If I treat with any of you it would only be with her.

This was astounding. But then Henry had always been unconventional.

'There is nothing for us to do,' said the Queen. 'We have to give way to him. He must have Katherine.'

She sent for her daughter.

'The King of England is demanding your hand. You are smiling. It seems to please you.'

'I liked him well,' said Katherine, 'and it is time I married.'

The Queen laughed. 'I think you may resemble me in more ways than one. Write a note to him. Tell him how you long to speak with him. Our position is desperate. He will be in Paris soon if we do not stop him. But he must not come in war.'

Katherine sat down as bidden and wrote a note to him. She had greatly regretted not seeing him for so long for their brief meeting in the pavilion at Pontoise had given her the desire to see him more than anything in the world.

It was a bold letter for a princess to write, but she was dealing with a bold man.

'He will want more than Katherine's hand,' said Burgundy.

The terms would be harsh but they must accept them. Katherine's dowry would be the crown of France after the death of her father. The King of England should on the marriage become Regent of France.

Henry was overjoyed. It seemed that his goal was reached.

When Katherine was brought to his tent he unceremoniously swept her into his arms.

'My lord, my lord,' she protested but she was smiling contentedly.

'At last,' he cried. 'I have dreamed of you, Katherine. A pox on these people who have kept us apart so long.'

She was no longer the young girl Isabella had been, but how she reminded him of her. Isabella had died at twenty-two years of age, poor sad Isabella; and after all the delays Katherine herself was nineteen years old.

'I swore I'd have you the minute I first met you in the tent at Pontoise,' he told her.

'I know,' she said. 'I hoped it too.'

'Katherine . . . Katherine . . . what a lot of battles I had to fight to get you!'

'I trust you will consider the fight worth while, my lord.'

They were delighted with each other. He was thirty-three years old. Not a young man any more.

'By God's truth!' he cried. 'I have a lot to make up for.'

In the church of Notre Dame in the town of Troyes Henry with the Queen and Katherine were present at the signing of the treaty. Henry looked magnificent in burnished armour and Katherine was now deeply in love with him. The King of France was unable to be present, but that was so frequent an occurrence that his absence was scarcely noticed. There on the high altar France was surrendered to Henry of England.

Then the pair were betrothed and Henry solemnly placed a priceless ring on Katherine's finger. He insisted that she now be in his care, for he did not trust the French and in view of everything they had surrendered he felt that even if those who had made the bargain adhered to it there might well be some rebellious faction which would try to take his well earned spoils from him.

He insisted that the wedding should not be long delayed.

It was a glorious June day when in the church at Troyes he and Katherine were married. There was universal rejoicing because all saw in the marriage an end of the war which had tormented the people for so long.

It had ended as honourably for France as could be hoped for it did not seem quite so humiliating to surrender to the husband of their Princess as it would to a stranger.

Henry was determined to do honour to his bride. He had ordered that the most sumptuous preparations should be made.

The French watched in amazement. Their own preparations were grand but more restrained. More elegant was their verdict but at the same time they admired the ostentation of the English.

'It would seem that he is the King of the whole world,' was the comment.

So Katherine was his. They held hands and he smiled at her with a passionate intensity. She was delighted. She did not resemble Marie. She liked what she saw in her lover's eyes.

The Archbishop went through the ceremony of blessing the marriage bed; and there was the ceremonial putting to bed. There was a procession to the bedside and refreshment was brought to the happy pair. They drank the wine and soup according to the old French custom; and in due course they were alone.

'This is the moment for which I have longed since I first set eyes on you,' said Henry.

And Katherine was content.

DEATH OF THE CONQUEROR

Katherine lay at Windsor, awaiting the birth of her child. The King of course was still at war. The marriage had not brought the peace all had prayed for. The new Dauphin perhaps could not be expected to relinquish his rights and determined to stand against the treaty. Moreover it was hardly likely that all Frenchmen would calmly stand by and see their land handed over to the English even though their mad King was to retain his title until he died.

So Henry was now in France awaiting the news of the birth of their child.

She was happy. She was meant to be a wife. She and Henry were well matched. She laughed to hear of the adventures he had had in his youth when everyone thought it would be disaster when he came to the throne. He was a man of passionate desires—whether it was in the bed-chamber or the battle field. He was a man who could become obsessed by an ideal; to her he was a conquering hero. She did not care that he had subdued her father and her country. She regarded her brother, the Dauphin, as an enemy because he was Henry's.

Thus had Henry claimed her as his own and they were both delighted with the marriage.

He had given her a magnificent coronation and she had been crowned in Westminster Abbey by Archbishop Chicheley on a cold February day. The banquet that followed was the most sumptuous that had ever been served in the great hall at Westminster.

Henry was determined to do her honour.

And soon afterwards to the delight of them both she had become pregnant.

Her baby was to be born in December.

'You must be with me when our baby comes into the world,' she told Henry; but he laughed at her and she knew that if he felt it necessary to go into battle even she could not detain him.

Conquest was his life. He was a great lover but a soldier first. The prosecution of a war meant more to him than anything else. Her kinswoman Joanna who had been Queen to Henry's father was still imprisoned in Pevensey.

Henry believed in witchcraft and he told her that Joanna had practised it against him. He only half believed it to be so for he had always liked his stepmother until he needed her money to help him to make war.

He was ruthless. She knew that. But he was a man . . . every inch of him; and she was gratified to have him as her husband.

When she had ridden out beside him she had been thrilled; when his eyes had sought hers in an assembly her heart leaped with pleasure. There could be no doubt of the love between them.

He was going away again. She could pout and express her displeasure but he took no notice. His presence was needed in France.

'And you will not be here for the birth of the child,' she complained.

'You will bear it without me,' he said.

'Then as soon as I am able to I shall come to you. You will not be able to prevent that.'

He laughed at her. 'It may well be that I have no wish to,' he answered.

She was amused when he began to have suspicions about the birth of the child.

He had been listening to astrologers.

'There is a cloud over Windsor,' he said. 'They predict it will be there in December. Katherine, our child must not be born in Windsor. It is an ill omen.'

'Stop here and make sure it is not born there.'

He laughed again and kissed her.

But all the same he had gone away to war.

And now here she lay . . . in Windsor. He would not stay with her while her child was born. Very well, she would deliberately disobey him.

He would not be angry; once the child was born he would forget its birthplace.

It was a magnificent castle; fitted to be the birthplace of Kings. She wanted a boy—a King to follow Henry. It was what they both wanted. And why should it not be born in Windsor?

Henry's favourite ancestor, Edward the Third, had been born here. They had called him Edward of Windsor, and if she had a son she would call him after his father. He should be Henry of Windsor.

And so she was brought to bed and in due course her son was born.

She called him Henry after his father.

'A plague on their prophecies, my son,' she said. 'My little Henry the Sixth, you are going to be another such as your father.'

When the news was brought to Henry he was filled with delight. A son! Was that not what every King desired? He had his fair and passionate Katherine and how like her to add to her perfections by giving him a son!

'The Queen insists on calling him Henry,' he was told.

'That does not displease me,' he said with a smile. 'Long live our young Henry the Sixth.'

'And may he not come to the throne for many a long year, my lord.'

The King was silent suddenly. He said: 'Where was he born?'

They hesitated to tell him knowing his uneasy feelings.

When he would have it from them he turned white—not with anger but with fear.

Then he said slowly as though someone else was speaking through him:

'Henry born at Monmouth
Shall small time reign and much get
But Henry of Windsor shall long reign and lose all.'

He looked with astonishment at those who surrounded
him. And then he added: 'But as God will, so be it.'

'My lord,' said his brother Gloucester. 'Are you well?'

Henry put his hand to his brow. 'A strangeness came
over me,' he said. 'It was the news that the boy had
been born at Windsor. I asked the Queen not to lie-in
there.'

'Windsor, my lord? It is a right fitting place for the
birth of a Prince.'

Henry clapped his brother on the shoulder. 'You are
right, brother. What matters it? A fine boy, eh. And a
Henry.'

Six months after the birth, Katherine prevailed on
Henry to allow her to join him. The baby was left in the
care of his nurses and she set out, accompanied by the
Duke of Bedford and an army of twenty thousand.

Thus as a queen should she travelled across France
sending messengers on in advance to tell her husband of
her coming.

When Henry heard that she had arrived in France he
was filled with mingling joy and dismay. For some months
he had been feeling ill and he could not forget how
rapidly his father had been attacked by disease.

His was not an illness of disfiguration. He was suffering from the dysentery which he had seen ruin so many
of his soldiers. It left him limp and exhausted. He was
advised to rest but he would not do so, assuring himself
that he would throw off the indisposition which he refused to believe was anything but temporary.

He sent to the Queen to tell her of her daughter's
arrival and as the King was enjoying one of his lucid
periods the two of them joined Henry and rode with him
to meet their daughter.

Katherine was shocked to see the change in Henry
and declared that it was time she came to him for it was
clear that he needed looking after. He smiled wanly, and
declared that he had far too much to do to become an
invalid.

They travelled on to Senlis and there Katherine insisted that he rest.

'Nay,' he answered, 'I cannot rest. Nor can I dally with you, sweetheart. Your brother, who calls himself the Dauphin, is about to battle with my ally the Duke of Burgundy. I know Burgundy expects and needs my help.'

'Forget it for a while,' pleaded Katherine. 'The doctors say you need to rest.'

He smiled at her. 'You are a temptress, my dear Queen, but I am not to be lured from my duty.'

'When do you leave Senlis?'

'At dawn,' he said. 'Come, let us retire now. The night is too short.'

So they retired but during the night he became very ill and she knew that he could not travel at dawn. He fought off the lassitude which overtook him and called for his armour.

Although he could scarcely stand he was dressed and ready to ride out, and set out at the head of his men for Melun, while the Queen went back to Rouen.

But as he neared Melun it was borne home even to him that he could go no further. It was no use pretending that nothing was wrong.

They prepared a litter for him and he was taken back to Senlis.

Henry knew that there was little time left to him. He believed he had displeased God in some way for he was only thirty-five years old. It was young to die and his work not completed. He had come farther than any English King before him. He had been himself a greater warrior even than Edward the First and Edward the Third. His people loved him; the crown of France was almost in his grasp and now he was to die.

His conscience smote him. He had caused his father great anxiety. In his youth he had lived without thought of anything but his own pleasure. John Oldcastle had expiated his past follies; he had died a martyr. But he, the King, what had he done? He had all but won France but for some divine reason he was not going to be allowed to complete the task.

He wanted to ask forgiveness of all those he had wronged. He wanted to know where he had failed.

He remembered his stepmother suddenly. Joanna who had been accused of witchcraft—not because there was any evidence against her but because he needed her money to help prosecute the war.

He must make amends. He must do it at once while there was time left to him.

All must be restored to her.

He sent for his scribe. He must write as dictated. All must be restored to Queen Joanna and she must be released from captivity. He knew that she had been wrongfully accused.

'Let that be done without delay,' he commanded.

He felt better after that.

He sent for his doctors. 'Tell me, am I dying?' he asked.

'There is always hope, my lord,' they answered.

'I want the truth,' he answered. 'Do not think to spare me. I want to know how much time is left to me.'

'Sire,' was the answer, 'you must think of your soul for unless it is the will of God to decree otherwise you cannot live for more than two hours.'

Two hours, he mused. Only two hours left to me. What of my son . . . a baby still? 'Send my brother. Send my uncle Exeter.'

They came and stood by his bedside.

'John,' he said, 'you have been a good brother to me. Be as good a friend to my son as you have been to me.'

'I will,' said Bedford.

'And my good Uncle of Exeter. You must be Regent of England and guardian to my son. As you love me care for him.'

'You may trust me,' said Exeter.

'Is that Warwick I see there? Our good cousin, be the governor of my son. Teach him what he should learn. Do this in memory of me, I beg of you.'

Warwick fell on his knees. 'My dear lord,' he said, 'if this must be then I will serve him as I served you.'

'I have good friends,' said the King. 'John,' he went on, 'you must comfort my Queen. She is young; she is the most afflicted creature living. Care for her.'

'I swear I shall do as you would have me,' said Bedford.

'Then there is no more for me to do but to die in peace.'

And so he died.

* * *

Katherine was stricken with grief. She was twenty-one years old and looked younger in her melancholy.

The King's body was placed on a chariot drawn by four horses and with a cavalcade of mourners was taken to Abbeville. It was an impressive procession for round the chariot rode four hundred men at arms in black armour, their horses covered in black velvet and their lances held with the points downward. The rest of the mourners were clad in white and they walked slowly carrying lighted torches and chanting funeral dirges.

They passed from Abbeville to Montreuil and so to Calais. When they reached Dover they were met by processions of bishops and priests and so they brought the King home to his capital city.

He was buried in the chapel of the Confessor in Westminster Abbey and a chantry was endowed in his honour.

As soon as the funeral was over Katherine hurried to Windsor to see her child.

He had been nine months old when his father had died.

She took him at once to London and rode in a carriage through the streets with him seated on her lap. They had curled his little hands about the sceptre but they could not put the crown on his baby head.

It did not matter. The significance was plain. Henry the Fifth was dead and the disastrous reign of Henry the Sixth had begun.

BIBLIOGRAPHY

Armitage-Smith, Sydney	*John of Gaunt*
Aubrey, William Hickman Smith	*National and Domestic History of England*
Bryant, Arthur	*The Medieval Foundation*
Church, Rev A.J.	*Henry the Fifth*
Costain, Thomas B.	*The Last Plantagenets* *The Pageant of England 1377–1485*
Davies, J. D. Griffith	*King Henry IV*
Davis, W.W.C.	*England Under the Angevins*
Froissart, Sir John	*The Chronicles of England, France, Spain etc.*
Gairdner, James	*Lollardy and the Reformation in England*
Green, John Richard	*History of England*
Guizot, M. (Translated by Robert Black)	*History of France*
Hume, David	*History of England from the Invasion of Julius Caesar to the Revolution*
McFarlane, K.B.	*Lancastrian Kings and Lollard Knights*
Ramsay, Sir James H. of Bamff	*Genesis of Lancaster*
Stenton, D.M.	*English Society in the Middle Ages*
Stephen, Sir Leslie and Lee, Sir Sydney	*The Dictionary of National Biography*
Strickland, Agnes	*Lives of the Queens of England*
Wade, John	*British History*

Waugh, W.T.   *The Reign of Henry V*
Wylie, James Hamilton *History of England under*
                     Henry the Fourth (Four
                     Volumes)

ABOUT THE AUTHOR

Jean Plaidy, who is Victoria Holt, resides in England. This is her seventeenth novel for Fawcett and the eleventh book in the Plantagenet saga.

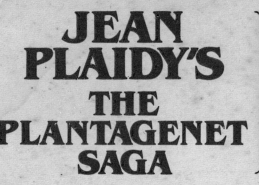